PRICE OF A PRINCESS

Alexander Boyd acted rather than argued. He grabbed James's reins and tugged. "Come, Sire!"

Mary, kneeing her beast's flanks, cried, "No! No, I say. Stop him!" It was Kennedy whom she so urged.

That lord, the King's cousin and her own, at one remove, made an indeterminate gesture, part shake of the head, part shrug. Then he seemed to decide, and urged his mount over nearer to the King's again, which was being pulled round. His hand went out.

Swiftly Sir Alexander twisted in his saddle and lashed out with his fist, striking the older man on the shoulder, and all but unseating him with the vehemence of the blow. At the same time he spurred his horse into vigorous motion, back towards the woodland, and perforce dragged the boy's beast with him.

Immediately all was changed as to tempo, urgency, atmosphere. There arose exclamations and shouting, much clamour and jerking of horses' reins and heads, much concern; but also a deal of uncertainty. For all the men there knew each other, had their links and friendships – and the reverse to be sure. For her part, Mary Stewart spurred after her brother without delay. Lord Kennedy, breathing stertorously, biting his lip, remained where he was.

James, reins wrenched from his not very firm hands, was clinging to his saddle-bow for support, and looking back over his shoulder. "Mary!" he cried, "Mary – do not leave me!"

"I will not!" she shouted after him, and heeled her mount the harder.

Price of a Princess

Nigel Tranter

CORONET BOOKS
Hodder and Stoughton

Copyright © 1994 Nigel Tranter

First published in Great Britain in 1994
by Hodder and Stoughton

First paperback edition published in 1995
by Hodder and Stoughton
A division of Hodder Headline PLC

Coronet edition 1995

The right of Nigel Tranter to be identified as the Author of
the Work has been asserted by him in accordance with the
Copyright, Designs and Patents Act 1988.

10 9 8 7 6 5 4 3 2 1

British Library CIP

Tranter, Nigel
Price of a Princess
I. Title
823.912 [F]

ISBN 0 340 60994 X

Printed and bound in Great Britain by
Cox & Wyman Ltd, Reading, Berkshire

Hodder and Stoughton
A division of Hodder Headline PLC
338 Euston Road
London NW1 3BH

Principal Characters in order of appearance

James the Third: Youthful King of Scots

Princess Mary: Elder sister of above

Gilbert, Lord Kennedy: Great noble, brother of former Bishop Kennedy

James, Lord Hamilton: Great noble, Head of the house of Cadzow

Sir Alexander Boyd of Duncow: Keeper of Edinburgh Castle

Thomas, Lord Boyd of Kilmarnock: Elder brother of above

Thomas, Master of Boyd: Son and heir of above. Later Earl of Arran

James, Lord Livingstone: Great Chamberlain

Lady Annabella Boyd: Sister of above

Patrick Graham, Bishop of St Andrews: Primate of Scottish Church

Princess Margaret: Younger sister of the King

Alexander, Duke of Albany: Younger brother of the King

John, Earl of Mar: Youngest brother of the King

Andrew Stewart, Lord Avondale: Chancellor of Scotland

Patrick Fullarton: Son of the Coroner of Arran

Andrew Durisdeer, Bishop of Glasgow: Envoy

William Tulloch, Bishop of Orkney: Envoy and interpreter

Rob Carnegie: Shipmaster

Christian the First: King of Denmark, Norway and Sweden

Martin Vanns: Grand Almoner

Princess Margaret of Denmark: Daughter of Christian and Dorothea

Magnus, Archbishop of Nidaros: Metropolitan of the North

William Boyd, Abbot of Kilwinning: Another brother of Lord Boyd

Archibald Douglas, Earl of Angus: Chief of the Red Douglases

Elizabeth Boyd, Countess of Angus: Daughter of Lord Boyd

Nils Larsen: Danish merchant

Wilhelm Schoenbach: Senator of the Hanseatic League

Lord Haliburton of Dirleton: Privy Councillor

1

The hunt was well past Duntarvie, and now heading almost due
southwards towards Niddry Seton, downhill through undulating
country of scattered woodland, the stag a notable runner but
carrying a splendid head of antlers, well worth this long pursuit,
the deerhounds still unable to run it down or corner it. Some of
the more experienced horsemen might indeed have been able to
use knowledge of the land to head it off, in this western part of
Lothian, but could scarcely do so ahead of the King – who was,
not unnaturally, less experienced, being of only fourteen years.
Nor was His young Grace the best of riders as yet, being a
studious and less than vigorous youngster, unlike his late and
impetuous father, James the Second of that name. Even his sister
had had to rein in on occasion at his side, for Mary Stewart was a
more vehement character and, at seventeen, a fine horsewoman.

They had already come more than five round-about miles from
Linlithgow, and it looked as though there would be more miles
ahead of them before they killed, if ever they did, with the stag
showing no signs of flagging.

The Lord Kennedy, at the other side of the young monarch,
pointed and panted out, "The burn, Y'Grace. Niddry Burn.
Water. That . . . our best hope . . . I judge. Quarry making for
. . . water, belike." A man of later middle years, now inclining
to corpulence, *he* was not having to rein his, his breathlessness
very evident.

"A burn? A river. Will we have to cross a river?" James
demanded, a little anxiously. "Is it . . . deep?"

"The Niddry is nothing that our mounts cannot take, Jamie,"
the princess reassured as they pounded on. "It is the boggy edges
that we will have to watch for. Where the deer can cross lightly,
but our beasts' hooves will sink in."

"Right, Highness," Kennedy agreed. "A pity that Seton . . .
did not come . . . this day. He knows this country best . . ."

They were approaching thicker woodland from a lengthy

1

downwards slope; and already the stag and pursuing hounds were disappearing into the trees. Mary was having to restrain herself and her mount from forging ahead, as were others behind – although she perhaps was the only one there who could have outridden her brother without seeming guilty of *lèse-majesté*.

Actually it was the girl, the only female present, who perceived the situation first, or at least was first to utter it. "Look – men!" she exclaimed. "There, within the trees. Many men. Mounted."

Kennedy stared, his sight scarcely as keen as that of the young woman.

"Who are they?" James asked, ever ready to be alarmed.

"They will be the Lord Seton's people," his sister suggested. "We are near Niddry Seton here. I have been here before. But for these woods we could see his castle, I think."

"Should we not halt? There are many. In case . . ."

"The Setons are your good friends, Sire," Kennedy said. But he did seek to slow down his pace a little, although that was not easy with them all thundering downhill, many of the other huntsmen close behind. Any sudden reining in, and the foremost could be ridden down.

Then Lord Hamilton's voice sounded from their backs – he was usually to be found as near to the Princess Mary as he could decently get. "It is Boyd! I see the Boyd banner. And Somerville. See – there is the white on blue of Somerville."

All who might have been apprehensive relaxed at that, as they saw horsemen emerging from the trees under colourful heraldic flags. Lord Boyd of Kilmarnock was a trusted supporter of the crown, and his younger brother, Sir Alexander, more prominent in national affairs, was indeed Keeper of Edinburgh Castle, the second most important citadel of the land. But it was strange to be intercepting the royal hunt thus. They must be bearing some vital news to account for it.

Their fine stag looked like escaping, in these circumstances.

There were about a score of horsemen coming slowly to meet them. Everywhere now the more numerous huntsmen, by unspoken consent, were drawing in their mounts, recognising these ahead as friends.

Lord Kennedy, whose brother, the late renowned bishop who had more or less ruled the realm for both the young King and his father, gave no impression of annoyance at this interruption of their sport. "It seems . . . we must leave . . . this chase

meantime, Sire," he advised. "These . . . would not be here
. . . thus . . . without cause." The Lord Boyd's son and heir,
Thomas, Master of Boyd, was after all contracted to marry Lord
Kennedy's daughter.

The two groups drew together, and not a few hands were
raised in greeting, for all knew each other well enough. There
was cap-raising towards the monarch and his sister.

"We regret the spoiling of Your Grace's sport, Sire," one
of the newcomers announced, with a flourished bow from the
saddle, not the Lord Boyd but his brother, Sir Alexander, a
fine-looking man of early middle age, richly dressed. "But the
matter is important."

"It is no matter," the youth said. "I think the stag was winning
away." He was no great one for hunting, this James Stewart.
And indeed this day's hunt had been something of a surprise
altogether, at least to his sister, proposed suddenly by Kennedy
as a relief from the admittedly boring business of the annual
Exchequer Audit, which had been going on for three days at
the palace of Linlithgow, and at which, by established custom,
the monarch had to be present. She had been glad enough to take
part in it, for she loved the chase, even though she did not always
relish the kill itself. But her brother had not been enthusiastic.

"We were on our way to Linlithgow, Sire, when we heard of
this hunt," the Lord Boyd said. He was a heavier man than his
brother, massively built and square-featured. "We understood
you to be at the Exchequer Audit there. But perceived the hunt
coming down this way."

It occurred to Mary Stewart to wonder, then. How had these
lords, from Edinburgh, heard of this hunt, which had been
decided upon only this morning? And had assumed that the King
would be with it? She did not voice her questions, however.

"Your Grace's presence is urgently required at Edinburgh."
That was the Lord Somerville, a younger man, of somewhat
haughty bearing.

"Why that?" somebody asked, from the ranks of the hunters
behind.

Lord Boyd frowned. Then glancing over at all the interested
faces of the listening horsemen, waved. "It is a privy matter. Of
some . . . secrecy."

"Shall we return to Linlithgow, then, and consider the matter?"
the Lord Hamilton said. "His Grace agreeing."

3

"No, my lord. And Your Grace. There is some urgency in this. Better for His Grace to come with us to Edinburgh now."

"But . . . the others? The Chancellor, Lord Avondale – he is at Linlithgow. Livingstone, and other lords of the Council. They must be informed."

"No time for that," Sir Alexander Boyd said crisply. "A messenger has arrived from Edward of England. From Carlisle. His mission requiring the royal reply and signature."

"The Chancellor, then, must hear of it. We are but five or six miles from Linlithgow . . ."

"No!" That was definite. "We must go at once." This was not the normal mode of speech where the monarch was concerned.

Kennedy, strangely, said nothing.

Mary wondered the more. There was much here that she did not understand. She scanned the faces of the newcomers. Of the score or so, most were men-at-arms, a mere escort. As well as the two Boyds and Somerville there were two others whom she knew slightly, Andrew Hepburn, Master of Hailes, and Andrew Ker, heir to Ker of Cessford, both daredevil young men, Borderers. But there was one whom she did not recognise – and she certainly would have done so had she seen him before, for he was the most handsome young man she had ever set eyes upon, well built, tall, bearing himself proudly and seemingly almost amused by the present situation, certainly in no awe of the company he had joined.

She was reverting to a consideration as to how this party could have known of today's hunt, when she realised that the good-looking stranger was eyeing her with frankest interest, all but assessingly. She was used to admiration, of course, not only as a princess but as a very lovely young woman, tall also, slender and lissome but amply rounded, dark-haired and fine-featured, her grey eyes large and expressive. Those eyes met the young man's, and they locked for a moment or two before she turned back to her brother.

James was indeed addressing her. "Must I go with them, Mary?" he asked. Ever since their mother, Queen Mary of Guelders, had died three years before, the young King had looked to his elder sister for guidance, help and comfort, a somewhat bewildered youngster requiring much support and fondness, no very adequate monarch for a nation as turbulent as

4

Scotland, and following a headstrong father. It was to be feared that he would never be a forceful monarch.

"Wait!" she said, and turned to Lord Kennedy who, since the good bishop's death a year before, had more or less assumed the duties of the monarch's principal adviser. "Such haste? Could the English messenger not have been brought here, to His Grace? Rather than the King having to go to *him*?"

Kennedy looked uncomfortable. "I know not, Highness. Perhaps he was wearied with long riding." That sounded feeble indeed.

Alexander Boyd reined his horse closer, to speak low-voiced. "This is important, Sire and Highness. The messenger must return to Carlisle, whenever he is sufficiently rested. King Edward is urgent. He leaves for the south. Prithee, come!" And he actually reached out for the reins of the boy's mount.

"No!" Mary declared. "Jamie, I say that we should rather return to Linlithgow. First. Here is something strange." She turned, tossing her long hair back from her brow, a habit of hers. "You, my Lord Kennedy – say you not so?"

That man hesitated, glancing left and right.

From behind, Hamilton spoke. "I agree with Her Highness. Back to Linlithgow."

Alexander Boyd acted rather than argued. He grabbed James's reins and tugged. "Come, Sire!"

Mary, kneeing her beast's flanks, cried, "No! No, I say. Stop him!" It was Kennedy whom she so urged.

That lord, the King's cousin and her own, at one remove, made an indeterminate gesture, part shake of the head, part shrug. Then he seemed to decide, and urged his mount over nearer to the King's again, which was being pulled round. His hand went out.

Swiftly Sir Alexander twisted in his saddle and lashed out with his fist, striking the older man on the shoulder, and all but unseating him with the vehemence of the blow. At the same time he spurred his horse into vigorous motion, back towards the woodland, and perforce dragged the boy's beast with him.

Immediately all was changed as to tempo, urgency, atmosphere. There arose exclamations and shouting, much clamour and jerking of horses' reins and heads, much concern; but also a deal of uncertainty. For all the men there knew each other, had their links and friendships – and the reverse to be sure. For her part, Mary Stewart spurred after her brother without delay. Lord Kennedy, breathing stertorously, biting his lip, remained where he was.

James, reins wrenched from his not very firm hands, was clinging to his saddle-bow for support, and looking back over his shoulder. "Mary!" he cried, "Mary – do not leave me!"

"I will not!" she shouted after him, and heeled her mount the harder.

There was a notable confusion of riders on that grassy slope, decision and indecision equally evident. Amidst the cries and beat of hooves, Mary heard the thudding crash of a horse falling behind her, and glancing back saw the two Andrews, Hepburn and Ker, reining back from the sprawling, kicking mount of the Lord Hamilton, who himself was now asprawl on the grass, clearly having been ridden down by the pair as he came after her and James. She almost drew up, to go to his assistance, then perceived that her brother's need was the greater, and pounded on.

Another horseman was coming fast from behind and drawing level. She saw that it was Fleming, another important lord.

"Better back, Highness," this one jerked. "No ploy . . . for a woman!"

She ignored him.

Then she realised that a second rider was close at her other side, the handsome young man whom she had noted earlier. And he was laughing, the only one there to be showing amusement. He reached over to pat her arm, their mounts almost touching.

"I salute you, lady!" he exclaimed. "Spirit! Fear nothing. All will be well."

"James!" she panted. "The King."

"He will be well enough, also. Here's to your spirit! I like it."

Mary, just then, could do without compliments, and rode the harder.

The Lord Fleming dropped back – but not the girl's good-looking admirer.

They were almost up with Sir Alexander and the young monarch now, and she called out reassuringly to her brother. Boyd looked round, frowning.

"All is well, uncle," the young man shouted. "Hamilton took a fall! Others . . . less eager! Save this princess. All in order."

Which was a strange way of describing the situation.

Level with James, Mary cried, "Fear nothing, Jamie. They will not harm you, the King."

Tense, anxious, the boy shook his head.

As they entered the woodland she looked back, expecting pursuit. But there was none. The hunt-followers were clustered round Kennedy, Fleming and Hamilton and other lords. All seemed to be more or less stationary, Hamilton mounting his horse again. Indecision triumphed, apparently. Or connivance!

The Boyds and Somerville were by no means glancing back apprehensively.

Presently, deeper within the trees, Lord Boyd's party pulled up, to consider the position – and it was at Mary Stewart rather than at the abducted young sovereign-lord that they stared, obviously put out and at something of a loss by her presence.

"Highness," Lord Boyd said, "I regret that you have been . . . troubled. By this. That was not intended. This way is best for His Grace. But you . . . ! This is no concern for a woman." He changed that. "For a young lady such as Your Highness."

"What *is* this concern, my lord?" That came out strongly, if a little breathlessly, with another toss back of her dark hair.

"It is for . . . for the realm's weal, Highness. And His Grace's own. That, I do promise you. And you, Sire. It, it had to be this way. Lest there be . . . difficulties." Boyd was clearly having his own difficulties, with this delivery.

The Lord Somerville was less troubled. "Better that you get back to Linlithgow, lady," he said curtly.

"I stay with His Grace," Mary told them simply.

"But, Highness . . . !" Boyd wagged his head. "Best indeed that you return . . ."

"No!" That was James Stewart, in agitation.

"This is man's work, Highness. In the kingdom's cause. For betterment therein," Sir Alexander Boyd put in. "His Grace will be very well with us."

"Perhaps, sir. Although I doubt it, by this present! But His Grace has suffered much, the deaths of his royal father, and his mother, none so long past. He must not suffer the loss of his sister also! If he goes with you, I go also."

There was muttering and growling amongst her hearers, but another voice spoke up, that of the next youngest person present after the monarch and Mary, the so handsome stranger.

"This lady is brave as she is fair, uncle. And could aid us all,

7

with the King. A useful friend!" And he flourished a bow at the girl. "Let her bide, I say."

Alexander Boyd shrugged, and nodded towards his brother. "Come, then. We have wasted sufficient time." He still retained the reins of the King's horse.

Lord Boyd looked doubtfully at Somerville; but it was clear that his younger brother was the strong character and the real leader here. He gestured onwards.

In the woodland track there was room only for riders to go two abreast; so Mary, unspeaking, drew in immediately behind Sir Alexander and her brother. She found her personable admirer at her side.

"I am Tom Boyd," he said. "And find Your Highness to my taste!"

"And I find nothing of this to *my* taste, sir!" she told him, and looked firmly away.

He laughed. "My taste in women seldom errs, I think! You will come round to it!"

She did not have to answer that, for along the track before them appeared three of the hunt-servants and two of the deerhounds, evidently coming back to discover what had happened to the hunt. At sight of this party with the young King these drew up and pulled aside, in astonishment and uncertainty.

The Boyds and their friends ignored them entirely, as they trotted on.

The track led them, presently, down to softer ground and then to a shallow ford of sorts over the Niddry Burn, up beyond which was the major road between Edinburgh, Linlithgow and Stirling.

They had some ten miles to go to Edinburgh, and it was not long before they could actually see their destination away eastwards ahead of them, for its great fortress-castle, atop its lofty rock, stood out as a landmark from afar. Mary's self-appointed escort pointed to it.

"You will know yonder citadel, lady?" he asked. "*I* find it less than comfortable."

The girl did not answer.

He went on, cheerfully. "We must seek to make it more suitable lodging for a princess. And, to be sure, for our liege-lord!" There was something like mockery in that last.

She did rise to that. "Lodging, sir? I thought that we went but to sign papers and speak with an English courier?"

He laughed. "That was as useful a pretext as any. A little longer stay will be called for, I think!"

"What do you mean?"

"Why – only that the realm's business may take some of its sovereign's time. And if Your Highness prefers to bide with him – for which praises be, I say! – then you may require some comforts in Edinburgh Castle, lady. And some comforting, perhaps!"

She stared at him, as they trotted along. "Do I take you aright, sir? Is this then some shameful . . . device? Some unlawful and treasonable seizure and constraint of the King? For the advantage of . . . these!"

Still he seemed to find amusement in even that dire challenge. "Not how my father and uncle would name it, I swear! Say, rather, for the advantage of all the kingdom and the King's folk. Even for His young Grace's self. Better keeping than he has been in, from those old men, the Kennedys."

"You mean that you and yours are going to hold James? To rule the realm, or seek to, through him, as your prisoner!"

"Never prisoner, no. Guardians, perhaps. His advisers, counsellors. Needful guardians. Since Bishop Kennedy died, the rule of this land has been but slack, has it not? Or so my father and uncle declare. Allowing much of ill to arise. So now there is to be . . . improvement. Should we not rejoice?"

Her lovely features set, Mary Stewart digested that as best she could.

He reached over to pat her sleeve. "If you do not like it, Highness, it is perhaps not too late for *you* to turn back. Go back to Linlithgow. I will escort you most of the way, if need be." But that also was announced with a laugh which held mockery.

She tossed back her hair. "I stay with the King," she said.

"And I am glad of that! Heigho – I have found Edinburgh dull indeed after my Kilmarnock and Ayr. You will improve it, I have no doubt!"

She shook her head wordlessly, seeking to order the tumult of her thoughts. Responsible as her nature, training and circumstances had made her, for a girl of seventeen this situation was upsetting to say the least. And the young man's familiarity of tone and manner were insufferable. Yet, presently, she turned to him.

"You say that it is your father and uncle who lead in this . . . felony and folly! And you come from Kilmarnock? A Boyd?"

9

"I told you – Tom Boyd. I am Thomas, Master of Boyd, yes. At your service, to be sure."

"I see. So – you are deep in this plot also?"

"Not so. A mere onlooker, Highness, unconcerned with affairs of state. I prefer affairs of the heart!" He waved a flourish. "I came from Dean Castle, our house in the west, only a week past. And now, this! So unexpected a satisfaction!"

"Unexpected, sir? I think not. Much about this day's doings I deem strange indeed. Planned in advance, well planned. I have noted much. No sudden whim of you and yours. This hunt, see you. It was only decided upon this morning – or so it seemed. To enliven the dull work of the Exchequer, for James. Yet your father said that he knew of it. And some of the lords in the hunt itself have acted very strangely. The Lord Kennedy himself. And Fleming. Hamilton alone sought to prevent this, this outrage. I think that the others knew that it was planned. Or some of them."

He glanced at her more carefully, at this, assessingly. "Perhaps these recognised it as for the best?" he suggested. "After all, they know my father and uncle. He, my uncle, is married to Janet Kennedy. And I, would you credit it, am supposed to be be marrying Kennedy's youngest daughter one day! Plain of face and person as she is!"

"Whom do I condole with, sir? You – or her! But . . . could my Lord Kennedy so betray his trust? His brother, the bishop, would turn in his grave, I think! To yield up the King so – he, his protector and supporter, since the bishop died . . ."

"There are more sorts of betrayal than one, lady. Before ever Bishop Kennedy died, his brother had a band with my uncle. And Fleming. And the Earl of Crawford. Each to support the other in all matters and interests – all save, to be sure, such as might be against the interests of the crown. And this present, I am assured, is in His Grace's best interests! Much so. Where, then, is the betrayal?"

"Words, sir! Words do not alter deeds. I have heard of these bands, between lords. And mislike the sound of them. Fleming also, you say? He, too, held back, there. But Kennedy – his is the greater betrayal. He is keeper of the King's royal castle of Stirling. James's home. And mine. Brought us to Linlithgow, for this audit. Arranged this hunt – and then hands over his charge to Sir Alexander Boyd . . ."

10

"Who is also keeper of the other royal castle, of Edinburgh! A fair exchange! What is so ill in that?"

"Do not play with me, sir! But – tell me this, pray. You who know so much. Why did Sir Alexander strike Lord Kennedy back yonder? When he reached out to James."

The master shrugged, but grinned too. "You should ask him that yourself, Highness. Myself, I was surprised. But I jalouse that it was a kindly blow, well meant! A precautionary gesture, shall we say? Lest aught went wrong. Hamilton was questioning. So – none could accuse Kennedy of . . . perfidy. But ask Sir Alexander."

"I do not think that I would place more faith in *his* answers than I do in yours, Master of Boyd!"

"For one so fair, you are hard, hard, Highness. But we shall convince you of our goodwill, never fear. I, in especial!"

Her head-tossing was eloquent.

The road being broader here, as they neared the city, Mary took the opportunity to spur forward level with her brother, at the other side from Sir Alexander. The boy turned to her anxiously.

"Is it . . . is it well, Mary? Why this? I do not understand. Lord Kennedy? Lord Hamilton? Where are they? They have not come . . ."

"I have explained to His Grace, Highness, that we act only for his weal, and that of his realm. As I have heard my nephew telling yourself. Heed us."

She eyed him, above her brother's troubled head, heedfully indeed. For this man deserved heed, in more regards than one. He was able, strong, dangerous, yet attractive, if scarcely as brilliantly handsome as his nephew. Moreover, not so long ago he had been her mother's lover – or one of them. When King James the Second had died, at the bursting of that cannon at the siege of Roxburgh, aged only twenty-nine, he had left a very beautiful young widow of the same age, Mary of Guelders, of strong character and talents and equally strong desires, with no lack of personable would-be partners. Her elder daughter had not failed to be aware of it, and to recognise the problems and dangers involved, in royal circumstances. This had, perhaps, helped to make Mary Stewart the more mature for her age.

"I cannot think, sir, that you go about your well-doing in the most leal and kindly fashion for His Grace!"

"It was necessary." That was brief and discouraging of further discussion. They rode on in silence – save for the Master of Boyd, who continued to discourse in lively and amiable style.

In due course they reached the West Port of the walled city, and passing through, trotted down the narrow streets to the Grassmarket, under the towering crags of the castle rock. Then up the steep climb of the West Bow into the Lawnmarket, with its tall gabled tenements and the booths of its traders and craftsmen, to the tourney-ground which led up to the lofty citadel itself, walls, towers and gatehouse frowning across the deep water-filled ditch and over the town and farflung prospects of land, hills and sea. It was extraordinary how alike it was to the castle of Stirling, the royal family's principal seat and home.

There was little homely however, once across the drawbridge and within the ramparts, about this fortress, grimmer than Stirling's and scarcely welcoming. James and his sister had been here before, of course, but had never lodged in it, the Abbey of Holyroodhouse, a mile to the east, providing preferred accommodation for royal visits.

"We do not go to the abbey?" Mary asked, as they clattered up the cobblestone ascent to the upper courtyard.

"His Grace will be safer here," Sir Alexander said.

"Safer? In his own realm of Scotland? His Grace has been safe enough, until this day!"

"The abbey would not be . . . suitable, lady."

"I do not like it here," James declared.

"We must take good care of Your Grace and Highness." That was the nephew. "The city folk could be lacking in respect."

The girl turned in her saddle to eye him witheringly.

Strangely, when they drew rein outside the governor's quarters, it was the Lord Boyd who took over from his brother. He had ridden ahead all the way, without word with the royal pair. Now, dismounted, he gestured them within.

"You will find the lodging well enough here, Sire. We had not looked for a lady, but it will serve, to be sure. I shall have a woman sent for, to see to your needs. All will be well."

"Well for whom, my lord?" Mary spoke for her brother. "We were very well at Linlithgow and Stirling. What is your purpose in bringing His Grace here? Sir Alexander says that it is for weal. No more than that. Are we not to be told more?"

"The realm requires better rule, Highness. Since the Bishop

12

of St Andrews died it has drifted, the ship of state lacking a firm hand on the helm. It is intended to improve on that."

"*Your* hand, my lord?"

"With others, yes. Many others."

"But in the King's name?"

"To be sure."

"And the Privy Council? And parliament? Do these not . . . signify?"

"They will . . . approve. In due course. These matters have to be devised in stages, lady. All will be done lawfully, I assure you."

"Will be? But has not been done so this day, I think!"

Boyd glanced at his brother and son. He seemed now to be in charge, but less sure of himself than had been Sir Alexander. "We shall put all in order. Have no fears, Sire." He avoided the girl's eye. "We shall do all to Your Grace's best advantage. Now . . ."

His son came to his rescue. "I will show Their Highnesses to their quarters," the master said, bowing. And taking two royal arms, he ushered them within from that doorstep.

Mary shook her arm free, even if the bewildered young monarch did not.

They were conducted along a vaulted passage to a door which opened on to two intercommunicating chambers, windows facing north across the Nor' Loch and the rolling grassy, cattle-dotted slopes which sank down to the shores of the Scotwater or Firth of Forth. The rooms were sparsely furnished, one with a table, chairs, benches, chests and wall-closets; the other a bedroom – but with only one bed, although a large one. The master waved to it all.

"You will do very well here, no? We will make all more comfortable, I promise you. Refreshment will be sent. And attendants. It will be *my* pleasure and honour to attend you, to be sure." It was at Mary that he looked, smiling.

The young woman managed that flick back of her hair, so telling. "When His Grace, or I, summon you, sir!" she said coolly. "Jamie, give the Master of Boyd permission to retire.

"Yes," the boy said. "Yes. Go away, sir."

The man spread eloquent hands, then changed the gesture into a flourishing bow, as he bent low – but never losing his grin.

"At your royal service!" he declared. "Always." And backed out.

Brother and sister, alone at last, eyed each other, his face crumpling, hers set, tight-lipped. Then she stepped over to clasp and hug him.

"Jamie, lad – I am sorry. Sorry! For this that they do. It is shameful. But they will not hurt you. Never think it. You are the King. They need you, to advance their plans. Whatever these are. So they will do you no harm. Be strong. They must cherish you, gain your help, or they lack the authority to act as they intend. I will be with you, always, aiding you. Fear not."

He shook his head. "I do not understand. When do we go home? To Stirling?"

"I do not know. They may bring them here. Or Lord Kennedy may keep them safe there. We shall see. But . . . keep courage, Jamie. You are their sovereign-lord. Crowned King of Scots. They have sworn allegiance to you. They cannot do without your goodwill. Remember that, always. Now . . ."

A knock sounded at the door, and Thomas Boyd ushered in two servitors with trays of viands – cold meats, oatcakes, honey, a flagon of wine. He drew up chairs to the table, three chairs. It looked as though he was intending to eat with them.

"That will be sufficient, sir. His Grace and I prefer to rest now. And eat alone," Mary told him.

"As you will." Waving the servitors aside, he poured out goblets of wine for them, before taking genial leave.

There was a key in that door, on the outside, and the girl took it out and, transferring it to inside, turned the lock. They had had enough of company for one day.

Sitting down, food untouched, suddenly she was overwhelmed, and sinking forward, head on arms, she sobbed, quietly. It had all been a dire and testing experience, and she had held up, played the princess and the elder sister as best she could, for Jamie's sake. But although no weakling and with her own understandings of due and suitable behaviour, she was of no hard or over-proud nature, no arrogance in her. And she was still only a young woman of seventeen years, King's daughter or none.

"Mary – are you, are you unwell? What is it? Mary, do not cry!"

She looked up, pulling herself together, to muster a watery smile at the boy's worried face. If Mary was in some ways

14

older than her years, James was the reverse, an unsure and hesitant youngster, clever in book-learning and amenable, but always requiring guidance and backing.

"It is nothing, Jamie. I am but tired from long riding. And talk with these lords. You also, to be sure. Food and drink is what we require. And rest. Come – eat you. We will feel the better. We have had a long day of it."

"Yes. I hope that we will go home tomorrow. If we were to ask that man, the one that you call the master – will he take us, do you think? He is much better than the others. Kinder."

"Over-kindly, by half!" she declared. "But, no – I do not think that they will let us go very soon. They have taken too much of trouble to get us here. Or you – for *me* they do not want. But I will not leave you . . ."

"That one, the master, likes you well."

"It is but his manner. A man who makes much of women – and expects much! Do not heed him greatly, Jamie."

They ate, once they had started, more heartily than they had thought to do, young bodies demanding sustenance, for it was dusk now, of a July evening, and they had not eaten since breakfast.

A knock sounded at the door presently, and when Mary signed to ignore it, Thomas Boyd's voice sounded.

"Candles, Highness. Lit. You have locked this door?"

"Yes. Leave them there."

"A pity. I would wish you a good night. Both."

"Well, you have done so, sir."

"And nothing such for *me*, in return?"

"Others, who have had a better day, I think, can give you that!"

"Cruel!" That, however, came with a laugh. "Sleep well, then." They heard his footsteps fade.

"There is but the one bed!" James said, questioningly.

"Then we must make the best of it, must we not? It is large. And we can do without the candles!"

"I . . . I have never slept in a bed . . . with a girl."

"Nor I with a boy! But we shall not die of it!"

"How, how shall we do it?"

"Just as you bed always. There is plenty of room for both of us. Without coming closer than you wish! Go you first, and undress. Call me when you are bedded."

15

Doubtfully the monarch did as he was told, and entered the bedroom. His sister went to the window, to gaze out over the darkening prospect.

She sought to gather and discipline her tumult of thoughts, impressions, questions, fears. These Boyds were clearly hard and dangerous men. And she and Jamie were completely in their power, whatever sort of a face *she* had put on it – no happy situation, however much she sought to reassure her brother. But she had been right in insisting on coming with them. He needed her, as never before. She owed him all her aid and care and support. For, strangely, was he not her own liege-lord and sovereign, as well as her brother, James, by the Grace of God, King of Scots! Of the oldest line of monarchs, possibly, in all Christendom. But she was worried, also, about her two younger brothers and sister, at Stirling. Was Kennedy to be trusted to look after them now . . . ?

A somewhat uncertain call came from the next room.

James was lying close to one edge of the huge bed, with the covers up to his chin, his clothes in a heap on the floor. Going over, she stooped to pick them up and arrange them in some order on a settle. She sat on the end of this, to draw off her long riding-boots – for of course, she was clad as for the hunt, unsuitable as these clothes were here and now.

Then she undressed. She was well aware that the boy, almost a youth, was watching her, for it was not so dark yet in that room that she could remain in any degree unseen – and at fourteen he was old enough to be interested, however shy about his own unclad appearance. He would have seen his *young* sister unclothed, no doubt, but Margaret was only seven, a child yet. Mary was no prude, no prim maid, and not unaware that she was well made, entirely womanly; and while she was not going to flaunt it, nor was she going to hide it foolishly.

Naked, she climbed into the great bed – and saw that the boy was seeking to draw still further away. "I will not bite you, Jamie!" she told him. "Have you said your night's prayers? No – then do so. And you will feel better." She reached over, to pat his arm.

He was silent for a while. Then presently he said, "Mary, you are kind. Thank you. For coming with me."

"Now – go to sleep, Jamie. Goodnight. All will seem better in the morning."

It was surprising how short a time it was before his deep breathing told her that he slept, whatever his anxieties. For herself, she lay long awake, pondering. If only their mother had been still alive, she would have been able to deal with all this, known what to do. This might not have happened then, of course, especially with that Alexander Boyd there. She was strong, able . . .

Mary was, at long last, about to drop off, when with a muttering, James turned over, and a hand came groping out towards her. Rousing herself, she leaned across and drew him to her, and he came, wordless. She clasped him close, hushing him – not that he spoke.

So they lay, silent. And strangely, now she slept almost as quickly as did he.

2

Up and dressed before James was awake, Mary went to unlock that door, after making use of the garderobe and sanitary chute, a new determination about her. Outside sat a serving-woman, half asleep, with jugs of steaming water, basin and towels. She said that she would be back with the breakfast when her ladyship was ready. Thanking her, Mary took the water to the bedroom and washed thoroughly, having partly to undress again. James wakened and watched, but this time with little sign of embarrassment. Nevertheless, when she had finished, and told him to rise and wash also, with breakfast coming, he would not get out of bed until she had left the room.

The outer door was still unlocked, and when a knock sounded she opened, and found four persons standing there, the woman, the two male servitors of the evening before, and Thomas, Master of Boyd again.

"Ha, Highness, a very good morning to you!" he greeted cheerfully. "I hope that you slept well? Here is the best this castle will rise to, to break our fast. We will do better in future, I promise you; but here is porridge, cream, eggs, cold venison and bread. Also ale, if you so desire." And he took a tray from one of the men and led the way in. Thereupon, he proceeded to set out all on the table – and Mary noted that it was three places that he set again. This was a determined young man, clearly. That made two of them, then.

But this morning she did not curtly banish him. For one of the decisions she had made last night, before she slept, was that, in this difficult situation, it would be wise to make use of almost the only asset they seemed to possess, apart from the royal status, and that was the so evident eagerness of this so handsome character to be friendly. Too friendly, no doubt, and she must keep him in his place, if possible. But that place might well be useful, helpful. So although she did not exactly smile upon him, when thanking the servants she did not dismiss him with them. Instead she called to James to come, that breakfast awaited him.

Owl-eyed, the boy came through, to be bowed to deeply and greeted warmly. He was not yet fully clad, and tousle-headed and barefooted – as indeed was his sister, her long riding-boots unsuitable wear for breakfast. She felt, to be sure, distinctly at a disadvantage, sartorially, her hunting-jacket discarded meantime and the sleeveless bodice she had worn beneath looking rather ridiculous above the heavy, long and full skirt, and revealing as to figure into the bargain. Whereas, despite the hour, the young man was dressed brilliantly, in the height of fashion. This was no help.

"You are very . . . attentive, sir," she said. "I wonder why? The others a deal less so!"

"It is my pleasure, Highness. And my leal duty." That to James. "I would wish all to be to your satisfaction, as far as is possible. While you are here."

"Yes. And for how long *are* we here? Against our wills."

"That, I fear, I do not know. And, no doubt, you will come to see that it is for the best. And be less displeasured."

"I doubt it, sir."

"I, at least, will seek to pleasure you! And Your Grace. To my best ability. And I am practised at it, see you!" That was added with a wave of a hand. "Now, shall we eat? While this porridge is still warm."

The King, for one, required no second invitation. He sat down to porridge and cream without delay.

Mary, although of a good appetite, was less eager. "If we are here for some time, sir, we require clothing, gear, attendants . . . other than yourself! These are at Stirling. Why must we be at this Edinburgh Castle? Why do you and your father, and the others, not go there instead of us being held here? Surely your purposes could be served equally well from Stirling?"

"The decision is not mine, Highness. But the rule of the king-dom has been from Stirling, since Bishop Kennedy died, and has not been . . . of the best. Good. Strong. It needs improvement. And those who failed to lead fittingly, hold Stirling. So, the new rule will be from Edinburgh. And better, surer."

"And *your* part in it?"

"Myself, I am but a looker-on. My father's son, my uncle's nephew. But anxious for your welfare. Sire, more porridge?"

19

"So – His Grace and myself are, in fact, your prisoners here! Is not that the truth of it?"

"Not so. Never think it. All will be done for your comfort . . ."

"Such as a second bed provided, perhaps?"

He raised eyebrows. "You prefer that? I swear His Grace does not! How fortunate and happy a bedfellow! I could wish . . . !" He sighed. "Ah, well – another bed, if so demanded. Possibly other apartments, an extra chamber. We had planned only for His Grace. We shall send to Stirling for your clothing and attendants. But meanwhile, I will have my sister, Annabella, come from Kilmarnock to be Your Highness's lady-in-waiting. She is a mite younger than yourself, I think – but sixteen years. But not uncomely or lacking in manners. And she could bring women's clothing with her."

"I see. And meantime we remain in this fortress, like cooped fowl!"

"Scarcely that, to be sure. With suitable guard, His Grace can ride abroad – for the King of Scots must not go unprotected, must he?" A chuckle. "Venison? And you, Sire? As for yourself, Highness, I will escort you where and when you will. Hunting. Hawking. There is the royal forest of the Holy Rood, around that great hill here, Arthur's Seat. The Braid and Pentland Hills also, I am told, are good for the chase. And lochs for wildfowling. We could go visit my sister at Tantallon, down the coast – she is Countess of Angus. No need to play the cooped fowl – you the fairest bird to fly this land!" And he bowed across the table.

"I find your empty compliments wearisome, sir. Boyd deeds do not match your words!" She rose. "I have had a sufficiency now, of provender as well as of talk! His Grace, I think, also. James, will you again give the Master of Boyd leave to retire?"

Mouth still full, the monarch nodded.

"Heigho – dismissed! But I shall be back, presently, to see if you would desire to go riding. It is a fine day. Too good to sit indoors."

"Yes," James answered for her. "I would like that. Could we climb that big hill yonder?"

"Arthur's Seat? I doubt whether we could get horses up to the top, Sire. I have never been there. But – a royal command, and we can try!" He turned to salute the girl. "In an hour, shall we say?" He took his leave, all smiles.

"He is very good," the boy asserted. "I like him, Mary."

She reserved her own opinion as to that. But she certainly did not wish to be immured in these two rooms all day. And at least she had clothing for riding.

In due course, then, their so diligent squire came to usher them out to the upper courtyard, where about a dozen men, mounted and wearing the colours of Boyd, awaited them, with their horses. There was no sign of Lord Boyd or Sir Alexander. The master made a great show of hoisting Mary up to her saddle, with considerable clutching, and taking the opportunity to murmur that it was a pity about the guard, but it was unthinkable that the monarch should go about without due and proper escort. She replied that she understood perfectly – and the first smile she had bestowed on him was a mocking one. She added that she was quite capable of mounting her horse unaided.

They rode down to the gatehouse and out across the tourney-ground beyond and into the Lawnmarket. The walled city of Edinburgh was highly unusual in its siting and layout, being in the nature of a mile-long ellipse, narrow, and flanking a central spine of rock which ran down from the castle-fortress to the Abbey of Holy Rood and the open woodlands which surrounded the extraordinary towering peak of Arthur's Seat and its cliff-girt outliers. From this central spine, which comprised the Lawnmarket, the High Street and the Canongate, alleys and lanes and wynds branched off, inevitably all downhill, left and right, like herring bones, with tall tenement housing rising everywhere, and all but meeting each other overhead, darkening the alleys, with booths and workshops and ale-houses in the arcaded basements, the town-houses of great ones, lairds and prosperous citizens on the first and second floors, and the teeming warrens of the lesser folk soaring six and seven storeys above; so that, although the city, within its sheltering walls, did not cover a great deal of area, it housed a notably large population in its restricted space.

Interested enough in what they saw, they rode down High Street, past the Mercat Cross, the High Kirk of St Giles and the Tolbooth to the Netherbow Port. Beyond this was the Canongate, strangely, a separate burgh belonging to the abbey, although there was no break in the housing. Down this they came to the Abbey Sanctuary, a girth or place of refuge for offenders against certain laws, debtors and those awaiting trial. Then they were at the great abbey and monastic establishment itself, founded by James's ancestor, David the First.

"I do not see why, if we must remain in this Edinburgh, we cannot lodge here, in the abbatial quarters," Mary said. "I have been here before. My father always bided here when in Edinburgh. The place is spacious, comfortable, much better than up in that castle. Better for all. The Lord Abbot would welcome us."

"It is the matter of security, see you," Tom Boyd told her. "These great monkish buildings, spread as they are, in gardens and orchards, cannot be guarded as can the castle. You must see that."

"Guarded against whom? The citizens of this Edinburgh are not going to attack you. Or us."

"Others could seek to do so."

"So! I think that you mean the lords from whose care you . . . stole us! Or some of them? You fear that they may seek to win His Grace back? The Lords Kennedy, Fleming, Hamilton, Crawford and the rest?"

"Not Kennedy or Fleming, I think."

"Why? They were our guardians. Still are, for our brothers and sister."

"We have our bands with them."

"Ah, yes – your bands. These bands are so strong? They bind and tie all hands? Stronger, it seems, than your oaths of allegiance to your sovereign-lord!"

"No-o-o. They are strong, yes. They bind lords to mutual support, not to injure each other's causes. Saving, to be sure, treasonable offences against the crown."

"And doing what you did yesterday is not treason against the crown? Forcibly abducting the King!"

"Not so. What was done was for the King's good. And the realm's."

"I think that you play with words, sir. You stole His Grace from those the Privy Council chose to guard and guide him, the monarch. For *your* ends, not his. And the Lords Kennedy and Fleming also, with others, did not seriously oppose you. Because of their bands with you. Hamilton tried – but perhaps you had no band with the Hamiltons? So – you fear reprisals. As well you may! And so we must be kept secure. Prisoners in yonder castle!"

"Save us, if you are hard to convince, Highness! While Scotland was being well governed, by your royal mother and Bishop Kennedy, there was no need for this. But now, the lords at Stirling are weak, feeble. The realm drifts. The Lord of the Isles and the Earl of Ross actually swear allegiance to the English, so long as they are left to hold all the Highland west and the Hebrides. And the Earl of Dunbar *bides* at the English court, and threatens invasion of the borderland. With a child King, the realm needs a strong hand, and has not had it, this sorry year."

"And could that not have been arranged decently, in order, by the Council and parliament? Not this unlawful grasping?"

"The other was talked of, yes. But no agreement was reached . . ."

"Even with your banded friends?"

"Not so that it was sure. Firm. As it had to be."

"So you have been tying men's hands, with your bands! For long. In preparation. All a plot! To move when all was ready. Now you hold the King, but fear reprisals. I think that you are a little unsure of your hands, you Boyds!"

"Not me, lady. I am but my father's son. Not consulted. But I say that you are hard on us. This was only a necessary device, a means to effect the required change. All will be put in order, you will see. A parliament will indeed be held. A new Council sworn . . ."

"When?"

"A parliament requires forty days of notice to be lawful. And the King's signature and seal. So that it will be six weeks yet before all is settled . . ."

"Six weeks! In yonder prison!"

"Is this prison-keeping?" He waved at all the parkland, woodland and steep whin-clad slopes. "Am I not doing my best for you?"

She relented a little. "As gaoler, you are more . . . friendly than your kin, perhaps! But we are prisoners, none the less."

James had been showing little interest in this conversation, gazing around him as they rode, especially up at the abruptly climbing hillsides beyond a small lochan from which wildfowl rose as they drew near.

"Can we not get up there?" he asked. "I would like that."

"We might try, Sire. But the last part, I think, will be too steep for horses. And rocky. And for ladies, belike!"

"I can climb hills as well as any," Mary declared – although

23

admittedly she was not clad for this, with her long riding-skirt and boots. But then neither was the young man, in his fine clothing. "Why not do that another day, Jamie, when we are better clad for it? Today remain a-horse."

"I agree," Tom Boyd said. "But I am told that we can ride quite high, round the far side of the hill. Up beyond this loch. They say that there is another loch up there, set high. And still another, large, far below, providing much sport for hawks."

Disappointed, James acquiesced. His was not an assertive nature. If the guard, behind, heard any of this, they would be relieved, no doubt.

Leaving the low ground, they trotted on by a climbing track up the eastern flanks of what was really a small range, with all the Lothian plain of Forth spreading before them now, to the green Fawside and Garleton Hills, the leviathan-like Traprain Law, the isolated conical peak of North Berwick Law and the mighty stack of the Craig of Bass soaring out of the waves beyond, then the limitless plain of the sea, a glorious prospect indeed, which had the monarch exclaiming, for he enjoyed beautiful things and showed a burgeoning talent for drawing and painting.

His sister, whilst appreciative of scenery, was more concerned with the situation into which they had been plunged.

"Who leads, in all this?" she asked. "Your father or your uncle? Sir Alexander appeared to be the leader, yesterday, the younger as he is. Yet, at the end, the Lord Boyd took over command, it seemed."

"My uncle is the man of action, my father has the wits! Uncle Sandy is the soldier, the knight-at-arms, the tourney-master. He has been called an ornament of chivalry! Your royal mother, I think, found him so?" He glanced sidelong at her. "Which gives me hope!"

When he got no response to that from Mary, he went on. "My father plans and judges and sees ahead. They make an effective pair."

"And you?"

"Why, I seek to learn from both. But have my own notions." He laughed, but eyed her keenly. "What, may I ask, is *your* position, Highness? I heard that you were contracted to marry an Englishman, their King indeed, Edward. King meantime, at least! Although with these Wars of the Roses, as they are called, who knows."

She tossed her head. "That is by with. It was but talk. Talk between my mother and Margaret of Anjou, Henry's Queen. A match for this Edward. I was not consulted. Now, with my mother dead, all that is forgotten."

"How blessed a relief! We must do better for you than that! To wed an Englishman! Even their King."

"*We*, sir?"

"The Council. The parliament. The realm. Scotland's fairest and most proud daughter, marry English! Never!"

"I hope to wed whom *I* will, sir – not who others may choose."

"Well said. My own attitude, entirely. My father formerly contracted me to that pale young Kennedy female. But I have persuaded him otherwise . . ."

"There is a heron!" James cried, pointing to a long narrow lochan they were now approaching, high in a sort of hanging valley. "And a flock of teal. Mallard amongst them. And – yes, it is a goose, only one. Is it a greylag? Or a pinkfoot?" The boy was good on birds.

His companions could not inform him.

"The hawking here will be excellent," the master said. "I will send to Kilmarnock for my falcons."

"We have many at Stirling. Will you bring them to us, sir?"

"I will see if it is possible, Sire. But – I have plenty. Fine birds. We will have good sport."

Soon they were out of that loch-cradling valley and able to look down far below, where there was a quite major sheet of water ringed with reed-beds, with beyond it more low hills beginning to lift up towards the lofty serried ramparts of the Pentlands.

"That will be Duddingston Loch, the largest here," they were told. "You see – you will do well, very well, at Edinburgh."

James at least was beginning to think likewise.

Back at the castle they found a second bed being installed in their chamber, a smaller one, necessarily further restricting the space in the bedroom. Refreshments were produced for them but no large meal was served, word being given that they would feed presently in the great hall – with His Grace's agreement. Tom Boyd seemed less than elated over this, obviously preferring a private threesome. Mary declared that if that was to be the way of it, then she must have clothing other than her riding-gear. To go dressed so would look ridiculous. Could the master not find some women's garb for her, about this castle? It need not be handsome or even especially well fitting. But she was not going in that scanty bodice, heavy skirt and long boots!

Approving of this request, the man went off to see what could be found. Unfortunately the female members of his family had been left at Kilmarnock during this venture; and his father was a widower. There *were* a few women in the citadel, however, in addition to servants. He would see what he could do.

When he came back almost an hour later, he brought a buxom, bold-eyed lady with him, both bearing armfuls of clothing and shoes. This was Isabel Cunninghame, he introduced, a friend. She was perhaps a little larger than Her Highness, but they might be able to make something here fit reasonably well. A tuck here and there? Shoes might be more of a problem. They should go through all, and try them. He led the way into the bedroom, the newcomer skirling a laugh.

Mary gestured for all the gear to be put on the new bed, then turning, pointed to the door. "Thank you. But we shall essay this the better for your absence, Master of Boyd!" She called, "Jamie, summon the master to you."

By royal command, however vague and non-spontaneous, the man had to leave them, protesting, to more mirth from the newcomer.

In fact, the dressing situation was less difficult than it might have been, with quite a choice of garments and sizes, and only minor adjustments required, presumably not all the offerings pertaining to this Isabel Cunninghame. A leather belt helped to reduce the waist-fitting, and the bust excess was not great, for Mary was quite well developed there, and a silken shawl served to hide any maladjustments. The footwear was less simple to fit, but by using ribbons to tie soft leather slippers in place, a fair comfort was achieved. So, arrayed in an olive green velvet skirt, a more ample bodice under an open quilted doublet of brocaded purple and gold satin, and that shawl, Mary sallied out to face male inspection – and found herself, in fact, concerned that the effect should be favourable.

The man clapped his hands at the sight of her. "Bravo!" he cried. "Here is wonder, delight! The vision fair! You gladden the eyes, Highness. And . . . more than the eyes!"

James could not have been less interested, at least in his sister's appearance. "The master was telling me that Boyd means fair, comely, Mary. The Erse, *boidheach*. And he *is* fair, comely, is he not? They come of the old Celtic people, before ever the Stewarts came to Scotland. Or the Bruces. Is that not notable?"

"The master is fair of talk, at least! Over-fair, I think!" But she did not frown as she said it. She turned to thank the Cunninghame woman for her help. Whereupon the master took that woman's arm and ushered her to the door.

"Come, Isa," he said. "I will be back for Your Grace and Highness shortly, to conduct you to the hall. When all is in readiness."

Mary noted that, as they passed out, the lady's hand went up to stroke Tom Boyd's head and neck affectionately.

When in due course they were escorted to the great hall of the castle, scene of many a parliament, it was to discover that quite a banquet had been prepared and a large company assembled to partake of it. A trumpeter sounded a flourish, and all stood as the monarch entered. In place of the Lyon King of Arms – who of course was at Stirling – Lord Boyd himself came to lead the royal pair up past the long table and bowing guests to the dais-platform at the far end, which they mounted, and where a group of notables awaited them. One was a short, corpulent, red-faced man wearing a handsome cloak and a chain of office, and bearing a cushion on which lay a golden key. This was the provost of the city, who thrust out the cushion to James, bowing as low as his build would allow, all but upsetting cushion and key in the process.

The boy, who had never been given the key of a city before, glanced at Mary for guidance. She nodded, and murmured, "Take it. Then put it back." Her brother lifted it up, admired it, declared that it was very heavy, and returned it to the cushion.

"Sire, come and sit here," Lord Boyd directed.

There was a throne-like chair at the centre of the dais-table, somewhat large for this King of Scots. To him there were brought the magnates who had stood waiting, the Lords Somerville, he who had taken part in the abduction, Hailes, and Livingstone, with the Master of Hailes and Ker Younger of Cessford. All now made respectful obeisance towards the sovereign.

The Boyd brothers seated themselves on either side of James, with Mary between Sir Alexander and the master. Much attention was paid to the boy.

A quite ambitious meal was served, entertainment proceeding

throughout down beside the long table, in the form of fiddling, dancing and a gypsy with a dancing bear. Sir Alexander addressed little of his attention to Mary, but she heard him enlarging on the military arts to James, and promising to organise a tourney for his edification shortly. It was evident that efforts were now being made to gain the sympathies and goodwill of the youngster, as well as holding his person.

The master made up for his uncle in attentiveness to the young woman, so much so that, removing a hand that was stroking her wrist, she asked him why he had not brought his friend Isabel Cunninghame up here to sit beside him; she could be seen placed well down the lengthy main table. Laughing, he told her that Isa was well enough where she was, and not over-particular as to the company she kept. Ask Uncle Sandy!

Mary did not pursue the matter, but sought to maintain her cool distance-keeping, difficult as this was in physical terms.

James ate heartily, enjoyed the bear's antics particularly, and listened to his two mentors, clearly appreciating all this new-found care and solicitude.

With the eating over and the entertainers beginning to repeat themselves, Lord Boyd, turning in his chair, signed to the waiting trumpeter, who thereupon blew another flourish. From the end of the dais-table the Lord Livingstone rose, and came along with a paper, ink-horn, quill and metal seal. He was Lord Chamberlain, and had been at Linlithgow for the Exchequer Audit. Now he was here; so he must have been in league with the Boyds, although not taking part in the abduction. He presented the paper to James, opened the ink-horn, dipped in the pen, and handed this to the young monarch. Boyd explained that this was the official summons, to the kingdom, for a parliament, to be held in forty days' time, requiring the signature and seal of the King. Would His Grace sign there at the bottom?

The boy looked quickly along at his sister. It was obvious to her that this was the real reason behind this evening's activities, James's co-operation now essential. If he refused, what would they do? Was there any point in refusal? Would not a parliament, in fact, be advantageous? Once the realm's parliament met, they could hardly keep the sovereign-lord a prisoner any longer. This entire situation should be bettered, regularised. Anyway, they might force James to sign, one way or another. Half shrugging, she nodded, wordless. The boy somewhat laboriously appended his signature, the quill rather spluttering ink.

Livingstone took the document, declaring that he would have wax prepared and the seal appended, and bowed himself off. Boyd rose and indicated that James should do so also. All then had to rise, when the monarch stood. Clearly the evening's importance was over. Amidst more trumpeting and bowing, the entire dais-table group escorted the monarch to the door – whereafter, however, the Master of Boyd was left to take the royal pair back to their quarters, their importance abruptly dispensed with. James, however, was well pleased with it all, almost excited.

Tom Boyd, of course, would have come in, to continue the evening's entertainment in his preferred style, but Mary was quite firm in directing otherwise. He did, then, kiss her hand, and was proceeding on up her arm, when she twitched it away.

"Go back, sir, to yonder hall," she advised. "You have gained your ends sufficiently for one night, I think! And you will find more . . . accommodating company back there, no?"

He sighed, shaking his head at her, but went.

Having to shorten her brother's encomiums on the evening's satisfactions, especially his approval of the bear-dancing and the promise of a tournament, Mary got him off bedwards. She hoped that she had done rightly in guiding him to sign that summons to parliament. But . . . these ones would have achieved it anyway, somehow, she had little doubt. A parliament, although obviously necessary for these Boyds' plans, was also best for James himself and the nation. Had she shaken her head, then, and James refused to sign, they might have separated her from him, as a hostile influence – which would have been a grievous development.

When, presently, she in turn entered the bedchamber, it was to find James, as before, lying in the large bed. It was later and darker than the previous night, and she was able to discard her borrowed clothing in more privacy. She went over to give the boy his goodnight kiss. He clung to her for a little, in her nakedness. She was making back for the smaller bed when he spoke.

"Will you not come back, Mary? To this bed. There is much room. It was good, last night. Was it not? Together."

She hesitated. Had she not been talking about suitability, earlier? Was this suitable? Yet . . . if James wanted it, was there any harm in it? He was going through a very upsetting experience, for a boy. If it helped him to feel her, his elder sister,

29

close, a reassurance, was it wrong? And herself – she could do with a little togetherness perhaps. These last two days had been . . . testing. She went round to the other side of the great bed, and got in.

James reached out to her, but taking his hand, she did not encourage him to come closer. He said, "Will the master take us climbing that hill tomorrow, Mary?"

"He might . . ."

"If I said that it was my royal command, would he do it?"

"That is hardly a subject for a royal command, Jamie!"

"If *you* asked him, he would. He likes you."

"We shall see. I am not eager to ask favours of that one! He is over-eager for favours from *me*! These Boyds are ambitious men, Jamie. They act of a set purpose. They need you, the King. As when they had you sign that parliament summons. I think that was right to do. But you will have to beware of them, not trust them too greatly. The master is very friendly, but you must watch him also."

He yawned. "A tournament would be splendid. I hope that they have one. Would they let me take part? Not just watch? What could I do?"

"Tournaments are for grown men, Jamie. Jousting on horseback, with lances. Swordplay. Duels. Archery contests. I do not see that you could take part in any of these. The last, perhaps. You could practise with a bow. I could show you. I have done a little archery. Not that I am good at it. I do not think that you have ever tried it?"

There was no answer. The King of Scots slept.

The next day was wet, and scarcely suitable for climbing hills, to Jamie's much disappointment. But the indefatigable Tom Boyd, who appeared to conceive it his pleasure, if not his duty, to be responsible for keeping the royal pair entertained, took them on a tour of the fortress itself. They started with the extraordinary topmost structure of all, a tiny chapel perched on the naked summit of the vast rock, severe, plain within and without, its whitewashed interior containing little more than a simple stone altar, a holy water stoup, a lectern and a kneeling-stool. This was Queen Margaret's Chapel, he explained. Why so small, so modest, when built by a Queen, he did not know, for the good King David's mother had erected the great Dunfermline Abbey, where the Bruce was buried, and other major shrines; but this place was considered to be very holy, for some reason, nevertheless. He was not very strong on matters religious, himself, but no doubt there was some reason . . .

Mary, although no know-all, took the opportunity to demonstrate that they were not all ignoramuses in the royal family of Stewart, and was quite pleased to be able to suggest that if indeed the Boyds were of the old Celtic race, as their name indicated, then the master ought to know what this chapel represented. She had never seen it before, but had heard of it. Queen Margaret Atheling, of the English royal house, believed that Almighty God must have sent her to Scotland for some especial purpose – after all, she was on her way to Hungary, her mother's home country, when their ship was driven ashore in a storm, and Malcolm Canmore, King of Scots, had captured her and, captivated in turn by her beauty, had wed her. She believed that God's purpose must be her conversion of the old Celtic or Columban Church, which had been Scotland's Kirk for five hundred years, since Columba's time, to her own Roman Catholicism. And, almost single-handed, this young woman in her twenties had achieved this, and turned the Scots to Rome. Whether this was indeed God's will was doubtful, for the old Church had suited the Scots people, independent folk who took but ill to domination in spiritual matters from the Pope, cardinals, archbishops, bishops and legates and nuncios, preferring their own monastic abbots, and small shrines to the grand abbeys and cathedrals of Rome. However, in middle life, when disaster took her husband and eldest son from her, and her favourite youngest son David was a captive hostage in England, with another son deserted back to the Celtic faith, Margaret came to doubt the rightness and wisdom of what she had done. She became all but an anchorite, shutting herself away, castigating herself, all but starving; and when sickness overtook her, holed herself up in this castle, and built this tiny, simple chapel, in the ancient tradition, for her dying worship. So this, not the great abbeys of the land, was her final statement of faith, possibly remorse, a monument to a woman's flexibility of mind.

James was not very interested in all this, but Boyd was, not so much probably from the religious or even historic aspect but in that the young woman knew of it and had elected to tell him. He said that he would not forget it and, patting her shoulder, added that it was a blessing that women could change their minds!

From the chapel they went down to the Governor's House where, it seemed, the Boyd family were installed. While they did not examine it all, although by no means palatial it was obviously a deal more comfortable and well appointed than were the quarters presently allotted to James and his sister – a point on which Mary did not fail to comment.

Boyd had his own answer to that, waving an eloquent hand. "If *I* had my way, Highness, you would be *sharing* these lodgings with me, I do assure you!" And she could take what she would out of that. Her tossed hair was as eloquent as his arm-waving.

Their next stop was at the fortress prisons, a row of dark, underground cells cut in the solid rock, provided with staples and iron chains, all fortunately empty at this juncture. Glad to get out of that horrible place, Mary could not resist a comment.

"At least you did not instal us *there*, prisoners as we are!"

Even she had to acknowledge his quick thinking and spirit when he answered, "Never. That is folly. But, even there, it would have been my pleasure to join you!"

Passing their own quarters, across the square from the palace building with its great hall, galleries and armoury, he took them down to see David's Tower, easternmost of the eight towers of the citadel, built by Margaret's youngest son, David the First of proud memory. And here he showed them the renowned cannon, Mollance Meg – which greatly intrigued James, if not Mary. She had something of a horror of such things, for it was, of course, the explosion of a cannon which had killed their father, who had been all too interested in artillery. Young James knew of this great piece by repute, the mightiest in Scotland, and recited for Boyd's benefit its story, how it had been constructed by a Galloway blacksmith on the orders of Maclellan of Bombie, and made powerful enough to smash through even the walls of Threave Castle, the seat of the Earl of Douglas who had slain Maclellan's father. This it had achieved, its huge ball, the weight of a Galloway cow allegedly, said to have taken off the hand of the Fair Maid of Galloway as she sat at meat with the earl. The castle had fallen, and its lord with it – and since he was the enemy of the King, that James had bestowed on its maker the farm of Mollance, formerly Douglas's, in gratitude. The smith's wife's name was Meg, and so the great piece had become known as Mollance, or Mons, Meg, and was brought to Edinburgh and installed here, the monarch's pride. Tom Boyd almost certainly knew all this, but he listened attentively to the boy. Made of staves and hoops of iron and mounted on a low trolley, it was impressive only by its size, weight and story; yet Mary's companions obviously found it fascinating – which led her to consider, not for the first time, the difference of what might impress males as distinct from females.

The rain had now ceased, and nothing would do but that, in the afternoon, they must climb Arthur's Seat, wet grass or none, Mary's protests about unsuitable footwear being dismissed by her brother as feeble. So, with the strongest of the borrowed female shoes which would approximately fit, they set out, horsed and with the required escort again, down through the town to the hillfoot, the enthusiasm one-sided indeed.

The master had been told that if they turned up from the parkland of the royal hunting forest, between a knoll called the Haggis Knowe and St Anthony's Chapel, just before they reached the first of the lochs, St Margaret's, they would find a rising valley which would take them almost two-thirds of the way up, still mounted, before they had to leave the horses and clamber. The floor of this quite wide valley had to be carefully skirted on the right, for it was waterlogged, indeed it was known as the Hunters' Bog; so the riders had to pick their way, James urgent, Boyd consistently cheerful, Mary patient and the escort glum.

Up on the final shoulder of hill before the ultimate steep and rocky peak, they dismounted, for a windy conclave. None was really dressed for climbing, the master probably the best so, even James having only riding-boots; and clearly none of the escort was properly shod for this – nor eager to make the attempt. However, the guard was there only to ensure that the monarch was not the target for any recapture attempt, and the climbers would be in sight throughout, so it was decided that the men could safely be left with the horses, and their three betters go on alone. The top of Arthur's Seat was hardly likely to be the scene of any reprisal raid.

So they set off, the King leading and determined to show his prowess, Mary kilting up her skirt and shaking off the master's helping hands.

It was indeed a steep and rough ascent, with much of bare stone and moss, slippery after the rain; and the wind, from the south-west, in their faces, did not help. Soon all were panting, and even James glad to pause with increasing frequency, the young man urging the girl not to overdo it, to go slowly, and when she breathlessly declared that she was perfectly able to master this hill unaided, pointing out appreciatively that her heaving bosom gave the delightful lie to her assertions.

Grasping tussocks and outcropping stone, and seeking to use the sides of her ill-fitting shoes rather than the toes to aid her, Mary pulled herself up. With perhaps three hundred feet to surmount, and so steep in parts that they had to pick a circuitous route rather than going straight up, it was a demanding business, with false crests to contend with. She would have copied her brother, who was largely going on all fours, but perceived this as undignified for a woman, princess or other, particularly with a man all too anxious to give her physical support. She was no weakling, but found it a trial.

At the summit, at length, it was probably worth it, however, so tremendous was the prospect on every hand and, yes, the sense of achievement, James capering about in triumph and exclaiming, and the master taking the opportunity to clutch the girl, to steady her against the wind's buffetings, in necessarily all-embracing fashion. There were these varieties of reward.

Going down again was as difficult as coming up had been, if less exhausting, slipping now the danger, and Mary not ungrateful for a hand on occasion – especially when, all but involuntarily, it was *her* hand which once shot out to prevent Tom Boyd from falling. That made her feel better, strangely enough. James was on his bottom as frequently as on his feet, but shouting his mirth.

Mud-stained, breathless and wind-blown, they reached the horses again, to their escorts' ill-concealed smirks.

That evening, when the master ushered in their meal, he brought news. It had been decided that he should go to Kilmarnock on the morrow, to the Boyds' Dean Castle there, to bring back Annabella Boyd, a supply of women's clothing for Mary, and to exchange some of their fighting men for a new batch – these being mainly the sons and brothers of tenant farmers and field-workers, cattle-herds and the like, who could not be away from their other duties for too long at any one time. It was suggested that Mary Stewart went with him, to select the clothing and other plenishings which she might wish, and for the chance to get out of their cramping quarters for a while.

She hesitated. The opportunity to go riding free appealed, even though she recognised that she would have to be constantly on her guard over Tom Boyd's advances throughout – but was she not that anyway? And she was reasonably confident that she could cope with him. But James . . . ?

The boy at once asked whether he could go also, to be told that unfortunately that was not possible in the circumstances. The royal protests were immediately forthcoming, when the master revealed that this had been foreseen by their captors, by declaring that Sir Alexander was desirous of discussing the tournament details with His Grace; and also, if he would wish it, give him some instruction in the martial arts, swordplay, lance-aiming at targets on horseback, archery and the like. This, of course, much altered James's attitude and priorities. When could they begin, he demanded?

Mary, for her part, asked how far it was to Kilmarnock – since distances she could see might complicate the issue as far as she was concerned, if an overnight halt was required. She was told, quite casually, that it was some sixty-five miles, but no really difficult riding – to which she replied that she had ridden further than that in a day ere this; and her mare was of excellent quality.

The man eyed her carefully, and shrugged.

3

The following morning they were up betimes, with James suddenly anxious and having to be reassured by his sister that she would be back in but three days and all would be well. He was to pay careful heed to Sir Alexander over the arms exercises, for these could have their dangers; but to remember always that he was the King, and not to be persuaded to anything that he judged unsuitable. This matter of suitability was becoming something of a preoccupation for that young woman.

The boy was a little tense at the parting, for he had never hitherto been left alone for more than an hour or two lacking the support of members of his family; and Mary asked herself whether she was in a way failing him, doing the right thing. But it was too late to change her mind now, and the boy was probably the better of learning to stand on his own feet on occasion; she must not seem to cosset him too protectively.

They rode off with a party of some two score men-at-arms, some of these of the Arthur's Seat escort, a cheerful company glad to be going home, the master in dashing mood. Fortunately it was a fine sunny morning.

They left the city by the Grassmarket and West Port, and took the road south-westwards as though making for the northern skirts of the Pentland Hills. Tom said that there were two or three routes they could follow, but the easiest as regards terrain for fair riding, although not the shortest, he reckoned was by the drove-road to Lanark by the upper Water of Leith, the Pentland hillfoots, the Crosswood and Medwyn Waters, to Carnwath and so to Lanark. From there, over the moors to the Avon Water and Darvel, it was but another score of miles to Kilmarnock. Put thus, it sounded no major journey.

The men-at-arms were on the whole well mounted, for the Ayrshire land of the Boyds was notable for raising cattle and horses; but Mary was afraid that they might hold them back nevertheless, her own and the master's animals being of course especially well bred. It was not so much their speed that she was concerned with, but the ability to cover the long journey in one day. An overnight stop could present opportunities for her companion to press his unacceptable attentions – although the possibility of putting up at some religious house or hospice did occur to her, where presumably women would be kept apart from men anyway. Or would they be? She had never been in such situation before. Were there any religious houses between Lanark and Kilmarnock? And if so, would such be prepared to entertain some forty men-at-arms? She could hardly put these queries to Tom Boyd however.

Not that there was much opportunity for converse at the pace they rode, her companion certainly not limiting his pace for whatever reason. No doubt he too was glad to escape the restrictions of the last three days. He led with a spanking canter for the first few miles, before settling down to a fast but steady trot, which ate up the distance satisfactorily. It was a good feeling, of a summer's day, the larks trilling and the curlews wheepling from the heather.

This road, made for cattle-droving, although flanking the hills all the way, nowhere rose very high, the moorlands on the whole providing fairly firm going, and the valleys, being those of cascading hill-streams, not boggy. So they made excellent time, with a minimum of talk.

When, after three hours of it, they reached Carnwath, to water and rest their mounts, Tom remarked that she was a good horsewoman to add to her other attractions. She pointed out that, with the father she had, she had to be – the late James being of an impatient and impetuous nature, to put it mildly.

They reached the River Clyde soon thereafter, and followed this most of the way to Lanark, where they fed after a fashion, at three ale-houses, for forty men-of-arms called for the facilities of more than one, and Tom Boyd was apparently not the kind of man to stint his supporters. Then on, still in the Clyde valley, to the inflowing River Nethan, up which they turned. They were here mounting to a central watershed of south-west Scotland, where many rivers were born, new country for Mary. They had to pick their way over dividing ridges and escarpments, none high, from one valley to the next, to maintain their true direction, from Nethan to Candor to Avon, the most difficult part of their journey, but picturesque. Thereafter reaching Strathaven, they

37

followed that river for a dozen miles up to the highest point of their journey, where Wallace and Bruce had fought some of their fiercest battles against the invading English, in the Loudoun Hill area; indeed Boyd pointing out the site of Wallace's camp, and asserting that he had Wallace blood in him.

Over this pass they were into the valley of the Irvine Water, a major stream, which would bring them almost all the way down to Kilmarnock, by Darvel, Newmilns and Galston, the final dozen miles. It was only early evening, so there would be no question of having to halt for the night, to Mary's distinct relief. Although what conditions would be like at Dean Castle remained to be seen.

Saddle-sore and stiff, but not too weary, they came at length, with the dusk, in sight of the town of Kilmarnock, its smokes blue haze to the evening. But they did not enter it, swinging off northwards to reach the Kilmarnock Burn in about a mile, where in open meadowland the tall, massive, square keep of a castle rose out of a high-walled courtyard enclosure, extensive, with its own parapet and gatehouse. At first glance it did not appear to be a very strong defensive site, however powerful-looking and impressive was the fortalice itself; but closer approach showed that meadowland to be largely waterlogged, and the Kilmarnock Burn used to provide a wide moat around the castle. An easily defendable causeway crossed this to give access. A dean or hollow might be no typical position for a stronghold, but Dean Castle was obviously not lacking in strength.

"Our poor house is perhaps no abode for a royal princess," the master observed, as they rode up to the gatehouse. "But we shall do our best to cherish you therein."

"I shall be surprised, sir, if it is not more comfortable than the quarters you allotted us at Edinburgh!"

"Not *I*, Highness. That was my elders' doing. And they had not looked to entertain a lady."

They had been dropping off men-at-arms for the last two or three miles, and it was only a small group which now passed under the gatehouse archway and into the large cobbled courtyard lined with lean-to outbuildings. Their approach evidently had not gone unobserved, despite the dusk, Boyd colours presumably sufficiently evident, for the drawbridge had been lowered and the portcullis was up, and a girl stood watching, waiting, up on a small stone platform projecting from a first-floor doorway. At some distance out from this a flight of steps rose, and from its top a removable wooden gangway crossed to the doorstep platform. The Boyds clearly could be concerned with their privacy.

"My sister Annabella," Tom said. "A saucy piece – but with her parts." Leaping down from the saddle, he went to aid Mary from hers.

Waving a hand, but with a smile, at his upstretched arms, she deliberately turned to the other side, flung a leg over the saddle as modestly as she might, and slipped to the ground unaided, there to brace her somewhat travel-aching shoulders. Let the Lady Annabella perceive, from the start, some hint of attitudes.

At least the man could not be prevented from taking her arm to escort her up those steps. "Anna," he called, "here is a guest indeed – Her Highness the Princess Mary, sister to His Grace the King."

The girl awaiting them was not handsome like her brother, but not unattractive, round-faced, sparkling-eyed, with a wide, smiling mouth and dimpled cheeks, less tall and slender than Mary but well built. Her examination of the other, crossing the gangway, was humorous rather than impressed.

"You fly high, Tom!" she greeted, and made an incipient curtsy.

Standing behind, in the iron-grille-guarded doorway, were now to be seen two small boys, aged eight and six. The master had not mentioned that he had brothers, only that their mother had died three years before.

"These are Sandy and Archie, scoundrels both!"

Mary offered them all a tentative smile. None of the offences committed by the older Boyds could be laid at *their* door, at least.

"You have come far this day?" the Lady Annabella asked, standing aside to let the visitor enter.

"All the way. From Edinburgh. So – food and drink, lass. We have scarce eaten since."

"So far?" the girl exclaimed. "Then you are a notable horse-woman, Highness. I do not know whether *I* could do the like."

"You will have to," her brother told her. "For you are coming back with us!"

"I am . . . ?"

"Yes. That is why we are here. If the princess will have you! You are to become a lady-in-waiting, Anna. So be on your best

39

behaviour – less than excellent as that may be!" He kissed the girl however, and slapped his young brothers' shoulders. "In, in!" he commanded. "Do not stand there staring."

Mary spoke. "You have a forthright brother, Lady Annabella. *I* was not long in discovering that. Forthright and . . . pressing!"

"Like most dogs, his bark is worse than his bite, I think!"

"Enough! Food, I say."

"I would prefer that I might wash first," Mary said.

"As you will." Annabella hesitated. "Not knowing of your coming, Highness, I have no chamber prepared. So – you had best come to mine, meantime. Sandy, go down to the kitchen and have Jeannie send up hot water to my bedchamber for the princess. Sufficient."

"And for me," the master added. "I think our mother's room for Her Highness, Anna."

The younger girl led the way upstairs two flights, pointing out one of three doors on the first landing in passing, which she said would be the chamber for Mary. That young woman noticed that the man entered one of the others alongside. On the floor above, she was ushered into a room, less than tidy with scattered clothing, but well enough furnished, particularly with a fine, large canopied bed, cupboards and chests, and its own seated garderobe in the thickness of the walling.

"I will make use of that, if I may," Mary said, pointing to the last, and did not wait for permission. Such a facility had not been available since Lanark.

The other laughed. "Even princesses can be so incommoded, then!" she commented. "Hot water will be up shortly. I will seek to see to all, for your comfort."

When Mary emerged, she found the other girl gone, but a pail and ewer of steaming water awaiting her, with towelling. She was thankful to disrobe partially and wash, having something of a preoccupation with cleanliness, something her brothers and sister found strange.

When Annabella came back and Mary was drying herself, she eyed her up and down frankly. "You are well made, Highness," she observed.

"You think so? You Boyds seem to be . . . concerned with such matters!"

"Oh, I did not mean to offend, Princess. I . . . admire!" She moved over to a doored cupboard, which she threw open. "Some of my clothing may fit none so ill, if you would wish to change, after long riding. Take whatever you require. I will go down and prepare the bed in the chamber which was my mother's."

Mary looked up, and over. "I think . . . if you do not mind it . . . I would prefer it here. With yourself. Here is a large bed. Room for both. And pleasant female company! If you do not find it to your displeasure? I will not disturb you."

The other blinked, but then smiled. "Surely. I used to share a bed with my sister, before she married. If you so wish it, Highness."

"I thank you." Mary moved over to scan the clothing in the wardrobe. "I fear that I cause you much trouble, Lady Annabella. I am sorry. But all this was no notion of mine, to come here. Your brother urged it on me."

"I can see why." That was simply said.

"Can you? The master is . . . urgent."

Annabella gurgled a laugh. "Yes, he is. And apt to get his way. But *you* will be a match for him, I think!" She paused, and threw up a hand to her mouth. "Oh, I did not mean, by match, a, a match of that sort . . . !" Her voice tailed away.

"I understand. Think naught of it. Now, this dark grey gown would fit me adequately, I judge – if I may borrow it?"

"To be sure. Anything. I fear that I am not provided as would be a princess . . ."

As they descended the stairs to the castle's hall for their meal, and passed the first-floor doorways, Annabella grinned and pointed to two of these. "I think that I know why you chose to sleep in *my* room!" she said.

"As to company of a night, I choose my own, yes."

Below they found Tom waiting with what patience he could muster, with the serving-woman Jeannie spreading a very adequate repast of soup, cold venison again, sweetmeats and cream, with wine. He eyed Mary's change of clothing critically, observed that her good looks transformed even the dull grey, but that the skirt was on the short side – on *her*, the better for that!

Annabella winked openly and sighed loudly.

The travellers did full justice to the provision, Annabella, having already eaten, contenting herself with the wine. The small boys had disappeared. When it was over, Mary announced that it had been a long day and her couch called. Gallant, the man rose to pull back her chair and aid her up.

41

"I will escort you to your chamber," he informed. There was a giggle from behind.

At the first-floor landing, he went to open the door next to his own, but Mary proceeded on to the next flight of stairs.

"A good night to you, Master of Boyd," she called back over her shoulder. "I have elected to share your sister's bed, of her kindness. I have been deprived of women's company and chatter, you understand. Sleep well."

She heard his exclamation, and glanced briefly back. The man was staring after her, expression eloquent of various emotions. But at his sister's tinkled laughter, humour of a rueful sort triumphed.

"Women!" he cried. "I vow you will make ill bedfellows . . . and keep each other awake!"

They proceeded to climb the stairs.

Undressing, they made a delectable pair – so much so that Annabella remarked cheerfully on what Tom, or any other man, was missing. Mary decided that she liked this girl.

In bed, and certainly not shrinking away from each other, she was further confirmed in her estimate, as they talked together easily, companionably. The younger girl admitted that she had known something of the design of her father and uncle to seek to obtain the keeping of the young King, and her doubts as to the propriety of it all; but she had learned no details. Mary recounted the tale of the hunt and forcible abduction, and the fact that clearly the thing had been arranged with the co-operation of Kennedy and the other lords, save it seemed Hamilton, and their shameful inaction at the deed; to which the other commented that their mutual-aid bands, tying their hands, had been well prepared. To Mary's charge that these had made unworthy guardians of the monarch, Annabella suggested that perhaps the Boyds might prove better ones, despite this doubtful start.

They left it at that, and soon thereafter Mary slept.

In the morning, the master, after pointed enquiries at breakfast as to whether they had passed a disturbed night, did his sister snore, and suchlike witticisms, announced that he had to go round the Boyd lands to collect a new batch of men, or at least pick them and order them to assemble here, well mounted, next morning early, for their journey back eastwards. So the young women would

42

have to entertain themselves. They could decide what clothing and gear they wanted to take back with them, and Anna, who was good at falconry, could select three of his favourite hawks, for sport at Edinburgh. Very much the master, the master went off about man's work.

Mary spent a pleasant leisurely day with the other girl and the two small boys, being shown over the castle and its surrounding gardens, orchard and pleasance, admiring the hawks and hounds, and going over much clothing left by previous Boyd women, from which Mary was not too proud, in the circumstances, to accept some for her use. She found a distinct affinity developing between herself and Anna, and they quickly were on first-name terms, save in servitors' company; after all, they had much in common. Both had lost their mothers at about the same age, and had had to try to act as such to young brothers and sisters; both were horsewomen, fond of hunting, hawking and outdoor activities; both girls of spirit. For a lady-in-waiting, Mary decided that she was fortunate with this one.

Tom got back for the evening meal, evidently satisfied with his mustering activities, and reporting that the hay harvest was almost all in and the oats well advanced with full heads. Keeping up the high standard of horseflesh was his one problem, his father having taken the best for his own trip eastwards; and not all their tenants, farmers and herdsmen breeding the highest quality. Some of his recruits' beasts would almost certainly not be able to cover the distance to Edinburgh in one day, so he had decided to take only the best-mounted with them on the morrow, leaving the others to come on at a slower pace.

They spent the evening agreeably enough, the vaulted hall lit by candles and a small birch-log fire, with music and singing, Anna playing the harpsichord and Mary not refusing to pluck the strings of a lute, accompanying herself in songs Scots and Flemish, learned from her mother. Tom proved to have a fine tenor voice and a quick ear for picking up melodies, refrains and choruses, demonstrating loving and amatory passages with gestures and embraces, suitable or otherwise, mainly directed at their guest, and difficult to reject when playing on instruments. Later, he gave a display of Scots dancing, very agile, and inevitably sought Mary as partner, to Anna's music. This, to be sure, involved much hugging and clasping and birling. The young woman, while seeking to keep this within bouncing bounds, could not but acknowledge his untiring persistence.

When it came to bedtime, and with an early start in prospect, of course the man could not fail to suggest that Mary would be better bedded in the other room than with his unrestful sister – with predictable answer. Probably he felt that it was incumbent on him to try, at least.

The girls discussed men and their ways and foolishness at some length before sleeping.

They were a deal less talkative in the early morning of a dull, grey day, saying goodbye to the two small boys, left in the care of Jeannie, a motherly soul of whom they were obviously fond. The troop of mounted men was waiting for them beyond the causeway, cheerful enough, apparently looking on this interlude as something of a holiday. Selecting about a dozen of the best horsed to accompany them, the master told the rest to follow on at their own speed, and rode ahead.

They followed the same route as they had used to come, and although there were spots of rain soon after they started, it came to nothing, and by Lanark there were even glimpses of sunshine. Anna rode well, and they were not delayed by pack-horses, for Tom had distributed the bundles of clothing and gear being taken amongst the men-at-arms. Each of their betters carried a hooded and jessed hawk at wrist, the birds remarkably little trouble.

They took slightly longer on the return journey than on the outward, this not on account of Anna but on the quality of the escort's horses; but even so they reached Edinburgh before the city's gates were shut for the night – not that the master would have worried about demanding the watch at the West Port to open up for them.

James welcomed them effusively – not, it seemed, because he had greatly missed his sister but in order to recount at length his adventures and prowess in various branches of the martial arts, particularly archery and quarter-stavery, the pleasures of tilting at hoops and pegs, with lances, and the saddle-posturing necessary to avoid the impact of enemy assaults. He had not so much to say about swordplay, the great two-handed weapons being rather heavy for his young wrists, and the short stabbing variety suitable only for men-at-arms. He found the shields heavy also, but Sir Alexander had promised to have a lighter one made for him, painted with the red Rampant Lion on gold. He was loud in

44

his praise of the said Sir Alexander, who had said that he would organise a tournament in the royal honour in a week or two.

In all this the monarch more or less ignored Anna as irrelevant, and was even a little superior in his attitude to his sister, such matters being of course beyond womenkind.

Getting the boy to bed thereafter was a delayed process, especially as no provision having been made apparently for quarters for Anna, and suitable lodgings in the fortress limited to say the least. It was evident that she had to share the royal rooms, meantime at least, Mary nowise objecting. So the obvious procedure was to put James in the smaller bed and the two girls share the larger – at which the monarch was not enthusiastic. However, the pleasures of watching the two young women undressing made up for that, with Anna nowise bashful.

The girls continued to get martial talk across the bedchamber, with scant response, until tired, they slept.

Next day, the master took them all to try out the hawks at Duddingston Loch, the large one on the south side of Arthur's Seat, a third of a mile long and half that across, and surrounded by reed-beds. It was a great place for wildfowl, varieties of duck, the occasional goose, herons, swans and sometimes oyster-catchers and other waders from the nearby Scotwater of Forth. So there was always plenty to fly hawks at; the problem was retrieval, both of the prey and of the hawks themselves. If the alarmed fowl flew off inland, as it were, it was not so difficult, for the horsemen could ride after them to collect; but if they took refuge in the high reed-beds then it was otherwise, and retrieval all but impossible, for the reeds grew out of mud and surface water capable of bearing neither horse nor man. This was why Tom had brought only his best-trained hawks, those which could be relied upon to return to the hawker after a strike, not to go down and seek to devour their prey. Falconers, the trainers of hawks, had to be expert at their task; and the sportsmen also, for they had to be selective about which wildfowl to loose their hawks at.

James knew all this, of course, but the master reminded him of it as they rode out to Duddingston. The secret was to keep the hawks hooded until a high-flying duck or goose soared off away from the loch, or a group of such, ignoring the low-fliers which would be apt to settle again on the water or in the further reeds. Heron and swans were less of a problem, for these were not so apt to come down again in the reeds but tended to flap away in a wide circle, to come back to the disturbance-point to see if it was clear. They were slower fliers also, and so more readily caught up with by the hawks; but of course they were much larger, stronger, and less easy for the hawks to kill.

The party was seven-strong, for they had brought along three of the Kilmarnock men to act as tranters, or retrievers. With only the three hawks, the two young women agreed to take turn about with one of them.

James was all excitement as they reached the loch, at its west end, near the monastic property of Priestfield, a grange belonging to the Abbey of the Holy Rood. Since that abbacy was a royal appointment, the King did not have to seek permission to hawk and hunt here. Before ever the horsemen got close to the reed-beds, the duck began to fly up with a great quacking, in ones and twos and groups. These all went off low, some even skittering along the surface of the water, eastwards, to the King's disgust.

"Wait you," the master advised. "These are but the easily scared ones. See – we will ride a little into the reeds. Not far, or our beasts will get bogged down."

The boy urged his horse on impatiently, and before he had gone a dozen yards a heron rose, a great grey bird with long legs trailing behind, to flap off seemingly lazily after the ducks' swift wing-beating, rising to only some twenty feet or so.

"Right! Fly!" Tom cried.

The boy, in his excitement, fumbled with his hawk's hood, and got its jesse, the leg strap, already loosed, caught in his fingers; and in those few seconds' delay, a pair of mallard burst out nearby and soared up, quacking. The hawk, freed, saw these as its prey, and launching upwards beat wings to gain height rather than going directly after the ducks. These were heading southwards, not down-loch.

"Stupid bird!" the monarch exclaimed. "Look – it has gone after the wrong game! And it is too slow! They will get away. It will lose them. And the heron get away too . . . !"

"Give it time. It needs height. Till then, it rises. Then it will fly swiftly enough. It will not lose sight of them." The man turned to Mary, who was taking first turn. "The heron!" he jerked. Then he turned to one of the men, and pointed wordlessly after the pair of mallard. That individual spurred off.

Mary had been ready, jesses loosed, and had the hood off her bird with a flick, almost throwing the hawk after the larger bird,

46

now at least one hundred yards away. Again this hawk began to mount at a fairly steep angle, whilst the heron increased its distance.

"Never fear," the master cried. "Better to let the heron gain some distance. We do not want it brought down in the water. Without dogs to retrieve it . . ."

"I have been hawking since I was a child!" she returned. "Save your breath! Aye, and your eyes!" She pointed over to the right, where another heron, no doubt the first's mate, had risen out of the reeds to beat off southwards.

Cursing, the man unhooded his own hawk and flung it after. There was mocking laughter from Anna.

So, within mere moments, all three hawks were in the air, and climbing.

The term hawk-eyed was proven to be no misnomer. Those birds, although firstly concerned with gaining height, never lost sight of their chosen quarry, despite James's fears and impatience. Once sufficiently high, and well above their hoped-for victims, they could plane down at a slant at fearsome speed, and drop on their prey from above for the kill.

The two other retrievers were already riding off after the birds, one due southwards over the parkland, the other along the reedy shores of the loch. The four remaining backed their horses a little way on to firmer ground, and waited.

"Your pardon, Highness, for seeming to instruct you," the master said, waving a hand. "I had not realised that you were so knowledgeable about hawking."

"My mother was enamoured of the sport, and taught me," she replied. "She taught me about men also, sir. And was experienced with them likewise!"

"So there you have it, Tom!" his sister chuckled. "Beware!"

Unabashed, he inclined his handsome head. "I may always hope that Her Grace's daughter might be as kind as was Queen Mary of Guelders!" he replied. "I must seek my uncle's guidance!"

Which might be said to even the score.

James, uninterested in this exchange, let out a whoop. "See – *your* heron, Mary!"

At the far end of the loch, Mary's hawk had got above the first heron, and dropped like a stone upon it, to strike at the base of the long outstretched neck in an explosion of feathers. The larger bird, three times the size of its attacker, plunged downwards in an ungainly sprawl of wings and legs, whether killed or not they could not tell at that range. Unfortunately, it fell into the water, although not far from the shore.

"A pity! If that hawk had but waited just a little, it would have been over the land," Tom declared. "I do not see your tranter getting through those reeds to collect it." He turned to observe the progress of his own hawk.

"*I* can swim," the King announced. "I will get it."

"Jamie, what nonsense!" his sister exclaimed. "It is not worth that. If the man cannot get it, leave it . . ."

"There goes mine!" the master cried. "Into those trees. Down. The tranter will get that one, to be sure."

"Look!" Anna called. "Here is *your* hawk, Sire. Returning." She pointed. Quite high, a hawk came to hover above them, and then circled down to them, coming to flutter wings above the man, not the boy.

"Good bird! It knows *me*, not you." Tom held out his gauntleted arm, for the creature to land on. "See – duck's feathers caught in its talons. It will have killed."

The bird settled on the man's gauntlet and folded its wings. He handed it over to James, who took it and hooded it, stroking its back feathers approvingly.

"Your hawk is better trained than mine," Mary observed. "See – it has come down and landed on the heron. What now?"

Tom frowned. "It is because the heron has fallen in water, I wager. The hawk will be unsure. Perhaps it will come, presently . . ."

They could see that tranter on his horse, stationary amongst the reeds perhaps seventy yards from the birds. They all commenced to ride round the loch thitherwards.

"I will get them both!" James asserted. "I will swim."

"Not so, Your Grace. That would never do."

"I will . . ."

"I forbid it, Jamie," Mary declared. "A King cannot do such a thing!"

"If any has to do it, I will," Tom said. "But the hawk may come back. The heron can lie."

When they reached the man, the hawk still rode on the heron's back. The latter had ceased to flap.

"Can you swim, man?" the master asked.

"No, lord, I canna. And it's ower soft for the horse. Thae reeds . . ."

Cursing, Tom whistled through his teeth and held up his gloved arm. But the hawk remained where it was.

"Devil-damned bird!" its owner muttered. Dismounting, he began to strip off his doublet.

"No need to go to such lengths, surely?" Mary protested. "It will come in time, no?"

"It may not. And it is a valuable bird – too much to risk losing. It is a haggard – a wild-caught adult, and could go wild again. A female peregrine . . ." The man was kicking off his riding-boots now.

"I say that he is but eager to display to you his matchless man's body!" Anna suggested.

"Why can *he* do it, if I may not?" James asked plaintively – but none attended to the royal demand, being frankly intrigued by the master's progressing disrobing.

Tom's own hawk was now circling above the party, possibly itself somewhat confused by its flier's behaviour, unusual in that sport. Anna whistled to it expertly and held up her leather-protected arm, and the bird dropped down to settle on it obediently; it would know her as well as it did him. Just then its tranter rode up, with a dead heron. But this passed barely noticed by the onlookers, as the Master of Boyd stepped out of his breeches and stood naked on the grass, a notably well-formed figure, wide of shoulder, narrow of waist and hips, with quite an abundance of hair on chest and at groin. He made no attempt to hide his masculinity, but nor did he flaunt it, before striding down to the first of the reeds.

"A pity to spoil all that revelation with mud, is it not?" his unreserved sister observed. Mary remained silent.

Plunging into the high reeds, Tom's feet and ankles quickly began to sink in and emerge with each step, black before the greenery hid him, and his progress was indicated only by the waving of the rushes and the noise of his squelching. Then, and rather thankfully, they heard a major splashing – for that mud could have been deep enough to endanger the man – which indicated open water reached, although, because of the height of the reeds, they could not see the splasher.

"Are you duly impressed, Highness?" Anna asked.

"Folly, I think. But sportive folly. There he is, out."

With a strong over-arm stroke the man came into view, with only a dozen or so yards to the birds.

"He swims well," Mary said. "But how will he deal with the hawk, while swimming?"

"The good Lord knows! But if any could, Tom can."

"You admire your brother more than you seem to, I think, Anna!"

The man reached his objective. They saw him swim round the birds, prospecting the situation. Then he turned on his back, using his feet to propel and steady him. The girls saw him stretch out and up one bare arm for the peregrine to jump on to – and both winced as they recognised what those sharp talons could do gripping naked flesh. The hawk obediently transferred itself to the arm, kept high. Then he grasped the long legs of the heron with the other hand, and paddling round in a semicircle, still on his back, commenced to kick his way to the shore.

"He has them both!" James cried. "The heron is dead. Good! Is that not splendid?"

The young women did not deny it.

Tom splashed his way into the reeds with his burdens, the tranters hurriedly dismounting to go down to the edge to relieve him. Presently the waving greenery parted to reveal him, hawk held high, heron dragged behind, black well above the knees, and much elsewhere, with clinging mud, but grinning triumphantly. Something not unlike a cheer came from the watchers, Mary included.

A tranter took the heron but the master took the offending hawk to his sister, then turned back to the loch's edge to splash himself with water to wash off the mud. He paid particular attention to his hairy groin. Mary transferred *her* attention to Anna, asking whether she intended to fly the errant bird any further.

Tom answered for her. Yes, they would go round to the other side of the loch, once he had his clothes on, and try a sally or two from there. Perhaps, if that peregrine misbehaved itself again, one of the ladies would choose to act the swimmer? Anna could swim, he knew. And, pulling on his breeches, he looked enquiringly at the other girl.

Mary told him that, although she *could* swim, she was less concerned to demonstrate her prowess than he seemed to be. Then, glancing round, she changed her tune.

"You are hurt!" she exclaimed. And flinging her leg over

saddle, she slipped to the ground and went to him. Black mud was now being replaced by red blood from a gash in his arm. Those talons had indeed sunk in.

"It is nothing," he asserted, wiping away the blood with the other sleeve of his silken shirt. "A scratch, only."

"Nonsense! It is deep. There is dirt in it. Come." And taking his hand, she drew him down to the water's edge again. Perhaps that peregrine had served him none so ill, after all.

Although protesting vocally, the man by no means held back; this was the first time that she had voluntarily taken his hand. Telling him to stoop, she bathed the gash with water thoroughly, examining it for any remaining mud. Then, ordering him to hold the sleeve-silk padded firmly over it, she left him to walk back along the lochside a little way. "Come," she commanded.

"Why? What is this?"

"Meadowsweet," she called back. "Much grows in this marshy place. I saw some nearby. There it is. Beside those yellow flags."

Mystified, he followed on.

She stopped at a clump of golden iris. Beside this was another clump of growth, long-stalked weeds with small white-flowered heads. Plucking a handful of these flowers, she raised them to her mouth and chewed at them. Then, putting the resultant paste on to her fingers, she turned to take his arm, remove the pad of silk, and spread the paste on the gash.

"There. That will staunch the bleeding and aid healing," she said. "Hold the cloth on it again. Firmly." She led the way back to the horses without further remark.

"Well, well! So you are physician as well as all else," he commented. "Who would have thought it?"

"Not that. But my mother taught me of this of plants. As she did other things. In Guelders they are wise about the like. Meadowsweet grows there also. Other plants she showed me, with their merits. Coltsfoot, tormentil, buckthorn berries, even nettles . . ."

She helped him to put on his doublet carefully, so that the sleeve held the padding in place. Mary was then for turning back for the city, but James's complaints were loud. Tom backed the boy, saying that he was very well and quite able to continue with their sport, especially so well looked after as he now was.

They rode on east-abouts round the foot of the loch.

In the event, there was precious little more sport for them on the north side. There were fewer reeds here, no herons, a couple of swans which merely paddled out into mid-loch – and swans were not hawkers' sport save when they flew. Some duck they did put up, but most of these only squattered across the water to the other side. One pair of teal did rise high, however, and swinging round in a circle, beat up as though climbing the steep hillside behind, obviously making for the high-set Dunsappie Loch up there. James had his hawk after them promptly – to the scowls of his tranter, who was faced with the daunting task of following up that difficult slope, and the Lord knew how much further beyond, to try to retrieve any kill; and all for a small teal.

With no more suitable game starting up, and the hawk returning presently, whether successful or not they could not tell, the party left the poor man to it. Enough for one day. The master did not admit that his arm was stiffening. Two heron and one mallard drake represented the day's bag.

That evening, Thomas Boyd joined them again for the meal. Clearly he considered it his duty and privilege to see to their provision and to eat with them. By the way he held his arm it was evident that it was sore, but he made light of it.

James was very vocal over the day's activities, much impressed with the man's swimming act, and saying that he had never tried to swim on his back. Would the master teach him? There was a loch below the castle rock, he had seen – the Nor' Loch. They could go there next day.

Mary told the monarch not to be impatient. It would be some days before the master's arm was fit for more swimming or lessons. Tom declared that he would be happy to oblige, but thought that the Nor' Loch was scarcely the place to do it, being the destination of much of the city's refuse and excrement. In a day or two he would take them to Restalrig Loch, near to Leith, where one of his uncle's lairdly friends, Logan of Restalrig, said that there was excellent fowling and no reed-beds. They could both hawk and swim there. Although, for swimming, the seashore would be better, did they not think, less muddy?

Mary had her doubts on this subject.

4

Two wet days intervened, to the King's disgust, and indoor entertainment had to be devised for him – the young women being more able to interest themselves, at this juncture largely with needles and thread, adapting the Dean Castle clothing to fit Mary better. They were summoned, however, to watch James's efforts at mastering the arts of quarter-staff, throwing-spear, hand-ball, skittles and the like. The master's damaged right arm was a disadvantage in this, so his uncle had to be brought in on occasion, when he could spare the time. Just what Sir Alexander was busy at elsewhere was not clear, but frequently he was away from the castle. James assumed that he was off arranging details of the promised tournament. It was noticeable that Lord Boyd himself seldom presented himself to them, almost all contacts being with his brother. It had always seemed, indeed, as though the younger was the real leader in it all. Mary said as much, one time, to Thomas, and got a careful reply, whether accurate or not, to give her the impression that there might be some hostility between the two brothers, possibly the elder resenting the prominence and driving force of the younger. Yet this entire policy, if that it could be called, on the bands between lords and the taking into custody of the young monarch, was evidently of the Lord Boyd's devising, Anna asserted.

Having Anna always with them improved matters for Mary greatly, not only in companionship, aid with James and other helpful services, but as regards her brother's ever-pressing attentions. Tom just could not make himself quite so suggestive and demanding with her about; and, the girls quickly becoming good friends, Anna recognised Mary's need of her in this respect as in others, and took her side against over-active masculine advances, making something of a joke of it all, which helped the older girl. The master was as much in their company as ever, but as far as Mary was concerned, conditions improved considerably.

After the rainy days, they went hawking at Restalrig Loch and had better sport than at Duddingston, thanks partly to the lack of reed-beds; also the fact that Logan of Restalrig, a swarthy man of middle years, joined them with his own hawks and dogs, these last able to retrieve fowl which fell in the water. The shores of the loch were somewhat muddy however, moreover directly under the windows of its castle on a rocky knoll, which rather inhibited the idea of swimming, to Mary's relief.

Another day, they went hunting deer in the Pentland Hills, a few miles to the south of the city, and although they failed to make a kill, lacking trained huntsmen, they had two exhilarating chases over steep hillsides, screes and high moorland, to lose their quarry both times in wet peat-bogs in which horses and men could not follow.

James declared that he preferred life at Edinburgh to that at Stirling, where he had had to spend overmuch of his time being tutored in dull subjects such as Latin, French and handwriting.

Then, one day in late August, Sir Alexander announced that the looked-for tournament would be held in two days' time. Great was the excitement, hawking and hunting paling into insignificance for James. It could not be on any large scale, in the circumstances, he was warned, no great assemblage of lords and knights being advisable from the Boyds' point of view; moreover the tourney-ground before the castle entrance was of only modest dimensions. But for the boy it was all a great event, his first — for his father had been too busy with real warfare for tournaments, and his mother scarcely that way inclined. And it was being organised in his name and honour. He would be allowed to take part in one or two events himself; and his sister was to be the traditional Queen of Beauty, and to bestow the awards and prizes.

There were fervent prayers for good weather.

The great day dawned, dull but not raining, and for once the King was up betimes, even though activities were not due to start until noon. He had to inspect the lists, the stand erected for the Queen and principal onlookers, the pavilions for refreshment and gear-changing and the like; and impatience prevailed thereafter until proceedings were to start. Eager as he was to be involved, the boy was informed that it was unsuitable for the monarch to be seen awaiting the arrival of others; he would have to make a staged appearance once all were assembled. He would then be escorted out with due ceremony.

So the King of Scots had to wait, fretting, while shouts arose, trumpets blew, cheering echoed from beyond the gatehouse.

At length the Lord Boyd arrived, to make one of his few appearances, and conducted the royal party out, under the gatehouse arch and across the drawbridge, to a fanfare of trumpets. The open space beyond was thronged with people and horses, flags and banners flying, half the city seeming to be present, children yelling, dogs barking, a lively scene.

The provost, magistrates and deacons of guilds came forward to greet their young liege-lord, with much bowing. Instead of the key of the city he was presented this time with an illuminated scroll – which he did not so much as glance at, being intent on greater things than paper. Then he and his sister, with Anna, were led to the stepped platform, with seats, from which they could view the contests. Around this were clustered the nobility and gentry, with only one or two of their ladies, and there was more bowing and curtsying. The Lords Somerville, Hailes and Livingstone were there, their sons and lairds and a number of knights and lesser magnates. Also the Abbots of the Holy Rood and Melrose and the Prior of Soutra, to add Holy Church's dignity to the occasion. Mary guessed that this was all as much an exercise in gaining public acceptance for the Boyds in national affairs as an entertainment for the young monarch.

They were escorted up the steps to the platform, amidst cheers from the crowd, to seats behind a table spread with chaplets, bouquets and posies of flowers, with ribbons and tokens, as prizes; also flagons of wines, with sweetmeats. The red and gold Lion Rampant standard was erected to fly above them – but with two other banners only a little less large on either side, the blue with red fesse-chequey of Boyd.

Despite all the respect and attention, James was still agitated. He did not want to sit up here, being a spectator; he wanted to take active part. Tom assured him that all would be as he wished. The churchmen had to have their say first.

The three clerics mounted the steps, and the Abbot of the Holy Rood held up his hand for silence. Apart from dogs and children he got it approximately. He then intoned a prayer for God's blessing on their sovereign-lord and his realm, on his royal sister, and on all who worked for their weal. Also upon this day's activities and knightly prowess. Whereafter the other abbot gave a comprehensive benediction for all present, James fidgeting the while. This was not what tournaments were for, he asserted.

There followed a great marshalling of horses, and the Lord Boyd came to conduct the King down to the head of this cavalcade, leaving the women on the platform. The boy was then mounted, and flanked by the two Boyd brothers, he led a procession round the tourney-ground behind four trumpeters blowing lustily, to the huzzahs of the populace. Back at the royal platform again, all except James bowed to Mary, the Queen. This ended the preliminaries, and Tom, as Master of Ceremonies today, announced the first contest, which would be a display of knightly skills between the Lords Somerville and Livingstone.

This took a little while to develop, since the said two nobles had to retire to a pavilion to change into armour, covered by heraldic surcoats, their horses also suitably and colourfully caparisoned. As tourney-jousting went, this was to be a mere demonstration, for these lords, one the Chamberlain of the realm, were much too important to risk the physical injury quite frequently resulting from such bouts. But presently coming out to place themselves at opposite ends of the ground, lances held high, at a single blast of a trumpet they lowered these, and shields held before them, spurred their mounts into a trot, then a canter, to bear down on each other in impressive style, armour gleaming, to the cries of the onlookers.

James, agog, demanded whether they would kill each other, adding that he did not much like the Lord Somerville anyway. Mary assured him that this was unlikely, this being a gesture rather than a serious trial of strength. She was proved accurate in this as the two charging duellists came together, each jerking his beast's head a little aside so that they would pass close by rather than collide, and at the same time raising their heraldic-patterned shields high to act as targets for the lances. Even so the impact was forceful and resounding, so much so that Livingstone's lance shattered, and Somerville's shield was jerked from his arm and fell to the ground. The contestants pounded on past each other until they could rein in their mounts, and then turned to bow, first to each other and then towards the royal platform.

It was now Mary's duty to declare the verdict, advised by the Master of Ceremonies.

"I would think Livingstone wins, since Somerville's shield fell and he became as it were disarmed," Tom suggested.

"No – it was a draw," the girl decided. "If they had continued the contest, Livingstone would have been at the mercy of the other, having no lance. I declare a drawn contest."

"A draw, a palpable draw!" the master shouted, to a mixture of cheers and boos from the onlookers.

The two contestants came, to dismount and climb the steps, to receive posies from the Queen, who made tactful praise of their efforts.

After more trumpeting, the master announced that there would now be a very special event, a three-a-side jousting between Sir Alexander Boyd of Duncow, one of the flowers of chivalry, Boyd of Bonshaw and himself, against the Master of Hailes, Hepburn of Waughton and Hepburn of Whitsome. This would be won by whichever team first unhorsed one of the others, by whatever means.

There was a stir at this unusual announcement, five young men against one of middle years. Mary found herself a little concerned over Tom taking part, when his right arm was still not entirely healed, some infection having swollen the wound. But he asserted that it would not incommode him, it being almost back to normal. James and Anna wished him well.

Adam, Master of Hailes, who led the opposing team, was one of those who had taken part in the abduction at Niddry. Once armoured, he led his Hepburn colleagues to the far end of the enclosure. Sir Alexander Boyd placed his kinsmen on either side of him, and gave them their instructions. At a sign that all was ready, the trumpet sounded and the six horsemen, lowering lances, charged.

This time there was no attempt to avoid headlong clash, and the two teams, riding neck-and-neck, cannoned into each other in mid-ground with a resounding crash. There was seeming immediate chaos, men all but unseated, lances askew, two shields falling, both Hepburns', Boyd of Bonshaw's horse staggering back on its haunches and seeming almost to topple but recovering itself. The impetus was maintained, however, in some fashion, and although raggedly, each trio did emerge, to proceed on a little way before being able to rein round and face each other again, now not very far apart. It was to be seen that Bonshaw had lost his lance altogether, whilst Tom's had a third of it snapped off.

Sir Alexander wasted no time, but with barely a pause for recovery or instructions, led his two back against the other group, spurring fiercely. The Hepburns, two lacking shields but all having lances intact, recognised the danger of being ridden down if they were not in forward movement themselves, and heeled their mounts to meet the next onslaught.

This time the collision was less dire, insufficient speed having been attained. The horses were now wary also, not having enjoyed the previous impact, and took their own avoiding action. As a result, the clash was scarcely headlong, partly slantwise indeed, but this had a major effect nevertheless; for it meant that the long, unwieldy lances, aimed for direct contact, tended to miss their marks – this to the Boyds' advantage. Whereas these three still had their shields, and these could be used almost as battering-rams. Both Tom and his uncle tossed away their lances, and reining round as best they could, rising in their stirrups, leaned over to smash their shields against their opponents, with all their force and weight, all but unhorsing themselves in the process. But the tactic succeeded, for the Hepburns now found their useless lances only a handicap, in the road, and without shields to counter the attack, took the smashing weight of it on their armour-plated torsos. The Masters of Hailes and Whitsome toppled over out of their saddles, and fell with a crash to the ground.

Boyd of Bonshaw was less fortunate than his fellows. Having no lance, he had drawn his sword. He sought to slash this at his chosen opponent, but achieved only a glancing blow because of his mount's swerve. And Hepburn of Waughton, a big, powerful young man, managed to find some use for *his* lance, swinging it round in a driving arc, not point-on, to smash it against Bonshaw's back with force enough to unseat him. He in turn fell heavily.

The three survivors sought to control their quivering mounts, and reined up.

Mary raised her hand, beckoning to the trumpeter to sound an end to the contest, lest there be any more mayhem. It was obvious that the Boyds had won, two against one, however unorthodox their methods. The two victors came trotting over towards the platform, while men ran out to deal with riderless horses and assist the vanquished to their feet, often necessary in heavy armour. The two Hepburns rose, to stand shakily, but Bonshaw lay still.

When Sir Alexander and his nephew dismounted and climbed the steps to the table, Mary was gazing past them, and pointing.

"Your friend," she exclaimed. "He lies there."

The others looked back. "He will be but stunned," the knight said. "Often a fall in armour can do that. A mouthful of wine will revive him."

"I hope that is all that it is. I have to congratulate you two on your win, sirs. However oddly achieved! But . . . perhaps you Boyds usually contrive your achievements oddly?" That was said significantly. "Here, then, are your so Boydly earned chaplets!"

They took their floral tributes, bowing.

James was chattering eagerly. "That was good, good! Is the other man dead?" he asked, all but hopefully.

"I think not, Sire. He was only knocked out of the saddle. That would not kill him. Bonshaw will be well enough presently . . ."

"When do *I* take part?" the boy demanded. "You told me that this was to be *my* tournament. I want to do something."

"Your Grace's turn now," Sir Alexander assured. "We will have the tilting at targets. You will show your skill, Sire, never fear."

Mary and Anna were dividing their attentions between concern for the master's arm and watching to see the person of Bonshaw being carried to one of the pavilions. Blood trickling down Tom's wrist they had not failed to perceive, and although the man declared that he was very well, they were insisting on him discarding his steel gauntlet and rolling up his sleeve. The swollen talon wound had burst open, no doubt with the impact which had broken his lance, and it was looking decidedly unpleasant.

"No more tourneying for you this day!" Mary declared. "Go and have this seen to by the physicians . . ."

"It is nothing . . ."

"It is not nothing. Forby, it stinks! So perchance the blood-letting will help it. But I have no meadowsweet here! It requires a salve. See to it. And have word sent to me, as to how is your friend Bonshaw."

"Yes, Princess. Your word is my command! Always!"

She eyed him levelly. "Indeed? *You* remember that. As will I!"

Sir Alexander went to divest himself of his armour and to direct the arrangements for the next contest – nothing so dramatic as the last but a trial of skills nevertheless. Gallows-like posts were erected in the middle of the ground, and from the cross-trees of these hung ropes, two to each post, these ending in circlets woven of reeds and flowers, of about six inches diameter, which hung and swayed in the breeze.

59

These were the targets and hoped-for trophies. There were five such posts.

The first batch of contestants were lined up, mounted, ten of them, the King placed on the extreme right. He was given a shorter, lighter lance than the others, with no armour worn. He almost dropped it, in his excitement. Those with him included young Ker of Cessford and the Master of Somerville.

At the first blast of the trumpet, all lowered their lances, to point; at the second, the line spurred forward, if somewhat raggedly – to Tom's criticism.

This was meant to simulate an onset in battle, and the targets the enemy line. So the riders were placed close together, to form a fairly solid front – and this, of course, was a handicap in their lance-aiming, with jostling and the necessity for careful horse-management to avoid contact, bumping. This was why James had been placed at the outer end, so that he might be less concerned with collision.

The less than lateral line beat down on the targets. The object was to spear one of the circular wreaths on the lance-point, no easy endeavour with the things swinging, the horses' up-and-down cantering, and neighbours so close as to be distracting – as in war. In fact, at that first drive, only two of the ten gained their trophies, and James was not one of them.

However, this was not unexpected, and while the two winners trotted off to present their wreaths to the Queen and be given chaplets in exchange, the other eight were lined up at the other side of the arena and given a second chance. And this time the King, and three others, did achieve success – and great was the royal delight, as he went to receive a small posy from his sister.

Another ten, of lesser rank, then were marshalled – and these, in fact, did rather better, keeping a straighter line, four winning their trophies in the first run, two in the second. From the platform, James was able to point out to the girls errors made.

Thereafter it was time for a change in the programme, with archery the sport. Butts were erected, with curtains of sheepskins hung behind, to prevent stray arrows going on to injure onlookers beyond. The monarch was anxious to demonstrate his skill in this also, and did fairly well – although, as it happened, not so well as did his sister who, after enquiring whether it was permitted for the Queen of the Tournament to try her hand in one of the events, showed that she was indeed expert with the bow and arrow; she

60

it was, in fact, who had given James his first lessons in the art. As the Master of Ceremonies, Tom Boyd thereafter presented her with a bunch of flowers, which he made a dramatic display of pinning on to her bosom, to cheering.

Quarter-staff duels followed, using six-foot-long poles, well greased, which were wielded in various strokes, sliding the grip up and down the shafts, to deliver and counter stylised blows and defences, with much swiping, whacking and dunting, but all done according to the rules, and requiring a quick eye and swift reactions to anticipate and thwart smites and to glimpse opportunities for return blows. James found this sport to his taste; but the difficulty here was in finding anyone suitable to exchange strokes with the monarch – who of course must not receive possible injury, but who, on the other hand, must not be given too obviously easy a win. In the end Thomas himself was appointed as acceptable opponent, his injured arm serving as sufficient handicap, shake her head over this as Mary would. Dozens of competitors took part, in pairs, but owing to the need for each couple to be carefully watched, for blows which did strike home, bungled strokes, quick recoveries and the like, to count for points, only three bouts went on at one time. So the entire contest took a considerable time, especially as the procedure was that the winners of each bout should then fight each other until one final champion was left. This, of course, again presented the difficulty of matching the King against all and sundry; so it was carefully decided that his bout with Tom should be declared a draw and neither should go on to the finals – to some protest on the boy's part.

There followed wrestling matches, in which few of the nobly born participated but which provided opportunity for much wagering. Then there was a wall-scaling competition – which again took time, since it demanded much preparation, timber palisades having to be carried out into the centre of the lists and fixed firmly in place. The object was for armoured contestants to lumber out, swords in hands, to seek to clamber over these ten-foot-high barriers, as though they were assaulting a castle's outer defences; no easy task, although productive of much hilarity on the part of the spectators. If one lost his sword in the process, fell heavily on the other side, or simply failed to get over at all, points were deducted.

James, who was small for his age, and had no armour which

would fit, could not take part, although in his eagerness to attempt it, he was allowed, at the end, to make a solo run, wearing a helmet and carrying a light sword. He did manage to get over his wall, but left helmet and sword behind.

The final episode was a massed double-charge, of practically all the horsed men present, from the two ends of the lists, banners flying, shields high, but with no intention of actual impact. This was less of a mere gesture than it might sound, for four score horsemen approaching each other at a fast canter, in a comparatively confined space, and seeking to pass through each other's lines without clash, was no simple exercise. And in fact three men, one the Lord Livingstone, the Chamberlain, were unhorsed in the process, and sundry banners fell to the ground. But it made a stirring finale to the day; although not to the evening, for a banquet was laid on in the castle for all the participants, and an ample if less ambitious feast spread in the tourney-ground itself, for all who cared to partake.

That night, as the master conducted the trio to their quarters, clearly in some pain from his arm but making light of it, Mary bade him goodnight, with her comment.

"A notable day indeed, Master Thomas. You Boyds do not lack cunning, I recognise! All this will much enhance your name and fame, I am sure. And have my royal brother thinking the better of you – which was your intention, no? For your further purposes hereafter!"

"Ah, me! Would that the Queen of Beauty was as caring as she is beautiful!" he returned.

She touched the damaged arm lightly. "*This* I am prepared to care for. Today has not furthered that, at least. It was folly to go jousting with it."

"If it arouses even such kindness in you, it was worth it, Princess. This enheartens me."

"It is your arm I am concerned with, sir – not your heart! Goodnight."

Anna dipped a curtsy. "Master of Ceremonies, Master of Boyd – but other masteries you lack, Tom. Perchance you will learn!" She blew him a mocking kiss.

It was September, and Mary had rather hoped that James had forgotten about demonstrating his swimming abilities, and the season for swimming for pleasure all but over, when, one sunny day, the master announced that the boy, having requested a visit to a seashore to spear flounders, flatfish, such as they did in the Ayrshire estuaries, he had accordingly made enquiries. He had discovered that there was a place at the mouth of the Figgate Burn, midway between Leith and Musselburgh, a mere four miles away. Would the ladies care to accompany them there? The sport might amuse them.

This put Mary into something of a quandary again. She enjoyed most sports, and had heard about this of spearing fish – they actually managed to spear salmon, from horseback, in the shallows of the Solway Firth, although this for flounders was done wading, she understood. She would like to try it, but if it entailed paddling about in the sea, it might well bring on Jamie's swimming ambitions. Not that she was against swimming – she enjoyed that also; but she foresaw complications with Thomas Boyd.

She decided that she was being feeble in this – and that young woman was ever against feebleness in herself as in others. Also, Anna wanted to go.

They set off down to the abbey again, and round the northern skirts of Arthur's Seat, to head eastwards by a well-defined road. The master explained that this was called the Fishwives Causeway, and was the route for two kinds of traffic, he had been told: the said fishwives of the fishing town of Musselburgh, who brought their menfolk's catches in creels on their backs, actually supported by straps slung from their brows – they might see some on their way, for there was a great demand for the fish in Edinburgh; and the other was the night-soil of the city, which was carted daily down to the market-gardens and fields of the Musselburgh area, for manure – a less than delightful conception but apparently productive. There was a tradition that this causeway had once been a Roman road, although that was doubtful; admittedly the Romans were known to have had a station at Inveresk, near Musselburgh.

Sure enough, soon after they reached a quite large stream, apparently the Figgate Burn, the banks of which their road followed, they passed a group of women, all clad in dark blue heavy cloth, and carrying on their backs large basket-work creels, obviously very weighty, these held in place by leather straps, dark with sweat, which were braced round their foreheads, a device which looked uncomfortable indeed but which the women, young and old, seemed not to mind, for they were all singing as they trudged city-wards, a cheerful band.

Tom was not making for Musselburgh, however, and where the road swung away southwards from the stream, in an area of rough pasture and gorse bushes where cattle grazed, obviously common land, they continued on down the burnside. Presently they came in sight of the sea.

The master had been told to seek out a couple of cottages of salmon-netters, in the Figgate Whins area, where they could borrow the necessary short stabbing-spears for their fishing. They had no difficulty in finding the houses; they had poles outside for drying the nets – and anyway, there were no others in sight. Two men were sitting outside, mending nets.

Of these the master asked if they might borrow spears, and for any advice on how best to go about the sport. When the fishermen heard that it was the King who sought their help, they promptly downed their tools and offered to come and instruct. This was well received, and dismounting, they left the horses with one of the men, while the other went to a shed and produced five spears, and led them down to the little estuary where the Figgate Burn entered the firth.

This was a pleasant place of rippling shallows, with the stream now fully fifty yards across, flanked on each side by long stretches of golden sand backed by small dunes.

The fisherman took off his boots, and explained, with much bobbing of head towards the young monarch. This fishing was done barefooted, by wading in the shallows. The flounders or dabs lay just below the surface of the sand, and the wader could feel with his toes and the soles of his feet the fish as they darted away. This movement set up a flurry of sand in the water, and the art was to stab down the spear swiftly into this, in the hope of spitting the fish. It had to be quickly done – and care taken not to spear the wader's toes in the process, easily done. The spears each had a little spur projecting near the sharp tip, and this, once in, held the fish secure. He would show them. There were usually lots of flounders here; they seemed to like the fresh water mixing with the salt.

Rolling up his ragged breeches, the man waded in towards mid-stream, and had not gone a dozen splashing paces before he suddenly plunged in his spear. They heard a smothered curse as the weapon came up empty; but only a few yards further and he stabbed again, and this time, when raised, he had a flapping flatfish impaled. Detaching it, he smashed its head against the shaft, to kill it, and proceeded on.

James was immediately agog, already kicking off his riding-boots and removing his hose. Grabbing a spear, he plunged in.

"Watch your toes, Jamie," his sister warned.

Thomas Boyd was not long in following him.

The girls eyed each other, and nodded in unison. Stooping, they too discarded their boots, and then raised their heavy riding-skirts to belt them to hang above the knees. Then they too laughingly waded in.

The fisherman had another dab now, and came with his catch to the King.

Before he reached him, the boy yelled out, "I felt one! I felt one! It wriggled. Where is it? I cannot see it."

"Och, they're just below the sand, laddie. You dinna right see them, just the bit birl o' the sand in the watter. You hae to be quick."

Tom let out a cry, and stabbed. But without result.

It was Anna who made the first kill — or not exactly kill, for when she drew her spear out it had a quite large flounder transfixed almost at the tail, and flapping wildly. She shouted for help, not knowing what to do with it, and Mary nearby was going to assist her when she too felt a wriggling beneath her toes, saw a little moving cloud of sand, and plunged in her spear. She felt the movement at its point, and lifting it out found that she also had a dab, smaller than Anna's, sand-coloured on back, with red spots, and white beneath, flapping. Unhooking it, she banged its head against the spear and it went limp.

Anna was still ineffectual in dealing with her vigorous catch, finding the fish slippery to grasp as well as over-active, she with the use of only one hand. Mary was even more handicapped, with her own fish to hold, but using the butt-end of her spear, she brought it down on the other girl's fish. Three times she had to do this before the creature was still, Anna giggling uncontrollably.

They both waded ashore, to deposit their booty.

Neither of their companions had in fact achieved a catch as yet, James complaining loudly that there were no fish where he was, and Tom shouting that the devilish brutes seemed to zigzag away so that he missed them. The fisherman however had another two.

The triumphant young women, wringing out their skirt hems which had got splashed, decided on another attempt. This time it took them longer, but eventually Mary skewered one, better than the last. Although Anna did get one, it was not properly impaled by the spur, and fell off before she could grab it. Despite much splashing about by the pair, they could not retrieve the fish, getting not a little wet in the process. They came to the conclusion that they had proved themselves sufficiently for one day.

Much humiliated, their male companions came ashore empty-handed, although the fisherman now had five. James asserted that the girls had clearly struck the lucky patches where the fish lay; and Tom took the opportunity to declare that it was all women's wiles, the ability to allure and ensnare flounders as well as men.

The fisherman presented them with his catch, which meant that they had eight fish which they could have for their evening meal. And then came what Mary had rather feared. James declared that the water had not felt cold. He liked to swim. There was lots of sandy beach. He wanted to go swimming – no doubt anxious to indicate that he was good at this, if not at flounder-spearing. Tom Boyd was not slow in supporting this royal edict.

The girls exchanged glances. Mary could by no means forbid it. "Swim if you wish," she said. "But not, I think, near these cottages." She looked at the master. "Your arm . . . ?" she wondered.

"The salt water will do it good," he asserted. He pointed. "Along there, where there are higher sand dunes."

Leaving the fisherman with the spears, and a coin in thanks, they walked along the shore in the Musselburgh direction.

At least there was ample privacy, a couple of miles of empty sandy beach backed by the lowish dunes, small waves rolling in and no rocks in sight. James was all but undressing as they went.

Quarter of a mile on, Tom suggested that this would do. The inevitable followed. "You will join us, no doubt?" he challenged the young women.

Anna gurgled.

Mary inclined her head. "I enjoy a swim, yes. As to joining you, scarcely that! You, Anna? We will go in further along there."

"M'mm. Not too far, I hope!" the man protested, James already half unclad.

A smile. "Shall we say we shall be within sight, sir! Come, Anna."

The girls went about another two hundred yards. "This will serve, I think," the elder said. "We will be . . . generous, no?"

"If I know my brother, he will come swimming along!"

"No doubt. But we shall be in the water by then."

They moved into the dunes to undress. When presently, naked, they ran down to the tide's-edge, they made a lovely sight undoubtedly. They could see the other two already splashing in the water.

Mary was quite a strong swimmer, and struck out vigorously, the younger girl less venturesome. When, tiring a little, she turned on her back to rest, legs in a gentle paddle, it was, as she anticipated, to see the man coming towards her, using a powerful over-arm stroke, whatever the effect on one of his arms. She smiled to herself.

"You swim . . . as well as . . . you appear!" he panted, as he came up.

"Ah, but then appearances can mislead, no? Especially under water. As you discovered with the flounders!"

"You do not . . . resemble a . . . flounder, even so!"

She turned over on to her front. "Should you not be looking to your liege-lord's safety, sir? In case he gets into difficulties." And she pointed.

"He seems to swim very well. He says that you taught him."

She had begun to swim shorewards, and found that he was accompanying her. So she changed direction, back towards where her brother was ducking and surface-diving. Perforce the man had to do the same.

"Your arm?" she enquired. "Does it not hurt?"

"A little," he admitted, possibly hoping for female attention.

"Then you were foolish to swim at all. And more so to have come thus far along."

"It was worth it," he averred.

Near the boy, Mary turned on her back again, and began to kick large fountains of white water with her feet. Under this screening, she waved to the man.

"I require no escorting back!" she called mockingly, and left them.

But the Master of Boyd was not readily discouraged. The girls were only just out of the water when he and James came running along the firm sand towards them – which set Mary and Anna running, in turn, for the cover of the dunes.

"Come running. To dry off," they heard, and ignored, that shouted invitation.

"I wonder . . . that they do not come . . . to help us to dress!" Anna panted, as they donned clothing over distinctly wet bodies.

"Was he always like this?"

"Tom is six years older than I am. But ever since I have known enough to watch him, he has been very strong on women. The castleton girls all had to beware of him – such as did not encourage him! My other brothers do not seem as though they will be like Tom."

"Boyds! Give them time . . . !"

Clad, they all returned to the horses. The King of Scots rode back with a string of eight flounders slung round his neck.

5

The forty days were up, and the parliament assembled. Right up to the last the Boyds and their allies were cautious. Usually parliaments met in the great halls of Stirling or Edinburgh Castles, but the Boyds saw possible danger in allowing all who were entitled to attend into the fortress here, and had arranged for the session to be held in the Tolbooth of Edinburgh. All the lords, barons, prelates, officers of state, commissioners of the counties and representatives of the royal burghs could take part, if so they desired. How many would do so on this occasion remained to be seen. And how many might be hostile to the Boyds, and what they had done? The carefully contracted bands would deal with not a few of the nobility, of course; but there were inevitably large question marks as to majorities. The Boyd hope was that most hostile or condemnatory ones would absent themselves, rather than come intending battle, in words or even deeds. So the atmosphere in Edinburgh that ninth day of October 1466 was tense.

The Master of Boyd however showed no sign of this when he came to escort Mary and Anna down to the Tolbooth, a tall, five-storey building set in the middle of the High Street near to St Giles High Kirk, through the crowded streets; the King, on this occasion, would be led thither in royal style, later, by the Lord Lyon King of Arms and his heralds.

The Tolbooth, despite its height and twin stair-towers, was scarcely the most illustrious venue for a national parliament, but was heedfully chosen as a difficult place to bring any large number of armed men against, in its narrowing of the street and with the booths of merchants abutting; the city crowds would bar the way and give any required warning. But the courtroom on the first floor was comparatively small for any such large gathering, more apt for the city council. But there was a gallery, and it was to this that the master took the two young women. Already it was full, with bailies, councillors and dignitaries not of parliamentary status, but seats had been reserved for the trio at the front. These two were the only women present.

The courtroom below was also filling up, and Tom was carefully identifying those present, although giving no sign of anxiety. Mary was aware of a general air of wary vigilance however.

They had not long to wait, with the space below becoming crowded and ushers leading lords, prelates and lesser magnates to their due places – which in fact were only rows of wooden benches, plain and less than imposing. A flourish of trumpets outside heralded the incoming of the official party. The crown, sceptre and sword of state could not be carried in, for these were still at Stirling Castle; but a substitute regalia had been improvised, the Earl of Crawford bearing aloft a great two-handed sword, the Earl of Argyll a marshal's baton on a cushion – these two both having been summoned back from England where they had been on an embassage – the Lord Somerville carrying another cushion on which lay a pair of golden spurs, and the Lord Livingstone, the High Chamberlain, bearing a scroll of unknown significance but looking impressive. These four came to stand in front of a table and throne, brought from the castle, erected on the judges' dais.

Another trumpet blast brought in the new Bishop of St Andrews, the Primate, Patrick Graham, and his colleagues of Glasgow and Aberdeen – notable as the only bishops present out of thirteen, to represent the support of Holy Church.

There was no sign of the Lord Boyd, although Sir Alexander sat in a comparatively humble position, as keeper of the royal castle of Edinburgh.

Then the final great fanfare. The Lord Lyon strode in at the head of his heralds, all gorgeous in their tabards, insignia and batons. And behind them, alone, came James, looking embarrassed and nervous, far from resplendent in his very ordinary clothing. He squeezed past the row of dignitaries to the throne, and sat down, biting his lip. Quickly his eyes rose to search the gallery for sister and friends.

"Poor Jamie," Mary murmured. "He will prefer swimming, even flounders, to this!"

"I hope that His Grace remembers his words!" the master said.

"He has words to speak?"

70

"Oh, yes. Important words."

"Then he will have been well schooled, I vow!" The boy had had a long private session with Sir Alexander that morning.

Lyon thumped his staff. "James, by God's grace King of Scots, ordains this parliament of his realm to be duly constituted and in session. I call upon the Primate of Holy Church to open the proceedings with prayer. God save the King!"

"God save the King!" all echoed.

Patrick Graham, Bishop Kennedy's successor in St Andrews bishopric, then asserted that they met on this very important occasion to make decision for the weal of the King's realm, and prayed that Almighty God would guide them in wisdom and prosper their conclusions. Amen.

The four lords bearing the emblems laid down these on a table near the throne, and bowing, proceeded backwards to their due seats. The Bishop of Glasgow, who was apparently to act Chancellor, or chairman, on this occasion, went to sit at this table, while a couple of monkish clerks scurried in, all bows, to take their places, with papers, at the other end of it.

All sat.

There was a pause. James glanced about him, anxiously, fairly obviously wondering whether *he* ought to be doing something. Mary felt for him.

Nobody else seemed to know quite what to do, either. Anna murmured, "Where is our father?"

"Wait, you," her brother advised.

The door by which the official party had entered was suddenly thrown open again, with something of a clatter, and in strode the Lord Boyd, alone. He was magnificently dressed, head held high. Straight to the throne he paced, ignoring the acting Chancellor at the table and Lyon with the assistants behind, and, in front of the King, sank to his knees and bending forward low, clasped arms about the boy's ankles.

"Sire," he said loudly, "I beseech you to tell me, to tell all here, whether Your Grace has conceived any indignation or offence against your humble servant and loyal subject, or against any of my companions, for our riding here to Edinburgh with you after the Exchequer Audit at Linlithgow? Answer, if you will, whether you bear any royal rancour or concern in this matter." This to the gasps of the company.

James moistened his lips. "I . . . *we* are not . . . we do not

71

so conceive, my lord. No. Not so. It, it was done by our royal command and desire. I say it, yes. Er . . . rise, my lord."

Boyd got to his feet, bowed deeply again, and went to stand behind the throne, nudging the Lord Lyon slightly aside.

"Save us – is that our father!" Anna exclaimed. "Abasing himself like that!"

"Wait, you," her brother counselled again.

Boyd tapped the boy's shoulder. "My lord Bishop?" James said then, hurriedly.

The acting Chancellor inclined his head. "As Your Grace commands." He consulted papers on the table put before him by the clerks. "This parliament of the realm, duly called by royal authority, is now in session. It has much of great import to decide and homologate. But first, His Grace has certain edicts of his royal will of which to inform you." He rose, and went to present one of the papers to the King.

James took it almost gingerly, looked up at the gallery, round at the Lord Boyd, and cleared his throat.

"I, James, King of Scots, do hereby make, make declaration," he read carefully, if with scant conviction. "For the necessary weal and gov . . . governance of my realm, I do hereby . . ." He seemed to lose his place and repeated, ". . . for the governance . . . I do hereby . . . declare, appoint and, and nominate, to be my royal governor and regent of my kingdom until I become of full age, the Lord Thomas Boyd of Kilmarnock. From this present. I . . ." His hands trembling obviously, the boy dropped the paper. Alarmedly he looked round at Boyd, who frowned, and gestured to a herald to pick it up as the monarch himself was stooping to do so. There were seconds of uncomfortable silence while the boy found his place again.

"From this present, I appoint the Lord Thomas to have governance of my royal person. Also to have the governance of my royal brothers, Alexander, Duke of Albany and John, Earl of Mar," he went on, at something of a gabble. "Likewise to take into his care my royal castles, each and all, the keepers thereof to, to deliver them into his hands forthwith . . . I . . ." He peered more closely at the paper, as though the writing thereon eluded him. "I do hereby pro . . . promul . . . promulgate, aye promulgate, as my royal will, that he, the Lord Thomas, shall have the execution of all my, my authority and justice, in my name, until I reach the age of twenty-one years. This, my, my sovereign will." With a

72

sigh of relief, James rose and went to hand that paper back to the bishop – an unscheduled move, which had not a few there hastily rising from their seats, since none should sit while the monarch stood. As James got back to his chair, Lord Boyd waved them all down.

"God save the King's Grace," he called.

There was a complete hush in that courtroom as the significance of the boy's reading sank in. Thomas, Lord Boyd, was no great magnate, not even an earl; and here he was suddenly, it seemed, complete ruler of Scotland. What had been declared on that paper, pronounced by the monarch before parliament as his edict and will, gave Boyd the control not only of the King's person but of everything pertaining to the rule and direction of the kingdom. He was now the Regent, with the monarch's powers delegated. That thought took a deal of digesting.

Mary turned to gaze at the master. "So – there was the aim of it all," she said, accused. "The regency! The Boyds to be rulers of the land. All to be subservient to Boyd!"

Even that young man looked a little uncomfortable. "For the good of all the kingdom," he asserted. "Since Bishop Kennedy died, and your mother, all has been weakness. No firm direction. This will make improvement . . ."

The Lord Boyd was speaking. "My lord Bishop, to business," he said crisply. There was no doubt now who was in charge.

Andrew Durrisdeer, Bishop of Glasgow, rapped on his table. "This parliament has to consider the due carrying out of the King's wishes for the best governance of the realm. Further, the Lord Boyd requires that these important decisions be recorded amongst the acts of the parliament, and provisions registered under the Great Seal of the kingdom, that there be no question as to the legitimacy and authority thereof." He did not ask for parliamentary approval of this, it was to be noted. Then, "Certain lords to be appointed, to have full power to act in the name of this parliament, until another is called to consider and approve the reforms instituted in the interim. Such parliament to be summoned early in the next year, 1467."

The Campbell Earl of Argyll was on his feet immediately. "I agree such provision," he said. "I nominate my lord Earl of Crawford to such council."

"And I second," the Bishop of St Andrews added.

"And I nominate my lord Earl of Argyll," the Lord Livingstone said.

"And I second," Crawford agreed.

"I nominate the lord Bishop of St Andrews, Primate." That was the Lord Somerville.

"And I second," Lord Hailes confirmed.

Like the rapid hammer-blows of a smith at his anvil, the names rang out, all the supporters of the Boyds, those with whom they had exchanged bands, their kinsmen and friends. The thing was done in almost less time than it takes to tell.

"Now, the matter of the royal castles," the acting Chancellor went on. "Some are known to be in the hands of those disloyal to the crown. Notably Dunbar, Lochmaben and Stirling. These are held respectively by Kennedy of Kirkmichael, Kennedy of Blairquhan and Gilbert, Lord Kennedy. These named to be requested to yield them up forthwith, and to the Lords Montgomery, Maxwell and Cathcart, as keepers."

"Considering that you were affianced to the Lady Janet Kennedy, you Boyds are hard on that house!" Mary observed.

"*Was* affianced – but no longer." That was brief.

"Fortunate Janet!" Anna commented.

No comment on these appointments came, however, from the assembly's members – who, no doubt, were busy making their calculations as on which side their bread was buttered.

"Parliament is now required to consider the important matter of the eventual marriage of the King's Grace," Glasgow's bishop went on, consulting his papers. "It was intended that, for the good of the realm, and peace with the realm of England, the King's sister, the Princess Mary, should wed Edward of York – this arranged by the late Bishop Kennedy." He glanced up at the gallery. "But now that Edward is King of England, he has wed a woman of the House of Lancaster." He did not add deplorably, but implied it. "Now it is proposed that our young sovereign-lord James be found a suitable partner, possibly one of the English royal family, York or Lancaster. Also the marriage of his brothers, the Duke of Albany and the Earl of Mar, be considered, whether to ladies of England, France, Flanders or elsewhere. Therefore this parliament is requested to appoint the Earls of Crawford and Argyll and the Bishops of Glasgow and Aberdeen to consider this matter, and report to the next parliament. Is it agreed?"

No disagreement was voiced – save by implication, and quietly, from the gallery.

"What is your Boyd motto?" Mary wondered.

Thomas raised his eyebrows. "Motto? Why? *Confido*, it is."

"I think that it should be changed to *I Waste no Time!*"

He shook his head. "In this matter I do not agree with my father. I see the King's marriage as best with Norway, or Denmark. For young Albany and Mar, who knows? But . . ."

"Norway . . . ?"

"Aye. It would solve much . . ."

But the bishop was speaking again. "For the future Queen, a suitable dowry must be offered. It is suggested that one-third of the crown's rents, with the use of the palace of Linlithgow, as was His Grace's late mother's portion, should be offered. Is it agreed?"

No contrary voice was raised, but the Primate spoke. "I would add the provision which the good King Robert the Bruce imposed, that as to dowry moneys, none should be permitted to be exported to England, whomsoever the lady. Lest it provoke . . . interference."

A dozen voices seconded that.

"As to this of moneys and exporting," the acting Chancellor went on, "it is important for the royal treasury, and the better care of the kingdom, that there should be greater export to foreign lands of the realm's goods and merchandise. This not only to fill all the empty coffers, and aid the public weal, but to pay for goods imported from other lands, in especial arms, wines, silks and other cloths, and other items which we ourselves cannot produce. This important matter has been but insufficiently considered of these last years. We must export more wool from the Lammermuir Hills, for which the Flemings cry out for their cloth mills. Also hides and salt-fish. In these Scotland is rich. Other goods also. A council to see to this. Who will so act . . . ?"

He was interrupted by an authoritative voice from behind the throne. "My brother, Sir Alexander Boyd of Duncow, will attend to that."

There was a moment or two of silence. This was the first mention of Sir Alexander's name so far – and for a far from resounding office, however necessary; dealing with mere trade, moneys, merchandise, would be considered below the dignity of most lords there. Anna looked past Mary to her brother.

"Uncle Alex, the Mirror of Chivalry?" she wondered. "*He* did not so choose, I think!"

The master said nothing.

Almost hurriedly, the bishop went on. "So be it. Sir Alexander Boyd to see to it. Lead a council, and report. Now – the matter of officers of state. justiciars, sheriffs of counties, customars and the like. This will, to be sure, take some time. Is it the wish of His Grace and of this parliament that the filling of these offices be dealt with now? Or at a further sitting on the morrow? For other necessary business will require a further session assuredly."

"I move adjournment. Sufficient for one day," the Lord Boyd announced – and only just seemed to remember to add, "if His Grace agrees?"

His Grace, bored by now, nodded hearty concurrence, and was on his feet before even Lyon signed for his trumpeters to sound.

All rose, although probably all did not realise yet that a new chapter had commenced in Scotland's eventful story.

Mary Stewart had some inkling of it, at least. "So now we know who rules the land! Thomas, Lord Boyd. Whoever *reigns*. But – what of his brother? Aye, and what of his son?"

"We shall see," the master said carefully. "At least there have been no interruptions from without." He sounded almost grim for that so confident character.

"You feared such?"

"Aye. Come, you . . ."

6

At first, in the days that followed, for the royal pair at least, it might almost have seemed as though that parliament had never taken place, so little difference was there in their conditions and daily programme. The only noticeable change was that they saw practically nothing of Sir Alexander Boyd, to James's disappointment – and they could not conceive that he was already away on his new duties as trade commissioner. Yet he was the Keeper of this royal castle of Edinburgh – or had been.

James had to attend two more sittings of the parliament, to his boredom; but the girls elected not to go, finding it scarcely enthralling.

The master, strangely, appeared to think as did they; of course he had no part to play therein, and was no born spectator. He preferred female company, it seemed, and presumably his father did not need him – as certainly was proved by the word coming from others, that Lord Boyd had now had himself appointed not only as Regent but as Chief Justiciar of the Realm and Lord High Chamberlain, this latter office giving him access to the monarch at all times. At any rate, the master continued to escort the young women assiduously; Mary was glad that in James's absence, Anna ever remained close. They went riding and hunting, especially in the Pentland Hills of which Mary had become fond, with the season now getting past for seashore activities. Tom was much his usual too-attentive self, never failing to seek to exploit every opportunity for amatory gestures, physical contacts and gallantry, yet there was something of preoccupation about him not previously noticeable. Anna saw it also, and did not fail to remark on it. She opined that it behoved them to watch out.

Then, only a week after the final sitting of the parliament, it was announced that all were to pack up and go to Stirling. It was an order, no royal agreement being sought. The Regent was now in full command. Not that Mary objected. Stirling Castle had been her home, scene of her childhood, where her belongings and clothes still were, set amidst a country she knew and loved. James was less pleased. He had come to like Edinburgh – and there was no sea at Stirling; but he was not consulted.

On 25th October they set out on the thirty-five-mile ride, a large and now fairly resplendent company, well escorted by armed men, with a lengthy baggage-train coming along more slowly behind. Sir Alexander Boyd presumably remained at Edinburgh. They passed Niddry Seton and Linlithgow, halfway, without comment.

It was almost dark when they reached Stirling and, tired and hungry, rode up through the narrow, steep-climbing streets of the town to that other fortress-citadel on its great rock-top, so like Edinburgh's but more commodious and less grim, the ancient seat of Scotland's monarchy, which dominated the waist of the land.

At the drawbridge and gatehouse an extraordinary scene was enacted, in the nature of play-acting but significant enough. Gilbert, Lord Kennedy stood there awaiting them, alone, a ceremonial rope tying together his wrists, but loosely. In his hands he held a bunch of great iron keys, not like the golden one the provost of Edinburgh had presented to the King. Bowing low, these however he did not offer to James, but came to Lord Boyd's horse and held them up to him. This was the first meeting of these two since the interrupted hunt. He said nothing.

Boyd eyed him, expressionless, but took the keys. Then he turned to the Lord Hailes, who rode behind him, and silently pointed, first at Kennedy, then into the castle before them. The Hepburn chief nodded, and urging his mount forward, stooped low in the saddle to reach down for the rope which tied together Kennedy's wrists – but not so very low, for that man raised arms to facilitate the process. Then, thus linked, the two nobles moved off together, one mounted, one afoot, over the bridge and under the gatehouse arch, gaoler and captive. Most obviously it had all been arranged beforehand.

"Your band with the Kennedys included this?" Mary asked the master, not troubling to lower her voice.

He shrugged, wordless, but his father looked round, frowning, before leading the way into the fortress, after the other two.

Dismounted, stiff and saddle-sore, at least it was good to be able to go, with James and Anna, to their own rooms in the palace block, infinitely more handsome apartments than at Edinburgh, and found their royal servants there to attend them.

Mary had a large bedchamber and anteroom, and James similar adjoining on the same floor. When Anna asked where she was to go, Mary declared that, unless she wished otherwise, she should continue to share accommodation with her; the great canopied bed was large enough for two, and there was ample cupboard and wardrobe furnishing for both. They had proved good boudoir companions hitherto, had they not? The other girl was more than agreeable, delighted; her brother might be less appreciative, they both recognised with small smiles.

The reunion with the other royal children provided an affecting occasion. Margaret was ten, a shy, gentle child, with little to say for herself; Alexander, Duke of Albany and Earl of March, a year older, was very different, a hot-tempered, opinionated boy, who rather dominated his younger brother John, Earl of Mar, aged only seven, but who had his virtues, being ingenious, quick-witted, clever — more so than was James, undoubtedly. They were all very fond of their elder sister, who had acted mother to them for three years; they had obviously grievously missed her these last months. They were now less excited over James's return, and at first a little suspicious and resentful over Anna — but soon they accepted her, and indeed found her good company.

As it happened, Mary, in her first weeks back at Stirling, had something of a remission from the attentions of Tom Boyd. Presumably lacking Sir Alexander's presence — for whatever reason, the brothers now appeared to be at loggerheads — Lord Boyd required his son to act for him where his brother would have done so before; and the master was sent off on various missions and errands for the new ruler of Scotland. With her young brothers and sister to look after again, and something of her old life to resume, Mary was kept a deal more busy than she had been at Edinburgh; but despite this, she had to acknowledge to herself, on occasion, that she missed the young man's company and challenge.

More than once, Mary asked Anna about the curious situation anent Sir Alexander Boyd. Although even that forthright and uninhibited young woman was reluctant to appear openly critical of her father, it did seem as though the elder brother had used the younger, who had so much more polish, style and good looks, with a gallant reputation, as against his own rather chill and colourless, not to say dull-seeming, self, to further his schemes and designs.

Possibly the elder was the more clever of the two, in fact; but the other had the more useful image and was the man of action. Now that Lord Boyd had got what he wanted, however, it seemed that Sir Alexander was to be dispensed with. There may have been jealousy involved. Mary was the less enamoured of the man who now ruled them all.

Her lack of approval was to be notably enhanced that Yuletide. One day, just before Christmas, James came back to their quarters from one of his now frequent sessions with the Regent and the Chancellor, now reappointed, Lord Avondale, to sign and seal documents, charters, edicts and the like, full of talk about this Lord Avondale, who was in fact a sort of cousin of his own, an illegitimate son of a former Duke of Albany, and who had been away in England and France acting as a special envoy. He had come home, and presumably thrown in his support with the Boyds, since he had been reappointed Chancellor of the realm. James quite liked him; but would have preferred the Master of Boyd to have been Chancellor, since apparently he had to see so much of him. It was a pity that he was away so much these days. He was good, interesting, very kind. He hoped that once he was married he would not be so often gone. It had been good at Edinburgh, much better . . .

"It will be long before you are married, Jamie," his sister told him, smiling. "That talk of marriage at the parliament was only policy, at this present. Much will have to be decided as to which realm will offer the best terms, which princess will make the best match for the King of Scots. Ambassadors will be sent out . . .

"Not *my* marriage, Mary – the master's. And yours."

"What . . . !"

"The master is going to marry *you*. Did you not know?"

His sister stared at him. "Marry? No!" she gasped.

"The Lord Boyd says it, so it must be so. Will you not like that?"

"No! No!" She turned abruptly, and went over to a window, to stare out, back rigid.

Anna moved over to her, and took the other girl's arm, silent.

Almost fiercely, Mary turned on her. "Did *you* know of this? All along? Has this been planned from the beginning? I will not! I will *not* wed him, I tell you! Never!"

Anna shook her head. "I am sorry. I knew naught of it. Tom has never spoken of it. Nor our father. But . . ."

"They cannot *make* me do it. I will not be sold, traded, like some new mare! This is too much – you Boyds go too far! Jamie, you must stop this."

"But why, Mary? He is kind . . ."

"He is a Boyd. Until three months ago I had scarcely heard his name! I am Mary Stewart, not some chattel to be married off at will."

"But you like him, do you not? And he likes you, I think."

"You know nothing about it. Marriage!" Mary turned, to glare at them both, so unlike her. Then she strode over to the bedchamber, entered, and slammed the door behind her.

The master arrived back at Stirling in time for the usual Christmas festivities, and was not long in presenting himself at the royal quarters, still travel-stained as he was from long riding. Had he seen his sister before he saw Mary, presumably he would have been warned of impending trouble; but Anna was with the other girl in their anteroom when he appeared, and in no position to sound the alarm.

"Ha – as beautiful as ever!" he exclaimed, and came to reach for Mary's hand to raise it to his lips, all urgent satisfaction.

She snatched it from him, and turned her back on him.

"Save us – here's no way to offer Yuletide greetings to the weary traveller from across the sea, no less!" he protested. "I've come from Arran itself. Have you not missed me?"

Mary did not reply, but moved further away.

"I have ridden from Dumbarton since disembarking, all but killing my horse, the sooner to see you, to salute you, to warm myself in your fair company! And now, this! What is to do?"

Anna spoke. "She knows. Her Highness has been told. This of . . . marriage."

That silenced him – but only for moments. "So-o-o! Our sire has spoken! I had hoped . . ." He shrugged. "Princess, I am grieved that you should have learned of this, this decision, thus. Not from myself, of my love and devotion. My seeking of your hand in suitable fashion, in humble duty and esteem . . ."

She whirled round on him. "Humble! You! Spare us more, sirrah! Let us be honest, at the least. *I* shall be honest with you, I assure you. I will not wed you!"

He eyed her distressedly, an emotion seldom seen on those handsome features. "Mary! Highness! Do not take it so. I am

81

sorry that it has come this way. My true caring and admiration. It is not as it should have been. However you heard of this projected match, the proposal should have been mine . . ."

"The proposal perhaps, Master of Boyd. The *decision* is mine. No, I say! And again, no!"

"But . . ."

"Master Thomas!" James, having heard the man's voice from his adjoining room, came hastening. "You are back. How good! We have missed you. Where have you been . . . ?"

It is to be feared that Tom Boyd quite failed in his loyal duty and respect towards his sovereign-lord, indeed ignored him completely.

"Mary, hear me," he pleaded. "Give me opportunity to express my feelings for you. You must have known of them, surely? I have not sought to hide my regard and fondness – aye, my love. These months you have been my joy, my need, my hope. I have not declared myself in words. But my strong desire and need of you must have been apparent to you. I have been waiting. Waiting until I had something to offer you, other than just myself, my heart. Now I *have* something. I could not ask the King's sister to be but Mistress of Boyd, to descend to that. But now I have Arran, the whole great island. Other lands also. And the promise that it shall all be erected into an earldom. Now you will be Countess of Arran . . . !"

"Think you that I care for Arran or any other stolen lands, sir? Or being your countess. I am of the blood royal, and will not be married off to any – at your demand, or your father's . . ."

"Mary," James said, "do not be so sore against the master. He has been good to us. Kind . . ."

"Be quiet, Jamie! You know not what you say. Know nothing of marriage and a woman's needs and concerns."

The boy bridled. "I am the King!" he said.

"And a foolish one! Spare me your guidance."

"His Grace is kind, Princess. Can you not be a little kind also? At least hear me out. For you are not a hard woman."

"In this you will find me sufficiently hard! What have you to say that you have not already said?"

"This. You, His Grace's elder sister, one of the two princesses of Scotland, will fall to be wed. To someone. Possibly a prince or even a King of some land. Or a great noble, here. It is always so – you know that. Call it your fate, if you will. The choice is

82

scarce likely to be yours. You know that also. So what would you? Myself, a man who loves you, is devoted to you? Or some stranger whom you know not, who may care nothing for *you*, only wish to marry into the Scots royal house?"

"As do you!"

"As does my father, *for* me. Myself, I want *you*, Mary – not Her Highness! And, and I think that you have found me none so grievous a companion, these months? At least, you know me, and my caring. Where you would not know another. And I am to be made a great lord – for none rank higher, in Scotland, than its earls, save only the dukes of the royal house. See you, you could do worse, Mary, in your marrying!"

"If I sought to marry – which I do not. And when – and if – I do, I will seek some say in whom I wed."

"You will find none more devoted than am I . . ."

Anna coughed and made a brief but complicated gesture, part shake of the head, part nod towards the door.

The man drew a deep breath, then shrugged. He bowed, and turned. "Have I Your Grace's permission to retire?"

"I will come with you," James said.

At the door, the master turned. "Think on it, Highness," he urged, all but pleaded, and went out.

Mary stared after him, biting her lip.

Anna discreetly left her alone.

In the days that followed, with traditional Christmas festivities prevailing, much feasting and entertainment, the question of marriage, if question it was, remained undiscussed. Tom Boyd sought to make all as it had been before, as far as the royal pair were concerned, or to seem so, a good companion. He organised amusements and sporting activities, although the weather was not of the best for such, spending most of his time in their company, whether desired or not – James at least encouraging him in this. But there *was* a difference. The man was less bold, less demonstrative in his attentions, less of touchings and sought intimacies, however heedful of the young woman's needs and desires. For her part, Mary, well aware of this, while by no means encouraging him, did not maintain too hard an attitude, too hostile a front, for all their sakes. It was not in her nature to do so, to be sure, and she recognised realities when she saw them. Also that he was trying to be placatory.

Twelfth Night came and went, the end to Yuletide. And as though to emphasise that festivity was now over, the very next day it was not the master who came to the royal quarters but Lord Boyd himself. He dismissed his daughter with a flick of the hand, and looked meaningfully at the King, who took the hint and retired to his own room.

"Princess," he said, without preamble, "I understand that you are informed that it is decided that you shall marry my son, Thomas. This for the benefit of all. He will be created Earl of Arran as from the day before the wedding, which will be on the last day of this present month. Certain details have to be arranged first, and of these I come to inform you – "

"I think, my lord, that you can spare yourself in this," the girl interrupted. "I have no wish to marry, the Master of Boyd or other."

Undoubtedly the Regent had been warned that this interview might not be all plain sailing, for he showed no surprise nor indeed any change of expression on his fairly consistently expressionless face.

"This is not a matter of wishes or preferences, Highness," he observed, flatly. "It is policy, state policy. Taken by the Council, for the good of the realm. His Grace's sisters should be wed, for many reasons, but first and foremost for the sake of the succession. Only two young boys represent the succession, both children; and boys do not always reach manhood. So, with His Grace not yet himself of marriageable age, although he must be affianced soon, it's important that the succession be strengthened, assured. So . . . ."

"So you, sir, would seek to have a grandson, a Boyd, to sit on the Scottish throne! The Kilmarnock lairds aspire to become royal!"

That did make the man blink. "Not so. That is not my intention. It is but a precaution. Ever necessary in the royal house, Princess. His sister, wed, will strengthen His Grace's hand, and His Grace's regency. You must see that . . ."

"But not necessarily to *your* son, my lord!"

"My son regards you highly. He will make you a good husband."

"A good husband, perhaps – but not for me!"

"For you, yes, Princess."

"No!"

"You cannot disobey a royal command, lady."

"*Command . . . ?*"

"Yes. The King has signed a decree to that effect. And to create the earldom."

She stared at him. "James . . . has done . . . that!"

"His Grace has, yes. At the Council's request."

Wordless now, the girl turned away.

The Regent, point made, went on, addressing her back. "There will be great benefits for you, Highness. You will be Countess of Arran. All that great island yours. Large lands in Fife, Lothian, Ayrshire and Galloway, also. Thomas will be one of the richest earls in the land."

"Think you that I care for that!"

"Would you liefer have wed an unknown foreign prince, lady? As part of a treaty?"

She did not answer.

"Kings' daughters seldom can choose whom they will wed," he told her. "I would say that you are more fortunate than most. Consider you that, I charge you." With the sketchiest of bows, he left her to her consideration.

7

Mary Stewart was not a fool, nor afraid to recognise and accept unavoidable facts. She had strength of character and will; but she knew how to bend to necessity. That is not to say that she thereafter surrendered meekly or became patiently accepting, reconciled to her fate. But, perceiving that she was not going to alter that fate, short of a miracle, she sought to adapt her behaviour so as to make the best of it, for herself and for others. Whilst making it clear, especially to Tom Boyd, that she was still no willing bride, she did not refuse all preparation for the marriage, nor make life miserable for her brothers, sister and Anna.

As for the bridegroom-to-be, he trod warily indeed for that man, still attentive but never assertive, not exactly apologetic but ever seeking to reassure, to allay fears, to indicate that his caring was real and included concern for the young woman's feelings. This was obviously difficult for a man of his temperament and lead-taking nature; and at times Mary was actually almost sorry for him, well aware of his efforts and strains.

It was towards James that she was most distant, finding it hard to forgive that he had been persuaded to sign the marriage documents, and charters of Arran and other lands, for Tom. She told herself that the boy did not fully understand, of course, that he had grown fond of the master, provider of so much that he enjoyed, probably thinking indeed that he was doing his sister a favour. But it rankled.

It was to be a most brilliant wedding, inevitably, Lord Boyd seeing it as the crowning evidence and symbol of his achievement and success, the flourished confirmation of the Boyd rise to supreme power. No expense was to be spared, no detail of the splendour of a royal occasion overlooked. These weeks of January were all too short for the scale of the arrangements, the provision of magnificent clothing, the preparations for feasting and the sending out of invitations to the illustrious – the haste was to have it all over before the fasting season of Lent. So the first weeks passed quickly.

Anna, not to mention the royal children, grew much excited.

There was a distraction however, before the due day. An envoy arrived at Stirling, from Norway. King Christian thereof sent, not felicitations and congratulations on the royal match, but urgent complaint. It was, as ever, concerned with those bones of contention, the isles of Orkney and Shetland. These clusters of islands, although lying off the north coast of Scotland, belonged to the Norse kingdom, and had done since Viking times, this despite the fact that they constituted a Scottish earldom and bishopric. Usually, the trouble was about the latter, for, because the Scottish Church had no Metropolitan or archbishop, the Archbishop of Trondheim, who called himself Metropolitan of the North, claimed spiritual jurisdiction over the See of Orkney. This was disputed by the Archbishop of York, who made similar claims – much to Scotland's resentment, the Scots prelates accepting the claims of neither, an ongoing clerical war. However, the present incumbent, William Tulloch, was a careful and diplomatic prelate, who got on well with the Norsemen. Unfortunately, William St Clair, Earl of Orkney, was of a very different character, a harsh and violent man, and the two seldom were in agreement. Now, according to this Norse envoy, the earl had actually laid hands on the bishop and locked him up in one of his castles, a prisoner – to the great offence of the Archbishop of Trondheim and King Christian; and, incidentally, when he heard of it, to the Scots Primate, the Bishop of St Andrews.

There was much concern at Stirling, not so much perhaps on account of Bishop Tulloch's fate as at the danger of trouble with Norway – for Scotland had only what amounted to a lease of the Northern Isles, and was considerably in arrears with the rental, one of the many problems of an all but empty treasury, finances neglected since Bishop Kennedy died. The last thing they wanted, at this stage, was King Christian's ill-will, and demands for indemnity – and payment of arrears.

Lord Boyd, faced with his first major challenge, in a sphere in which he had no least experience, sent for the Primate, from St Andrews. Bishop Graham, hastening to Stirling, not much more than a couple of weeks before he was due there to celebrate the royal wedding, was much upset, both at the outrage perpetrated upon one of his bishops, and on the Norse reaction, fearing that the Archbishop of Trondheim might do what had been threatened more than once before, petition the Pope to have the Orkney diocese removed from the Scottish Church to the Norse one, a dire development, especially over this question of Metropolitan status. Something must be done, and at once.

Lord Boyd's dilemma was acute, his courses of action limited indeed. The Earl of Orkney had to be dealt with, and vigorously, obviously; but that was not so easy, up there in his island fastnesses; and he was a formidable individual, apart from his hot temper – he had indeed been Chancellor of Scotland once. No sort of military persuasion was to be considered, even possible; so diplomacy it had to be. But who was to apply it, and what? The fire-eating earl had no regard for churchmen, obviously, to imprison a bishop; so there was no point in sending up the Primate or any of his fellow-prelates. Who, then? Boyd himself, although Regent, was only a Lord of Parliament, no earl, and undoubtedly the St Clair would refuse to heed any less than of his own rank. As it so happened, the Boyds' friends and allies and supporters included only the two earls, Crawford and Argyll, the Lindsay and Campbell chiefs, and these were both away on the embassage to seek a suitable bride for King James. The two others were keeping their distance, to see how this Boyd regime developed. Certainly none would or could go on this awkward mission to Orkney and Shetland.

It was the Primate himself who came up with a possible solution. He said that he would have proposed Sir Alexander Boyd for the task, as the sort of man old St Clair might listen to, soldier and known as the Mirror of Chivalry; but he recognised that a mere knight would probably not carry sufficient weight, even if supported by some of the lords. So – postpone the wedding, but have the Master of Boyd created Earl of Arran forthwith, and send him. He was a personable and effective young man, and about to be wed to the King's sister.

For want of a better suggestion, or indeed any other, Boyd agreed, and the master given his instructions. The wedding to be held over meantime, but not the earldom. The King would sign the necessary documents right away, and the new Earl of Arran, with, say, the Primate himself and Lord Somerville, would sail from Inverkeithing for Orkney, just as soon as a ship could be got ready. No argument was permitted.

88

Tom Boyd came to Mary with mixed feelings, obviously uncertain as to her reactions, whatever his own.

"Behold, Highness, an errant bridegroom indeed!" he began, with an attempt to mix apology with both concern and banter. "Matters of state are to give you remission, for a little while, of being wed to your unworthy suitor! I am to go to Orkney, to beard the earl thereof in his den, and seek to free the good bishop. This is not of my choosing, I do assure you. Indeed, it may be the end of me! The Earl William is said to be a fierce character, and I may end up sharing the same cell with the bishop!"

"I think not," she said. "The St Clair may be a hard man, but he would not do that. He was Chancellor of this realm once. He is bitter, yes, but may have reason to be." That was levelly said.

He looked at her curiously. "You sound as though you know more of him than do I?"

"Perhaps I do. Perhaps I have reason to do so. Since he represents, in some measure, a stain on my father's honour." She was looking away from him, but speaking firmly. She had heard something of what was to do this day in Stirling, from James.

"Your father? The King? The late King?"

"The same. This Earl William of Orkney had a sister who wed the Earl of Douglas, the seventh of that great line, James the Gross. And my father, with his own hand, stabbed the son of that sister, the eighth Earl of Douglas, with his own dagger, at a banquet here in this Stirling Castle. To bring down the great power of the House of Douglas, which he feared was threatening the royal power. That was some fifteen years ago – but it is not something that I can forget. I do not think that ever before had a King of Scots done the like. My father was . . . impetuous. He lived to regret it, I know. As must all of his family."

He reached out to touch her – but thought better of it. "I knew of the death of Douglas, yes, But not that he was nephew to this Earl of Orkney."

"He was. And because Orkney supported the Douglases, he lost much. He resigned the chancellorship. Also the position he held of Admiral of Scotland. Much else. So St Clair is a bitter man."

"I see. This will scarcely help my mission, then!"

"What is that mission? What do you go to say to him? What have you to offer St Clair? Since you cannot threaten him with men, with violence, in those far isles. You would require a great

89

fleet of galleys – which you have not got. Whereas he has. The other islesmen who have, the Lord of the Isles and his like, will nowise help you in this. Nor my lord of Argyll, I think. What have you got that the St Clair may want, as a price?"

"Lands. The offer of lands here in the south. And the threat of seeking to use the King of Norway's power against him."

"Think you that the Norse would not have done that ere this, if they were prepared to do it, rather than appeal to the King of Scots?"

"M'mm. You seem concerned, Mary? And knowledgeable about it all?"

"Not greatly so, no. But I heard my mother and Bishop Kennedy discussing a similar situation, when the earl gave up the chancellorship and the rest. They feared his power, allied to what was left of that of Douglas. I was young then, but I was interested. For the bishop took me to see the splendid chapel which St Clair had built at Roslin, near to Edinburgh, where the line hailed from. I said that a lord who built so fine a church could not be so ill a man."

"Roslin? I have not heard of this. A chapel?"

"One of the finest in the land. Renowned elsewhere – if not in your Kilmarnock!"

He grinned. "You think that I may survive, then? And our wedding be only delayed!"

"I can bear the delay, sir. However long!"

"I was afraid of that! Whereas *I* can not."

"May I at least hope that the marriage will now not be held until after Lent is past? If it must be, even then!"

"Oh, I think not, no. Easter is not until mid-April. So Lent does not start for six weeks yet. Lord help me if I am away for *half* of that time. It is but three days' sail to Orkney, they say – if the ship does not sink in the winter's gales! Two or three days at Kirkwall or Stromness or wherever the earl bides in those God-forsaken isles, and then home. I should be back in two weeks."

"I think that it will take you longer. Unless you have some strong lure to tempt him. More than any mere gift of lands. He has a sufficiency of lands already, I would say."

"Since you appear to know more about it all than do I – or my sire, I think – have you any suggestion as to what could well please the man?"

"It is scarcely for me to say. But . . . I would think that to assuage his hurt pride over what was done to him over the Douglas cause – for the St Clairs are notably proud – that would be best. He can hardly have back the chancellorship, nor want it now. But it would cost little to rename him Admiral, would it not? There is no Admiral of Scotland at present, I think? And he has the ships. And that might serve to help keep the turbulent Lord of the Isles in his Hebridean place, no? It could do the realm no harm . . ."

The master wagged his head at her. "Save us, here is a wonder! So young, so fair – and such wits! Such knowledge of affairs. A King's daughter, indeed. That might serve . . ."

"Also, there is this of the Roslin chapel. It is not only a chapel, of course, but attached to a collegiate church, if I remember rightly, with a provost and priests. If the Primate was to elevate Earl William in some way, or at least elevate his foundation of this collegiate church, as its patron, might this not please him? He is no young man, and will be apt to be considering his latter end, on occasion – as older men can do, they tell me. A raising of his status with the Church, after this of imprisoning a bishop, might well appeal to him – and help to release the poor prelate. To ensure for him some credit on the Day of Judgment!"

Tom Boyd was lost for words. "I think . . . I think that you should come with me to Orkney!" he got out. "You would make the best envoy!"

"A woman? Women are meet only to be men's playthings, and married off to whom men will!"

"Do not say that . . ."

"Is it not true?"

"No. And a plaything *you* could never be." He wisely changed the subject. "You will come tomorrow, to see me invested as Earl of Arran? Since it is only because of you, that I wed you, that so I am to be."

"If you will . . ."

In the morning, it was a somewhat abbreviated ceremony held in the great hall of Stirling Castle, with Thomas due to leave almost immediately thereafter for Inverkeithing, on the Fife coast, where a ship had been found for them, strangely enough by the Abbot of Dunfermline, whose abbey and lands, the richest in the land, did a great trade with the Low Countries, in timber, salt-fish, hides, and beeswax for candles. The Primate feared that it might smell somewhat of the hides, but it ought to be sturdy enough to get them to Orkney, and its shipmaster experienced and skilful. There was only a comparatively small company present in the castle to see the investiture, momentous as it was, the first creation of an earldom for many a day. All indeed could be accommodated on the hall's dais-platform.

The proceedings, however shortened from the traditional, had to be celebrated in two parts, for it was unthinkable that any man could be created earl who was not already a knight; so knighthood had to be conferred first. The Lord Lyon King of Arms dispensed with a trumpeter on this occasion, and thumped his staff on the floor to have all to stand – although all were standing already – for the entry of the monarch. James, on cue, came in. All bowed, and he was handed a sword by Lyon, who declared that by His Grace's royal command, Thomas, Master of Boyd, was to be admitted to the order of knighthood, in token of his services to the crown. The said Master of Boyd to kneel.

Thomas got down on his knees and James rather gingerly raised the sword.

"I, James, by God's grace King of Scots, do, do hereby . . ." He hesitated over getting the wording right. ". . . hereby dub thee, Thomas, knight." He brought down the flat of the blade rather more heavily than necessary on one Boyd shoulder, then transferred it to the other, with some risk to the recipient's head in the process. "I charge that you, you fulfil your knightly vows. Yes, and remain a good knight until your life's end." That came out in something of a gabble. "Arise, Sir Thomas." Thankfully he handed back the sword to Lyon.

There were murmurs from the company as the new knight stood, looking, for him, almost embarrassed. Considering the greater honour to follow, nobody felt that congratulations were convenient at this stage.

The Primate thought that a prayer might be suitable here, to mark the interval, and besought the Almighty to bless and cherish Sir Thomas Boyd, about to be raised to the rank of earl, by His Grace, on the eve of a most important mission on the King's behalf; and thereafter to prosper the said mission with divine aid, and bring all to a worthy conclusion, including the release and restoration of William Tulloch, Bishop of Orkney, presently in durance vile.

That over, Lyon thumped again, and declared that, with His Grace's royal permission, the sponsors for the bestowal of the earldom should stand forward.

The Lord Boyd, as Regent, and the Lord Avondale, as Chancellor, moved over to the King, the latter bearing a golden banner over his arm. Drawing this aside, he revealed beneath it a golden belt. This, most obviously weighty, he handed to the Regent.

Lyon bowed to James.

"I . . . we, James, King of Scots, having approved that . . . the elevation of the . . . *Sir* Thomas Boyd, to the rank and dignity, aye and the honourable estate of earl of my kingdom, do hereby . . ." Looking very uncertain here, he paused.

"His Grace names, appoints and raises the lands of the Isle of Arran." That was the Lyon, helpfully.

"Aye. I name, appoint and raise the lands of the Isle of Arran to the, the status of an earldom. And I hereby . . ."

Lyon coughed warningly, and the boy stopped.

"My lord Regent, and my lord High Chancellor, sponsors, will present the earl's belt to His Grace."

Lord Boyd stepped forward and held out that golden, gleaming trophy to the King – who, obviously unprepared for the weight of it, all but dropped it.

Actually this procedure lacked some authenticity. It was the custom for two earls to sponsor the newcomers to their ranks, but today no two earls were available. There were no great numbers of earldoms anyway, and some were vested in the crown itself, some in the hands of minors. And only Crawford and Argyll were openly supporting Boyd.

James took a deep breath. "I hereby call on the master . . . Sir Thomas . . . Boyd to, to kneel again."

Tom duly got down, and managed an encouraging smile to his liege-lord.

The boy raised the massive chain with difficulty, and as the other ducked his head, managed to get it over without actually striking Tom's face with it, to deposit it on one shoulder, the rest to be draped down to the waist at the other side. Earls' belts were not to be worn round the middle, but hung thus from one shoulder, intended for the better carriage of a heavy sword.

"I hereby create you an earl of Scotland and invest you with

93

the earldom of Arran, Sir Thomas," James got out with a rush. "Arise, my lord Earl."

There were exclamations all round as the new earl stood, adjusted the massive belt slightly, and bowing, reached for the King's hand, to take it between both of his own, in the traditional gesture of fealty, before backing away.

The thing was done.

Congratulations were now in order. Presently Tom came to Mary, where she stood with her brothers, sister and Anna. He searched her face almost anxiously.

"Your lordship!" she said. "Should I be overwhelmed by your increase in stature? Dazzled by more than this golden chain?"

"You, you do not resent it, Mary?"

"Why should I? Some of it will represent one more seal on my marriage contract! I can hardly escape you now, can I, my lord?"

He shook his head.

Anna kissed him, with a smile and a mock curtsy.

James came up. "What must I call you now?" he demanded. "Are you to be always my lord Earl?"

"Surely not, Sire. I was Master Thomas until this day. To Your Grace I will be proud to be Master Thomas always."

"Good! That is well. Mary, did I do it properly?"

"Very well, Jamie. I was afraid that you might stun his lordship with this chain!"

"It is heavy, yes. Do you wear it all the time, Master Thomas?"

"Lord, no! I hope not. I, I have enough on my shoulders!" And he glanced at Mary.

"My heart bleeds for you!" she told him, but lightly.

"Will you come to bid us farewell, Mary? And wish me success. Aye, and safety."

"To be sure."

"Glad to see the back of me, for a space?"

"As backs go, my lord, yours is well enough."

With that he had to be content.

Later, down at the gatehouse and drawbridge, the Primate, Lord Somerville and the new earl, with a small party of monkish clerks, servants and an escort, took their leave, to the advice and well-wishing of all. Tom bade farewell to the King first, and to Mary last.

"Well . . . ?" he questioned. "What is your word for me?"

"Safe journeying. A successful mission – remembering pride. Not *your* pride, but the St Clair's. I think that it will all turn on that."

"And . . . ?"

"Would you expect me to say haste ye back?"

"Not expect – but wish it, Mary."

"Very well. Haste ye back, Thomas, Earl of Arran."

He gripped her hand, kissed its back, then turned it over and kissed the palm, before swinging on his heel and striding off to his horse, only remembering, with a foot in the stirrup, to turn and bow towards the monarch. He did not wait for the Primate and the others, but urged his beast away.

Mary looked after him less calm than she seemed. As the others rode off, she raised that hand, to wave.

8

The weeks that followed were strange, in that all urgency seemed to have gone out of living, for Mary Stewart at least. The wedding preparations continued, but with less immediacy. She saw little or nothing of Lord Boyd or his colleagues, although James was frequently summoned to give royal assent to edicts and to sign papers. So the royal group had considerable time on their hands. Unfortunately, as so often in Scotland, the snow came as January passed into February, and this restricted excursions from the castle, under escort as these still had to be. There was a renowned sport, however, unique to Stirling Castle, known as hurly-hackit, in which the participants went tobogganing down a steep slope at the northern tip of the castle rock to a little green terrace meadow called Ballengeich, halfway down, where the two milk-cows for the fortress's inmates were pastured. This pastime was pursued sitting on the skulls of oxen, using the horns as handles to grip on the bumpy ride over the grass and outcropping stone, no gentle proceeding. But in snow, north-facing as it was, this slope became a deal more smooth than normal, and with rough sleds instead of the ox-skulls it made an exciting descent – one where steering was very necessary if minor disaster was to be avoided, for there were many large boulders, outcrops and miniature cliffs dotting the slope to be dodged – and fast-moving sleds are not the easiest vehicles to steer. So the royal sledgers, and Anna, had to be prepared for rough riding and upsets, but were by no means off-put by that, not in spirit however much they were apt to be in person. Young Margaret *was* the least enthusiastic, and never went on a sledge alone. The favourite sport was to have races, two sleds with three on each. Anna came to enjoy it, although scarcely as much as did Mary who, she declared, was determined to try to kill herself in order to avoid having to marry Tom.

During this waiting period Mary sought better to prepare herself to accept the inevitable as best she might. She told herself that countless women had had to do this down the ages, in every period and in every land, especially royal and noble women, married off for dynastic and policy reasons. Many undoubtedly had found their fate none so grievous. And she was possibly more fortunate than most, in that Thomas Boyd was a much more attractive man than many she might have been saddled with, young, good-looking and most evidently not only desirous but fond of her. She might have been landed with a harsh, sour, older man, who would have made her life a misery. This one might do that also, of course, once they were wed – although she rather thought not. And he could be good company, she admitted; indeed in this interval, she had moments when she actually missed him – at the sledging for instance, and of a long evening by the fireside. Sometimes she even worried about his present safety. More often she wondered what he would be like in bed. She had no actual experience in this, to be sure; princesses were apt to have their virginity emphasised, for obvious reasons. But her mother, a lusty woman, had told her not a little, and not all of warnings and the need for care, but of pleasures and indeed delights also. Often Mary Stewart lay awake of a night beside the sleeping Anna, wondering what it would be like with brother exchanged for sister.

There was, of course, no means by which the people at Stirling could learn how the Orkney mission fared. With varying degrees of anxiety, all waited.

Then, on a snowy Eve of St Finnan, a single horseman arrived at the castle on an all but foundered mount, having ridden from Inverkeithing, the port of Dunfermline – the Earl of Arran himself, having far outridden the Primate, Somerville and their escort in his haste to get back. And it was very clear that it was not so much the urgency of the news he brought as his desire to see Mary Stewart at the earliest possible moment – to his father's disapproval. It so happened that the young people were at their sledging at Ballengeich when he arrived, and he came hastening over to them, all still clad for hard winter's riding as he was. Mary, rising from her sled alone, at the bottom of the slope, all breathless and rosy-cheeked, was astonished to see the man come plunging, sliding, slipping down to her, frequently on his bottom, long riding-boots no help to him, an extraordinary sight.

Her companions above were waving and shouting.

He could hardly avoid cannoning into her – not that he tried. Even as she stared, he was upon her, and she was caught up in his arms bodily, in headlong, stumbling career, to stagger on a few yards together and then collapse into the snow in a heap, the man on top.

"You . . . great . . . witling! Fool!" she gasped. If she had been breathless before, she was more so now.

"Fool . . . as to . . . you!" His own breath was scarce now. "In especial . . . as thus!"

"Had I . . . foreseen *this* . . . I would not . . . have prayed . . . for your return!" Even as she was, panting, she amended that. "Your *safe* return."

"You did that? Prayed? God be praised!" Almost reluctantly lifting himself off her, he rose, to aid her to her feet.

"I prayed for . . . the Primate and . . . Bishop Tulloch also!" she pointed out.

He still held her by the arms, all but devouring her with his eyes. "It has seemed an age, endless . . ."

"Yet you are back sooner than we looked for you."

"Once we had gained our ends, I would have no lingering, I promise you! Bishops or none."

"You did succeed then?"

"Aye, he was none so ill. St Clair. I remembered your advice. His pride! Played on that. He is Admiral again, now. And the Primate made him Commendator of Roslin, which seemed to please him. Although not Bishop Tulloch! But we did get that one freed. He was scarce as grateful as we thought he should be. He is now off to Denmark, to see King Christian. But . . . enough of all that. This is not what I came hastening to tell you!"

"No? Yet it is good news. You earn your earldom!"

"Would that you said that with a kinder smile! I tell you . . ."

What he would have told her had to be postponed, for the other sled, with James and Anna aboard, came hurtling down to join them, amidst cries of greeting and a flood of questions. There could be no doubt about the man's welcome from these two, at any rate. He released Mary, whom he had been clutching the while, sketched some sort of a bow to the monarch, and returned his sister's kisses. Anna at least sought no account of his mission, although James was interested to hear how near to shipwreck they had been and whether the famous tidal whirls between Caithness and Orkney were as fierce as they were said to be.

Presently they all climbed back up the hill, to where young Alexander, John and Margaret awaited them, snowball fighting meantime. Tom admitted that he had never thought of sledging here – but then he had never lived in Stirling Castle previously. He would have to try it, later.

Back at the palace block, it was not long before the ex-envoy found his way to the royal quarters, changed as to clothing, presumably leaving the Primate and Somerville to report in detail to his father and the other lords, while he recounted his adventures to the younger folk. Actually, he did not make a great deal of it, over their meal, but he did describe the "rousts", as they were called, the whirlpools amongst the isles where the Atlantic tides met those of the Norse Sea, hazards for shipping indeed, not unlike the notorious Corrievreckan of the Hebrides. He told them of the mighty cliffs of Hoy, the swirling winds which prevailed, the multitude of the islands, treeless but not infertile, the rich fisheries, the friendly enough folk, more Norse than Scots with strange names, the small but sturdy cattle and horses, some of the latter barely larger than a dog.

James declared that he would like to go there, one day. Would Master Thomas take him? He had never been on an island, a real one. He was told that it might be possible, although Orkney and Shetland were the Norse King's territory and they might have to get especial permission. But meantime there was Arran to visit, and much to see there.

The mention of that island produced its own effect, on Mary at least, and while she did not ask the question foremost in her mind, and probably in Anna's also, James had no such inhibitions.

"Will we go there, after the wedding?" he demanded. "When is the wedding to be?"

Tom answered that carefully, for him. "It should be soon. As soon as possible, with Lent ahead. Weddings are not held in Lent. So, at Her Highness's convenience, the sooner the better."

"*My* convenience! You are most thoughtful, sir!"

"I rather conceived the time of the month to be important, Princess!"

Anna's glance darted from one to the other.

"You *would* think of that!"

"Would you have me not to care, Mary?"

She did not answer.

"Would a week hence serve?"

"As well as any. Since . . ." She left the rest unsaid.

"Everything is all but prepared. This delay . . ." He looked at her almost appealingly. "It will be none so ill, Mary."

She changed the subject. "Tell us more of Orkney and Shetland. And the St Clairs. This earl's father, Henry St Clair, played guardian to our grandfather, James the First, when his uncle Albany sought to slay him as he had slain his brother Rothesay, to gain the throne for himself, a vile man. So we Stewarts have our links with the Earls of Orkney. That one suffered much for us."

"He took our grandfather to safety on the Bass Rock, in the middle of the sea," James added. "Near to North Berwick. Until they could go to France. We saw the Bass from Edinburgh, from the top of Arthur's Seat. I would like to go there, one day."

"One day, Sire . . ."

Later, when Tom left them for his own chamber, a tired man after his long day and journeying, he contrived a private word with Mary.

"See you, my dear, do not dread this of our marriage, I beseech you! It will not be so ill, I swear it. For you. For me, I can scarce wait! But I recognise your . . . fears. Apprehensions. I am willing to be . . . patient. To consider you."

"You Boyds are always considering, my lord!"

"No – not that! I mean it, lass. I know that this is no desire of yours, however much it has become mine. But *you* consider. Together, we shall make it . . . serve."

"Serve? Who serves who, my lord Earl?" Then she relented a little. "But I thank you for your intended reassurances for an unwilling bride. I am, shall we say, partly reconciled to my fate! Almost. And I perceive that I might have had a worse one! Let that suffice, for this night."

He half nodded, half shrugged, and reached for her hand to kiss it as he had done before, back and front, and left her.

The Chapel Royal of Stirling Castle was modest in size however splendid as to style and decoration, and was packed on this occasion. No expense had been spared, no detail and embellishment overlooked. The guests were illustrious as they were numerous, even though there were not a few notable absentees, for this being a royal wedding, not merely a Boyd one, some who were not in fact in favour of the Boyd faction were present, as a mark of respect for the crown, all clad in their finest. The church was lit by candles innumerable, hung with banners and standards, and rich with the scent of incense. Instrumentalists and a choir of singing-boys made sweet music.

There were four small preliminary processions. First came the Lord Lyon King of Arms and his four heralds and trumpeters, leading in Alexander, Duke of Albany, John, Earl of Mar and the Princess Margaret, to seats at the front. Then came the clergy, led by the Dean of the Chapel Royal and the Primate, with four bishops, four mitred abbots and sundry priors, who moved into the chancel. Then a single blast of trumpet ushered in the bridegroom and his father, and two young Boyd brothers, Tom magnificent in blue and white velvet of their heraldic colours with the red and white fesse-chequey as a silken sash over his right shoulder and his golden earl's belt over the left; his father notably plainly dressed by comparison. There was no sign of Sir Alexander. The younger Boyds went to seats beside the royal children, while their father and brother went to stand centrally before the chancel steps.

There was a distinct pause, which produced some shuffling of feet, murmuring and even a few sniggers, before Lyon signed to the two trumpeters who, waiting, promptly produced a tremendous flourish of a fanfare – which shook the rafters and actually brought down some bat-droppings and dust on distinguished heads. But even when this ended there was some delay, to the frowns of Lord Boyd and some anxious looks from the bridegroom, before the vestry door opened to admit King James, more handsomely garbed than he had ever been, a golden circlet round his brow, and on his arm, his sister.

Mary, however unenthusiastic a bride, had never looked more lovely. She was dressed all in white damask with the raised patterns in gold, having little other decoration, but superbly cut and fashioned by the best dressmaker Stirling could boast. The coif, which sat lightly on her long, dark hair, was simple but beaded with pearls from the River Tay, a gift from her father to her mother. She held her head high, features unsmiling but nowise sour. James looked the more nervous and excited of the pair. Behind them came Anna, glancing all around cheerfully.

All stood – and must remain standing while the King did.

To the choir's chanting, James led his sister to Tom's side, that man turning to her eagerly and receiving an inclination of her head and a direct look which was almost questioning. Anna stood a pace behind.

So they waited, while the Dean, from before the high altar, opened the proceedings with prayer to the Almighty, that He might bless what was being done this day. An anthem followed.

Then the Primate came forward to stand before the five principals. He declared that they were here together in this place, in the sight of God, to enact a great matter, no less than the union of two of God's children to be made into one, one in the sight of God. This was a notable and enduring mystery, the entry into the estate of holy matrimony. Man might pronounce it, all unworthily, but only the Almighty Father of us all could make it real. It therefore was not to be entered upon lightly or with lack of due understanding. Was that recognised by the present applicants for the sacrament of marriage?

Tom shot a swift sideways glance at Mary, cleared his throat, and made an approximately affirmative noise. The girl said nothing, but meeting the prelate's eye, raised her brows slightly.

Bishop Graham presumably accepted that as sufficiently positive, for he went on.

"Marriage, as well as for the union of two persons to be one hereafter for all time, is also for the procreation of children. Offspring to be raised for the service of God, and nurtured in the fear of the Lord, if the union is blessed with children. This must be understood by those who seek their Maker's blessing upon their union. Is it so understood?"

Again the man's swift look at the woman. This time she returned his glance levelly. Neither spoke.

The bishop no doubt was aware of something of the situation between these two, since he had been Tom's close companion on the Orkney visit. At any rate, he appeared to be content with their reception of his statements. He in fact seemed to speed matters now, as though having made his point, he was concerned to spare the couple anything more than the essentials. Almost businesslike, he asked who gave this woman to wed this man?

James said that he did.

The vow-repeating, after the Primate, followed, Tom's strong, Mary's merely a slight movement of her lips. Then, for the ceremonial of the ring, with the bridegroom having no other supporter than his father, Lord Boyd handed over the symbol to his son, and stepped back beside Anna. James did the same.

Fitting that ring on the girl's finger, so almost defiantly thrust out, had even Tom Boyd's hand trembling a little. But he got it in place, and squeezed *her* hand thereafter, searching her face.

Another hand raised, the prelate declared that these two, Thomas and Mary, were undoubted man and wife, in the sight of God and of all men. He signed to them to kneel, and with a hand laid on both heads, blessed them in the name of Father, Son and Holy Spirit.

The kneeling pair could scarcely believe that that was all, that the deed was done.

The Primate turned to the altar, and on that cue the choir broke out into a joyful chorus of hallelujahs and hosannas, which went on and on, while high above them all the chapel's bells rang out. Long the resounding praise and thanksgiving went on, and even Mary was not exempt from some emotion as they rose and stood. For his part, Tom seemed as though he was going to take her in his arms and kiss her rapturously, but with an effort contented himself with kissing that beringed hand.

"Your hand . . . in marriage!" he got out.

Anna did not hesitate as her brother had done, but flung her arms round the bride, in a mixture of tears and laughter. James, as yet not at the kissing stage, pecked at his sister's cheek and backed away to safety. The Lord Boyd looked grimly satisfied but made no gestures.

A nuptial hymn from the choir, and a general benediction from the Dean, completed the proceedings.

Led by the monarch, the Earl and Countess of Arran paced down the aisle to the west door, his arm in hers, to the congratulations and plaudits of all.

The banquet which followed was on a scale seldom seen in Scotland previously, in richness as in variety, with ongoing entertainment of performers, dancers, acrobats and musicians, as well as set scenes of masques and play-acting, all this ordered by the Regent although not devised by him – he was scarcely that way inclined; but by another brother, William Boyd, Abbot of Kilwinning, who was having his abbey erected into a regality, with all the financial and other advantages accruing, a man of talents in more than religion. He sat at Mary's left at the dais-table, an entertainment in himself, even though she had some difficulty in concentrating on his witticisms and anecdotes this evening, an unlikely brother for Lord Boyd. Tom, at her other side, was not as attentive as he might have been either; the thoughts of both tended to be elsewhere.

Indeed, throughout what to him seemed a never-ending trial of patience, that young man's glance was more often towards his new wife than on either the entertainers or on his rich food and drink. And, considering his normally confident, not to say ebullient, nature, a sort of apprehension could not be concealed, indeed more apprehension than was apparent in his partner – although perhaps she was merely becoming better at hiding her feelings. He kept glancing sideways at her, rather than any gazing or consistent eyeing; he did not actually address her much, but frequently his hand went out to touch her arm or squeeze her wrist. Mary did not return these gestures, but nor did she move hand away; and once or twice she met his glance and nodded slightly.

James, at the other side of Tom, with the Regent on his left, at least fully enjoyed and appreciated the proceedings more adequately. This, in time, oddly enough, in part contributed to the bridegroom's impatience and concern – for with the King present, none might rise and leave the hall before he did, without his express permission; and he seemed in no least hurry to do this. Normally a newly-wed couple could, and did, leave a nuptial feast considerably before the end, to frequently outspoken advice and comments from the guests; but this was not possible here.

At length, with James applauding vigorously and demanding a replay of an acrobatic display by four almost naked performers, two of each sex, presumably considered by the abbot as suitable wedding-night entertainment, Mary took pity on her new husband, recognising that putting off further was not going to aid *her* in any way. She did what only she there could do. Briefly touching Tom's elbow, she rose and went behind him to her brother's back and stooping, murmured in his ear.

The boy looked up, surprised, but listening, shrugged and stood. All had to rise, the music stopped, the acrobats paused in an uncomfortable stance, and silence descended save for the growling of deerhounds under the tables, squabbling over bones.

"My sister . . . the princess . . . Her Highness the Countess of Arran . . . she has my royal permission to leave my presence. And, aye, Master Thomas, Earl of Arran," he announced somewhat uncertainly, and sat down.

Cheers and laughter sounded from the crowded tables down the length of the hall. Thomas rose, bowed to the monarch, and taking Mary's arm, led her down from the dais-platform and on down that length of the hall, nodding right and left to the sallies and guidance offered, crude as much of it was. Mary played the princess, possibly her last opportunity to do so that night.

Out into the February dark and wind, they hurried across the palace yard's flagstones to the opposite wing, a long handsome range of building, at the north end of which were the royal apartments. But it was not to these that the couple now headed. The man's quarters were at the other end.

Mary, in fact, had never been in Tom's rooms, and now entered them with mixed feelings. She found them spacious and comfortable enough, lamps lit in both chambers and fires burning brightly in each. She was surprised to find Anna waiting in the outer one. She had not seen her leave the hall. It was a kind gesture.

"Highness." The girl dipped a curtsy. "At your service, as always!"

"Thank you, Anna." She looked from sister to brother. Whose unexpected notion was this?

"All is prepared. Warming-pans in the bed. The morn's clothing laid out. Bed-robes to hand. Also towels. Warmed water. Cloths." That seemed to Mary to be rather spelling it out.

Evidently Thomas thought so also. "We shall manage," he said shortly.

"No doubt. *You* will not find it all so . . . strange!" Anna answered. "But we do not all have your experience, brother!" Smiling, she turned to Mary. "If you need me, Highness, there is also a bell on the floor by the bed. I shall be in the chamber along the passage. His Grace will have to do without near company tonight."

"You are kind, Anna . . ." It occurred to Mary that perhaps Anna was not herself wholly without experience in such matters.

Raising a hand, the other girl departed.

Tom drew a deep breath, looked at his companion, but found no words.

"You have been very patient, husband," she said. "Now – it is my turn!"

"Patient? I hope . . . I trust that patience is not what you will find necessary. It need not be so ill, see you. Others have not found it so, Mary. Or, leastways . . ."

"And you will have, shall we say, instructed not a few?" When he did not answer, she shrugged. "Well, Thomas, I see naught to be gained by delay. Now, shall we seek our couch? So well prepared for us!"

He eyed her questioningly, as though he had scarcely expected *her* to take the lead in this matter. He gestured towards the open bedroom door. "Do you wish . . . to go first? To, to make ready? To . . ." he left the rest unsaid.

"Do *you* so wish?"

"No-o-o."

"Then come, my lord of Arran. And of myself! Since I have, I think, much more to, to undergo this night, let us not make much of this. After all, you have seen me unclothed, in the sea, have you not. And I you, running along that fishwives' beach!" And she preceded him into the other chamber.

It was less brightly lit than the first, but the fire was even better, indeed the birch-log flames producing much of the lighting. A massive urn-like sitting-bath stood before the fire, with a lidded pail, from which steam curled, beside it. The bedclothes were turned back, with bed-robes lying there, the other conveniences listed evident. There was even a flagon of wine and beakers on a chest nearby.

"Your sister is very thoughtful. And . . . knowledgeable. For one of her years," Mary commented, going over to the fire. "How think you – the firelight? It is more kindly, perhaps, than these candles." Not waiting for his assent, she went and snuffed out the four candles with her fingers.

He stood watching, silent.

She removed the lid from the pail and dipped in her fingers, to clean them of the soot. "It is sufficiently hot," she reported. "After all this day's events and excitements, I vow a bath will not come amiss. How say you?" She was removing her coif now.

"If you . . . yes."

"Help me then, with this gown. At the back . . ."

Still remarkably silent for that man, he stepped over, and making something of a fumble at it, undid the buttons at the rear of that splendid damask dress.

She moved aside and let the gown drop to the floor, and so stood in her knee-length linen shift. This she raised, to take off

106

garters and to roll down and remove her silken hose. Stooping to gather up these, with her gown, she went over with them to one of the chamber's chests, laid them thereon, and then slipped off the light shift from her shoulders and let it fall away, to stand quite naked.

"Pour the water, Thomas," she directed – although her voice thickened just a little as she said it.

Tom Boyd did not move. He was staring, quite frankly staring. And he had something to stare at indeed, for she had, by any standards, a quite superb body, beautifully proportioned, from her long, graceful neck and sculptured shoulders down to full, rounded but not heavy breasts, well apart, tipped with generous pink aureolas and nipples. Below, her stomach was by no means flat but firmly rounded above a dark triangle which notably served to emphasise the white of long and shapely thighs to slender calves and ankles. No man could do other than stare. She made no foolish attempt to hide any of herself.

"Water, my lord," she repeated.

He mumbled something, and went over to the pail and bath, while she waited.

When he had done it, and turned back to her, he found words. "You are beyond all beautiful! A joy to behold. Perfection itself!"

"Scarcely that, I think. Although it is not for me to point out my failings!" She moved across to the bath, and he took her hand to help her step into it, and steady her therein.

The nearness of all that warm loveliness seemed almost to affect his breathing, the more so perhaps in that her own was not unaffected by the situation, as the slight stirring of her bosom testified.

"I . . . I . . . it is not too hot? The water . . . ?"

"No. It is very well. One of those cloths, if you please."

He hurried to pick up what proved to be a towel, and at her pointing this out, changed it.

"May I . . . could I . . . it would give me great pleasure to bathe you. Wash you down." That came out in a rush. "If you would permit it? I have never . . . so done."

Mary stooped to dip and squeeze the cloth in the water – and the change in posture in itself added further enchantment and stimulation for the man, front and rear.

"I do not see why not," she decided. "If you so wish." She handed him the wet cloth.

He took it, swallowing audibly, seemed doubtful as to where to begin, and bent to wet it further, although it scarcely needed that. Whilst down, he evidently decided to start thereabouts, as the least taxing probably upon them both. Sinking to his knees, he began to wash her feet, her ankles, her calves.

She looked down on his bent head. "Is this normal usage? A wedding-night custom?"

"I do not know. All I know is that I, I rejoice in it." He moved his busy hand higher.

"You are very thorough, at least, sir!"

"You do not mind it?"

"I think not, no."

"Do you sit down. There is not a great deal of water."

"And you are spilling some, splashing it over. To make it less. No, I will remain standing."

At her groin and middle he was careful indeed, clearly anxious not to offend; but round the back he allowed himself more scope, more freedom, almost lovingly massaging those firm rounded buttocks with the cleavage between. Then, making something of a show of re-dipping the cloth, he rose to his feet, to tackle those challenging breasts, which became the more so when she raised her arms high that he might wash below them.

"As well that all be done . . . properly," she murmured. "If that is the apt word!"

He found no answer, other than active but far from rough hands – for he now seemed to be requiring both – that cloth tending to figure less prominently than did his fingers. Her bosom had never been so meticulously bathed before. When he appeared to be about to repeat the process, she took the cloth from him.

"My face I can deal with myself," she observed. "The towel now, if you will." And she stepped out on to the floor.

Emboldened now by what he had achieved, Tom did not hand over the towel to her but started on the drying treatment himself, patting and dabbing and gently rubbing in a comprehensive coverage, until she declared that there was surely no least drop of wetness left on her, and she was going to bed. Would he put a couple of logs on the fire . . . ?

Mary all but ran over to the wide bed and got in under the blankets and between the sheets, to cover herself, somewhat belatedly, perhaps.

Tom busied himself with the fire.

Watching him, the girl said, "I will let you bathe yourself!"

He shook his head, decidedly. "I think not. I will not trouble with it. Tonight. I bathed before the church, the wedding. I, I have better things to do!" He was divesting himself hurriedly, as he spoke.

It did not take him long. He had indeed some small difficulty in removing his fine velvet breeches, for masculine reasons – but for the same reasons wrenched them off vehemently. And for his part there was no tidy picking up of discarded clothing and putting it on a chest. Observing this last, Mary transferred her gaze to the flame-flickering on the painted ceiling rafters.

He came to the other side of the bed and jumped in. At once his hands reached out for her – but not to grope nor to draw her to him, only to hold her.

"You are . . . well enough?" he asked, seeking to keep the urgency out of his voice.

"Well enough? I am washed. And naked. And, and wed to you! Is that not sufficiently well for you?"

"I mean . . . see, Mary, I know that this is not of your choosing. That therefore it could be . . . difficult for you. Something of a trial, perhaps. Yet . . ."

"Yet it is my duty now. And your right. Is it not?"

"I would have you to think, to *feel*, otherwise." His hands began to slide lightly over her soft warm skin. "There should be pleasure in this, lass. For you, surely, as well as for myself. Will you not . . . seek it so?"

"If you say so, I will try."

His hand continued to caress. At her breasts she did not stir, but when it moved down and down below her midriff to her groin, she drew quick breath, and stiffened.

His own breathing was growing the more evident by the moment, stronger, deeper, as he sought to hold himself in. He was moving over to her now, gripping her. She remained rigid, as that exploring hand went probing.

"My dear, my dear!" he almost groaned. "I . . . I . . ."

Mary could not fail to recognise his need, his urgency, that he was undergoing his own testing struggle, however different in character from hers. She forced herself to aid him a little, even as he was presumably trying to aid her.

Then he was on to her, above, his hand superseded, and basic masculinity took charge. She almost bit *his* lip instead of her own as he forced his way. She knew sudden hurt, yes, but more hurt of mind, of her inner self's privacy, integrity, than of her violated physical person, and twisted beneath him, this way and that, in her extremity.

He was panting, gasping, blurting out incoherent words, but so active upon her, his weight so heavy, his sheer dominance over her so overpowering, that she lost all sense of anything but his mastery and ascendancy over her, his undeniable demand, under which she could do nothing but accept. And as it went on, the acceptance grew the less hurtful to her pride, as to her body. A sort of yielding grew in her, a feeling of self-immolation, and yes, wonder in some measure.

Then, suddenly, his gasping changed to a strange cry of mixed triumph, fulfilment, relief, and yet somehow regret also, as the pent-up pride of his manhood burst its bounds, his struggle over. And in that strange, violent, aggressive moment she nevertheless felt all woman as she had never felt before, receiving if scarcely receptive, as, in his final throes, he more or less collapsed upon her, chest heaving now to match her own.

As he lay upon her but still within her, spent, where she was anything but, she gazed up at the firelit ceiling and wondered. She was surprised to feel no offence, no real resentment, however much her physical discomfort. She did not speak.

At length the man did. "I am sorry! Sorry, Mary. That, that I had to . . . could not . . . contain myself. Gave you no time. Overbore you so, so hardly. I sought to wait, but . . . I am sorry, lass."

She rather wondered what he meant by giving her time. Time for what? She had been as prepared for his assault as she would ever be. What would further waiting have availed? She did not answer him other than by patting his sweating back a little.

He lay some moments longer, while his breathing became more normal. Then he rolled away, to lie at her side, on his back, although one hand still held a breast.

Mary stirred a little, moistening her almost bruised lips.

Presently he asked, thickly. "You are . . . well enough?"

"Well . . . *enough*! Yes."

"I am sorry . . ." His voice tailed away. He sounded sleepy now.

Still she stared up at the ceiling, herself far from sleepy and relaxed, going over and over what had happened to her, her mind

110

darting this way and that. This, then, was what was meant by losing one's virginity, her innocence. She had, of course, heard women's talk of this, and not usually with any signs of great concern. She had not failed, to be sure, to wonder what it would be like. Was it so grievous once the mind was schooled to accept it? All women, or most, had to go through with it. Many, no doubt, almost rejoiced to suffer it – that is, if they loved the man, or themselves felt the desire for him. Or of what it could lead to.

Presently the clutch at her breast relaxed, and Tom's breathing deepened in sleep.

Long she lay, wide awake, pondering, wondering. This then was marriage, this sleeping man her husband. She had taken vows before God, however unwillingly. Did a lifetime of this stretch ahead of her? Was that a cause for dread? Her own mother had not felt that way, assuredly. From all accounts she had had many lovers once her husband died – or, if not lovers, at least bedfellows. Including this man's uncle. That was no road to follow, surely; but there could be *something* to be learned from it all? This, of possible pleasure in the act . . . ?

How long Mary lay thinking thus there was no knowing, before there was a stirring at her side and that hand came reaching out once more.

"Mary," she heard. "You, you sleep?"

"No."

"You are very lovely. Desirable. And patient, too. I am grateful. I failed you then. But – not again. I shall not fail you again, my dear."

She shrugged, under the hand which had begun to caress her bosom again. "I did not esteem you . . . failing!" she said. "You seemed sufficiently . . . active!"

"Aye, too much so! I had waited for you, desired you, ached for you, overlong, you see. So that I was at, at bursting-point! But that is over now. Now we shall do better."

As he moved close again, hands only a little less eager than heretofore, she realised that what he meant by not failing her again was not that he would not use her again, and right away. The not-failing was to be otherwise. What? How? Her ordeal for this night was not over, then! If ordeal it was . . . ?

Tom Boyd changed his tactics indeed. He threw back the bedclothes, so that they both lay bare, all her lovely nakedness

111

fairly apparent, even though the firelight was much less bright now, although the room was comfortably warm. Then he began to kiss her, not just on the lips now but comprehensively, all over her person, lingeringly, lovingly, in no haste. She did not seek to stop him, since this was presumably him not failing her again, even when he told her to turn over, so that he could start on her back. Besides, she had to admit that it was not an unpleasing sensation.

Then commenced as comprehensive a fondling of her, high and low. This continued for some considerable time – not that it seemed overlong for the still somewhat apprehensive girl. But clearly he knew what he was doing – had not Anna said that he was an experienced lover? So perhaps this was meant to be an aid to her, as well as to himself, and certainly she sensed his masculinity nowise reduced. For herself, something of a strange and not unpleasant lassitude seemed to be coming over her – no doubt lack of sleep, after a long and tiring day, beginning to tell? Not that she felt actually sleepy herself . . .

He talked quite a lot while this was going on, quiet, murmurous talk, hardly soothing but certainly reassuring, whispering endearments, declaring love, admiration, fascination. She realised that she was finding no real fault with it all.

Then, with this continuing, he found his way on top of her again. But now there was no hasty aggression, only a sort of playing and testing – so much so that she began to feel that it would be better if he got it over with, since it obviously had to come. She was scarcely impatient, but . . .

And then, with his assertion becoming stronger, more commanding, abruptly, almost without warning, she knew a great surge of feeling, emotion, urgency, desire, need, a demand indeed such as never before experienced or even imagined could be hers. Aware of it, then, the man responded strongly, as a man should, and like flood-gates opening, her own woman's tide overwhelmed her. She cried out, clutching his shoulders convulsively.

They moved as one, as Tom Boyd cried out also, for the second time that night.

Thereafter, he muttered no apologies, nor did Mary Stewart put her wonder into words, although she stroked his shoulders which she had clutched, till he slid over.

112

"Man . . . and wife!" he got out, before he was part asleep again.

She nodded, all but questioningly, at that. Soon she also slept, not caring about those down-turned bedclothes.

9

It was Anna who wakened them, belatedly, next morning, having dismissed the servitors who brought the hot water and breakfast viands. She knocked, entered, and eyed the pair on the very rumpled bed interestedly, assessingly.

"The sun is up. Perhaps you should be also?" she said. "Unless the night was too ill for your rising? Yet I heard no call for my services."

Mary yawned and stretched, frankly. "I think that we have survived it," she gave back. "But – ask Thomas."

The man opened one eye. "Why the haste? Begone, Anna." He turned his back on his sister – and then his hand went out to touch and caress Mary's white shoulder. "Begone!"

The young woman beside him, becoming aware now of the signs, rose quickly and jumped out of bed, reaching for the fallen bed-robe to cover her nakedness. Smiling, she pointed to the bath.

"Some warm in last night's water will serve," she suggested. "For only I used it!"

"Ha! So that was the way of it!"

"Begone!" repeated her brother from the bed.

"Not so, my over-weary lord of Arran! So weak and worn! I am Her Highness's lady-in-waiting, and have Her Highness's care to consider, if you have not." She was carrying forward the steaming pail. "Perhaps you should not have wed a princess?"

Mary was quite glad of the other girl's attentions this morning, for she had not failed to note the gleam in the man's eye. "Thank you, Anna," she acknowledged. "And, now that we are good-sisters, I think that we can forget the Highness, save in company."

"As you will, Mary." Anna busied herself with laying out the daytime clothing and carefully folding the wedding gown, while the other, discarding the bed-robe after all, washed herself all over, as carefully, but turning her back on the others. Anna came over with a towel.

From the bed Tom watched the two girls interestedly and a little ruefully, so obviously did they work together – and *his* interests would be apt to suffer.

When, the drying over, Anna was assisting with the dressing process, he made further protest.

"Off with you, girl! *I* do not require, nor relish, a lady-in-waiting."

"Wheesht, you!" his sister returned. "Your princess's hair has yet to be seen to." And she brought brush, comb and mirror.

"You can comb your own hair, Mary, can you not?" And then, with a jerked exclamation, he climbed out of bed. "Anna – go!"

Mary smiled. "Wives have their rights, as well as husbands," she observed.

At sight of her brother's state of aggressive nudity, Anna emitted a squeal of feigned shock, and made for the door, but scarcely in a hurry. She looked back, indeed, with a typical gurgle.

"Breakfast is here. You both need it, I swear!'

At the bath, Tom reached out to take Mary in his arms and to kiss her eagerly. "Lass, I thank you! I thank you, indeed. For last night. For your, your patience, your help, your forbearance. You were very kind."

"Was it indeed all those, Thomas? I but sought to . . . play my part, however unlearned."

"You did well. But – you did learn a little, no?"

"I think it, yes. I recognise that I received some . . . tutoring!" Very much aware of the male pressure against her middle, she disengaged herself. "Now, I will go and aid Anna with the meal."

"Save us, what is the haste? The least that you can do, surely, is to wash *me*, as I washed you last night."

Glancing down, she pushed him away. "I think not, my lord. Lest there be . . . problems. Enough tutoring for the moment!" And she fled.

Thereafter, breakfast, distinctly delayed, was interrupted by the arrival of the monarch. James came not so much to see how the newly-weds had survived the night as to enquire when they were going to Arran. It was usual for a bridal couple to seek to betake themselves off on their own for a few days, and they had decided that, despite the time of the year, a visit to the new earldom would be suitable and useful. But James had declared that he wanted to come with them – and besides this being in the nature of a royal command, it would have been difficult to deny, since Arran, up till now, had been a crown property, part of the royal earldom of Menteith and Knapdale, which the Regent had persuaded the boy to alienate

Tom told him that there would be some matters to see to first, but that they would be going in a day or two. The first of March was St Marnock's Day. Would not that be an apt time to go, since he came from Kilmarnock? The King had no views on that, and his only other comment was that they were very late with their breakfast.

Mary was very much aware of the glances which came her way that day from the castle's inhabitants; however, she did not have to mingle greatly with the company there, and the Regent kept his distance. These two would never be friends. The younger royal children, less affected even than James by the wedding and its consequences, were clamouring for their favoured sport of hurly-hackit, of which they had been deprived these last few days inevitably, and which they were not allowed to engage in unattended, for safety's sake. Their elder brother supported them in this, so quite a proportion of the day following the so important event was spent hurtling down and climbing up, both breath-taking, the steep slope above the Ballengeich terrace of the fortress. The snow had gone, so the sleds were exchanged for the traditional ox-skulls with their curving horns, which actually made more manageable and manoeuvrable vehicles, if less comfortable to sit on. The snows had left the soil, such as there was, slippery, muddy, and many were the tumbles, upsets and rollings-down, an odd sport for royalty, with dignity at a minimum, clothing derangement normal – and female legs apt to be much in evidence, however muddied.

The new earl was good at it, but was glad enough when he could decently claim that he had many arrangements to make for their Arran expedition, and brought the entertainment to a close.

That night, Mary received further tutoring, and learned not a little, physically and mentally. Perhaps the latter was in fact the more important now, in that, once her mind and inner self were prepared to accept the physical side of it all, the satisfactions began to come of their own accord. Tom's care in the matter was evident and she appreciated it – although he clearly nowise lacked his own satisfaction, and at certain stages was less than gentle.

It did not make for undisturbed night's sleeping, however. Anna's kindly enquiries were variously received.

An improvement in the weather enabled the royal party to get out on horseback. One of the drawbacks of living in a rock-top fortress, however finely housed and comfortably furnished, was the sense of constriction, of being closely cooped up behind stone walls, trying for active folk and young people especially – hence the popularity of hurly-hackit. Being able to ride abroad, weather being kind, was a great relief. And Stirling's vicinity was even better than Edinburgh's, since the town was much smaller and open countryside more swiftly available. And there was great choice all around. To the south lay the great Tor Wood, next to Ettrick in the borderland the largest forested area of the Lowlands. East of that were the meanderings of the Forth, before it changed from river to firth, where the great victory of Bruce at Bannockburn had been won; here careful riding was required, because of the pools, bogs, ditches and marshland, but which made exciting territory to explore, if the tracks were held to, hunting country, with deer abounding and even wild boar quite frequently to be seen. Northwards, once across the ancient Stirling Bridge and mile-long causeway beyond, where William Wallace had gained *his* victory, all the foothills of the Ochil range were available, although the upper ground here was still snow-bound, the peaks dazzling in the sunlight. But it was westwards that there was most scope for them, for, over twenty miles stretched the vast flood-plain of the Forth known as the Great or Flanders Moss, a strange land unto itself – although land perhaps was not the most apt description – of some one hundred square miles, waterlogged miles, through which the river wound its way, spreading here and there into ponds and pools and even lochs, but more often mere swampland and brush, with islands of firmer ground, some quite large, all again swarming with deer, boar and wildfowl. James, hunting-mad, looked upon it all as next to heaven, and deplored that it was not now the hunting season. He knew it fairly well, of course, and was so eager to show Master Thomas his favoured areas that he almost would have put off the Arran trip until he had demonstrated all.

But, King or not, the Arran arrangements stood, and on the first day of March, a dull but not cold morning, the party of

117

four set out, with the necessary small escort. They would head for Kilmarnock again, for the first night, although the shorter sea crossing would be considerably further north; but Tom had his reasons.

The going was somewhat poorer than on the previous occasion, the melted snows having left the ground muddy and soft, with no real frosts as yet to firm it. But they were all good horsemen, and it was of course different territory to cover from the last time – indeed none of them had ridden from Stirling to Ayrshire. The most direct route would be south-westwards through the Gargunnock Hills and Campsie Fells to Glasgow, and thence on in the same direction. But with snow still lying fairly deep on the hills, it was decided that they would in fact be quicker to go by the more round-about way, by the Tor Wood to the Carron valley at Denny and then round the foot of the Kilsyth Hills, by Kirkintilloch, and so to Glasgow, some thirty miles. There would still be almost another thirty miles to Kilmarnock, but used to long riding as they had to be, Tom did not have to make a challenge of it. The escort, on somewhat less mettlesome steeds, probably did least well – but these Boyd retainers, carefully chosen, were not going to be outdone by women if they could help it.

They reached Glasgow, after an early start, by midday, and making use of the royal prerogative, called at the bishop's palace, beside the mighty cathedral-church of St Mungo, for sustenance. Bishop Durrisdeer was not in residence but the provost found them excellent provender, and would have provided more if they had not had to press on, to cover as much ground as possible before darkness reduced their pace. Tom remarked that the churchmen always knew how to look after themselves – as witness his uncle of Kilwinning.

They again had some high ground either to surmount or avoid, inevitably, this being Scotland, but this time there were no really major heights, so they took the direct road, having to climb after Rutherglen by the Mearns heights and the Earn Water, over to the Fenwick Water, Hamilton country this, and down eventually, with the dusk, to the low ground of the River Irvine, where they could just discern the white cone of Loudoun Hill away to the left. Weary, mud- and spume-spattered, they rode up to the Dean Castle gatehouse in the half-dark – and with the drawbridge up and portcullis down for the night, had some difficulty in gaining entrance to courtyard and keep.

That night, despite tiredness and saddle-ache, Thomas Boyd was somewhat more aggressive than heretofore. Perhaps it was being in his own house that did it. At least Mary considered this, and whilst not actually chiding him, suggested that no doubt in this chamber he had had so many other young women that he felt spurred on to make comparisons and to demonstrate his virility?

Perhaps that was *her* weariness of body speaking?

They rested for a day at Dean, for the Lord Boyd had given his son instructions to see to various neglected matters here. Moreover, the horses required and deserved remission. Mary and Anna had a women's day to themselves, for James elected to accompany Tom, king and new earl making a large impression on the vicinity.

The following morning, after a more leisurely night, they were off again, still south by west, ten miles to Ayr town. This was not the usual port of embarkation for Arran, too far south, but it was where the Boyds, quite mercantile nobles – indeed only ennobled for one generation before – kept their three merchant-vessels, for trading with Ireland, Cumbria, Man and even Wales, when the English were not at war with Scotland, and would not act pirate. These were larger craft than normally plied over to Arran, Bute and Cumbraes, from Irvine, Ardrossan, Largs and the like, but with the dozen of escort, the party had sixteen horses to transport and these were necessary.

The port of Ayr was quite large and thriving, and the monarch for one was much excited by it all, his first real experience of shipping and seafaring. Arran, although its white mountains looked large, indeed all but dominating the wide Firth of Clyde, might have been as far voyaging as to Orkney itself for young James Stewart.

Only one of the Boyd ships was in port, and busy loading tanned hides and salt from the local salt-pans. Its skipper was somewhat put out by the demand to halt this and put the travellers across the twenty miles of sea to the port of Lamlash in Arran. But the authority behind the requirement was undeniable and the grumbles muted, however much of a nuisance those horses represented for the crew.

It took a while to effect, but presently, sails hoisted, they sailed out of the harbour and river mouth, to head north-westwards. This was not too difficult, for the wind was consistently south-westerly and only minimum tacking was required. No great seas running, as sometimes there could be in this firth, nobody was seasick.

Mary was interested in all that she saw; but also in what their reception was going to be like at Arran. She had not realised that the island was so mountainous, and wondered what sort of an earldom this would make, more apt for goats and deer than for themselves by the looks of it. Also how the islanders would react. It had been part of the royal lands, yes, the present Earl of Menteith, a distant cousin, forfeited and in England – or the place could not have come to Thomas. But she, at least, had never heard of any member of the royal family visiting Arran or even mentioning it. Presumably there would be a land steward. How would such see them? Tom expressed no least worry about that.

The crossing was uneventful if scarcely pleasurable, even though a fitful sun did appear and made their destination look the more dramatic with its great shadow-slashed snow peaks, wooded valleys and green but narrow coastal plain. It was a larger island, obviously, than Mary had realised, almost a score of miles long and perhaps half that in width, hilly throughout but the major mountains in the northern half, rising to mighty summits. The lower, southern end, which they approached from this angle, was cliff-girt, with rocks and skerries and little bays, more typical of the Hebrides. Tom named various landmarks, although he admitted that he had only been on the island once.

They were heading for Lamlash and its great bay, one-third of the way up the eastern side. This was the best landfall, for the bay was sheltered by a notable lesser island, providing a safe anchorage whatever the wind direction.

Well before they reached this haven, Tom pointed out, on the very southernmost clifftop, Kildonan Castle, a small, stark hold. There it was that King Robert the Bruce, their royal ancestor, one hundred and fifty years before, had awaited the fiery signal from the Ayrshire coast to bring him across by night to commence his seven-year desperate struggle to free his occupied kingdom from the English invaders, after his earlier defeat and almost exile. Yes, they would visit it one day. There would be much to see on this great isle.

Beating up the coast, the shipmaster having to deal with down-draughts from the hills so close, they came to Lamlash Bay; and Mary for one was surprised to discover that what had seemed to be just one more pointed hill, close to the shore, was in fact a mountainous offshore island, with the inner bay tucked in behind. This was Holy Isle, they were told, so called because there was a renowned and ancient monastery thereon, founded by Ranald of the Isles on the site of the hermitage of the famous St Molas, come from Columba's Iona. This they would visit also, in due course.

This Lamlash Bay itself was notable, having sheltered many a fleet in its time, but especially interesting as where that other Orkney overlord, King Haakon of Norway, had reassembled and rallied his host of galleys after his defeat by Alexander the Third in 1263 at the famous Battle of Largs. James was enthusiastic over this. Had other predecessors and ancestors of his been here, besides the Bruce and Alexander?

They landed at a sizeable jetty, backed by a long, straggling shoreside community, more than just a village, obviously occupied mainly by fisherfolk, with boats drawn up on the curving sandy beach and drying nets much in evidence. This was not the chiefest place on Arran, it seemed; Brodick, where there was a larger township, another port on a more exposed bay, and the main castle of the island, being three miles to the north. They would ride there forthwith, where they ought to find the steward of the lordship.

Bidding the shipmen farewell, and mounting, the party rode northwards, starting to climb almost at once. Obviously there would be much climbing on Arran. Their road turned away from the coast, which here swung out to a headland, the northern horn of the bay, and quickly rose between small hills, these notable in being dotted with many standing-stones, cairns and stone circles of their ancient Pictish ancestors, who evidently had found the island to their taste. Mary, interested in the Picts, or Albannach as she preferred to name them, said that she understood why St Molas had come here. They must come back and examine these. Tom said that he understood that there were plenty of others of the like, elsewhere.

That was true, for they saw others as they began the long descent to what was obviously a major valley coming down from the western heights to enter another bay, this shallower and more

121

open. Clearly there was a township where the glen opened to the sea; and up on the high ground beyond was a red stone castle, their immediate destination.

Clattering through the strung-out village, and raising surprised stares from the folk – clearly the islanders were unused to horsed parties, with ladies and men-at-arms – they mounted the steep slope beyond and came to Brodick Castle on its spur of hillside. There was no sign of watchful wariness here, the gates open and drawbridge down, and looking as though it was usually thus. They rode into the courtyard, Tom hallooing loudly.

Servants appeared, and then a young man of about Tom's own age came to the keep's door, most evidently astonished. He was carelessly clad but clearly no servitor. .

"Ha, friend – is the steward here?" Tom called. "I am Thomas, Earl of Arran." He said that a little self-consciously, the first time that he had had to announce the fact. "And here is His Grace, the King. And the Princess Mary, my countess."

The other's eyes widened and his jaw dropped a little. "Eh . . . ? You . . . is it . . . ?" He recovered himself, as he took in the fine clothing, the splendid horse-harness and the two pennants bearing the royal and Boyd arms carried by men of the escort. "Yes. Yes, my lord. And, and Your Grace!" He contrived a bow of sorts. "I greet you. I, I will get my father. He is within." He turned to leave them there, then recollected suitable and respectful civilities. He waved to the staring servants. "Aid them down. His Grace. The ladies. The earl . . . and see to the horses . . ." Then he departed.

They dismounted, not waiting for help, Anna declaring that that young man deserved their pity – but was none so ill-looking.

Presently a stocky man of greying head and stern expression appeared, with the other behind him, to eye the visitors carefully before making brief obeisance.

"Is this true? That it is the King's Grace? And the new Earl of this Arran?" he demanded.

"Think you any would claim it if not true, man?" Tom asked him. "Are you steward here?"

"Yes, my lord. I am John Fullarton of Kilmichael, Coroner of Arran. I act steward also, and have done these many years."

"Good. Then you will be able greatly to aid and guide us. But the Fullartons are an Ayrshire house, surely? Of Dundonald?"

122

"A forebear of mine wed a daughter, a bastard daughter, of an Earl of Menteith, and was appointed Hereditary Coroner of Arran and also steward here." He looked the other up and down. "I have heard of your appointment, my lord." That sounded questioning, as though the man was wondering whether his position now was in doubt.

Tom nodded. "I shall need a steward, sir – if scarcely a coroner!" he said. "So, if it serves us both . . ." He left the rest unsaid. "Now, there are quarters for us, in this hold? Suitable for His Grace and his royal sister?"

"Quarters, yes. I can have them made ready, my lord. And Sire. Unused for long. But . . ."

"I understand. We shall not be over-particular, meantime, Fullarton. Will my men find quarters here? Or will they return to Brodick?"

The other counted the escort. "I say that they would do better downby," he decided. "And, my lord, Brodick is the name of this castle, see you. Invercloy is the name of the village and haven."

"Ah, I stand corrected, Master Coroner! You can feed us all here?"

"To be sure. We can find a sufficiency. Then my son here will take your people down to Invercloy and find them lodging. Come you, within, Sire, and my lord and ladies . . ."

Brodick Castle proved to be very like Dean, only somewhat smaller, very similar as all these fortalices were, as distinct from the great fortress-castles like Stirling, Edinburgh and Dumbarton. A vaulted basement contained the kitchen, dairy and storage cellars, a turnpike stair led up to the great hall and withdrawing-room on the first floor, and there were three storeys of bedchambers above, the last attics within a parapet and wall-walk. John Fullarton, they found, had a cheerful, bustling wife, who presumably had been listening somewhere in the background to the exchange at the door, for she seemed to know the position and seemed quite prepared to cope, bobbing curtsies, smiling and waving hands about. Mary and Anna declared that they would help if required, but she shushed them away. She had lassies to aid her, she assured, down in the castleton. She would have a meal prepared for them forthwith, even though much of it would be cold, with water heated for washing, and while they made use of these she would have their bedchamber readied. How many would they require? Themselves, they used only two, their son Patrick's and their own. There were six others above . . .

She was told that three would serve. And they would be happy to eat in the kitchen meantime.

No, no, the lady asserted. She was obviously much more forthcoming than was her husband, possibly something of a blether, but seemingly her wits and hands could be as busy as her tongue. The Fullartons themselves used the withdrawing-room to live in, she informed, so the hall was free for the visitors. She would have a fire lit there right away.

The newcomers decided that they were fortunate, after having arrived thus without warning. The young man Patrick took them upstairs to select their rooms while the meal was being put together. They found the castle only fairly basically furnished, but when girls appeared with armfuls of blankets and sheets, and men with baskets of logs for the fires, they perceived that they were going to be comfortable enough.

They sat down to a substantial meal of hot soup, cold venison, bread, oatcakes and honey, with home-brewed ale to wash it down, Patrick and his mother waiting on them assiduously, the former paying particular attention to Anna – who indeed more or less asked for it, by her glances and reactions. James, mouth full, announced that he liked Arran, Brodick and the Fullartons.

The hall, large and bare and draughty as it had seemed when first they arrived, looked much better with a great log-fire blazing and candles lit, and the travellers stretched themselves pleasantly in front of it, while Patrick took the escort down to Invercloy, where the River Cloy, in its glen, reached salt water, and the community was strung along the shore, as at Lamlash. Indeed,by the look of it, all the communities, of this side of the island at least, would be so placed, for there was seemingly little breadth of land between the mountainsides and the sea.

When Patrick came back, it was to announce that his mother would be bringing them hot drinks of her honey wine before bed, a speciality of hers. He was clearly a friendly young man, and Anna kept him talking. He was able to tell them something of what there was to be seen and considered on Arran, and they realised that he would make an excellent guide, such as they were undoubtedly going to require.

The honey wine proved to be potent stuff, despite its sweetness, and sent them off to their couches more heavy-eyed than they had already been. Fires in each bedroom welcomed them.

Sleepy or not, Tom Boyd was not going to waste a bedding, especially as their couch was somewhat smaller than that at Stirling, which made for closer proximity. Mary, without actually reaching any heights of excitement, was no way aggrieved, and sank to sleep thereafter almost as quickly as he did.

Tom had a consultation with the Fullartons, father and son, next morning, as to the state of the island, its extent, its revenues and how it was administered, Mary sitting in on this and asking her own questions, since this great property was in the nature of a dowry for herself. In time, James burst in, demanding when they were going to go see and do something? He wanted to climb those mountains, especially the pointed one.

Tom agreed that this would be something that they might do; but there was a lot of snow up there meantime, and it might be better to wait awhile. A survey of the island first would be best, he suggested, and since it had a seaboard of no less than eighty miles, they were told, that was going to take some time. John Fullarton proposed that, to get some notion of the place as a whole, they should take a ride westwards over the spine of the island, from the crest of which they would see much, and then down to the western coast, which was very different from this eastern side, more exposed to the winds but not the seas, because of the shelter of the long Kintyre peninsula; and it had much more low ground. Patrick would show them.

This programme was acclaimed. The question was, whether to take their escort with them? They scarcely required them here, indeed would be better without them; but they might get into mischief, idling down in the clachan. Fullarton reckoned that his islesmen and fisherfolk could well look after themselves.

So the five young people set off, in very much a holiday mood. They rode down to the village in the forenoon sunlight, to tell the Boyd men-at-arms that they were not required, but to behave themselves, and then turned westwards. They found that although the community was called Invercloy, it was actually at the junction of three glens, that of Cloy being the southernmost and largest. Glen Rosa, which probed up behind the castle, was the north one, but it was the central one, Glen Shurig, which they took, heading due westwards and starting to climb almost at once, its burn cascading, its well-defined track the main access between the two sides of the island, and apparently called the String. Mary declared that this was obviously a Lowlander's corruption of their Gaelic ancestors' word *streap* or *streapadair*, which meant ladder or climb, to a pass. She knew of other similar names in the Highlands, usually called struie. Tom was impressed by his wife's erudition and interest in the past.

They saw plenty of signs of that distant past on their climb up Glen Shurig, Pictish burial-cairns, standing-stones and, right at the summit, a grass-grown fort with three layers of ramparts and ditches. Not that they spent much time on examining this, so stupendous was the view which here burst upon them. In every direction the prospect was breathtaking. Before them, the land sank into a widening valley, which itself opened on to a much wider coastal plain than on the eastern side, with the blue, firth-like Kilbrannan Sound beyond, six or seven miles wide, bounded by Kintyre, the longest peninsula in Scotland, almost seventy miles of it. This last was hilly, and so not to be seen over from here, save for a gap of lower ground to the south, across which they could glimpse the vast plain of the ocean, the Atlantic – and, according to Patrick, on a very clear day, the shadow which was Ireland itself. Stretching southwards from this summit was a great jumble of hills and valleys, leading the eye to the sea again, the mouth of the Firth of Clyde, with the Ayr and Galloway coasts and the isolated stack in the midst which James asserted was like the Bass Rock in Forth, and was told was the Craig of Ailsa. Northwards were the mighty ranked snow-peaks, starkly challenging in their proud aloofness.

All explanations, pointings and questionings, they proceeded down to what they were told was the Machrie Water, leading to Machrie Bay.

Pictish relics became even more numerous, circles, inscribed monoliths, cairns, tombs. When Patrick learned that Mary was especially interested in these, he told them that there were so many on this western side as to defy description. At Tormore, for instance, above Machrie Bay, there were actually eight stone circles, some with as many as a dozen monoliths still standing, all connected, of course, with sun-worship. He pointed to a prominent headland to the south-west, which he named Drumadoon, on the summit of which there was an enormous Pictish fort covering no fewer than twelve acres. And carvings

126

and inscriptions everywhere. Tom admitted that he had never realised that the Picts, or Albannach, had been so numerous, so active, so concerned with setting up monuments, not just uncultured barbarians. Mary told him that he should be prouder of his Boyd Celtic heritage.

Down on the low ground, quite fertile here, with cultivated rigs and grazing cattle, they crossed from the Machrie to another river, the Black Water of Clauchan, on the bank of which they were shown another feature, a burial-ground made out of a stone circle, notable for a different kind of inscribed stone, with Christian symbols. This was the grave of St Molas, of the Holy Isle, who came from Columba's Iona to convert Arran's Picts, and lived allegedly to the age of one hundred and two. This monumental stone had been brought from Iona itself, as suitable token.

They rode on south-westwards for another couple of miles, to Drumadoon Point, and there ate the provender Patrick's mother had made for them, within the tiered ramparts of the huge fort above the foaming tides of the Kilbrannan Sound – this, they were informed, called after another of Columba's missionaries, St Brendan. Indeed, the folk of these parts called themselves Brandanes, after Brendan and this long arm of the sea.

Anna remarked that Arran seemed to be a very holy place, with so much sun-worship and saint-worship. Were they all as saintly today? And Patrick was a saint's name too, was it not? Even though a far-away Irish one!

The young man rose to that, pointing out that St Patrick was a good Scot, or at least a native of Strathclyde, born near Dumbarton in what were now called the Kilpatrick Hills, before ever he went to convert the heathen Irish. So Columba, coming over from Ireland a century or two later, was but repaying a debt. Did her ladyship object to saints? There were very muscular ones, he judged!

James, who found all this talk of Picts and saints something of a bore, wanted to know what the hunting was like on Arran, whether they went in for hawking, and whether Patrick had ever tried spearing fish, flounders? Thomas, for his part, was more concerned with having details of lands, properties and wealth-production pointed out to him. This western side seemed to be much more fertile, with not a few farms, holdings and grazings. Were their rents and dues properly assessed and collected? Patrick assured that this was so, his father looking after that, and making account to the crown commissioners – and now no doubt to his new lordship. This side of the island did produce more grain, beef and mutton; but the east had much better fishing, and of course trade with the mainland. There were a number of small lairdships on both sides, vassals of the earldom, his father's own Kilmichael one, Machrie here, Kilpatrick, Dougrie, Shiskine and others. All of their holders, no doubt, would come to pay respects to the new earl – and to His Grace of course – when they heard that they were here. There was, however, one property which would not send a representative – that of Lochranza, in the far north of the island. This was a strange situation.

Demands for the reason brought forth a significant story – with the young man glancing sidelong at the monarch and his sister. It seemed that His Grace's royal father, for some reason, had, some fifteen years before, granted Lochranza Castle and its estate to Alexander Lord Montgomerie, alienating it from the rest of the island lordship. He had no sure notion why, although there were tales. But all the rest of Arran's hundred thousand-odd acres remained with the crown, save these four hundred. And he pointed northwards, beyond the high peaks.

Mary at least guessed what had lain behind this, the same old sorry story. Fifteen years ago, 1452, was the same year of the bringing down of the Douglases. Lord Montgomerie had no doubt assisted at the grim murder of the Earl of Douglas at Stirling, by the King, her father, and fell to be rewarded or quietened, paid off. Thus was Scotland governed, on occasion. She did not say so, however.

Tom, for his part, was concerned. He would have to see his uncle about this – for it happened that Lord Montgomerie had married Tom's aunt. He had not known about this Lochranza. He could possibly exchange some other lands on the mainland for it. He could not have a ridiculous bite out of his earldom like that.

Their midday break over, Patrick led them southwards above the shoreline and into the hillier country again. This was little less rich in relics, and he pointed out a cashel at Kilpatrick Point, one of the early Christian monastic settlements of the converted Picts, long deserted but clear enough. And so onwards, down towards the southern tip of the island. Mary asked whether they were going to be able to visit that Kildonan Castle they had glimpsed from the ship, where the Bruce had waited for the signal to return to the mainland to start his long campaign; but was told that this would be too far for them to ride this day, if they were to get back tö Brodick before dark. They would turn northwards soon now, to go up the Sliddery Water, and this would lead them through the central hills eventually to Lamlash Bay. Even so, that was a ten-mile traverse. Kildonan would have to wait.

There was somewhat less to see on this north-eastwards route, apparently known as the Ross Road, through a positive welter of hills, with the waterfalls of the Sliddery most of the way testifying to the steepness of the ascent. But even here there were Pictish remains. Arran, Mary declared, instead of being named after *aran*, the Gaelic for a kidney – which admittedly was almost exactly its shape – should have been called Eilean Albannach.

Much more aware of the size and character of Tom's earldom, they came down to Lamlash Bay again, with the dusk. Mary, commenting that it was a strange name, learned that it was really only another corruption, of Eilean Molas, the saint's isle. James tried that on his tongue, and wondered why there should have been two languages in Scotland. Explanations and examples kept them going all the way to Brodick.

They could well have reserved that discussion on place-names, Picts and Albannach, Scots and saints, until a later occasion, for there followed two days of continuous rain and winds gusty but warm, with outdoor pursuits contra-indicated, and the filling-in of time something of a problem, especially where James was concerned. Tom had much debate with John Fullarton over the island's profitability and where improvements could be made, having the local lairds over to meet him, and the like. Meg Fullarton did her best to make the accommodation more comfortable, as well as over-feeding them. Patrick was good company and consistently informative – as well as good at contriving to disappear with Anna on occasion. And Mary sought to curb her brother's impatience, and to instruct him, in so far as she was able, in his realm's long story. She had also to attempt a certain amount of impatience-curbing where Thomas was concerned, this of a different sort, especially in the evenings, when her husband saw little point in sitting by the hall fire when they might be more effectively employed elsewhere.

It was on the second evening, however, with the rain stopped at last and the skies clearing that, venturing outside for a breath of fresh air, they could hear a sort of distant roaring sound which none had noticed before. Patrick told them that this would be the Glenrosa Water in spate, that all the rivers would now be in flood, but the Rosa more especially so, since it drained the high mountains to the north, where the snows would have been melting fast. This of course had James agog. Would the snow indeed be gone? Could they go climbing? Patrick was a little doubtful, but if they went up to the summit of a nearby hillock they would be able to see the great peaks. By royal command, they marched over the wet terrain to ascertain – and sure enough, only small patches of snow were left on the high tops ahead. That was it, then, James declared; they would go climbing on the morrow. Patrick warned that the ground would be very wet and slippery, but such feeble attitudes were brushed aside by their sovereign-lord. They would go.

In the morning, the question of suitable clothing and footwear for the girls inevitably came up, and James was for declaring their attendance as unnecessary anyway. But Mary, and to a lesser extent Anna, was not to be thus discarded. Heavy riding-habits and long, high boots were quite out of the question for climbing, and their house-shoes quite inadequate. It was Meg Fullarton who provided an answer, even though she seemed to think that high-born ladies should not contemplate such activities. Nevertheless, as a girl she herself had gone climbing on rocky hills on occasion, and had found the common rawhide brogans apt enough for the exercise. Some of the castleton lassies would have such footwear, to be sure; and since they were tied on with lacing, they could be made to fit well enough. She herself could lend them rough and shortish homespun skirts, which would serve – if the ladies were prepared to wear them? So the two girls went down to the castleton cottages and had no difficulty in borrowing brogans which, by their lacing design, could fit almost any woman's foot.

Thus equipped, the six of them mounted – for they were taking one of the men-at-arms to take care of the horses – and rode over to Glen Rosa. The lower glen was pleasantly wooded. They crossed the still-swollen river by a ford near some standing-stones, the water almost up to their horses' bellies, the track being on the west side. Soon the valley began to narrow in to what was practically a deep gorge, with the mountains growing ever steeper and taller on either side, so much so that the narrowed sky seemed able to let in but little light. Soon there was only scanty room for the track beside the drumly water; indeed, from the debris, it was evident that this would have been impassable the day before. Some three miles up from the ford they passed a sizeable waterfall, its thunder all but shaking the gorge.

The glen was in fact remarkably straight and, Patrick said, probed for over five miles directly into the heart of the mountains, as though making for the pointed peak which was James's chosen objective. This apparently was named Cir Mhor, the great crest or coxcomb; and although it was not the highest, Goat Fell, nearer on the right, being this, it was certainly the most scenic and dramatic. Actually it was possibly the most easy of access too, since this Rosa's headstream rose right up on its east flank, in almost a straight line, all they had to do was to follow the waterside up. What the going of the upper reaches would be like remained to be seen, and would determine how far they could get the horses. Thereafter, it would be just steep climbing, for about five hundred feet, and by curving round a little it ought to be possible to avoid scaling the summit cliffs. If they had been climbing Goat Fell, or almost any other of the peaks, they would not have been able to get the horses nearly so far.

The river forked some four miles up from the ford, and the track deteriorated with its branching. They took the central burn, and could now see it running almost directly ahead of them, right up into a corrie scooped in the side of the pyramidical peak, an exciting prospect. How far would they get the horses?

The melt-water had left very soft and muddy ground, over which their mounts had to pick their way carefully. But the higher and steeper they went, the more firm was the surface, this because it had been washed down almost to the grey granite bedrock. It was scarcely ideal terrain for horses' hooves, but it made possible riding, and they in fact got their beasts almost another mile up before it would have been dangerous to go further.

Dismounting, they left the animals in the care of their groom, and started to climb.

After a reasonably moderate start, it became quickly steeper, so that soon hands as well as feet were brought into action. The girls found their borrowed brogans were very effective, indeed more so than the men's boots, since they were softer of sole and this allowed the toes to play their part. When James found his sister actually ahead of him in the climb he was distinctly put out, and Mary began deliberately to hold back. The two young men, perceiving the situation, also restrained themselves, for this was to be the monarch's day. Patrick found much opportunity to assist Anna, who laboured rather more than did her mistress, being shorter in the leg and plumper about the middle.

Nevertheless, soon Mary was panting, as indeed were they all – only the girls' physique made this the more apparent. James seemed to require, or at least take, fewer rests than did the others now, which allowed him to get satisfactorily ahead. They were getting into patches of snow and ice, very slippery.

There were cliffs around the summit, and the boy was for scaling these also, but Mary insisted that this was highly dangerous and to be avoided. He grumbled about feeble females, but allowed himself to be diverted round to the right, where there was a gap in the cliffs with a steep crevasse between. Normally this would be scree-filled, loose small stones, but it had filled likewise with snow, which at this height had not all melted away. So the scree was covered with semi-frozen snow, into which they had to dig their toes to gain footholds. Now the men's boots proved a deal more effective than the girls' brogans, and much assistance and hoisting ensued, amidst gasps, slippings and clutchings.

Eventually this was surmounted however, and now there was only the final pinnacle, largely bare and broken rock, demanding more clambering. James was, of course, first on the top, shouting and gesticulating his satisfaction, pointing at all the peaks around, monarch indeed of all that he surveyed. And it was, by any standards, a tremendous prospect, a world apart, of aloof crests and crags and ridges, rearing above deep, shadow-filled troughs and valleys, tier upon tier, daunting in its so utterly impersonal-seeming preoccupation with only space and sky.

But almost equally daunting was the cold wind up there, and they did not linger. It had taken them less time than anticipated, and James was eager for more, to go on and climb other mountains now that they were here. His companions were less keen, and it was pointed out to him that getting back to their horses from other peaks might well be very difficult, with all these gorges and cliffs. Patrick, as a compromise, suggested that they might make a traverse of the mighty ridge which stretched southwards from this summit for well over a mile, a lofty, narrow, roof-like feature flanked by tremendous precipices on both sides of a very narrow spine. It was called A' Chir, from the same derivation of Cir Mhor, and merely meant the comb, rather than the coxcomb; and certainly the serrated escarpment could be said to resemble a great comb.

Mary was a little concerned for her impetuous brother as they proceeded along that dizzy ridge, so narrow, with awesome drops on either side, a fall down which could result only in death; and by pretending that it was for her own safety, she clung to him. The knowledge that they had to retrace their steps along this, for there was no other way down, save by climbing another great mountain ahead, did not help. But the sights and vistas were so enthralling, breathtaking, that it was probably worth all the dreads, however thankful the girls were when at last they won back to Cir Mhor.

There was still the descent to the horses, a slipping, sliding progress with much disarray of Meg Fullarton's skirts, short as these were, in consequent hilarity.

They returned to Brodick well pleased with themselves, despite a certain amount of minor bruising. Some limbs might be a little stiff on the morrow.

The morrow saw them heading northwards again, but this time along the coastline, and mounted all the way. Thomas wanted to see this Lochranza Castle, which he looked upon as filched from his earldom, and to be regained if possible. The road thereto clung to the shoreside's low cliffs mile after mile, passing the small, isolated community of Corrie, and at length, after six or seven miles, at Sannox Bay, swinging inland up Glen Sannox. As well that it did, they perceived, for the coast directly ahead now looked grim indeed, all broken precipices and great rocks, with foaming reefs below, which Patrick declared extended all the way to the very northern tip of the island, known as the Cock of Arran, a headland of fierce challenge, like a fist shaken in the face of all the Highland west.

This Glen Sannox, probing westwards, was itself long and rather featureless, rising after about three miles to quite a high pass, with a drop thereafter, another three, to a sea-loch which they could see gleaming ahead. That was Loch Ranza, a remote and difficult place to reach indeed. Tom wondered why anyone had ever built a castle here; and Patrick said that it had been a hunting-seat for the Menteith earls, on the site of a more ancient fort no doubt so placed to protect the north of the island from Viking and other invaders. Mary suggested that it was hardly worth Tom approaching Lord Montgomerie about.

However, when they reached sea-level and found a small scattered community, with the fortalice sitting on a spit of land jutting into the loch, they perceived it to be a more attractive place than they had assumed, however isolated. The castle itself they found to be all shut up, and looking as though it had been that way for long. It evidently did not have a resident keeper; but Patrick took them to a rather larger house amongst the cottages of the castleton, where an elderly man greeted them respectfully enough, and on learning that he was in the King's presence, hastily escorted them down to the castle, with the keys, they being followed by a small crowd of staring folk to whom strangers were obviously a source of excitement. Their guide admitted that he had not seen Lord Montgomerie there for three years. He was getting old for stalking the stags perhaps; and that was Lochranza's principal attraction apparently. When he did come, it was by boat from Ayrshire, north-abouts. There was a jetty near the mouth of the loch.

The visitors explored the quite large castle, with its tall square tower and L-plan, and found it sparsely furnished and chilly, but with its own interests and possibilities. All agreed that it could be made into quite a comfortable house. James had pricked up his ears at the mention of stags and hunting, and had to have it explained to him that this mountain terrain, although good for the deer, meant that they had to be *stalked*, not hunted on horseback as he was used to doing. Stalking had to be done on foot, or even on bellies, by individuals, not parties, armed with cross-bows, to get close enough to the wary deer to be within arrow-shot, a very different proceeding from horsed huntsmen with hounds chasing the game. They *could* be killed in deer-drives, but this took much organising, many men and massed marksmen, not easily achieved in a place like this. The monarch's interest waned.

Thomas wanted to see the extent of this Lochranza property and its possibilities, so they did not return as they had come but continued on round the coast westwards and then southwards, with the mountains rising close on their left. One brief gap in that mighty wall Patrick called Glen Catacol, and then the hills closed in again and they were pressed almost to the shore, mile after mile. The new Earl of Arran recognised that this northern

134

half of his territory was a deal less valuable than the rest, however fine its scenery. But he was still determined not to let it belong to someone else if he could help it, even an uncle.

Eventually they won back to the more populous and fertile areas of Dougrie and Machrie Bay, and thereafter returned across the String Road to Brodick, after a total of some thirty miles' riding.

That evening, Tom declared that they could not stay on Arran for very much longer. His father had made it clear that a week or so away would be the limit, not so much on account of his own, or Mary's, absence, but because the King was needed in fairly constant attendance with the Regent, in order to sign documents and give royal assent to edicts, charters and other measures of government. Actually Lord Boyd had been loth to let James go with them at all, but the boy had been insistent. Now Mary said that she hoped that they would not leave the island without making the visit to Kildonan Castle at the southern end, which meant more than all the rest in Scotland's story. Tom promised that they would go the next day. Meanwhile he would get Fullarton to send one of the Invercloy fishing boats over to Ayr, to have their ship come for them two days hence.

Windy again, and threatening rain, they rode south next morning, by Lamlash once more, and another great but shallower and unprotected bay beyond called Kiscadale, to the very southern coast, different again from all the rest, all cliffs and reefs and skerries, with offshore islets, one of these quite large, apparently called Pladda, where Patrick said another saint had had his hermitage or diseart, St Blaize. With Kildonan itself called after one more, St Donnan of Eigg, Anna remarked that the Arran folk must have been especially wicked – and possibly still were – to have acquired so many missionaries sent by Iona to save their souls!

Past the impressive Dippin Head they came to Kildonan Castle on its clifftop site beside one more stone circle – no doubt why it was there, for the Celtic saints, following Columba's own example, were apt to use these sun-worship circles as sites for their own cells or little churches, continuing the theme of worship but making it Christian to replace the unknown god represented by the sun; and the castle had been built nearby by the Lords of the Isles. It proved to be abandoned now, indeed part ruinous. But the visitors explored it interestedly, trying to decide out of

135

which east-facing window the great Bruce had watched for the fire on the Ayrshire coast fifteen miles away, in 1307, with arguments about who would be with the King at that time.

The rain developing and looking as though it would continue, they proceeded no further along the south-coast cliffs but turned back for Brodick. It was on the way there that Anna came out with her proposal – which no doubt she had been hatching in her mind these last days. Why not take the good and useful Patrick Fullarton back with them tomorrow, to Dean and Stirling? If he would come? As an earl, Tom should have at least one attendant always available. And they got on very well together, did they not?

Her brother, eyeing them both, grinned. *He* would be glad of Patrick's company, yes. Perhaps that fine fellow would not want to leave Arran, however, and his father's house? He had a full life here, did he not?

By the speed with which the other young man answered this it was fairly evident that the suggestion had not come as a complete surprise to him. He promptly asserted that he would be glad to join his lordship's household in whatever capacity, and would be honoured to be so appointed.

Mary caught Anna's eye and wagged her head, but not censoriously. James obviously approved, and said that he would teach Patrick how to fly hawks, spear flounders and joust at tourneys. It was all as easy as that.

So the next day, when they took leave of the senior Fullartons, it was to relieve them of their son's presence meantime. If the parents were displeased they did not show it; John Fullarton was not one for showing his feelings anyway, and his wife was proud that her son should be thus raised in stature and move into the royal household.

When the ship, in due course, was reported as having entered Lamlash Bay, the party collected their men-at-arms, useless as these had been – and who seemed quite reluctant to leave Invercloy, getting their own appreciative send-off from the villagers, especially the womenfolk – and rode off southwards to embark, promising that they would be back. Oh yes, they would be back.

All sailed for Ayr well pleased with the Arran situation.

10

Tom and Mary found themselves in a rather strange situation when they returned to Stirling. The King's presence was necessary – but theirs seemingly was not. Lord Boyd was ruling Scotland almost single-handed, although of course he had the advice of such as Avondale the Chancellor, Somerville, Livingstone, Hailes, Bishop Graham and other lords temporal and spiritual. But basically he was a loner, and kept all the reins of power in his own hands, a strange man. He seemed to have little need for his son. And yet it was that son whom he had elevated to the rank of earl, married to the King's sister, and endowed with vast lands, while he remained only the Lord Boyd. It was as though he intended the House of Boyd to be amongst the most illustrious in the land hereafter, but he himself was quite content with *power*, as Regent. After all, he could equally well have had himself appointed an earl, and taken over all these properties, for he could get James to sign anything. But that did not seem to be his way. The future might be his son's; the present was his alone.

So Tom and his wife found themselves in little demand at Stirling, save for occasions when a show was to be made, banquets for ambassadors, visiting papal representatives, feast-days and the like. They were neither of them of the sort who could appreciate inaction, a lazy acceptance of life or continual pleasure-seeking. Hurly-hackit, hawking, hunting in season, and exploring the countryside were all very well, but such an existence palled, especially for Thomas. So, fairly soon after their return, they set off again on a series of visits of inspection to the other properties which his curious father had incorporated in the earldom – and these were many indeed, former crown lands, the estates of forfeited families such as Douglas, Dunbar, Menteith and the like. In Ayrshire alone there were Dalry, Noddsdale, West Kilbride, Monfodd, Stewarton, Terrinzean, Turnberry and Rosedalemuir. There was another offshore island, smaller than

137

Arran, called Meikle Cumbrae, in Buteshire. There was Nairston in Lanarkshire, Caverton in Roxburghshire, Teiling in Angus and Polgay in Perthshire. All these fell to be visited sometime, and with nothing else apparently required of him, Thomas might as well see to it now. They represented much wealth, undoubtedly. Anna and Patrick, now a firm friend of them all, accompanied them, and sometimes but not always James – for on the longer trips, it was the Regent's preference that the King was not far from his side for more than a few days; and when James was with them, an armed escort was obligatory, just in case some other ambitious lord or group thought to copy the Boyd example and stage an abduction.

So passed the spring and early summer, with much travelling and seeing places new, interesting enough usually but scarcely satisfying the Earl and Countess of Arran.

On their return to Stirling from a visit to the former Douglas property of Caverton in the borderland, they discovered that the two earls, Crawford and Argyll, had at last returned from their prolonged survey of the princesses of Christendom seeking a possible bride for King James. They had been thorough enough in their search, it seemed, but were not too happy with their findings. They had been to France, Spain, Flanders, Burgundy, Savoy and, of course, England. Young women they had seen and inspected, tactfully of course, but without conviction that they had found the right one for James Stewart – or at least for his realm. After all, the boy was still only fifteen, which meant that the suitable age bracket was very restricted. Someone even three or four years older would scarcely be apt, and bairns younger than, say, twelve likewise. And it so happened that there was a dearth of available princesses within the twelve-to-seventeen age group just then. They did bring back the names of one or two possibles, but these were of ducal rather than royal rank, and probably a little below the standard felt suitable for the King of Scots, on the most ancient throne in Christendom.

And the English situation, which might have been best in the national interest, was still complicated by the Yorkist and Lancastrian dichotomy, two men calling themselves King of England, and the outcome by no means certain, although Lancaster was supreme at the moment. It would be unwise to plunge for a daughter of either house until the position was assured.

A council was held to consider the earls' reports. Also to decide upon another matter. King Christian of Norway had sent another envoy, none other than the now-freed Bishop of Orkney, William Tulloch, to demand the payment of the Orkney Annual, as it was called – although annual was scarcely an apt term for the rental to Scotland of the Northern Isles, since no payment had in fact been made for over twenty years, and the arrears now amounted to an astronomical figure. The bishop, on release by St Clair, had apparently gone to Norway and Denmark to complain, and to ask for financial help for his ill-used see from his Metropolitan, the Archbishop of Nidaros at Trondheim. And now he had been sent back by King Christian, to Scotland, with this demand for payment of the Annual and at least some of the arrears. It seemed that Christian, never rich in moneys, was himself in dire financial straits, owing to the heavy costs of bringing the rebellious Swedes under his control.

At this demand, the Council was in fact more concerned than in finding a wife for young James. Thomas, who as an earl now automatically sat on the Privy Council, was discussing all this with Mary that evening, declaring that it was a pity that they had ever got the wretched Bishop Tulloch released, to cause all this trouble. But the young woman looked thoughtful.

"Perhaps the good bishop is doing us none so ill a service?" she suggested. "Good might come of this. If we Scots were to use our wits."

"What do you mean?"

"I mean that your Privy Council might solve both of its problems. See you, King Christian of Denmark – or Norway, I never know which he should be called – has a daughter, I am told. Young. He might like it well to have her a Queen."

"Marry *her* to James?"

"Would she not be as good as any?"

"She would bring no fine dowry, that one, such as is always looked for. Christian is always short of moneys. Always has been – why he wants this Annual from Scotland so keenly. *His* treasury is as empty as is ours. He has to keep a large army always in Sweden, to put down rebellion. The Swedes and Goths want independence . . ."

"I know all that. It is why I say this. Send him a token payment only. Not all the arrears, but this year's Annual. *Take* it, rather than send it. And see this daughter, Margaret. I think that she is

139

of twelve years, perhaps thirteen. If she seems suitable, propose possible marriage with James. And her dowry – the Orkney and Shetland Isles!"

"Lord!" He stared at her. "Save us – why, oh why, did I not think of that? The Northern Isles. To become part of *this* realm, not Norway's. Here is a wonder, yes. What a head you have on that lovely neck, lass! *You* should be James's regent, I swear! But – would Christian agree, think you?"

"Offer a treaty of mutual support also. That would tempt him. And could help Scotland too, on occasion. But not against the Swedes, or we could be called upon over often. If the English, these Lancastrians, become too powerful, they may come to assail Scotland again, as they have done in the past. We have been spared that for some time. Then the Norse, with their great fleets, could be useful allies."

"Ye-e-es. That too. Here is notable thinking. Why has it been left to a young woman to think of it?"

"Women are none so lacking in wits as often men assume! And we so often have more time left us to think! But this cost no great cudgelling of brains. It is but dealing, trading. What each has and each wants. You Boyds were traders once, were you not?"

"Aye. I will put this to my father. There is one matter that may halt him, I think. The Annual. You say make one payment, for the Northern Isles. This realm's treasury is almost as empty as is Christian's, I fear."

"The realm's perhaps. But what of others? The Boyds'? Yours, my good Earl of Arran? Other lords'? All these fine lands you have acquired, with your wife! Their wealth. Surely the Scots lords could dip their hands a little way into their coffers, for once? Loans to the treasury? To pay the Annual. How much is it?"

"Thirty thousand silver florins, I think."

"Is that beyond this Scotland? What of Holy Church? The Church is rich. And the merchants, the trade guilds. This is to gain a bride for their sovereign-lord. And win the Northern Isles."

Tom rubbed his chin. "We shall see. *I* would give something, yes. As a loan . . ."

Next day he took the suggestion to his father. Lord Boyd, as anticipated, saw the virtues and possibilities of the project, but jibbed at the provision of money, private moneys. It was unheard of for individual lords, or others, to pay for state requirements out

140

of their private pockets. He would consult others, but . . . He was not paying siller out of the Boyd revenues!

Tom said that he would be willing to make a contribution. Say of three thousand florins.

His father forbade it flatly. Then it would be expected of himself. That was not the way.

But the planted seed did bear a harvest of sorts, for a day or two later the Regent announced that, having discussed the matter with others, he had decided that the general conception was a good one – the Norse match, the Orkney and Shetlands bride-payment, and the rest. As to the Annual, whilst none were agreeable to paying it from their own pockets, it was agreed that the one-year sum should be found. Since the treasury was in no state to produce thirty thousand florins, the suggestion was to make parliament responsible for it, the Three Estates each to raise ten thousand, barons, Church and burghs. This would, of course, entail calling a convention of the said Estates – and that required forty days' notice. That would take them into October; and allowing for time for the moneys to be found, after that was no time for long sea voyaging. So an embassage to Norway would have to wait until the spring. But meantime, they could send an envoy, probably this Bishop Tulloch, to Christian, informing him of what was proposed, to prepare him and keep him quiet until then. If he refused it all, at least they would be spared the raising of the moneys . . .

Told of this, Mary declared that for men of sufficient drive and initiative to abduct a King and his sister and take over the rule of a realm, the Boyds were remarkably feeble where money was concerned. Could taxation not take care of the matter, if private coffers were too closely guarded?

Tom explained that tax-gathering was a perquisite of the lords and sheriffs of counties, as commissioners – and the very word indicated that their commission was an important part of it, part of their own revenues. Why, indeed, the treasury was so empty! Besides, any increase in taxation would require the assent of parliament.

The young woman shook her head over all this folly. But she had other matters than state affairs to preoccupy her just then – for she was fairly sure that she was pregnant.

This news set Tom Boyd in a stir indeed. It seemed never to have occurred to him that this might be the result of all their love-making – not so soon, at least. But he was greatly pleased nevertheless, indeed evidently proud of himself, a begetter of offspring. And promptly he began to treat his wife as though she was a tender plant, to be protected from every wind that blew, fussing over her, concerned for her every comfort and care, and enquiring daily for her state. Mary assured him that she was no fragile flower, that this was indeed a woman's fulfilment, not some dire hazard; besides, if she calculated aright, the birth would not be until Yuletide. Meantime, she was perfectly able to lead a normal active life.

Reassured, Thomas declared that they would call his name James, after the King. Not Grizel, she asked? She had always liked that name!

So the late summer passed into autumn, the hunting season much preoccupying James at least, so that the royal group spent much of their time mounted, in the Flanders Moss, the Tor Wood or on the skirts of the Highland mountains. There was talk of making a return to Arran, for a spell, and sampling its sport, but this came to nothing, Tom worried about sea-sickness and waves upsetting his wife. They did however make the short crossing to visit the island of Meikle Cumbrae, and found it attractive and interesting, with more ancient Pictish relics – not unnaturally, since its name, originally Cymri-ay, meant the isle of the Cymric or Welsh-speaking Celts. Four miles long and half that in width, it was like Arran in miniature.

Then, in October, the necessary parliament was held, at Stirling, a brief affair, little more than a formality intended, which, with those in power making their wills very evident, duly accepted the proposal of a Norse match for the King, and acclaimed the notion of the Northern Isles as dower. The raising of the Annual was a deal less popular, but when the Primate, Bishop Graham of St Andrews, led the way by promising ten thousand florins from Holy Church, and the burgh representatives, after consultation, agreed to find the same, the lords and barons could scarcely refuse. So the thing was passed. The Three Estates would find the Annual by Yuletide, and have it available for the embassage to take to King Christian thereafter, when sailing conditions permitted.

Mary, her condition not yet very apparent, sat in the great hall gallery listening, and smiled a little. No hint was given in the proceedings that the entire project was of *her* devising.

Under other business however, there was an unlooked-for development. Bishop Graham, without actually saying so, made it evident that he looked for reward for leading the way over the Annual contribution. He, like his predecessors before him, was much concerned over the grave matter of Scotland's non-Metropolitan status in Holy Church. It was an offence, a stone-for-stumbling and a constant danger, the English in especial always using it as an excuse for their claims to paramountcy over the northern kingdom. They claimed that the Archbishop of York was the most northerly Metropolitan and therefore the Church in Scotland was subject to himself; whilst the Archbishop of Nidaros, or Trondheim, asserted that *he* was more northerly still, and that he was Metropolitan over Scotland's Church. This folly should be ended, and the Scottish Primate, himself, raised to the status of Metropolitan, the see of St Andrews made an archbishopric. He perceived the present traffic with Norway as opportunity to effect this. It would require papal agreement and authority, of course, but that might not be too difficult to obtain, if the Norse archbishop accepted. Perhaps some inducements might be offered? If Norway was losing the bishopric of Orkney anyway, some arrangement might be come to. York would never agree, to be sure, but Nidaros might.

Was all this any concern of this parliament? the Chancellor asked. Was it not merely a matter for the churchmen?

The Primate thought that it *was* the realm's concern, since the English ever used their claim to spiritual hegemony to back their claim of regal suzerainty. But no more moneys would be required from the parliament; that at least was the Church's responsibility.

Relieved, the non-clerical members concurred. Bishop Graham declared that, in the circumstances, it might be best for himself to join the prospective embassage to Norway in the spring, to negotiate with the archbishop there.

One final matter was raised by the Earl of Crawford. Suppose that the embassage to Norway and Denmark was to be unsuccessful? King Christian might not agree to the proposed match. The princess might prove unsuitable – as had others they had considered in their travels. The Norse might not agree to the Northern Isles as bride's portion. Or they might demand full payment of all arrears of the Annual – for these the envoys would have to require to be remitted. In such case, the negotiations would fail. Should not the envoys therefore be given instructions and authority to proceed further in search of a royal bride?

This was agreed – although just where the said envoys should further go was not specified or obvious, since Crawford and Argyll had already covered most of the possibilities.

That completed the business, and parliament adjourned.

Mary could not but find the next two months somewhat wearisome, as her condition imposed increasing restrictions. However, she was interested, intrigued in her state and in what was growing within her, the development of her body, the changes in its functions. She even began to feel an identification and affection for the creature which stirred and kicked within her, and duly reported progress to her husband. Thomas, for his part, continued to be almost too considerate, the proud begetter of James Boyd, Master of Arran – as he was wholly convinced was the situation. Mary gave up warning him that it might be a girl.

So the monarch had to do without his sister's company at hurly-hackit, hunting and hawking, and often his Master Thomas also. Even Anna felt that her place was at Mary's side most of the time, although she was told otherwise. So it came about that Patrick Fullarton became James's most constant companion, a strange development for the young islander of no very lofty parentage. The armed escort, of course, was never far away.

It was on Hogmanay, the last day of the year, that Mary went into labour, and there was question whether the new Boyd was going to be born in 1467 or 1468. In the end it was the latter, after a delayed and taxing travail, that birth was achieved, and James, Master of Arran did indeed appear. Happily he was a perfectly normal child, and with excellent lungs – which he soon made apparent – and Stirling Castle was set to rejoicing, bonfires were lit and the New Year celebrated even more enthusiastically than usual. Lord Boyd himself unbent sufficiently actually to commend his daughter-in-law, and assess his grandson held in Anna's arms.

Mary smiled tiredly, and slept.

11

For Mary the months that followed were a joy, the infant preoccupying her as nothing before had ever done, a wonder and a delight, a gurgling and uncomplicated little creature of wide blue eyes, quite a lot of fair hair, dimpled fists, spreading fingers and toes, and dribbles, much dribbling. He got a lot of attention – indeed, Tom became quite jealous, complaining of neglect.

They decided to refer to him as Jamie, which meant that Mary had to stop calling her brother that; anyway, the monarchical dignity was now beginning to make the childhood name unsuitable. The King too found his little namesake something of an intrusion, depriving him of his sister's company, since *he* did not want to be always playing second to the moist brat. Anna also became a devotee of her nephew and consequently was less available for expeditions and sport – which had its own effect on Patrick Fullarton. Such was the impact of the new Master of Arran.

As it happened, the Lord Boyd it was who helped to make the royal objections of less consequence, even though not deliberately. For some time he had been indicating, as the King's guardian, that James had been spending overmuch time on outdoor pursuits and neglecting studies suitable for a young monarch. He had had his tutors at Stirling, before the abduction from Linlithgow, and was reasonably well educated and well read; but these had been dismissed. Now the Regent, who hardly approved of Patrick as royal esquire, produced another young man, another Boyd indeed, named John, or Father John, recently entered into holy orders, actually a nephew in blood of his own, an illegitimate son of the Abbot of Kilwinning, of a studious and artistic frame of mind, indeed erudite and artistic. Fortunately he was also of an equable and friendly nature and James rather took to Father John. So that winter and spring he passed more time in mental rather than physical activity, although Tom and Patrick did frequently go hunting with him.

Tom himself had preoccupations to share with his father and the rest of the ruling group, other than preparations for the Norse venture – which looked like being somewhat delayed owing to the slow accumulation of those thirty thousand florins. This was because of trouble in the north, and worrying. Admittedly clan feuds and internecine fighting were endemic in the Highlands and Islands, and did not normally greatly concern the rest of Scotland. But this outbreak was different. It was the Lord of the Isles again, and his behaviour outrageous.

John MacDonald, Lord of the Isles and former Earl of Ross, had always been a wild and uncontrollable character – and possessed, of course, of vast manpower and a great fleet of galleys, the greyhounds of the sea; and with royal blood in his veins. As a young man he had been ambitious indeed, actually entering into a private treaty with the English Yorkist Edward the Fourth, whereby he would aid Edward to conquer Scotland and thereafter he would have all north of Forth and Clyde to rule as independent prince, this he considering himself to be already. Fortunately the Wars of the Roses had intervened and the House of York had come down, so that Mary's father had been able to subdue the Islesman in some measure, although not having large fleets at his disposal, had not been able to take over the Hebridean seaboard and isles. He could and did deprive John MacDonald of the Ross earldom but the Lordship of the Isles was different, a hereditary style and title, not a lordship of parliament, and this remained with the awkward John. He had since lain quiet, as least as far as the rest of the kingdom was concerned, although he made his presence felt all over the Highland west and over into Ireland. But now, he had, for reasons unknown, suddenly led an expedition of armed Islesmen far from his own fastnesses and down into Atholl, there to storm and take Blair Castle, capture the Earl and Countess of Atholl and take them off prisoner to his island of Islay.

This extraordinary assault could not be ignored by the crown authorities, not only because Atholl, in Perthshire, was only seventy miles as the crow flew north of Stirling, but because John Stewart, Earl of Atholl, was in fact closely linked with the ruling house, his mother having been Joan Beaufort, widow of James the First, who had married the famous Black Knight of Lorn after the King died.

Yet, what was to be done? The realm had no fleets of galleys, and without such the Western Isles were safe from any Lowland attack – always one of Scotland's great weaknesses. So they could by no means hope to overcome John MacDonald by force and thus rescue Atholl and his wife. If anything was to be achieved it would have to be by negotiation or guile. But what had they to offer the Islesman? To give him back his earldom of Ross, now merged in the crown, would be to ask for further trouble. What else?

It was Mary again, with wits presumably inherited from the longest line of kings in Christendom, who suggested the answer to that, to Tom. The small but ancient kingdom of Man? It had long, in theory, been part of the realm of Scotland, ceded by Norway in 1266; but situated where it was, not far off the Lancashire coast, and nearer Wales and Ireland than Scotland, without the required fleets and shipping to maintain the connection, the island kingdom had been more or less abandoned to its fate. Invaded sometimes by the Irish, the Norse pirates, sometimes by the English, it had suffered under a variety of overlords, and was at present held by an English lord named Stanley, who called himself King thereof. But it was still Scots territory by treaty. If John of the Isles was given charter of it to add to his lordship, he might well jump at it, even if *he* thereafter called himself King of Man. After all, his great ancestor, Somerled, the first lord, had conquered Man once. And its transference would not damage the Scots realm.

This suggestion, for want of any other, commended itself to the Boyds. Mary was not so pleased, however, when it transpired that it was the Earl of Arran whom the King, or at least his Regent, elected to send north to negotiate in the matter. And on this occasion, his wife, with a new baby, could not accompany him.

Tom himself was a little doubtful; but he did see it as something of an adventure and challenge. Anyway, he could not refuse a royal command. He would take ship from Ayr, using a couple of other Boyd vessels as escort – puny as these would seem against the Islesman's galleys – and sail for Islay. It was late April, and the seas should be reasonably manageable, even the Sea of the Hebrides. Evidently John MacDonald had found them so! It should not take so very long. Once a-sail, they should be at Islay, the most southerly of the major Hebridean isles, in three days or four at most.

So it was parting, their first since the wedding. Patrick would go with Thomas. Also Andrew Stewart, Canon and Sub-Dean of

Glasgow, Atholl's younger brother, and reputed to be a persuasive negotiator and no humble cleric. Mary realised that she was going to miss her husband, young Jamie notwithstanding.

In the event, she did not have to suffer Tom's absence for long, for he was back in just twelve days, with extraordinary news. According to Sub-Dean Stewart, God had taken over the situation, as the result of his prayers, no doubt. All was well, and his brother and sister-in-law released and indeed by now back in Atholl. Apparently, after immuring the earl and countess at Finlaggan on Islay, John of the Isles had sailed off with his galleys for Ardtornish Castle on the Sound of Mull, for purposes unknown. And off Jura and Scarba, where the Atlantic winds swept through the gap where lay the notorious Gulf of Corrievreckan, a most violent storm had struck the fleet, with disastrous results, sinking most of the ships, and with them all the rich plunder stolen from Blair-in-Atholl. The chief's own vessel had foundered, but John had unfortunately survived. He was now somewhere in the more northerly Hebrides licking his Heaven-dealt wounds. The visitors from the Lowlands, landed on Islay, had had little difficulty in freeing the captives. And all at no cost to themselves. A miracle indeed.

None disputed that.

Now all efforts were concentrated on completing the raising of the thirty thousand florins for Norway. The Church, with its traditionally full coffers, had paid up promptly in full; and the merchant and trade guilds of the cities and towns were well ahead with their collections. It was the lords and barons who were delaying and grumbling, and Thomas was now despatched on a series of visits, to collect, no very enjoyable task, and by no means entirely successful.

There were other problems. The Primate fell ill, and clearly could not face a long sea voyage and a stay in a foreign land; so a substitute prelate had to be found, to negotiate with the Archbishop of Nidaros. In the end Andrew Durisdeer, Bishop of Glasgow, was selected for this delicate duty. Then suitable shipping had to be arranged and prepared, quite a squadron, for it was recognised that this must be an illustrious and numerous embassage, to impress the Norsemen that Scotland was a realm worthy of having their princess as its Queen. These vessels were to be assembled in Leith, the port of Edinburgh; and this involved visits of commissioning and inspection.

It was strange how, without any real debate on the matter, it was assumed almost from the first that Mary would accompany her husband on this great expedition. Even the Lord Boyd saw that it would be advantageous to have the King's sister as one of the envoys – and, to be sure, it was her idea in the first place. For his part, Thomas was not going to be parted from his beloved wife for weeks, possibly months. Moreover, her wits in matters of statecraft had been proved, and might well be very useful in dealing with the Scandinavians.

It was the parting from the infant Jamie which troubled Mary, of course. For she could by no means take the baby with her, she had to admit. So the child had to be weaned at seven months – for it was July before all was ready – and a kindly nurse found for him. Anna would accompany her mistress; but Tom's other and older sister, the Countess of Angus, promised to look after her small nephew, at her husband's seat of Tantallon Castle on the Lothian coast near North Berwick. She had had babies of her own, and so was to be relied upon. But it was going to be a wrench . . .

At length, all was ready, and on 27th July the large concourse set out from Stirling for Leith, the King and a lofty entourage accompanying them to see them off. Mary had had her fraught private parting with little Jamie earlier. It rained, to the disadvantage of all the fine clothing.

After spending the night in Edinburgh Castle, they rode the two miles down to Leith and boarded the five vessels awaiting them in the haven there, where the Water of Leith entered the Forth estuary. James, coming aboard with the voyagers to inspect his sister's ship, declared not for the first time that he wished that he was going with them. This, of course, was not possible, for if King Christian proved uncooperative, or his daughter turned out to be unsuitable for any reason, the presence of the Scots monarch would complicate matters direly.

The vessel, the *Tay Pearl*, from Dundee, although sizeable and stout enough, and cleaned and furnished to best effect, would provide scarcely palatial quarters for a lengthy voyage; but Mary for one did not complain. It was the best, and largest, of the five, at least.

The Arrans' fellow-passengers on this vessel were the Chancellor, Lord Avondale, and the Bishops of Glasgow and Orkney, the latter's position somewhat equivocal since, although he was a Scot, he ranked as a Norse citizen, and paid allegiance to King Christian as well as being a prelate of the Norse Metropolitan, a position all hoped would shortly be amended. But he ought to prove a useful go-between.

James would have lingered aboard, but learned that even kings had to pay homage to tides, and the shipmasters were anxious to be off. So farewells were said, the first time the young monarch had been parted from this sister for any length of time, mooring-ropes were cast off and sails hoisted. That Mary was, in fact, going off to try to find him a wife, hardly seemed to interest him.

For better or for worse, Mary's notion, that time, was being put into practice.

12

Watching the Bass Rock, North Berwick Law and, more important, Tantallon Castle where little Jamie was going to be cared for in the interim, fade from sight, Mary Stewart realised that she had never actually been out of sight of land before, and found it a strange experience, so much that was familiar left behind, so much unknown lying ahead. Not that she in any way dreaded what was to come, indeed she looked forward to it, in the main; but with so much that she held dear left there in Scotland, and always the possibility that she might never see it again, it was a sobering thought. Jamie? Ought she to have left him, have come on this venture . . . ?

Tom, Anna and Patrick seemed to have no such wonderings – whatever Avondale and the bishops might have – their thoughts, questions, hopes, all ahead; although the present featured too, especially for Anna who, as they left the comparatively sheltered waters of the Scotwater, or Firth of Forth, for the wide ocean of the Norse Sea, passing south of the Isle of May, and the ship began to roll and heave, wondered whether her stomach was going to let her down, together with hopes that the ship itself would not do so either.

The shipmaster, a rugged Dundonian named Rob Carnegie, seemed entirely confident at least, his only concern that the present prevailing south-westerly wind, helpful for their sailing, might change into the east and so delay them and entail much tacking to and fro. He was not a little impatient too with one of the other vessels of the little squadron, slower than his own *Tay Pearl*. They had over six hundred miles to go to Copenhagen – where Bishop Tulloch said King Christian would probably be found – and he had reckoned on averaging one hundred miles each twenty-four hours, provided no real storm blew up. But if the ships had to keep together, and some lagged . . .

That first evening, in the low-ceiled stern-cabin which was to be their one public apartment, seeking to adjust their interiors to the motions of the vessel, and none save the much-travelled Bishop of Orkney eating much, Tom sought that prelate's guidance on the strange diversity of the triple Scandinavian kingdom, with its three capitals, and where lay the priority? After all, it was usually called Norway, at least in Scotland, and its inhabitants Norsemen; and this was the Norse Sea. Yet apparently they were heading for Copenhagen, which was the capital of Denmark. Also sometimes Christian was referred to as King of Denmark. And presumably he was King of Sweden also. All very confusing. What was the King's true and preferred style? And where did Finland come in?

Bishop Tulloch agreed that it was difficult. Actually Christian, as former Duke of Schleswig-Holstein, part of Denmark, preferred to be called King of Denmark. Yet Denmark by no means included Norway. And Sweden insisted that it was a separate realm. All making for difficult governing. The terms Norsemen and Danes had been used loosely down the ages to describe the same people, although in fact they were different, but both sea-raiders with, as was to be expected, the more southerly Danes raiding in England and southern Scotland, as well as on the Continent, and the Norse northern Scotland, Iceland, the Isles and Hebrides and Ireland. Yet even so, there was this curious mix-up of names – scarcely to be wondered at perhaps, in that the two nations' warriors looked and sounded so similar, and behaved almost identically. At least the term Jutes had faded, although most of the raiding Danes came from Jutland. Probably the most notable and long-established confusion of the names was that of the Normans. These were not Frenchmen, although they soon adopted the French language, but Norsemen, so called, who had invaded and settled in northern France, yet in fact were Danes from Jutland. So, many of Scotland's leading families, claiming to be of Norman descent, were really of Danish extraction, including the royal Stewarts themselves who, before they came from Normandy and in due course became High Stewards of Scotland and married into the Bruce house, had been Stewards of Dol in St Malo.

The bishop's hearers pondered on all this but were not greatly the wiser.

When they sought their bunks that night, Tom was concerned to find that their vessel did not rise to double beds, with consequent necessary adaption of his nightly procedures, somewhat cramping his style. Mary was patient, even helpful.

The wind, fortunately, stayed in the south-west and the weather was on the whole kind, so that the ships made good time and the passengers could stroll the decks or sit on the sheltered sides of the upper-works. That other vessel, from Dysart in Fife, proved to be something of a laggard, and the *Tay Pearl*'s master frequently had to order shorten sail to allow it to catch up. But otherwise the voyage proceeded uneventfully and pleasantly enough, and stomachs soon accepted the motions of sea and ships, as they sailed into August. There was, of course, an insufficiency of matters for active folk to attend to. Mary was probably the only one embarrassed thereby, in that her husband found love-making a very constant preoccupation.

On the fourth day out there was considerable stir at the sight of land ahead, with congratulations to the shipmaster on the short time taken. But Rob Carnegie was less impressed. Had it not been for the Dysart lugger they could have been this far the day before, he asserted. That was Skagen Head, or the Skaw, the most northerly tip of Denmark. Despite that, they had a long way to go yet, and probably the worst part of the voyage, for round that headland they turned southwards into the Kattegat, the narrow sea between Sweden and Denmark, down which the tides raced as through a funnel, and strewn with islands and reefs, no mariner's delight, one hundred and fifty miles; and then through the tortuous Oresound before they could reach Copenhagen in Zealand.

Indeed, when they rounded that long pointed beak of the Skaw, they felt the difference very promptly, the ships beginning to pitch fore and aft in short, steep seas, with the wind no longer consistent but sweeping this way and that between the land-masses. They were told that in some measure the Kattegat resembled the Hebridean seas, only the land on either side was not mountainous and so there were fewer down-draughts and tidal overfalls; but because this overgrown sound entered the shallow Baltic Sea at the other end, the tidal forces themselves were greater, a deep sea linked with a shallow one.

They had to tack their way down this, winds now less favourable, and, such being the dangers of the waters, they anchored for the night in the sheltered lee of the island of Anholt, till daylight. From there on, the land drew ever closer on each side, and passing the famous Elsinore, at the tip of Zealand, by midday they were in the narrows of the Oresound, now with the Swedish coast as close as the Danish. Through the throat of this, they swung westwards into the bay, really a sea-loch, of Copenhagen, journey over.

If the visitors expected their arrival to cause any stir in the Danish city they were disappointed. No doubt groups of ships were for ever entering Copenhagen harbour, a notably lengthy one, the capital of a great seafaring nation and the principal centre of Baltic trade. They were more or less ignored, even though the *Tay Pearl* flew the royal standard of Scotland at its masthead, until, seeking berthing accommodation amongst the host of shipping already harboured there, a harbour-master's barge came out to enquire their business and docking requirements. The announcement by Bishop Tulloch, in Danish, that they had come from Scotland to visit King Christian, did not seem to make any major impression either, but they were guided through what almost seemed to be the streets of the city, penetrated by the elongated series of docks and basins, to tie up eventually amongst tall warehouses, and there left. A less splendid reception to the sea-king's domains would have been hard to imagine.

Bishop Tulloch was nowise put out, however – presumably ceremony was not a Danish, or Norse, preoccupation. Taking Patrick Fullarton with him, they set out on foot, necessarily, for the Christiansborg Slot, or palace, the King's favourite seat, no great distance off apparently.

The others had some considerable time to wait. And when their emissaries did reappear, it was not on foot or as they had gone, but from behind as it were, and by water. They came in a handsome, long-oared barge, colourful with gold and black paintwork, and in the company of a soberly dressed individual who proved to be the palace chamberlain.

He welcomed them in his King's name, but only briefly, for he did not speak any tongue that they understood, and the bishop had to translate. They were to leave most of their people in the ships here, and only the principals to go, in the barge, to Christiansborg Slot, until accommodation was prepared for the rest, possibly elsewhere.

So there were some decisions to be made as to who should go and who should stay, with certain feathers tending to be ruffled. Eventually a party of about one dozen embarked on the barge and were rowed by a narrow lane-like offshoot, a canal evidently, between two churches and various other buildings, to a suddenly opening area, with its own pier, which proved to be the gardens entrance to a long and massive edifice, somewhat featureless but obviously strong, which appeared to be their destination, Christiansborg Slot, or castle, quite unlike any Scots castle or palace. However plain, and not unlike some of the warehouses they had passed, it was commodious enough and no doubt defensible.

Here the chamberlain led them to a rear wing, facing another canal which acted as a moat. They were shown into a number of rooms, linked by a central passage, all fairly sparsely furnished, the walls hanging with the skins of animals rather than tapestries. They seemed to have these premises to themselves. Servants came with hot water, cold meats and some sort of fiery and potent spirits. They were told that King Christian was to house and would grant them audience in due course.

They were still settling in, awaiting their baggage being brought from the ships, when a big, burly individual, reddish-fair of hair and with a shaggy beard, appeared unannounced, shouting greetings. He came on the two young women first, partly unclad as they were and washing themselves, but seemed no way abashed at that. He hooted laughter indeed, and seemed almost as though he was going to advance and assist at their ablutions, addressing them in a tongue which they did not understand.

Mary was not the one hastily to cover herself up in maidenly modesty and blush, but nor did she flaunt herself.

"Whom do you seek, sir?" she asked. "My lord Earl of Arran is in another chamber." She pointed along the corridor. "With my lord of Avondale and the bishops."

"Ya! Ya!" the big man all but roared. "Beeshops. Lords. From Schottland. Goot! Goot! Womans. Schottishe womans!"

"Yes, sir." Mary gestured along the passage again. "They are there, the lords from Scotland."

But the visitor showed no inclination to leave them. "Goot womans!" he observed appreciatively, observed in more than speech. "Most goot womans."

Anna giggled, following Mary's example and covering up somewhat.

Their approver was only partially distracted by the arrival in the doorway of Tom and Bishop Tulloch. He waved a hand towards the girls, and said something vehement in his own language.

It was the bishop who answered, and bowed low as he did so. It dawned on Mary that this was evidently someone very important.

"His Majesty of Denmark," the prelate added.

Blinking, the young women curtsied.

Christian chuckled and launched into a peroration, pointing at the girls separately, back and forth, apparently comparing attributes. Clearing his throat, the bishop gave an approximate translation, most obviously embarrassed.

"His Majesty declares you beautiful. Both. Variously. He, ah, welcomes you to his realm. I will tell him who you are, Highness . . ."

The King, learning Mary's identity, was but the more appreciative, striding forward to clasp her to him in what amounted to a bear's hug, but an exploratory bear, and planting smacking kisses. Then he did the same for Anna, in slightly lesser degree, as was suitable. Clearly the Danish monarch, whatever else, was not concerned with protocol and keeping royal distance, perhaps a hopeful sign for their mission.

Tom and Avondale were then presented, and Bishop Durisdeer appearing, likewise. The King was affable, but less demonstrative than to the young women. He came back to them, now approximately respectable as to dress, to pat their shoulders with lingering caresses. Then laughing heartily, he headed for the door, shouting back something which Bishop Tulloch said was the command that they would all dine at his table that evening and drink their fill – this last the prelate adding with a little cough.

Thomas declared that he reckoned it as well for Scotland's cause that he had brought his wife along – but that it looked as though he would have to watch the said wife as keenly as any hawk, in this Denmark. Perhaps that was to be his only role.

Later, in a vast dining-hall, they found conditions to be very different from those at home on such an occasion. There was no dais, for one thing, and no waiting for the monarch to appear for, although it was not evident at first in that crowded noisy gathering, Christian was already present, not sitting at any especial top table but at one part way down the hall, amidst a group of almost equally shaggy and hirsute characters, all singing loudly and beating tankards in time on table-tops, whilst three women danced up and down the said table-tops, as others were doing at adjoining tables, skirts lifted high and white legs flashing. There did not seem to be a great many other women present.

156

When servitors with laden trays apprised the King of the newcomers' presence, he rose alone and came to greet them, just a little unsteady on his feet, and bearing straight, or fairly straight, for Mary. He threw an arm around her and all but lifted her off her feet, to propel her onwards to the table he had left, while with the other arm he waved the others on behind him, to thread their way through the seated throng, which was now bellowing acclaim. No standing when the monarch stood here, it seemed, no signs of awe or reverence, but much hearty approval, the table-dancers for the moment neglected.

Mary was carried along to where Christian had been sitting, and there his table companions, right and left, were cheerfully waved up from their benches to go and seat themselves elsewhere, to leave vacant places for the new arrivals. Mary was sat down on the King's immediate right, and turning, he beckoned Anna, not Thomas, to sit on his left. The others could place themselves where they would. Stentorian roars demanded fresh supplies of meat and drink – the which was already, in fact, appearing behind them.

What had been a whole wild boar, roasted, tusked head still attached, was set before them, and with his own knife Christian cut a thick slice from the haunch and presented it straight to Mary's lips on the knife-point, with voluble if unintelligible comments. She dealt with this as best she could, and then, knife transferred to the other hand, she was given the King's slopping tankard to take a drink from. Wary of this last, for she had already sampled the Danish schnapps and found it potent indeed, she took only a sip, to her host's manifest disappointment. But he managed to pat her leg with the knife-hand nevertheless. Then he turned to deal with Anna in similar fashion, if with slightly less large a piece of boar. That one pleased him by gulping a considerably greater mouthful of schnapps.

A roasted goose was then presented to them, and again Christian insisted on dismembering it for them and feeding them portions personally, each bite with the tankard in support, as it were. Now Anna grew more discreet, as she perceived where this could lead.

One of the female dancers came to cavort in front of and above them, skirts kilted, and the monarch, peering upwards, gestured, and to emphasise his point, ran his hand down Mary's thigh. When it came back upwards and seemed to be going to linger,

157

she reached down gently to remove it, but smilingly, one royal hand upon another. The king laughed, and fed her more goose.

That meal lasted a long time, with supplies by no means running out. When the dancers tired, having ever increasing difficulty in stepping amongst the accumulating platters and dishes – and avoiding the clutching hands of admiring diners – they were replaced by jugglers and tumblers, which some of the company sought to emulate disastrously, to produce the greatest hilarity of the entertainment. It was that sort of evening.

With Christian becoming ever more affectionate, Mary, noting that others were rising and leaving the hall intermittently, whether departing or merely going to attend the calls of nature, decided that, since the King had been here before they arrived and did not seem to demand any permission to leave, enough was enough for one night. She told Christian that she was tired, after their long voyaging; then, realising that he had no notion of what she said, reverted to sign-language and, releasing one of her hands from his, put her two palms together, laid her cheek against them in the gesture of sleeping, and closed her eyes. Then she took a quick breath as she recognised that he might well take this as an invitation to join her in bed, and somewhat hastily rose to her feet.

Perhaps the monarch was in fact feeling the effects of the enormous amount of schnapps he had drunk, for he only grinned, put his own hands in approximately the same position, sought to rise and sat down again heavily. Curtsying, Mary signed to Anna to follow, and moved off to pick her way through the throng to the door by which they had entered – having to elude sundry kindly hands in the process, Anna, not entirely sure of her steps and the less elusive, behind. Thomas would no doubt find his own way, in due course. The bishops, she noted, were already gone.

That night the two girls slept together for the first time since Mary's marriage – and if Thomas had any objections, when eventually he arrived back at their quarters from the banquet, he did not voice them, possibly was in no state to do so.

While it might have been expected that the Danish monarch and his advisers would have been disinclined for any early prosecution of business after that evening's entertainment, in fact Bishop Tulloch came to inform Thomas and Avondale in mid-forenoon that King Christian awaited them, to hear the

158

Scots envoys' proposals. Tom, with a sore head, was scarcely ready for this, Avondale likewise; but they could nowise delay. In the circumstances, although it was unusual to say the least, they both felt that Mary should accompany them, her head undoubtedly being clearer than theirs – whatever Christian's reaction might be to a woman's attendance at a council.

In the event, the King clearly approved of a female presence, on this occasion at least when, after a wait outside the council-chamber, the Scots envoys were admitted, to find the Danish councillors not only already assembled, with the monarch, but, having half-empty tankards of schnapps in front of them, looking as though they had been there for some time. Mary recognised some of the revellers of the previous night in the dozen or so men therein. Clearly these Danes had strong heads.

Christian, at council, was not so very different from his normal outgoing and hearty self, hailing Mary with evident satisfaction, although on this occasion he fell short of having her to come and sit beside him at the table. But almost ignoring the men, he shouted welcome and appreciation – at least she assumed that was the case without understanding a word that he said.

This language problem the envoys had insufficiently considered hitherto – save for Bishop Tulloch no doubt. It seemed that none there, save he, knew the other's tongue. So everything would have to be translated by the prelate, with inevitable delays and possible misinterpretations.

Seated round the bottom end of the table, the Scots found brimming tankards placed before them, while their opposite numbers' were refilled. The newcomers were cautious now about schnapps, and merely moistened lips with it.

After a general and somewhat rambling introduction by the monarch which, according to Tulloch thereafter amounted merely that his council was prepared to listen to the Scots proposals, all eyes turned to Thomas, who, as earl and senior envoy, had to lead off. And that man was in something of a quandary. For, so far, they had seen no sign of the Princess Margaret, nor of any of Christian's family – and he was said to have a German wife, Queen Dorothea of Hohenzollern, who indeed had been the widow of his predecessor, King Christopher, and three young sons by her as well as this Margaret. The trouble was, of course, that if the girl was found to be unsuitable, for any reason, to be wed to the King of Scots, misshapen, ugly, lacking in wits or otherwise, these negotiations should not be begun; or at least should be confined to matters financial concerning Orkney and Shetland. But this condition was a difficult one to announce to the princess's father. Tom required a clear head this morning. They had scarcely expected the negotiations to commence quite so soon as this.

So he began by saying that they looked forward greatly to meeting the Princess Margaret of Denmark and, if all was to their mutual satisfaction, returning to Scotland with news of her and of possible marriage settlements, for King James's decision. Whereafter, a second embassage would no doubt come to complete the arrangements. That was the best that he could do at this stage.

The bishop translated equally carefully.

Heads nodded portentously round that table, and Christian looked assessingly, but at Mary rather than at the prelate or Thomas.

A grave-faced elderly individual, the most soberly dressed there, and possibly a cleric, raised voice. He wanted to know, Tulloch said, whether the Scots had brought with them the Northern Isles Annual and arrears? That was sufficiently blunt.

Thomas said that they had brought this year's Annual, yes – thirty thousand florins. Arrears were another matter, and this would require time and consideration.

Features lightened around the table at the mention of those thirty thousand florins, the King nodding his satisfaction. But the grave man lifted a finger. The arrears were of the greatest importance, he insisted, a vast sum now owing. This would have to be dealt with if negotiations were to go ahead. Possibly this individual was Christian's chancellor.

Bishop Durisdeer said that this inherited debt was grievous to both realms. But since it would take considerable time to raise the moneys, it would be most unfortunate if the proposed royal match was put off until further payments were made.

That might be so, the other agreed. But some substantial part of it would be required before decisions could be made.

King Christian caught Mary's eye and grinned cheerfully.

There was a pause. It had not taken long to reach apparent deadlock, despite the apparent amiability of the monarch.

Mary, encouraged by that look, spoke up, quietly but not in any way diffidently. "A wise merchant accepts a fair price for what he has to sell, rather than demanding more than the buyer can pay," she observed. "We are not merchants here, but the principle is sound, is it not? My brother's realm shows its good faith by bringing here the Annual, the first such payment for many years. Even if your princess is not to become Queen in Scotland, the Annual stays with you. That is our pledge. For your part, do you not make some such pledge?"

When that was translated, Christian thumped the table. "Goot! Goot!" he exclaimed.

Most there nodded, but the soberly clad man was not impressed. Thirty years of non-payment of thirty thousand florins amounted to nine hundred thousand florins, he declared flatly.

At mention of such all but astronomical a sum, all present blinked and eyed each other.

Mary mustered a smile. She addressed the King, not the last speaker. "The heavens are high, Sire, and the multitude of the stars uncountable. As is the total of these arrears. And one as unreachable as the other. Such moneys are not to be found in all Scotland. Are they, here in your Denmark?" She did not wait for that to be answered. "There is surely more to this match, this league of the realms, than gold, silver, moneys, to count? Goodwill between the kingdoms. Alliance against the enemies of both. And Orkney and Shetland themselves. These are as a running sore on your realm, Sire, are they not? How much tribute does the Earl St Clair send to you? He imprisoned your bishop, here. Your Majesty could not free him. Or did not. Without warfare and armed men and ships. And have you not other needs for such? Would you not have *that* running sore healed, at the least?"

When Christian got the gist of all that, the effect seemed favourable, however little impact it appeared to make on his evidently principal adviser.

Avondale, the Scots Chancellor, took the matter of the Northern Isles further. "Orkney is a *Scottish* earldom, Your Majesty," he said. "The Earl William St Clair is . . . difficult towards you, as has been said. If, Sire, the earl was deprived of his earldom by our King James, and given another on the Scottish mainland, then would that not much comfort you?" This had been mooted by the Lord Boyd.

The monarch nodded vigorously, but the awkward member of the council looked severe. They required silver florins, not styles, titles, allegiances, he asserted.

Looking from one to the other, Mary, weighing the differences in character which she perceived between monarch and adviser, and making her choice of approaches, produced a tinkling female laugh.

"The Swelkie!" she observed, into the silence.

All eyes turned on her questioningly. That was a Norse word, *svelgr*, even if she pronounced it slightly differently. It meant whirlpool. No translation was needed.

She had these seafarers' interest at once, as she had guessed. "You will all know of the great Swelkie off the island of Stroma, in the Orkneys," she went on. This story she had heard often as a child. "It is famous. There was once a Swedish king named Frodi. He possessed a magical quern, a great hand-mill, which he had found. He called it his Grotti, for groats, grain, which he ground in it, amongst other things. But groats are also coins, are they not? Here, as in Scotland." She waited, while the bishop translated that.

"This Grotti ground silver, gold, as well as grain. But it also brought, or bought, peace for King Frodi, which was indeed its magic. But another sea-king, Mysing, of Denmark, envied Frodi and stole his Grotti. He used it for his own ends, but decided that it would also grind salt, and salt could be sold for much money in lands which had no salt seas. So he took his ships to Orkney, where as all know the sea is more salty than is the Norse Sea, from the Atlantic tides. And there he worked the Grotti. But that man did not know when, or indeed how, to stop it working, on the seas. And the Grotti ground salt in such quantities that it made a great hole in the sea-bed, and the salt filled his ships until they sank and the Grotti with them. They were never seen again. Thus was formed the Swelkie, the famed whirlpool. All because this King of Denmark knew not when to stop, when he had gained a sufficiency."

When the translation ended there was a great shout of acclaim and appreciation from around that table, Christian's the loudest, as he slapped the boards time and again. Mary had calculated aright. These Danes were a race of storytellers as well as seafarers, saga-makers. And here was a telling saga indeed.

The grave-faced cleric looked at the young woman hardly, recognizing that he had lost this battle.

Christian rose, announcing that they had debated sufficiently long for this day, and would consider well what had been said.

Then he came round to Mary, to clasp her to him, chuckling, patting, all but shaking her.

"Swelkie!" he cried. "*Svelgr!* Goot!" He reached down for her still-full tankard, raised it and took a draught, then presented it to her lips, evidently a mark of royal favour in this land, possibly a gesture similar to kissing. She sipped, but only a little, smiling and shaking her head. He emptied the remainder in one vast swallow.

They must all come and eat and drink with him, he declared. In one hour. This as the Scots party left the council-chamber.

"You have that great bear of a king eating out of your hand!" Thomas declared, as they went back to their own quarters. "Only – so long as that is *all* he does! That one would take you, if he might, I swear! You gain us much with him, yes, but do not let him go over-far, wife of mine! Or I see myself as wrecking this mission, and war between Scotland and Denmark!"

"Never fear, jealous one! I think that I have the measure of Christian of Oldenburg. He may be the sea-king here, but I am the daughter of kings also, the Bruce amongst them! I can look after myself. *You* remember that, husband."

"I never forget it, nor am allowed to." He squeezed her arm. "That of the Swelkie was a notable notion. How thought you of it, lass?"

"I was fond of the story in childhood. And reckoned that these are folk for stories. The Norse sagas, Bishop Tulloch says, mean more to them than Holy Writ! And Christian, whatever his name, is of the saga sort, that I am sure. So . . ."

"It served, indeed. And as did the other about merchants and prices to pay. You could be the Scots envoy here, on your own, Mary!"

"Me? A weak woman! Amongst all these fierce sea-rovers?"

"You are a match for them, I say, even though you have belike made an enemy of that man whom Tulloch says is the Danish chancellor. A match – whatever match we reach over Christian's daughter! Which, my dear, I think *you* may be best to enquire of him. When are we going to see the girl? All this may be but wasted effort if she is no worthy bride for James. Where is she? And her mother? This appears to be only a man's court."

"It is difficult to enquire of him when I do not speak his language. Bishop Tulloch would have to be beside us."

"Surely that can be contrived. Perhaps Christian himself would

163

wish him near – some of the time! So that you could know what he says to you, as well as feeling his hands! Ask you when we can see his daughter."

In the lesser hall, and with many fewer men present, again no women save Mary and Anna and no entertainers, they had no difficulty in getting Bishop Tulloch seated close to the King – although the latter still had Mary on one side of him and Anna on the other, so that he could pat and fondle both; but the prelate placed himself at Mary's right and Thomas on Anna's left. So that, in the absence of music, singing and dancing, all in the monarch's group could hear what was said. Schnapps was as much in evidence as heretofore. The Danes seemed to be able to swallow it more or less *ad lib*, largely without effect – unless of course they were all somewhat under the influence of it throughout.

They ate various cold meats, and a sweet which seemed to be composed of almost equal quantities of honey, cream, ground meal and some kind of wine which, potent enough as it tasted to the visitors, evidently required a lot of schnapps to wash it down. Mary again had to do a fair amount of gentle hand-removing and, by her giggles, Anna also.

Choosing her time, Mary asked, through the bishop, when they would have the pleasure of meeting the Princess Margaret? And, to be sure, the Queen Dorothea? She was told that this could be arranged at any time, almost as though it had hardly crossed Christian's mind. His wife and children were presently up at their summer palace of Helsingor, little more than thirty miles to the north – which they would have passed on their voyage here, where the Kattegat narrowed to the Oresound. They could sail there in a few hours. Mary said that they were all eager to see the possible future Queen of Scotland – assuming that all the moneys problems could be settled in mutual acceptance. To which Christian shouted, "Swelkies! Swelkies!" with roared laughter. Which seemed hopeful, at least. He also announced that there would be another banquet that night – which Mary heard without elation. If this was going to be similar to the previous one, she reckoned that the Scots party was going to require a little sleep that afternoon. Although bedding down with Thomas might not be so very restful, even so. Did all these Danes do their sleeping in the afternoon?

All agreed that the sooner they could persuade the King

to take them to Elsinore, or Helsingor as he called it, the better.

After only fairly brief love-making, the Arrans slept – but not before Mary suggested that, to abbreviate the royal advances that evening, if possible, they ought to contrive it so that there was not too much sitting at table for her. Suppose that they offered to demonstrate Scottish dancing to Christian and his folk? Demonstrate, and then perhaps seek to teach? That would get them up and about. Thomas wondered murmurously whether it would not result in still more clutching and fondling, but his wife pointed out that such ought to be spread amongst others, at least.

So, when the Scots presented themselves at the great hall again, and found all approximately as it had been the night before, and eating and drinking already started and table-top dancing again in progress, with the addition this time of dwarfs, both male and female performing antics, Bishop Tulloch, somewhat stiffly, informed the monarch that the visitors wished to contribute to the evening's entertainment by exhibiting Scottish dancing, which might well be rather different from Danish. Christian applauded, indeed seemed as though he could hardly wait. That did not prevent him from showing his usual appreciation of femininity throughout the meal's many courses, however.

When Mary, and even Anna, had had enough of this, she signed to Tom, who rose, and announced the Schottische dance, making an up-arm gesture and jigging his feet. Intrigued, all exclaimed and clapped.

There was a problem, of course. Typical Scots reels demanded multiples of four, eight, or even sixteen. Eight was the usual number, but since it was normal to have male and female partners interchanging, the female quotient here was inadequate. The embassage had brought many lesser members with them to Denmark – indeed, over-many, for it proved difficult to know what to do with them at Christiansborg Slot, and most were still using quarters in the docked vessels and sampling the attractions of Copenhagen otherwhere. There was sufficient here at the palace to provide an eightsome, to be sure, but only Mary and Anna female. It was decided that they should first demonstrate with a foursome, the two young women with Thomas and Patrick; and when the rudiments of the reel were perceived by the audience, some of the female table-dancers would probably pick it up quickly and join in.

Then there was the matter of musical accompaniment. There were fiddlers present, but these would not know the Scots tunes. No doubt these also would pick up the rhythms in due course; but at first there was nothing for it but for the dancers themselves, and their compatriots watching, to hum and sing the appropriate airs, however inexpert might be the vocalists. So the Scots, even the two bishops, about one dozen of them, were assembled in a cleared space, and Mary chose the best repetitive tune for them, having to sing it solo for the first few bars, her efforts nearly drowned out by King Christian's huzzahs of approval. Fortunately, Patrick Fullarton had a strong and tuneful voice, and quickly joined in, Tom's contribution vehement but less melodious. The others, with varying degrees of embarrassment, added their voices, a little raggedly at first, but soon settling to a rousing, sprightly rendering, the beat more important than the melody.

Mary, whose idea all this had been, had come prepared with belts for Anna and herself to hitch up their long skirts, as was necessary – this being greeted with enthusiasm by the onlookers. Then curtsying and bowing to partners, the four timed their start to the appropriate beat of the singers, and commenced their reel, circling first, then toe-and-heel skipping, arms held high, facing partners then linking arms and birling round, before exchanging partners in a figure-of-eight movement abbreviated into four, themselves chanting the tune as they danced, with the two men interspersing their contributions with high-pitched heuchs.

They repeated this sequence twice, with considerable energy displayed, the girls graceful, the men vigorous, until they had to give up their singing for lack of breath. But now the Danes were joining in vocally and beating tankards to the rhythm, so that the Scots singers and hummers were all but eclipsed and the actual air suffered although the beat strengthened and indeed quickened so that the dancers were forced to ever speedier exercise, the young women's bouncing breasts much admired, their hitching up of skirts likewise.

At length, panting, Mary called a halt and found much of their audience now on their feet, laughing and shouting and jigging in all but elephantine fashion, King Christian foremost. He came to Mary to hug her to him, kiss her comprehensively and seek either to still or to encourage her bosom, which was not clear.

Enthusiasm reigned.

Some of the table-dancers had now descended to the floor and were skipping about, and Mary managed to detach herself from the sea-king to beckon these to her and, still distinctly breathless, demonstrate the footwork involved – which they speedily picked up. Selecting two of them, she beckoned forward two more of the Scots party, to make up an eightsome. At the same time, Tom was guiding the fiddlers to produce an approximate version of the tune.

Out of all this the largest, longest and most detailed reel was attempted, distinctly chaotic as it proceeded but enjoyed by all, impromptu copies of it developing all around, the heuching yells in especial being highly popular.

This effort did not so much finish as deteriorate into a laughing, stumbling riot of limbs and persons, the schnapps undoubtedly contributing. All but exhausted, the original four gasped for rest.

But they reckoned without the monarch. Christian was agog to try his footwork and, more especially, his handwork, and nothing would do but that a number of eightsomes should be formed up, with himself, Mary, Anna and two of the table-dancers added to Thomas, Patrick, and of all individuals, Master Martin Vanns, Grand Almoner to King James, one of the deputation, a middle-aged but nimble cleric. Four circles were contrived – the available space would not hold more – and the fiddlers and singers ordered to strike up.

What followed all but beggared description: enthusiasm, Danish spirits of both sorts, and lack of room contributing to produce uproar, pandemonium and turmoil. Yet joy of an utterly uninhibited and deafening variety prevailed, whilst all semblance of eightsome reels disappeared, and whirling, leaping, tripping bodies gyrated, males clutching females to them, often with the latter's feet off the floor and clothing apt to become distinctly disarranged. Mary, seeking to keep Christian from complete possession of her person, wondered whether *this* notion of hers had indeed been a good one. Anna, with commendable self-immolation, did come to her aid, to Patrick's concern.

But even sea-rovers can tire, especially after a heavy meal, and these two young women managed to abstract themselves, and all but collapsed back at their places at table, restoring their clothing as best they could – not that the Danish ladies seemed to trouble themselves about that. They were even glad to gulp down some schnapps.

Schottische dancing was everywhere voted a major success.

The Scots party, or the loftier section of it, effected their escape shortly afterwards when the King left without any announcement, no doubt for the relief of nature. Moving off, Thomas observed that his wife was better at devising statecraft than evening entertainment. Mary rather agreed, but did not admit it. This night's cantrips would do their negotiations no harm, she contended, the Scots' popularity enhanced. There were more ways of winning their way than by bargaining over florins.

13

Whether out of this appreciation for the Scots or otherwise, they did not know; but Bishop Tulloch informed next morning that King Christian had to perform some duty that day at the town of Roskilde, some twenty-five miles to the west, but would take them to Helsingor the day following to meet his wife and children. They would sail there in the King's own ship. So they had a free day, and the bishop suggested a tour round Copenhagen. Mary was relieved to hear that there would not be another banquet that night.

They went exploring the city therefore, on foot and in holiday mood, walking its narrow streets, many of which were in fact also quaysides, for the town was honeycombed with docks and mooring-places, ships' masts and spars being as much part of the skyline as were tall gabled buildings. They crossed its canals by bridges, examining the traders' stalls and booths and sampling their wares, the bishop a competent guide. Meeting the people interested them, their interest obviously returned. Their identity presumably would be known, as some of the Scots from the five vessels which had descended upon their community. It was good to have a day free of responsibilities.

The following forenoon they were led down to board the royal ship, flying all sorts of flags and banners, something between a galley and a galleon, two-masted with great decorated sails but also with banks of long oars or sweeps. King Christian was already aboard, and welcomed them with schnapps, loud salutations and cries of "Swelkies!" Mary suspected that he might indeed think of her under that name, and was doubtful of being identified with any sort of whirlpool – although Tom made the inevitable comment about deep women in whom men could founder and drown.

It was the oars which had to be used to get the vessel out of the narrow waters of the canal and harbourage; but once the open sound was reached, the sails were hoisted and they headed almost due northwards in fine style before a south-westerly breeze.

They were never far from shores – they could not be, for this Oresound was nowhere more than a dozen miles wide, and narrowing as they proceeded. So Christian was able to point out landmarks on both the Danish and the Swedish sides, the Swedish city of Landskrona and the Danish towns and havens of Hellerup and Skodsborg and Rungsted. Then they were passing the long, low island of Ven, with the sound now beginning to close in to its bottleneck to the Kattegat, this dominated by their destination, Elsinore, on the one side and the Swedish Helsingborg on the other. It was well seen here why Swedes, Norsemen and Danes had become almost interchangeable terms.

The castle of Elsinore, really called Marienlyst, as distinct from the town, was dramatically sited on a cliff above the narrows, based on what had been a Viking fort, tall and challenging, the town a little way behind. There was a sheltered anchorage and good harbour below the cliffs, for this was a ferry terminal for one of the main Swedish crossings, the shortest, and there was much shipping. But there was a special royal quay where their vessel tied up, almost directly under the castle.

They could see a curling, round-about road to give access to the fortalice-palace; but there was also a steep flight of steps, largely cut in the naked rock, and down this, before berthing was completed, they saw two children come running, a boy and a girl, waving. The King's ship, with all its banners, would have been recognisable from up there for some time.

"Hans! Margrete!" Christian announced proudly, and bellowed a greeting.

So, presently, at the gangway-foot, the visitors made the acquaintance of her whom they had come all the way from Scotland to see, Margrete Christiansdotter, aged twelve years, standing beside her eight-year-old brother Hans – and relief was undoubted. For the girl, although not beautiful, was well built, open-featured and smiling, calling vehemently to her father, no handicaps in evidence. The boy was sturdy, stolid, unsmiling, probably shy.

The King caught them both up, one under each arm, laughing uproariously, bringing them kicking and wriggling to present them to the Scots, Margaret squealing, Hans looking away. Presumably they were used to this sort of treatment.

170

The envoys could scarcely pay suitable respects to the Prince and Princess of Denmark in the circumstances. They did their best.

Set down, the youngsters showed much less interest in the visitors than these did in the girl, being obviously determined that their father took the steep stairway up to the castle rather than the coiling roadway, seeking to pull him thence, Margaret laughingly. She seemed to be a normal, happy and uncomplicated creature, which was a comfort.

The monarch was evidently easily persuaded by his offspring, and the party found itself forced to tackle the taxing and dizzy-making ascent of the cliff, arriving at the top eventually breathless. Here they met Queen Dorothea, a strange, stern-faced woman to be the wife of the ebullient Christian, silent, reserved. It seemed that the daughter took after her father rather than her mother – which might be as well for young James Stewart.

This castle was nothing like so commodious as Christiansborg, nor prepared for entertaining large numbers of incomers, and it was discovered that the King intended to stay only for one night. With but two or three of his councillors with him here, it seemed that there was to be no negotiating of terms on this visit.

That evening, after a good meal but no banquet, Bishop Durisdeer reminded Thomas of the second objective of the embassage: that was to see the Norwegian Metropolitan, Archbishop of Nidaros, to seek to transfer the Orkney see to Scotland and if possible to persuade him to relinquish Metropolitan claims over the Scottish Church. This matter was very dear to Primate Graham's heart, and he had given Durisdeer authority to offer quite substantial Church moneys as recompense. Here, at Elsinore, they were only three miles from the Swedish coast, and Norway just to the north. He was not sure just where Nidaros was, but it seemed an opportunity to deal with this matter now and save time hereafter.

They debated this. Thomas was agreeable, but felt that this was a matter for churchmen, not for such as himself. He should stay with King Christian and seek to work on him to come to suitable terms for the marriage settlement, which, now that they had seen the young princess, should go ahead. And he would require Bishop Tulloch as interpreter. So . . .

Glasgow's bishop accepted that. He would go on to Nidaros on his own, and deal with the archbishop adequately enough –

for all senior clerics must have the Latin, and they could converse in that language. Only . . . He glanced over at Mary. Only – if Her Highness would be prepared to come with him, he felt that it would be a major help. She had proved her keen wits and persuasive powers, and might well be a very useful influence with the Metropolitan. Also would give himself added authority, as the Scots King's sister. Would the princess accompany him?

Thomas was not at all keen on this suggestion, but Mary was quite agreeable – if she indeed could be of any help in an important matter for Scotland. She would quite like to visit Norway, and she would be prepared to escape Christian's further attentions and banquets for a space.

Next morning they put the matter to the King. He said that they would be foolish to cross to Sweden here, and thereafter travel by land. In his realms, all journeying was done by sea, as far as was possible. Trondheim, where the archepiscopal see of Nidaros was situated, was fully five hundred sea-miles from the southern tip of Norway, Lindesnes, and there was no point in travelling up through Sweden. Besides, the Norse land was mountainous and cut into by innumerable fjords, over and round which they would have to make their way. Much better to sail in one of their own ships, from Copenhagen to Trondheim Fjord, in three or four days, not weeks.

Presently, then, they all took their leave of the Queen and her children, well satisfied with their visit, and sailed back whence they had come.

Rob Carnegie was quite happy to make a diversionary voyage to Trondheim, for he was having difficulty in keeping his idle seamen in order amongst the varied delights of Copenhagen. A couple of days later, then, the *Tay Pearl*, with Mary and Anna, Bishop Durisdeer and King's Almoner Vann, set sail once more northwards up the Oresound, now becoming a familiar waterway. They did not take any of the escorting vessels with them. Undoubtedly there was a certain amount of disappointed masculinity left behind them, also.

Through the Elsinore narrows again, and up the Kattegat, to round the Skaw into the Skagerrak they went, and there, finding themselves now facing into the prevailing westerly breeze, had to start tacking back and forth. This continued for fully one hundred miles, until they could round what Carnegie called the Naze and

Christian had named Lindesnes, the very southern point of long Norway. This, of course, much delayed them, but once round the great headland, with the wind astern, they made excellent time up the Norse coast.

And what a coastline that was. Mary had heard that it was not unlike their own Hebridean seaboard, but now saw that it was very different, mountains cut into by sea-lochs, here known as fjords, offshore islands by the hundred and skerries and reefs by the thousand, yes; but the mountains were steeper, barer, harder, the fjords narrower and darker, the islands rockier, less sand-fringed, the whole less colourful; but dramatic, spectacular. And it went on and on, seemingly endless.

For three days and nights thereafter they sailed up that extra-ordinary coastline, ever aware of its domination, of the effect of sun and shadow and cloud on those fierce, riven mountains and savage landscapes, where rock and sea seemed to battle eternally. They perceived no towns or settlements – presumably any such were hidden within the fjords; there appeared to be little if any coastal plain and few trees, even heather and the like, only soaring dark stone and white water and spray. Possibly some of the myriad islands supported inhabitants, but since they wisely kept well clear of these and their defending reefs and skerries, they saw no sign of humanity. The nights were short here, at this time of year, even shorter than in Scotland, for they were considerably further north now, drawing level with Iceland; so the travellers saw a sufficiency of that seaboard and wondered at it, recognising how it had produced a race of fierce sea-warriors, the Vikings.

The young women wondered also as to how Rob Carnegie knew where he was going, for this endless succession of great headlands, soaring peaks and chasm-like fjords, behind their screen of islands, was seemingly unchanging. How to know when they reached Trondheim Fjord? The shipmaster assured them that, although he had never been here before, he had had adequate directions. When the coastline eventually began to bend away eastwards consistently, they would find the mountains drawing back noticeably, and soon thereafter there would be three large islands quite close together, Smola, Hitra and Froya. Immediately beyond this last the Trondheim Fjord opened and they turned in.

It was the afternoon of the fourth day out that they came to three much larger islands than most that they had seen, and perceived the mountains indeed sinking into hills and greenery becoming evident on the slopes. The girls had not realised that the land had begun to trend eastwards, but the shipmaster had discerned it. Round the tip of Froya the *Tay Pearl* swung at right angles and faced the hidden entrance of a fjord wider than most they had seen hitherto.

Even so, that waterway was very different from most Highland sea-lochs, deep, dark and growing darker as the mountains into which it probed closed in again. It twisted and coiled also, so that it was seldom possible to see more than a mile or two ahead or behind. And it went on and on. Carnegie told them that Nidaros was said to be thirty miles up, no less, although perhaps only half that as the eagles might fly from the sea. Mary said, was it not an extraordinary place to site the ancient Norwegian capital? He agreed, but pointed out that probably defensively it could scarcely be bettered – and it was a sea-raiders' capital. In the old Viking days this fjord could be barred to invaders at a score of places. He was told that they used to have great chains across, which could be raised from under water to prevent shipping from getting past. And presumably there was some more level and fertile ground beyond these mountains.

Some fifteen miles up they found a narrow bay, at a bend in the fjord, in which to anchor for a few hours of night – for navigating these coiling straits in darkness would be hazardous indeed. After the great seas' motions of their voyage, it was strange to lie quietly in that black abyss amongst the beetling cliffs, the only sound being the faint roar of cascading waterfalls, of which they had passed dozens.

But in the morning, quite quickly they came to a major widening in their waterway, a great basin where branching arms opened into the lessening and retiring heights, and a notable river came in from the south, the Nid apparently, from which the town took its name. It would be an exaggeration to call the surrounding area any sort of plain, but it was the nearest to such that the travellers had seen since leaving the Swedish coast. There were meadowlands, low, swelling green hills, woodlands and cultivation patches, farmeries and a town of sorts which seemed to crouch under two great dominating buildings, a cathedral and a castle, the former unlikely seeming in such a situation.

When their vessel, approaching this inhabited area, rounded

a small peninsula, it was to find a harbour, behind a sea-wall, with jetties and quays and a neighbouring boat-strand for fishing boats. A number of ships were tied up here, but none so large as their own. Mary still thought it a strange place to be the capital of Norway.

They had some difficulty as to mooring, for the harbour-master and his men could speak only their own tongue, not being clerics. So much sign-language, gesticulation and shouting ensued; but Bishop Durisdeer, pointing up at the cathedral and pronouncing the name of St Olav and that of Magnus, which was apparently the archepiscopal name, eventually gained them permission to dock and land.

Watched by interested peasantry and fisherfolk and barked at by dogs large and shaggy, the bishop's little party started to climb up towards that extraordinary cathedral.

It was unlike any of the abbeys or churches of Scotland, massive, many-gabled, with pointed roofs and little spires. The castle was nearby, crowning another knoll, presumably the archepiscopal palace.

In some doubt as to which edifice to make for, the question was resolved for them by the appearance of a group of men coming down towards them, in no sort of style or order but looking enquiring. Foremost amongst them was a stocky, thick-set, square and elderly man, notably short of leg and long of arm, in nondescript clothing but with a silver crucifix hanging on a chain at his breast.

"Some sort of churchman," Bishop Andrew observed. "He should be a guide, if he knows the Latin." He held up an arm in greeting, and addressed the approaching party in that tongue, to the effect that they were a mission from Scotland seeking the Archbishop of Nidaros.

The answer was brief indeed, although in clear Latin. "I am Magnus," the thick-set man said. The young women, no Latinists, understood that.

They all tried to hide their astonishment. Anyone less like a prelate, let alone an archbishop and Metropolitan of the North, would have been hard to imagine; but from the way he declared it, this could be no other Magnus, common name as that was in Scandinavia.

Durisdeer and Master Vanns bowed hastily and sought to introduce themselves with suitable respect, the one saying that

175

he was the Bishop of Glasgow, before hastily amending that to mention first the Princess Mary, Countess of Arran, sister to King James of Scots, before reverting to himself and to Vanns as King's Almoner, representing the Primate of the Scottish Church, Patrick, Bishop of St Andrews. He did not trouble to introduce Anna.

The archbishop seemed nowise impressed, but smiled amiably at the ladies. He welcomed them to Nidaros, whatever the reason for their visit. Evidently he was a man of few words.

The effect, of course, was to make Bishop Andrew the more voluble. He explained that they were part of a larger embassage to King Christian, at Copenhagen, concerned with the proposed marriage of his daughter to the King of Scots; but that *his* especial mission was over the see of Orkney and the position of the Scottish Church, matters of concern for His Eminence. The bishop used that style somewhat doubtfully. It might relate only to cardinals? Was a Metropolitan archbishop of similar rank? He had never encountered one before. And Eminence did seem an odd title for this very unecclesiastical-looking individual. This as they all made their way uphill towards the castle, not the cathedral.

Where the roadways divided, Archbishop Magnus took Mary's arm, to guide her into the right-hand track – and retained his grip. That young woman was beginning to recognise that this was an effect she seemed to have on the other sex, why she was not sure; she certainly did not deliberately intend to captivate, although she liked men, or most men.

Bishop Durisdeer, who had not been notably loquacious hitherto on their embassage, now appeared to be impelled to speech, possibly on account of the need for careful Latinity. This was hardly the moment to launch into details of their mission and proposals, but he all but did so, the more so seemingly as he got little response from the other man. Mary, whose Latin was scanty indeed, did seek to help the bishop's so evident discomfort by interjecting a few halting words of goodwill and greetings of her own – which produced only a nod of the greying head and a squeeze of the arm, perhaps sufficient response. Almoner Vanns tried out a phrase or two on some of the other men there, and did get a reply in Latin – so possibly these also were clerics. Perhaps churchmen in Norway did not dress differently from other folk normally?

Thus they came to the castle on its hillock, no very palatial residence but strong enough. There the girls were handed over to a cheerful, motherly woman, presumably some sort of housekeeper, who conducted them to a tower wing of the fortalice, somewhat bare as to furnishings, but where two maids presently appeared to cater for their needs. Evidently there was no custom of excluding women from ecclesiastical establishments here. These spoke no Latin, so it was all a matter of smiles and gestures.

Mary and Anna wondered what they had let themselves in for. They had not anticipated anything like this.

They were, in fact, left to themselves for a considerable time, although log-fires were lit for them in their tower and ample food and drink provided. Eventually Bishop Andrew found his way to them, and seemed considerably more like himself. These Norsemen, although peculiar, were none so ill, he observed. They behaved very differently from the Scots clergy, or such English as he had met, and the archbishop was an oddity indeed. But they were nowise hostile and might well be prepared to negotiate. Clearly, for an archbishopric, this one was very poor in worldly goods. This castle showed it; and while he had not yet been over to the cathedral, he could even from a distance distinguish signs of neglect. So – moneys might speak quite loudly here.

He had established relations with one a deal more forthcoming than Archbishop Magnus, whom he took to be an archdeacon or the like, named Sverre. From him he had learned quite a lot, in a general way. This church of St Olav was the first Christian shrine to be established in Norway, just prior to the year One Thousand After Christ, by King Olav Tryggvesson, who adopted the faith, demoting Thor, Odin and the rest as the Norse gods. A descendant, St Olav Harroldsson, had had it raised into an episcopal see, and built the cathedral, the first archbishop being appointed in 1150. How the Norse had achieved this Metropolitan status when the Scots could not was unexplained. But certainly now there was a lack of endowments. If the country they had passed on the way here was typical of the rest of Norway, the lack of wealth was not to be wondered at. Where the other bishoprics were, how many and how rich, was not clear either. But Bishop Andrew was hopeful that what they had to offer would not be unwelcome.

Later, a visit was paid to the cathedral, the young women included. Although very different from Glasgow, St Andrews and Dunblane, the only such Mary had seen, or the great abbeys of Melrose, Dryburgh, Jedburgh, Arbroath and the like, it was a noble and imposing building in its own way, lofty, many aisled, roofing at a great variety of levels, the stonework well carved with curious effigies, gargoyles and masks, the ceilings all vividly painted. But the said paintwork was stained and peeling, the roofing leaked most obviously, and lack of due upkeep was not far to seek. The archbishop had not accompanied the visitors; they could see why.

Magnus was present at the meal in the castle which followed, no banquet but a very adequate repast of soup, venison, beef, salmon and curds, with the inevitable schnapps. Magnus did not behave as did King Christian, but he did seat Mary at his right hand and obviously approved of her. There was no real conversation, of course, but some rapport was mutual.

Instead of dancers and performing dwarfs they were entertained thereafter by grotesquely garbed skalds, reciters and singers; and although the words were unintelligible to the visitors, the scene in the torch-lit hall was memorable, strange.

The young women discussed all this that night in bed, much intrigued. But they missed their menfolk.

In the morning they went, on foot necessarily, exploring the neighbourhood, whilst Bishop Andrew and Almoner Vanns commenced their negotiations with the archbishop and his aides. The houses here were all of wood, which seemed strange in a country with so much stone available, the people interesting and interested, not unfriendly, the fisherfolk, their boats, nets and gear very similar to those of Scotland.

They were astonished when they got back to the castle to discover that all was finished, arranged, and successfully. Archbishop Magnus had been simplicity itself to negotiate with, indeed he seemed to have looked upon the Scots as a God-send. Not that he was soft or lacking in wits; but clearly he and his desperately needed money, and it had been only a question of how much. The Orkney diocese had sent him nothing for years, and was unlikely ever to do so. Lordship over it was purely nominal. So he had been quite prepared to cede it to the Scottish Church, for suitable recompense. And once that was accepted the matter of Metropolitan status lost any point. Magnus had wanted extra payment for his agreement to write to the Pope to that effect, and to suggest that the bishopric of St Andrews in Scotland be raised to an archbishopric, and its Primate incumbent made a Metropolitan. A certain amount of bargaining had ensued over that, but in the end ten thousand florins had settled the deal.

Bishop Graham back at home, whose great ambition this had been for years, would be joyous indeed. They could now return to Copenhagen, without delay, next day perhaps.

The return voyage lasted longer than the outward one, with the south-westerly breeze still prevailing and therefore almost continuous tacking necessary, but none there grumbled. They had completed their mission in much less time than had been anticipated, and achieved their ends. Not that Mary Stewart felt that she had contributed anything on this occasion.

Back at Christiansborg Slot they discovered matters to be proceeding less speedily but not unsatisfactorily. The proposal that the Princess Margaret should wed King James, if found suitable, had been more or less agreed in advance; Mary did not fail to note that her *brother*'s suitability was more or less taken for granted. These negotiations, again, were mainly about finance and material things. In royal marriages it was customary to provide substantial settlements, portions, dowries, on both sides, and such could vary greatly depending upon the wealth of the nations concerned. Clearly, however impressive the triple kingdom of Denmark, Norway and Sweden might sound, it was far from rich in money. King Christian had to spend large sums on keeping up what amounted to an army of occupation in rebellious Sweden. Moreover, he had made a policy of buying extensive lands in his native Schleswig-Holstein, to the south. So his treasury was even emptier than that of Scotland. Yet national pride and face-saving demanded a high-sounding exchange on both sides.

So while Thomas and Avondale came to agreement with Christian on principles without much difficulty, details were holding up final decisions, details of money, florins, basically, or the King's lack of these. He could nowise offer some tiny sum which would look feeble and unworthy. The Scots, being realists, did not look for large amounts, even if they seemed to do so; but they *were* interested in the ownership of the Orkney and Shetland isles, however unexpressed had to be this aim. They had got the length of agreeing to a nominal dowry on Denmark's part of sixty thousand florins, ten thousand to be paid forthwith, the rest forthcoming when possible; also the cancellation of all the

Orkney and Shetland arrears. In return, the Scots would give the palace of Linlithgow to the new Queen, with the castle of Doune of Menteith, and the revenues of all the lands pertaining – these to remain hers even if her husband should die before her. Also she was to enjoy the revenues of one-third of all the royal lands in the event of James's death, so long as she remained in Scotland and did not remarry the King of England or one of his subjects. Moreover, each monarch obliged himself to go to the aid of the other against all parties other than already made allies.

Thus far they had got, it seemed. The trouble was, it had become evident that at present Christian just could not raise the advance payment of ten thousand florins, despite the thirty-thousand Annual the Scots had brought him – and which presumably had been used at once to pay off pressing debts. Orkney and Shetland had not yet been brought up as a kind of surety, hinted at but ignored by Christian and his advisers.

Thomas was obviously very glad to see Mary back so soon, and not only for her person. He wanted her advice as to how to force Christian's hand over Orkney; it had been her suggestion in the first place, after all.

She pointed out that the Church's successful mission to Nidaros ought to help in this matter, to give Christian some saving of face, as his churchmen had already shown the way. She recognised that the actual secession of national territory was not easy for any monarch to grant; but Orkney and Shetland were far away and of little real value to Denmark. Some device was necessary to enable Christian to swallow this indigestible morsel not too painfully.

Tom impatiently asked did she think that he had not perceived this all along? But – what?

This of the ten thousand florins which Christian could not presently find, she suggested? Was he trying to raise it right away? And they waiting here for it?

Her husband agreed that this was more or less the situation. How long it would take, the good Lord alone knew.

Then, was not that the answer, she put to him? *Not* to wait; at least, not all of them. Leave quickly, before he could raise it. Say that it was necessary to return to Scotland for instructions, with even one-sixth of the dowry not forthcoming. Leave some of the party here, to show that negotiations were not actually broken off. Then come back later, with the outright request for Orkney and

Shetland as wadset and assurance of full payment? Would that not save all faces?

The man considered that, and then slapped his knee. "I believe that you have it, lass! As ever! To go home, and then back, with this demand. As though from King James himself. Keep Christian unsure meantime. Waiting. Even if he has raised the ten thousand by then, he will not have the rest, the other fifty thousand. Nothing more sure. Demand – or request – the Orkneys in pledge for that. Mary, my heart – bless you!" He hugged and kissed her.

"I serve you as best I can, husband," she observed. "Otherwise than you serve me, to be sure!"

"What mean you by that?"

"I mean that I think that I am pregnant again. Indeed, I am sure of it . . ."

"Glory be! Another of us! Here's joy. A girl, this time. When . . . ?"

"January, I would think."

"Then the sooner that we get you home, the better, lass. Before winter storms commence."

"It is only late summer, Tom. And I am no delicate creature. But, yes – for this of Christian and Orkney, yes. Soon . . ."

"Christian is going to miss you!"

14

They left Lord Avondale, Almoner Vanns and Bishop Tulloch at Copenhagen, and with Bishop Andrew, *his* duty done, set sail in the *Tay Pearl* a few days later, King Christian seeing them off amidst lamentations as hearty as the rest of him. But he would see them again . . .

The voyage home was much slower, again, than on the outward passage, heading into those westerly winds, but was otherwise uneventful, no actual storms encountered – save, oddly, when they entered the Scotwater, off the Isle of May, and there ploughed into heavy seas. This, Rob Carnegie informed, was not uncommon, with the Norse Sea's deep waters suddenly meeting the shelf of Scotland, and the tides spouting upwards.

They docked at Leith, and the Arran party went ashore, to hire horses for Stirling, while the *Pearl* took Bishop Andrew across to Fife, to report success to the Primate at St Andrews.

They all found it good to be in the saddle again, horses appearing to be but little used in Scandinavia where, like the West Highlands, most travel was done by water. They had been away little more than two months, but it seemed longer.

Their reception at Stirling Castle was varied. James and his brothers and sister were delighted to see them; but the Lord Boyd, who seemed preoccupied, was clearly disappointed that they had returned lacking final results.

No major developments appeared to have taken place during their absence. James complained that it had been very dull at Stirling without them, Lord Boyd not having let him do much hunting or hawking, indeed not allowing him to leave the castle much at all, and then only under strict and numerous guard. There had been very little interesting company, and altogether life had been dreary. He wished that he had been allowed to go to Denmark with them. They ought to have arranged it. He would have liked to have visited those lands. He asked them, now, for details as to the places and peoples visited – but Mary noted that he seemed quite uninterested as to details regarding his prospective bride.

In their own bedchamber that night, Tom told her that he was a little concerned about his father. They had never been close in any affectionate way, indeed his sire was not a man to show emotion or reveal himself. But now he was more withdrawn than heretofore, something most evidently on his mind. And clearly he was upset that they had not brought back a definite decision about Orkney and Shetland, and the assertion that it would all probably come right in due course not enough for him. Which was strange, for the matter of the Northern Isles was not, after all, of first priority for the ruler of Scotland.

The Arrans' first need, of course, was to visit Tantallon Castle, not so far from the mouth of the Scotwater where they had encountered the high seas, to see and collect the baby Jamie, whom his mother had greatly missed. They found the child well and developed notably in the interval, a joy to behold. Indeed Tom's sister Elizabeth was loth to relinquish him to his parents.

There followed, by royal command, a period of very active, almost continuous, hunting, hawking and riding abroad, in golden October weather, James determined to make up for the inaction of the summer months; and Mary, recognising that her condition would soon forbid such, prepared to humour him, Thomas, Anna and Patrick nothing loth. The Flanders Moss and the Tor Wood, in particular, saw a lot of them. Lord Boyd made no objection, so long as the King was available morning and night to sign his decrees and charters. The fact that he had not been allowed to go before, when Tom was away, looked as though he had been afraid for the monarch's safety, or at least security. An escort always had to go with them still, of course.

The first hint they had as to what was wrong with the Lord Boyd came from that man's brother – not Sir Alexander, who seemed to be acting the recluse now down on his Dumfries-shire property of Duncow in Nithsdale – but from the Abbot of Kilwinning. With Lord Avondale, the Chancellor, away in Denmark, it seemed that Boyd had had the abbot appointed acting Chancellor, so he had had to come not infrequently to Stirling – although, in fact, the elder brother was more or less governing Scotland single-handed. So perhaps his preoccupation was not to be wondered at. But possible trouble was building up, according to Abbot William, against the regime. Always, of course, there had been those hostile in some degree to the Boyd hegemony; but now there were rumours of meetings and associations, possibly indicating more positive reaction, with the King's two illegitimate uncles, the Earl of Atholl and Sir James Stewart of Auchterhouse, apt to figure the most prominently. Moreover, some who had formerly been close supporters of Boyd were now beginning to absent themselves from court, notably the Lords Somerville and Hailes. This was worrying for the Regent, and would account for much.

The abbot added that it was a pity that the Orkney and Shetland secession had not been brought to a satisfactory conclusion as yet, for the acquisition of these territories for Scotland would constitute quite a major credit for the regency, and help to damp down hostility. He, the abbot, urged Thomas to return to Denmark as quickly as possible, and bring back the good news, together with the royal bride. Such development would undoubtedly much improve his father's position.

Tom saw that, but nevertheless was not going to rush away. More important to him than any such matters of state was Mary's care and well-being. He just was not going back to King Christian until he had seen his wife safely delivered of their second child. Besides, winter was no time to make crossing of the Norse Sea. There was no shaking him on this; and Mary of course supported him.

In November they paid a visit to Arran, before the worst of the weather set in, James not permitted to accompany them on this occasion, to his vehement protests. All went well otherwise, Patrick happy to see his parents again, and with so much to tell them. That young man had developed considerably in the interim, in manners, in self-confidence, as esquire to the Earl of Arran. He had still not become any typical courtier, but association with such had given him a polish and assurance. Anna had had quite a lot to do with that also, undoubtedly. Almost certainly they were lovers, as well as firm friends; indeed Mary had more than once caught them in all but compromising situations. But it was certain that the Regent would not countenance his under-age daughter's marriage to someone as lowly as an Arran laird's son, and their association had to remain a private one. Both were of a cheerful and uncomplicated nature, however, and prepared to accept such satisfactions as were available meantime.

The Arran interlude was enjoyed by all, although Mary was suffering some pregnancy discomfort now.

On their return to Stirling and James's grumbles against the Regent, it was not long before the Yuletide preparations were afoot, concurrently with preoccupations with Mary's forthcoming delivery, which looked like happening earlier than anticipated, with more disturbance to her normal way of life than on the previous occasion. Thomas wondered whether all the voyaging might have been responsible for this?

In the event, Christmas festivities still ongoing, on the last day of 1468, the child was born, after a prolonged and difficult labour. It was, as Thomas had required, a girl, to be called Grizel. The baby was small but exquisite, perfectly formed and a delight to behold. Mary, although weak, rejoiced.

Lord Boyd was already pressing Thomas to return to Denmark without delay to finalise the royal marriage negotiations, brushing aside his son's assertions of the dangers of winter's storms for voyaging. But Tom did not lack Boyd willpower, and was determined not to leave until he was assured of his wife's full recovery and the new infant's good progress. There was no question, in the circumstances, of Mary going with him this time, much as she would have liked to do so.

It was not until the beginning of March that Thomas felt that he could put off no longer. Carnegie and the *Tay Pearl* had been on stand-by for weeks, on the Regent's orders, and this time they came up-Forth as far as Blackness, the port for Linlithgow, to collect the travellers, this to ensure a shorter journey from Stirling, so that the two young women might ride there to see them off, this even so Mary's longest spell on horseback since the birth.

The parting was not exactly tearful but reluctant indeed, much reassuring required on both sides, although it was not anticipated that the young men would be gone for very long this time, Tom's instructions being to bring back the princess quickly even though little or none of the dowry money was forthcoming. The bride, and the mortgage of Orkney and Shetland, were what was important, vital, now, for the Lord Boyd. Haste was the embassage's watchword.

They had to await the tide at Blackness, so far up Forth, so that farewells were protracted as well as exacting, at the royal fortress there, which frequently was used as a state prison, a fairly grim establishment. Thereafter, the girls waved and waved as the ship drew out into the estuary, even after they could no longer distinguish their men waving back, loth even to turn their backs when the *Pearl* was small-seeming indeed. Denmark then seemed to them a long way off, and sea-voyaging much more hazardous when they themselves were not going along. It was almost an ordeal to turn their beasts round for the twenty-five-mile ride back to Stirling.

15

In the months that followed, Mary had no lack of preoccupations other than wondering how her husband fared. With two little ones to nurture and cherish, and a very discontented royal brother to cope with, as well as a distinctly uneasy air about the court, and rumours of the regime's growing unpopularity amongst the lords and magnates, she had a sufficiency to concern her.

James was going through a difficult stage. He was now seventeen and beginning to wish to act the man, and, to be sure, the King. And Lord Boyd was not in any way conceding this, yielding no iota of his powers and authority as Regent, nor even making any superficial gestures of subservience towards the young monarch. Which was folly, to be sure, when others were doing so, for it would serve his cause nothing to make an enemy of his liege-lord who, in a year or two would be able to dispense with a Regent's services. Mary was scarcely in a position to tell her father-in-law so, but she did mention the matter to Abbot William who, shrugging, declared that he had said something of the sort to his brother but had made no evident impression. He confessed that he was worried somewhat, in his capacity as acting Chancellor; and other churchmen were telling him of opposition to the Boyds growing in the realm. The Regent was, of course, aware of this; but, ever a man alone, and assured of his own capabilities, which indeed were not inconsiderable, he believed that he could weather any minor storm meantime. And when the royal marriage was brought about and if Orkney and Shetland were added to the Scots realm by his arranging, he reckoned that the regency, and his own position, would be greatly strengthened.

More Boyds than these were having problems. For, some six weeks after Tom's departure, Anna told Mary that she feared that she was pregnant – if feared was the word. For, in a way, she was glad to have Patrick's child. That would be a joy, and it might well force, ensure, their marriage. But meantime, with Patrick absent in Denmark, it posed difficulties indeed.

Mary was not condemnatory, but she was less optimistic than the other over this of marriage. Knowing Lord Boyd's soaring ambitions for his family, she feared that even in these circumstances he would not allow his daughter to wed anyone of such comparatively lowly status as Patrick Fullarton. He had had his son created earl, and his other daughter was a countess. He would want Anna to marry some lordling of broad acres, she was certain. But she did not say so.

What she did do, however, was to speak to James. She did not reveal to him the pregnancy, in case he told others, but she suggested, almost casually, that since Patrick was so good and faithful an esquire to Master Thomas and indeed acting as an extra envoy at the Danish court, he, James, might confer the honour of knighthood upon him. He was the King, and could do this, irrespective of the Regent's wishes. Such was the royal right. Patrick deserved it, did he not? And they were friends.

James agreed at once. He would do it when Patrick returned. He would like that. No, he would not mention it to Lord Boyd. It would be a secret, a surprise to all.

Mary hoped that this rise in rank might help the Regent to accept the young man as son-in-law, especially if some grant of royal or Arran lands was to go with it.

In early June a ship from Denmark brought a letter from Thomas to Mary. He had hoped to be home before this, he wrote, but Christian's pride was delaying things. He just could not raise the ten thousand florins token, modest sum as this was; indeed it was rumoured that he had got together only two thousand. The envoys, as instructed, were quite content to come away, with the Princess Margaret and the wadset of Orkney and Shetland, but Christian felt that would make him look foolish, impoverished. His councillors were prepared to agree to this, and almost certainly the King would do so in the end. But it might take some little time more to bring him to it. Thomas hoped that they would be back within the month, however. Tell his father so.

In this extended period of waiting, two very significant developments eventuated, one personal, one national. The first was that, unfortunately, Anna's state began to show by the end of the month. Presumably she had miscalculated the timing. At any rate, her father perceived it, to his cold anger. And more than anger; she would not marry that low-born scoundrel, son of the Coroner of Arran as he might be. But she *would* marry, and forthwith. No daughter of Boyd was going to have an illegitimate child. He would find her a husband of as suitable rank as was possible, and such would be given sufficient reward to make the cost to him acceptable. There would be no argument, no choice. *He* would decide. His fool of a daughter had sacrificed all rights in the matter.

Needless to say, this declaration threw Anna, and to some extent Mary, into dire distress, all but despair. But there was nothing that they could do about it. The Regent wielded supreme power, and Anna was still under age. Thomas might possibly have been able to effect something, but Thomas was still far away.

The second significant event was a visit to Stirling by Bishop Andrew of Glasgow. He came privately to see Mary, not the Regent. And he brought grave news, from the Primate at St Andrews. Bishop Graham was a sick man and could not travel here himself; but he was concerned for the princess-countess who, he considered, had helped him gain what he so greatly desired, rule of the Orkney diocese from Norway and the renunciation of the Nidaros Metropolitan status over the Scottish Church and the promise of support for his own elevation to archbishopric by the Pope. In return, he desired Mary, and the King, to be secretly warned. The Boyd regime was almost certainly about to fall, and bloodily. An alliance of earls, lords and barons had been formed to unseat the Regent and take over the government and the charge of the monarch, indeed to arraign Boyd and his close supporters on a charge of treason for having laid violent hands on the King at that hunt. The alliance was very strong, and included many of the greatest in the land, led by the King's uncles, the Earl of Atholl and Stewart of Auchterhouse, and had been joined by the two earls who formerly supported Boyd, Crawford and Argyll. They were almost ready to strike, and when they did, the Primate did not think that the Regent would be able to withstand. They had even arranged to call a parliament, to arraign the Boyds for treason. That, of course, would require the royal agreement and attendance to be official, so it could not be summoned as yet. He, the Primate, had been approached secretly, and to some extent he would favour the move for, as the late Bishop Kennedy's nephew, he deplored the Boyd coup, although as Primate he had had to work with Boyd in the interim. His present sickness enabled him to take no active part in the planned uprising; but he knew that many of his fellow-bishops were in favour of it. He was anxious that the Princess Mary, who was married to a Boyd, should not suffer in all this, and so he warned her. But, if she would heed him, not to warn the Regent that she knew of it all. He, Boyd, was bound to be aware of some of it, but probably not its full extent. If he did learn how close this was to fulfilment and just how strong was the opposition, he would surely summon all the armed forces which he could muster and hide the King away somewhere to secure him, and use him as a bargaining factor. There could be war, civil war. So he urged the princess to seek her own and the King's safety, secretly, on whatever pretext, possibly going to Arran or to the strong, all but impregnable castle of Tantallon belonging to her good-sister's husband, meantime.

Thus Bishop Andrew.

Needless to say, this gave Mary furiously to think. She was not entirely surprised, save in the seeming immediacy of it all. She had sensed that trouble was coming, but had assumed that it would not come to a head for some time yet, and that Thomas's return with the Princess Margaret and the Orkney and Shetland secession would much improve the situation. But now it looked as though this might not be in time. This talk of an arraignment for treason, of course, was dire indeed – for the penalty for treason was execution. And Thomas, as son and heir to Boyd, could well be included in the indictment, whatever his services in the meantime.

What was she to do? It was all very well for Bishop Graham to advise her to take James away to Arran or Tantallon, but the Regent would never let him go. *She* could go, yes – but not James. And if the whole Boyd family was to be indicted before parliament, what of her own little Jamie, Master of Arran, who was after all a Boyd also?

Mary Stewart, usually so keen-witted as to ways and means, was here at a loss. She did not debate the matter with Anna, who had enough on her mind meantime, however hard she herself cudgelled her brains.

In the event, Anna was wholly otherwise preoccupied, for only two days later Lord Boyd told her that he had found her a husband, Sir John Gordon of Lochinvar, Baron of Stichel, who was prepared to wed her, child and all, in return for unspecified benefits. The wedding would take place immediately, in a week, no more, since she was swelling visibly and days counted, or folk would be talking. The fact that Anna had never so much as encountered Sir John Gordon seemed to be immaterial.

They met only three days before the wedding, a stiffly formal occasion, with Lord Boyd very much in charge. Gordon proved to be a wary young man, slight, narrow-featured, hesitant, speaking with a lisp. Mary guessed at once that in this strange match Anna would be the dominant partner, if partnership there was to be. Why he had let himself be brought into this situation was not divulged; but his father, now dead, had been the first Gordon, from the Merse, to move over into Galloway, where was Lochinvar, and perhaps his heir had succeeded to problems there and required financial and other assistance. At any rate, here he was, confronting with no confidence his reluctant bride, and carefully avoiding looking at her middle.

It was only a brief meeting, with Mary and James present, Lochinvar looking as eager to be elsewhere as did Anna. They would wed in the Chapel Royal here in Stirling Castle two days hence, in a quiet ceremony conducted by the Abbot of Kilwinning. Anna made but one commentary – which she had discussed with Mary beforehand; she was the royal lady-in-waiting, and intended to remain so, on the princess's orders, with her duties close to her mistress always. Mary confirmed that, there and then, whatever Lord Boyd thought of it. Probably he cared not, so long as his daughter was duly married before her child-bearing was known to all.

So the wedding took place in the ancient Chapel Royal, in the presence of the monarch and royal family, the Regent and very few others, none of the bridegroom's family attending, in a service remarkable for its brevity, vows exchanged in uncertain mutters. The meal thereafter was scarcely a feast, and got over as quickly as the rest. What was to happen then had not been spelt out, and Mary wondered how Anna would cope. But that young woman, once the knot was tied, showed her Boyd spirit and decision, for she arrived back in Mary's quarters after only a short interval, to announce that she had told Lochinvar – she avoided calling him her husband – that in her condition bodily relations between them were out of the question, dangerous to her and her unborn child. This was almost certainly erroneous, but the man had not demurred, indeed had seemed almost relieved. Where he had gone to spend the night she neither knew nor cared. But for herself she would pass it in Mary's bed, if she might.

So two forced-brides bedded down together that bridal night. One of them did dissolve into tears for a while. Mary would have comforted her by declaring that her own union had turned into love and happiness now, but recognised that this might seem to imply rejection of Patrick Fullarton. She contented herself with holding the other girl close, and consoling as best she might

The very next day, as though almost to rub salt into the wound, one of the smaller vessels of the Danish embassage's squadron, able to sail right up Forth as far as Carron-mouth, and so only fifteen miles from Stirling, brought none other than Almoner Vanns to the castle, to announce that the Earl of Arran and Chancellor Avondale, with the Princess Margaret, were on their way, and had sent him ahead to arrange for a fitting reception for the future Queen. They would dock at Leith in perhaps ten days, weather permitting, when it was hoped that the King and an illustrious company would be there to welcome Margaret to her new country.

This, needless to say, much cheered all at court, although Anna's joy was shot through with regrets and exasperation that the homecomers had not been able to arrive just a few days earlier and so possibly saved her from her ridiculous and unwanted marriage. However, she placed great faith in Thomas and Patrick, and prayed that somehow they might solve her problems for her.

Mary was overjoyed, to be sure, and hoped that from now on the entire situation would greatly improve. Master Vanns said that the Danish princess was well, friendly and apparently not at all upset by her fate and her uprooting, a cheerful youngster.

Then, only a few hours after Vanns's arrival, the atmosphere of well-being at Stirling was abruptly changed by the appearance of another unexpected visitor, Archibald Douglas, fifth Earl of Angus, the Lord Boyd's son-in-law, from Tantallon, a young man not yet out of his teens but of a vehement and impetuous nature, as befitted the Red Douglas chief. He brought grim tidings and urgent advice. The rebel magnates were massing in arms no further away than St John's Town of Perth, with their thousands, practically every earl in Scotland other than himself and Arran, under Atholl, Crawford and Argyll, with most of the lords and knights by the hundred. They had approached him for Red Douglas support, but he had temporised. The Earl of Dunbar, his neighbour, was with them – he had done the approaching. They would march in only a day or two, and nothing that the Lord Boyd could muster could withstand them. Stirling Castle, besieged, might hold out for a while, but escape would be impossible. They had issued orders for the arrest, imprisonment and trial before parliament, for treason, of the Regent and those still supporting him. They had already sent south, Dunbar said, to arrest Sir Alexander Boyd in Nithsdale, and the Abbot of Kilwinning in Ayrshire. They would demand the immediate surrender to them of the person of the King's Grace and his brothers and sisters. Angus advised prompt flight from Stirling.

Consternation reigned, even Lord Boyd for once uncertain, agitated.

Mary put the question uppermost in *her* mind. What of the Earl of Arran? Was anything being said about him? He was due to arrive back in Scotland in a few days.

The earl said that the word was that Arran was to be tried for treason along with the others, since he had taken part in the royal abduction near Linlithgow those three years before. Because of his services in the matter of the Danish princess, it was possible that he might escape execution. Who could tell? But he would be arrested and forfeited, most assuredly, once he had handed over the princess to the allied lords.

In the flurry of alarm, question and debate which followed, King James himself appeared to be the least upset. He, of course, was the least threatened there, for whoever won in this contest for power, they required him, safe and not hostile. He was the monarch, the symbol of all authority and governance. And he was already hostile to Lord Boyd, although not to Master Thomas. Whatever upheavals eventuated, his position was not in question.

Angus, at distinct cost to himself, made the suggestion. Let them all come to Tantallon with him, meantime. His castle was impregnable from the land, and the rebel lords would have no fleet of warships to assail by sea – not for some time, at least. From there, His Grace and the Regent might seek terms. He did not see the Boyd regime surviving, but once Arran, Avondale and the princess arrived, there might be something to bargain with.

The Regent shook his head, decision apparently made. That

was not for him. Boyd was not so easily beaten. He would go to his own country, Ayrshire, Kilmarnock, where lay his manpower and allies. He would raise added bargaining factors to the Danish match and Orkney and Shetland, armed men. He was still the Regent, appointed so by parliament, and as such still exercised the royal authority . . .

James broke in there. *His* was the royal authority, he declared hotly. He had had enough of being ruled by others. He was the King. And he was not going to Kilmarnock with Boyd, or anyone else. He would either stay here at Stirling, or go to Tantallon with Angus.

Regent and monarch glared at each other. In that moment, Lord Boyd lost the rule of Scotland.

Mary spoke. "I have two bairns to think of and care for. Anna here is in no state to be caught up in men's struggles and warfare. We will go to Tantallon with my lord of Angus, meantime. Until my husband arrives, James, I say that you should come with us. You will be best there until this upheaval is overpast. When the Princess Margaret arrives at Leith, she can be brought to you there, but a score of miles away. Her arrival in Scotland, after all our efforts, must not be turned into uproar. Perhaps, with Douglas guard, you could go to meet her? The nation's honour is at stake, here. And we owe it to the lass."

"Yes, yes – I will go to Tantallon," the King agreed.

Without another word to any of them, and without any sort of obeisance to his sovereign, the Lord Boyd swung on his heel and strode from the room.

The others eyed each other.

"I think that the sooner we leave, the better," Angus declared. "It is near to sixty miles to Tantallon, and the Lady Anna in no state for long riding. And bairns to be taken. We can win as far as Linlithgow this night. Then to Edinburgh . . ."

"Almoner Vanns's ship will still be at Carron-mouth after its long voyage," Mary pointed out. "Your castle is near to the haven of North Berwick, my lord, is it not? Could we not go that far, to the Carron, only some fifteen miles, and then use the ship to sail down the coast?"

"Ha! That would be better, yes. Well thought of! How long until you are ready, Highness? With the bairns?"

"Give us one hour . . ." she said simply.

James Stewart actually grinned.

16

Tantallon Castle, soaring, huge, on its high clifftop headland above the boiling seas, was as secure a hold as the young earl had claimed – it had had to be, with its stormy Red Douglas history. Landward, its narrow promontory was protected by a series of high ramparts and deep ditches, to keep cannon and cavalry at a distance; and seawards precipitous rock was sufficient defence, with offshore reefs and skerries to prevent any shipping coming close enough to be any danger, save by such as knew the tortuous channel amongst the hazards. Here the royal party arrived the following afternoon, bringing Almoner Vanns with them, a possibly useful go-between. There had been no objection made to their departure from Stirling by Lord Boyd, who had been making his own preparations to leave. That man was having to adjust his priorities drastically.

Elizabeth Boyd was glad and relieved to welcome her visitors, in especial her sister, and of course concerned over her untimely and odd marriage.

Mary's concern now was Thomas's situation, what he was coming back to, and what she might do about it, if anything. Somehow he had to be warned. How? The only possibility which she could conjure up was somehow to intercept his ship as it entered the Scotwater – which entrance, to be sure, was just off Tantallon. But the firth mouth was some fifteen miles across; and the ships might enter it in darkness.

Master Vanns could not do more than guess at even a day when the little group of ships might reach Scottish waters. Perhaps two days hence, depending on the winds, perhaps three. Mary wondered whether any signalling device might be effective to bring the ships close to the castle, but Angus saw little hope in that. They would almost certainly pass well north of the Bass Rock, for the seas between it and the Lothian shore were shallow and scattered with skerries and reefs, and thus would be too far out for any effective signalling. A beacon by night or smoke columns by day would be seen, but would not hold any significance for the travellers.

There was nothing for it, then, Mary declared, but boats out to intercept. There were fishing craft at North Berwick, she had seen. Two or three of these, patrolling the area between the Bass and the Isle of May nearer the Fife shore, ought to be able to ensure making contact with the ships – by day. But, by night? At this time of year there was little real darkness most nights; but even so it would not be easy to spot or to attract the attention of vessels, or to be seen by them. Would they, in fact, enter the Scotwater in darkness, if they were making to dock at Leith? Might they not lie off until daylight?

Angus thought not. It was less than two hours' sailing up to Leith admittedly, and they would not wish to arrive there by night; but any lying-off would be likely to be done in the more sheltered waters of the port itself. Why wait in open seas out here?

Mary was determined. Somehow she had to reach Thomas and warn him. The only way to be sure, or all but sure, was to go out in a boat and wait, go herself. Sail up and down between the Bass and the May, patrol. It might take long enough, days and nights. But she saw nothing else for it.

Angus had his own boat at North Berwick – Tantallon's cliffs were no place to tie up – and he said that she could use that, something better than a mere fishing boat although not much larger. They could get a couple of fishing craft to aid them; three boats beating to and fro would ensure that the ships did not get past unintercepted. They would have to take provisions, and pray that the weather was kind. It would be dull work and scarcely apt for a lady, however.

Mary brushed that aside. She was no flighty girl, twenty years now, and mother of two. She could fish, and while away the time with needlework, storytelling, talk with the oarsmen. She would do well enough.

So, with James and Angus, she went down to the township and haven of North Berwick, there to inspect the earl's boat and arrange with fishermen that there would always be two of their craft out assisting. Since all here were vassals of Angus, owing him service, there was no difficulty about this, and with more than a score of boats available, it was agreed that they should go out in twelve-hourly relays, relieving each other, although the earl's craft would remain permanently at sea until its mission was accomplished. They would start the next morning.

There was much discussion that night as to who should accompany Mary on her vigil. She declared that there was no need for any to do so, but the others were insistent. In the end it was agreed that her friends should take it in turns to keep her company. Since the fishing boats would be relieving each other twelve-hourly, it would be quite simple for the Tantallon group individually to come and go with these.

Also discussed, to be sure, was the likely fate and future of the Boyds. None there was very hopeful. The Regent was unlikely to be able to raise sufficient men successfully to put down or nullify this major uprising, especially lacking the King's personal assistance – and James was adamant that he had had more than enough of the Lord Boyd. If this parliamentary trial for treason did eventuate, there could be little doubt about the verdict. How Thomas might fare at that was doubtful, but neither of his sisters were optimistic. They both felt that he would do better to avoid any appearance, to flee the country meantime until tempers cooled and the King was established in a position to ensure his safety. Mary was not so certain about this, believing that the Orkney and Shetland acquisition and royal marriage would tell greatly in his favour; and was not he the King's brother-in-law, his and her son third in line in the succession?

No firm conclusions were arrived at.

In the morning they all rode down to North Berwick again, laden with food and drink, blankets and other gear. It was decided that Angus would accompany Mary for the first day, Anna coming out for the first night. Then James himself for the second day – although there were some doubts as to the suitability of this for the monarch, but he was determined – and John, Lord of Douglas, Angus's brother, for the second night. It was felt that Elizabeth should have women companions for the nights. Thereafter, if it was necessary, they could repeat the sequence.

The earl's craft was reasonably convenient, for it was of a fair size and had a screen to divide the fore-part from the rest, to give the lordly ones privacy from the oarsmen. Also there was a roofed-in portion at the bows, less than a cabin but fit to sleep under, or as shelter in wet weather. A crew of four, and two manned fishing boats were awaiting them.

Hopes were expressed and farewells said, and the three boats cast off. Apart from other fishing craft dotted over the firth, no shipping was to be seen.

It had been reckoned that the best position for Mary's boat was the central one, with each craft beating up and down a three-mile stretch. That ought to cover the area between Bass and May Isle.

It was a day of breezes and sun and cloud, the sea wavy but not rough. It was quite pleasant in the boat, strange for Mary to be alone, behind that screen, with this young man whom she hardly knew, but who proved to be an agreeable companion and quite a talker. He became presently eloquent on the turbulent story of the Red Douglases, and how they differed from the Black. Mary had never quite understood how this, the lesser, junior branch, had survived when the senior had been so drastically brought low by her father. She now gained enlightenment. The Reds stemmed from an illegitimate half-brother of the second Earl of Douglas by a Stewart Countess of Angus, later married, this in the late fourteenth century. The two lines had never been friendly. Then, fourteen years ago, at the Battle of Arkinholm, which brought down the power of the Blacks, this Archibald's father, the fourth Earl of Angus, had been in command, acting for James the Second, this battle becoming known as "the Red putting down the Black". So the Reds had always supported the throne, and thus escaped the fall of the parallel line.

Mary suspected that there was more to it than that, but did not say so.

The time passed thus congenially enough. Shipping they did see, going and coming, but always single vessels, and none flying royal banners, as would be those bringing Scotland's future Queen. There was more than enough to eat and drink, and although attending to the calls of nature was less private than might have been desired, men and women used to long riding and travel were quite inured to that, and disinclined to fuss.

Rocked by the motion of the waves, they took turns at sleeping and watching during the afternoon.

When the two evening boats came out to relieve the others, one brought Anna. There was nothing to report.

Mary had slept in the afternoon so that she could remain awake much of the night, and she and Anna talked until late. The younger girl was, of course, much concerned about Patrick and what would happen to him. If Thomas was in danger, what of him? Would he not be more so, no earl or lofty one yet a Boyd supporter? Mary said that probably being less lofty would be in his favour, especially as the King was fond of him and had even promised to create him knight.

Anna slept in time, but Mary maintained her vigil, although their four oarsmen were to take turns at watching also. The eastern sky was lightening before she dozed off.

The daytime boats came out later than arranged, with James – who was no doubt responsible for the delay. There was also a relief crew for Mary's craft. Anna was taken back. It was today that Master Vanns thought the most likely for their squadron's arrival.

Mary found her brother a less interesting companion than the others, restless, quickly bored, complaining of this and that. Seventeen is a difficult age for most young males, not yet men but childhood well past, and the need for assertion apt to be evident. She would have indeed preferred to be alone, or chatting with her new crew. James's complaints against the Regent were unending. He would get free of him now, and he would show all who it was who ruled this realm. Mary warned that he had still some years to go before he was of full age, and a new regency might be little more kindly than the old one.

As the day wore on and only coastal shipping appeared, the King grew disenchanted. This was a waste of time, he asserted. Better that they should go to Leith and wait for the ships there, in comfort. If he, the monarch, took care of Master Thomas and Patrick – and the girl, to be sure – none would dare assail them. Mary doubted that, pointing out that once they had Princess Margaret and himself in their hands, the rebel lords would be concerned to make sure that the Boyd faction did not regain strength and seek the rule again, to their own hurt. Therefore they might well wish to get rid of Thomas, who could head up a resurgent regime even though his father had failed to do so.

Her brother held to his own views.

It was quite a relief when the Countess Elizabeth was brought out instead. She was of a very different nature from Anna, quieter, less ebullient and positive, but easy to get on with, the least assertive of the Boyds. They talked of babies and the upbringing of children, also men and their odd ways, and did not disagree. Thereafter they took turn about at keeping watch.

It was soon after sunrise, with the waters glittering in the level rays, and the two countesses waiting for the morning boats from North Berwick, when their oarsmen's shouts drew their gaze eastwards. Eyes shaded against the dazzlement, they took a little while to discern the sails of four ships, hull-down but fairly close together. The chances were that this was the Danish squadron at last.

The fishing boat to the south of them, nearer the Bass, came hastening to inform, in case they had not spotted the sails. The fishermen reckoned that they were still at least six miles off, but clearly approaching.

The patrolling craft to the north had seen them also and now came back. All agreed that the four ships were unlikely to be other than those they sought.

Mary was in a state of mixed emotions, agog to see her husband, now beloved, and concerned over the news she was going to bring him and the problems which would confront them thereafter.

As the ships drew near it could be seen that the largest and foremost was flying large banners, the Lion Rampant and the Saltire of St Andrew. That would be the *Tay Pearl*.

Angus had given Mary one of his own blue and white flags with the red heart, Bruce's heart, which the Good Sir James Douglas had taken on crusade and died defending, and this they now hoisted on their own short mast in case the ships treated them as mere fishing boats to be ignored. They rowed on an intercepting course, all three boats. Mary stood up in the bows of hers and waved and waved.

There could be no mistaking intentions. The leading ship hove to, and the others followed suit. Well before the Tantallon craft could draw alongside to the *Pearl* they could see Thomas and Patrick leaning eagerly over the side, waving back and shouting. Close by was Avondale and the young princess, surprise on all faces, greetings, questions being called. A rope-ladder was lowered.

An oarsman steadying this for her, Mary was first to ascend, hitching up skirts, seeking not to bark her knuckles on the timbers and to adjust to the sway of it. Before she reached the final rungs Thomas was bending over to grasp her wrists and all but hoist her over the bulwark and into his arms.

Incoherences prevailed.

Elizabeth climbed up. If Patrick Fullarton was disappointed that it was not her sister, he managed to hide it.

Greeting Princess Margaret, Avondale, the Bishop of Orkney and Rob Carnegie, Mary was inevitably delayed in explaining the reasons for this interception, Tom apparently assuming that it was merely a particularly dramatic welcome home. What she had to tell him could not just be blurted out before all.

She was about to instruct the two fishing craft to return to harbour, leaving the earl's boat, when who should appear but the Earl of Angus himself, coming out in another boat to relieve his countess. He too climbed up the ladder.

There was more delay until Mary could draw Thomas aside and indicate that she wished to talk to him alone – he no doubt assuming this to be for more intimate greeting. Nothing loth, he led the way to a stern cabin.

Within, he enfolded her in his arms, covering her face and neck and hair with kisses, hands as busy as his lips. She was far from finding this unwelcome, or lacking in response; but concern for what she had to tell him was strong. At length she sought to hold him at arm's length, and put a finger over his lips, both.

"Thomas, my heart," she got out, "here is joy, delight, wonder! But . . . pain also. Sorrow, my dear. For I have ill news for you. I bring pain and hurt, I fear. Why I am here thus. Shame it is, to spoil this our joy at coming together again. But – you must hear it, know of it."

He searched her face. "Trouble? Here? In the realm? My father?"

"Yes. Uprising. Rebellion, it might be called. A grand alliance of the lords, against the Regent. He is gone from Stirling. To Kilmarnock, to try to raise men, an army. To fight them. But will not, cannot, win in this, I think. Many have deserted his cause – Argyll, Crawford, Somerville, Hailes. Others. He has few friends now. Of all the earls, only Angus here, and yourself, are with him. And Angus has no intention of fighting, I would say."

"Fighting? War? Not that!"

"No, I hope not, pray not. But that was Lord Boyd's intention when he left Stirling. Four days past."

"I will go after him. Seek to turn him from this. Civil war, bloodshed, will serve nothing . . ."

"So say I. But, no – do not go after him, Thomas my heart. Not you. For there is worse to tell. They, the earls and lords, intend to call a parliament. Not only to bring down, change, the regency, but to indict you all, all the Boyds, on a charge of treason. For the abduction of James, that time. *Treason*, Thomas! That is the intention. It must not be! *You* must not be charged with treason. Yet you were there, when we were taken, near Linlithgow. I fear, I fear . . ."

"So-o-o! That is it. Aye, they would have me, yes . . ."

"They have sent to arrest your uncles, Sir Alexander and Abbot William. They will try to capture your father. *I* came away, with James and Anna and the bairns, to Tantallon. Here. So as to warn you. They will be waiting at Leith, for you and the princess. They will take you, nothing more sure. You must not let them get you, my heart."

"No. I see that. James – where stands he, the King, in all this?"

"He is here, at Tantallon. He greatly mislikes your father, who has used and constrained him. He will, I think, do nothing to aid Lord Boyd. But you, his Master Thomas, he likes. He will not stand out against these lords, I think, but will wish to protect *you*. He will go to Leith, he says, join them, and meet you and this Margaret, his bride. Says that he can save you. But – I fear not. They will see you as the one who might raise many against them. Your father is not popular, but you are. And our son Jamie, in line for the succession to the throne. They will, I judge, see you as dangerous. Seek to get rid of you."

"Yes, you are right. Who is behind all this? All the earls, you say? But there must be some in the lead. Who seek power."

"It is my uncles, I think, my bastard uncles. The Earl of Atholl and Stewart of Auchterhouse. Or so Bishop Andrew and Primate Graham say. They will resent the Boyds' power. Oh, Thomas, you have been away too long!"

"Aye." He took a turn up and down the confined space of the cabin. "You are right. I would be a fool to put myself in their hands now. I care not about my father's regency – that can go. I would not wish to rise in arms to try to save it, whatever *he* may seek. But . . . this of treason is bad, bad. They could hang me, for that. So – I must not go on to Leith." He shook his head. "Nor, I think, go to my father at Kilmarnock, or wherever he is gone. Nor, indeed, stay here at Angus's Tantallon. For anyone who gives aid or support or even shelter to one accused of treason is deemed to be in treason also. That I must not bring upon any."

She bit her lip, eyeing him.

"What is best?" he demanded. "Anywhere I go in Scotland,

and seek shelter, help, could gravely harm others. If I thought that we, my father's regency, his cause, had any hope of winning in this struggle, it might be different. But I do not. All along he has offended others, acted alone, kept all in his own hands, scarcely rewarded those who aided him at the beginning. I have told him so, but he heeded not. He can call on few friends now. Even Avondale here will not risk his neck for him, I think. So — where do I go now? Avondale can take the princess on to Leith. But myself — where do *I* go?"

For once Mary Stewart had to fail him. She just did not know, considering it all as she had done these last days and nights. "Over the border? England?" she suggested, but without conviction.

"What would that serve? The English, if they would let me bide there, would but seek to use me against Scotland. Make a traitor of me, indeed! They are the Auld Enemy still . . ."

They heard voices outside and Avondale called, to interrupt their privacy. Thomas went to the door.

The Chancellor looked worried indeed. "My lord of Angus, here, has told me something of what is afoot," he announced. "Here are grievous tidings. And just when we have completed our mission, with success. What is to be done? The Regent has fled. All is in chaos. None in control of the realm. The young princess . . . !"

"Aye, I have heard. This changes all. But not the royal marriage. Or Orkney and Shetland. You, my lord Chancellor, are in no danger. You will have to go on to Leith, with the Princess Margaret. And, to be sure, the King. He is at Tantallon, yonder. For myself, I cannot do so — that is clear. Where I will go I know not. Probably back to Denmark meantime. Yes, back to Denmark. I can seem to go, to announce to Christian his daughter's safe arrival in Scotland. I am, it seems, to be charged with treason! So I had better be furth of the realm until the situation is resolved, one way or another. I would be arrested at Leith, my wife says. You are different. You were appointed by parliament, as Chancellor. You were not my father's appointment. Yes, it is Denmark for me, again. They do not mislike me there . . ."

They all gazed at each other, Angus and his wife behind the Chancellor.

Mary spoke. "Do not decide on all yet," she urged. "Let us go ashore to Tantallon. The ships can wait here, can they not?

Time to think. And you will wish to see your bairns, Thomas? And the King. And Anna. There is no great haste to reach Leith, is there? They do not know there when you will arrive. Any more than did we."

"Aye, that is true. That is best," Thomas agreed. "The ships can lie off here for a few hours, while we make our decisions. These small boats will take us ashore . . ."

None controverted that, and a move was made to inform Carnegie, the Princess Margaret and the others, and to summon the fishing craft alongside again. A much enlarged group descended rope-ladders thereafter, the Danish girl greatly excited by this adventure.

On the way back to North Berwick in the earl's boat, Mary spoke quietly to Patrick Fullarton. "My friend," she said, "I have ill news for *you*, also. Apart from this of my lord Earl, and treason. Anna! She is here at Tantallon with me. So you will see her. But – she is with child."

He blinked, drawing a deep breath. "I . . . I . . . what can I say, Highness?"

"Say nothing until you have heard it all, Patrick. *That* is none so very ill! It is what followed. Her father perceived her state – she is fairly large with it, and he has a keen eye. He was wrath. He had her to wed, and at once. No choice given her, no time. He would not have her with a bastard . . ."

"Wed! Anna! God in heaven – not *wed*! Not Anna, my Anna!"

"Yes, wed. He found a man to take her, as she was. No doubt at a price. Sir John Gordon of Lochinvar. In Galloway. A weakling, I judge. But they were married, without delay. They have not slept together, nor even seen each other since the ceremony. But she is now the Lady Gordon. I am sorry, Patrick. But . . ." She left the rest unsaid.

Shattered, the young man clenched fists and stared away, as they approached the haven below the conical hill of North Berwick Law.

At Tantallon Castle there was no lack of drama and emotion, the King encountering his bride-to-be, Patrick meeting Anna, Mary and Thomas agitating as to what to do, Avondale concerned for his own future; all at first, distraction, jumbled talk, uncertainty. But since so much fell to be decided, and for so many, Mary it was who presently suggested that they should all sit down round the hall table, like any council meeting, and discuss it quietly, in orderly fashion. This was accepted.

Where to begin? Thomas, rather than the King, led off, but since James was present it seemed suitable to deal with his situation first. The proposal was that he joined the ships and sailed to Leith with the Chancellor and the future Queen. But Mary queried the wisdom of this. Would it not be asked by the lords how he came to be on that ship from Denmark? That would lead to having to explain this call at Tantallon and Thomas's leaving the party. This in turn would implicate Angus. Better, surely, if James was to ride to Leith, with Angus and an escort. He would not be there so soon as were the ships, but that did not signify. He would not be expected to know when the Danish party would arrive. There he could greet the princess, who would presumably already have landed. The lords would be in some disarray, not knowing where the King was after leaving Stirling. His presence would reassure them, and at the same time avoid any suspicions over Angus.

That was accepted as making good sense, Avondale particularly affirmative. It would avoid any questions as to his own implication. But – what would he say about the Earl of Arran's absence?"

Mary said could he not declare that Thomas had received warning from his father? At sea. A fishing boat sent out to take him off the ship. Not necessarily from North Berwick. Just a fishing boat. To take him where, who knew? Possibly to join the Lord Boyd, wherever he might be. Avondale and the Bishop of Orkney, knowing naught of what was to do in Scotland, could nowise stop him, nor think to do so. They had come on to Leith with the princess.

None controverted that.

What then of Thomas himself, the biggest problem? That was answered promptly. He had decided. He would have one of the smaller ships turned around and sail back to Copenhagen. That would be best, meantime. He had made friends in Denmark, and got on well with King Christian. He would be safe there, until the situation in Scotland was such as to allow him to return home. He looked at Mary.

That young woman drew a deep breath. It had had to come to this eventually, and she had made up her mind, hard as the decision had been.

"I will go with my husband," she said simply.

They all eyed her, none forgetting her two infants.

"The children . . . ?" Elizabeth asked.

Mary inclined her head, swallowing. "I . . . we . . . must leave them behind, I fear. We cannot take little ones like that to Denmark, not knowing where we go from there. They must . . . remain here." Her voice almost broke.

Thomas reached over to grasp her wrist. "Bless you, Mary!" he said.

"I will care for the bairns," Elizabeth declared. "My brother's children."

All were silent for a space.

Then Anna spoke. "I go with Her Highness, as ever," she said. But she looked at Patrick.

"As do I, with my lord," that young man announced quickly, eagerly.

James it was who made question of these decisions, or of some of them. "I do not think that you should go, Mary," he said. "It is not . . . suitable. You are my sister."

"I am married to Thomas, James. Made one, in the sight of God. My first duty is to him. And you have another sister, and two brothers, still at Stirling."

"They are young. I say that I can save Master Thomas from any hurt. He should remain here, in Scotland. In hiding perhaps, at first. Until matters are settled. Then I will call for him."

"With respect, Sire, I will be a deal safer in Denmark!"

"You can call for him there, James, when all is settled. Better there. Here he could well be discovered, betrayed, or his father reach him and seek to use him. Denmark is best."

James scowled. "I could make it my royal command!"

"You could – but will not, I think. Not to *me*!"

Their eyes met, and he lowered his.

"You have four years yet until full age," she went on. "So another regency will be established. Others will make decisions for you. *You* may cherish Thomas, James, but others will not. If a parliament condemns *all* the Boyds for treason, as is mooted, your pleas for him will avail nothing. Better this way."

Angus, their host, accepted that as final. "When shall we leave for Leith, Sire?" he asked. But it was at Mary that he looked. "This day? Or tomorrow?"

"The sooner the better," Avondale put in. "The ships will be

206

at Leith haven in two hours or so. Her Highness, here, should be received in Scotland in due style. Some of the earls and lords will be there, no doubt. But His Grace should be present soon after."

"I agree," Angus said. "The ships can lie off here for a little longer. His Grace and I should ride almost at once. It is over twenty miles."

"Very well," Thomas declared. "All is settled, then. We can go our separate ways . . ."

"*Almost* all," Mary interjected. "His Grace may have forgotten, in all this upset. But I have not. He promised that he would knight our friend Patrick Fullarton, for his good services and lealty. It must be now. You agree, James?"

The King was nowise reluctant about this, at least, a demonstration of his royal powers and authority.

"Yes. To be sure. A sword . . . ?"

Angus could produce one without difficulty there, and amidst murmurs and exclamations and chuckles of delight from Anna, the astonished and embarrassed Patrick was ordered to kneel in front of his liege-lord, was then tapped on each shoulder with the blade, told to be upstanding, Sir Patrick, and to be and remain a good knight until his life's end – this all in something of a rush. Congratulations followed, with kisses from Anna, Lady Gordon.

Then it was partings, these indeed dire for Mary, to say farewell to her two little ones, tears flowing. The ship-party then left James and Angus to prepare for their ride to Leith, and themselves rode down to North Berwick harbour with such baggage as Mary and Anna could hurriedly assemble.

Back on the *Tay Pearl*, Thomas and Patrick transferred their belongings to one of the lesser ships, the *St Colm* of Inverkeithing. Then it was more leave-taking, from Avondale, the bishop and Princess Margaret – the last obviously bewildered by all this coming and going.

What the master and crew of the *St Colm* thought of their instructions to turn around and sail back to Denmark could be guessed at but was not expressed, in words at least. And what Mary's and Anna's thoughts and emotions were as their vessel beat round and left the other ships there, to head eastwards again for the open sea, were little more explicit – but sufficiently traumatic, for all that.

17

That voyage back to Copenhagen held a strange, unreal quality for them all. Behind was disaster, danger, confusion; ahead was none knew what, in the long run. But for the present, it was reunion, joy, leisure, ease and chosen company. The weather was fair, the winds light but favourable for eastwards progress, the July seas moderate. This smaller vessel provided less comfortable quarters than did the *Pearl*, but none complained.

Mary and Thomas had learned to accept happiness when it was available, not to pine for its permanency, not to look over-far ahead, love now accepted, acknowledged, trust assured, their pain at leaving behind the little ones shared. Anna and Patrick had each other, openly, at last, for how long they knew not, but to be fully savoured while it lasted, Anna's condition a bond rather than a handicap.

With westerly winds prevailing they made good time, and three days and nights after leaving North Berwick they were into the Skagerrak and rounding the Skaw, to sail southwards into the Kattegat.

They held a conference as to how much to tell King Christian. Could they pretend that all was normal and in order? That this was merely an embassage sent to inform him that his daughter had arrived safely in Scotland and would by now be married to King James? Would the Scots send an earl and his princess wife just to say that? Probably not. Should they be frank, announce the fall of the Boyd regime; but declare that this would nowise affect Margaret's position? Since Thomas would presumably not be able to return to Scotland for some time, this might be advisable, to explain a continued stay in Denmark Yet they did not want to be looked upon as refugees. It was not likely that Christian would expel them, for they had a good relationship with him. But, on the other hand, with his daughter new-married to King James, and Denmark now in treaty with Scotland, he would not wish to offend the new regency by seeming to harbour a fugitive. It was difficult.

Mary it was who again came up with a suggestion. Thomas had mentioned that, before he had left Copenhagen with Margaret, there had been word of trouble between the Hanseatic League, Christian's German mercantile friends, and England, over growing English trading with Iceland, which the League looked upon as their especial territory. Could Thomas not use this? Tell Christian that Scotland would support Denmark in *its* support of the League, against England? Admittedly there was a fifteen-year truce with England in force, with the present Lancastrian regime – but it was *only* a truce, no real peace, Border raiding still going on, and any stick to beat the Auld Enemy was not to be neglected. It would be safe to say that this would be Scotland's attitude, and it might well please the Danes.

Thomas, agreeing, took it further. He could make himself more than just a messenger, a carrier of tidings – but an ambassador. And not only to Denmark. He could offer to approach other princes of Europe in this cause. They would receive him, married to the King of Scots' sister. Supporting the wealthy and influential Hanseatic League would gain them acceptance. And Scotland would get to hear of it, and gain him credit.

This was accepted. Only Anna wondered. In her present state she could hardly go travelling around the nations of Christendom with them. Mary acknowledged it, and said that she should remain in Denmark until her child was born. Patrick could stay with her. Now, as *Sir* Patrick, he had some status, and they would be accepted as man and wife. Thomas could do without his attendance, for once.

So they sailed down the Kattegat with a degree of confidence.

This was in no way diminished by their reception at Copenhagen, Christian obviously pleased to see them back, especially Mary whom he embraced in comprehensive fashion. They had now, of course, no Bishop Tulloch to act as interpreter, but the King made his attitude, indeed his intentions, sufficiently evident – so much so that Mary was a little concerned, although Thomas seemed to consider her well able to look after herself.

They were allotted their old quarters in the Slot.

They wondered what was happening back in Scotland, and how the Lord Boyd and his brothers fared. The family at Tantallon would be safe enough, whatever transpired, in that impregnable stronghold.

They had to find an interpreter sufficiently expert in their own language before they could fully convey to Christian and his councillors what they had to tell, inform and propose – although Thomas had picked up a certain amount of Danish in his sojourning here. This took some time, but eventually they found a merchant, in the Ostergade, who had traded with Scotland as a younger man, and was able to translate with fair accuracy. In the interim Mary had to put up with much affectionate handling by the monarch of three kingdoms.

Their interpreter, Nils by name, did not seem in the least overawed by the company he now had to keep, and appeared to be able to get their instructions across adequately and to transmit reactions equally so. Christian and his ministers were clearly interested in what they had to say, and particularly so in the Hanseatic suggestion. The situation with the Hanseatic towns, Lübeck, Hamburg, Wisby, Rostock, Stralsund and the rest, was much concerning them. It seemed, in fact, that the League controlled the entire trade of Norway and much of that of Denmark and Sweden also – these Norsemen, in the past, considering that trade and industry and commerce were beneath the dignity of a warrior race such as themselves, a costly attitude it transpired in the long run. Now they were very largely dependent on the League for economic survival.

The Danish councillors were quick to perceive advantage in having a Scottish earl and princess to act as go-betweens with the Hansa leaders, who were clearly demanding much of them at this juncture. The Hansa was in a strange position, wielding enormous influence throughout Continental Europe yet having no armed force of its own. Lübeck in Schleswig-Holstein, the principal centre, ranked as a city state; but it had nothing more militarily effective than its town guard. Similarly with over one hundred other towns and cities. Now they needed men and ships in large numbers to prosecute their offensive against the English threat to their trading monopoly in Iceland, and were demanding much of these from Denmark, Norway and Sweden. Christian had men and ships a-many, of course – but he needed them nearer home than Iceland at present, for the Swedish nobles were rising against his overlordship once more, and this had to be put down.

He was planning a major campaign in Sweden, if possible to end the troubles there once and for all. This Hanseatic demand, which he was in no position financially to reject, came at a most inconvenient time. He was sending a deputation to Lübeck, to put this before the leaders there; but to have the Earl of Arran and his princess with it, indicating Scottish support against the English, and he now in treaty with Scotland, would be a valuable aid.

Even Mary was quite surprised at how aptly her proposal of ambassadorship had fitted into the situation here, all but heaven-sent, she felt.

Thomas wanted to know why Iceland seemed to mean so much to the Hanseatic League? After all, it was only a small outpost of the Norse domains, remote and with no large population for trading purposes. It was explained that it was not so much the size of the country that mattered but the principle which was at stake. These Hansa trading monopolies were all-important to them. Allow one to be broken or taken over, and who could tell what it might lead to? Other nations might follow the English lead, and the great trading empire begin to disintegrate. The English trade with the Low Countries was expanding; and although Hansa had no monopoly there, they did have major mercantile links. So something had to be done about this of Iceland.

And there was another point. Iceland's main wealth was in the fishing, salted fish its principal export. And the monopoly allowed the League to be sole supplier of salt, Lüneburg salt, mined there in great quantities, that city linked by canal to Lübeck. So Lübeck itself was directly concerned, the "capital" of the League.

Thomas could understand this very well, for, next to Lammermuir wool, salted fish and meat was Scotland's main export also, and the salt trade vital, although the salt was not mined but obtained from evaporation pans of sea water.

So, how soon was the deputation to go to Lübeck, for the Scots to accompany? In a week, they were told.

Perhaps fortunately for Mary's piece of mind, King Christian was to be over in Norway for the next few days, organising the mustering of men for the Swedish campaign; so that at that evening's banquet his attentions were pressing indeed, literally so, and she had to use all her ingenuity to retain approximate command of the situation without possibly offending the monarch – on whose goodwill, of course, so much depended. Thomas came to her rescue where he could.

In the days which followed, they made it their business to learn as much about the Hanseatic League as they could. Fortunately, their interpreter, Nils Larsen, was a great help, for, like all Danish merchants, he had to have strong links with Lübeck, and indeed had skippered one of their ships in the past. He could speak German. For a suitable fee he would be quite prepared to come with them on their visit to Schleswig-Holstein, leaving his sons in charge in the Ostergade.

He told them that the League had started modestly as a consortium of merchants in the Baltic area and the Lower Rhineland in the twelfth century, *hansa* meaning trade guild. It had quickly spread and grown, both in size and in its powers, as other merchants in neighbouring principalities and lands saw the advantage of a united front against powerful nobles, robber barons, pirates and the like, who looked upon unarmed traders as their natural prey. Soon the League had spread from the Germanic princely states to Poland, Lithuania and Russia – Novgorod being one of their main bases. The Holy Roman Emperor, Frederick the Second, saw the League as useful and gave it his protection, and other rulers followed suit. Actually one such had later chosen to renege and renounce them – and he a Dane, King Valdemar; but the League had called on others to aid them, and defeated him. That was exactly one hundred years ago. Since then, Denmark, Norway, and Sweden to a lesser extent, had adhered firmly.

There were great advantages in this, of course, especially for maritime nations. The League not only quelled brigands and pirates but built and maintained lighthouses, trained pilots for different and difficult waters to foster safe navigation, established trading and commercial bases in many lands, and gained valuable trading monopolies. They had even set up a base in London, the Steel Yard, but this had been under a cloud for some time. In Scotland, Berwick-on-Tweed served as an agency and toehold, the Flemings having established it there.

So this of aiding the League over England and Iceland was important. The English merchants could have joined the Hansa but had rejected offers and now were seeking to capture its markets, or some of them. This must be stopped. Wars had been started over less. A united show of strength was what was required, to warn the English off.

Thomas and Mary agreed that this was something which they

could fully support, assured that whoever was ruling Scotland now would concur – although they did not want to be advocating actual warfare.

Christian was not back from Norway by the time that the Danish deputation set off. Since Schleswig-Holstein was no great distance, and the visit not expected to last for long, it was decided that Anna could accompany them on this occasion. They would be going by sea, so she should be undergoing no risks. The leader of the party was Erik Johansen, who was what in Scotland would be called Vice-Chancellor, two other members of the Rigsraad or Council of States with him, one a bishop, together with representatives of the Copenhagen trade guilds.

They set sail on a sultry day in August, with a hot wind blowing from the south-east – which was not the best for this journey – to enter the Oresound. With a westerly or northerly breeze the one-hundred-and-seventy-mile voyage would have taken only one day and night's sailing, but thus it might take as much as three days, unless the wind changed, with constant tacking called for. This did not greatly concern the Scots, who looked upon the trip almost as a holiday. Nils Larsen proved a good companion, knowledgeable as well as friendly, and necessary of course for any communication with their fellow-travellers.

When they reached the Oresound and turned southwards, with the wind in their faces quite strong, the need for tacking became all too obvious, their shipmaster much concerned with his sails and steering. This way and that they had to turn, at steep angles, to make any progress, the navigation complicated by islands and their outlying reefs and skerries.

The channel of the Oresound widened in time to what was apparently called the Ostersoen or Eastern Sea, as they passed beyond the southern tip of Sweden. Here the going became notably rougher as they progressed, sizeable waves developing. Nils explained that this was not so much due to the wind as to currents. The waters of the Norse Sea had come racing down, channelled through the Skagerrak, the Kattegat and the Oresound, and here met a very different trend, the cold currents of the Gulfs of Finland and Bothnia sweeping down and round. The result, in this shallow Baltic Sea, was major turbulence. It would grow worse. Indeed, between the large island of Bornholm and the Lolland coast, it could be fierce and dangerous, although on this trip they would miss the worst area.

By darkness they had reached only the island of Stege, just beyond the tip of Zealand, and they put into a sheltered anchorage here to pass the night, since navigation of these waters in these conditions, and with much shipping abroad, could be hazardous.

It was good to be spared the heaving and tossing for their sleeping.

In the morning there was little change in wind and seas, and the tacking had to be resumed. But after some thirty miles of progress, however many more of actual sailing, they passed the last headland of Denmark, the Gedser Odde, and thereafter were able to steer more into the south-west. This helped considerably. Passing the first Schleswig island of Fehmarn and through what was known as the Fehmarn Belt, they progressed into the great Lübecker Gulf, now having to pick their way amongst more shipping than the Scots had ever before seen, indicative of the importance of Lübeck as the chiefest port on all the Baltic, possibly of all Germany.

At the northern tip of this vast bay was the Oldenburg peninsula, where King Christian had been count before gaining the Danish throne. This was now the Wendish coast, from whence had come the Wends or Vandals, of ancient savage reputation.

That long, wide gulf narrowed eventually to the mouth of the Trave River, which they now entered. Lübeck, it seemed, was some ten miles upstream. It was a wide river, which it needed to be to carry the amount of traffic using it. This entailed slow progress indeed; but even so they could hope to reach the city by nightfall, better timing than they had feared.

The Scots were interested in all that they saw. This was all very level, flat country, obviously fertile, highly cultivated, well wooded and populous, with villages and small towns prominent. But presently, outlined against the westering sunset, they perceived prominence indeed, the silhouette of a large city on a low ridge ahead, all soaring spires and towers and domes above long ramparts of gables, roofs and pinnacles, a dramatic sight. As Mary declared, it only required a mighty fortress-castle on a rock rising above it all to outshine Edinburgh or Stirling.

Their shipmaster nosed his vessel through a series of outer harbours on the river-banks, nine of them he said, and into the second of two inner havens directly under the massive walls and bastions of the city's defences. They could go no further because of bridges across the Trave. Erik Johansen decided that they should remain aboard ship that night, the hour too late to go seeking accommodation from the Lübeckers, although the city gates apparently were not shut of a night here. Surrounded by other moored shipping, and with much noise emanating from the dockside taverns, they passed a somewhat disturbed night.

In the morning, Johansen and his colleagues went to introduce themselves to the Hanseatic senators, as they were called, as distinct from the Lübeck councillors; and Mary and Thomas, with Patrick and Anna and Nils Larsen, proceeded on a tour of inspection of the city.

The first feature which impressed them, apart from the fact that it seemed to be divided into four distinct quarters, all very regular, was that it was all built of brick, and to a lesser extent, wood, no stonework evident save for a monument or two. They were so used to stone as the building material in Scotland that all this brick, in various colours, red, yellow, brown, even black, struck them as extraordinary, the architectural effects created with it highly decorative, elaborate. The streets were wide, compared with Scottish ones, with removable market-booths and stalls down the centre, the population obviously large and prosperous-looking, no beggars or vagabonds in evidence. Lübeck was a rich community, most clearly.

Brick-built although they were, the public edifices were almost overwhelming in their magnificence, no fewer than three cathedral-like churches towering over all, as well as numerous lesser fanes. Nils conducted them around, almost as proud of it all as if it had been his own native city – the pearl of the Baltic, as he named it. The Dom, dating from the twelfth century, the true cathedral, had two lofty steeples, more than four hundred feet high, he explained, as did the even larger Marienkirche nearby, this latter filled with priceless works of art and an altarpiece by no less than Hans Memling. The visitors had none of them heard of this character – but did not say so. They were in process of realising how ignorant they were about so much of European culture and history, how far removed from all this wealth, splendour and preoccupation with art, science, decoration and lore of many sorts they were in Scotland, where all was so much more essentially basic, although they were not backward in their own forms of erudition. To some extent they were like the Norsemen, tending to look down rather on trade

215

and industry; here they saw what centuries of trading success could result in. Not only in merchantry, to be sure, for here had been a centre of the Teutonic Knights; at least they had heard of these.

The third great church was the Petrikirche. It had only the one steeple, but this fully as high as the others. These three were all built of red brick; but nearby was the Rathaus, or council chambers, apparently only recently reconstructed, in black brick, and huge as it was handsome, with no fewer than five council halls, it serving both the city fathers and the Hansa senators. Presumably here would be the scene of the visitors' meetings.

On their return to the ship they found themselves to be instructed to transfer to a senate guest-house adjacent to the Rathaus, where quarters were awaiting them. Arrival there revealed accommodation more luxurious and commodious than any they had yet experienced, with attendants a-many. These merchant princes, since that is what they appeared to be, knew how to use their wealth, and to impress others.

Erik Johansen came to tell them that there would be a council meeting the following forenoon, which they were invited to attend. Meantime all the facilities of the city were theirs to use and enjoy. The Princess of Scotland was to be made especially welcome.

The visitors from afar were further impressed.

Next morning, when along with the Danish deputation they were ushered into one of the handsome halls of the Rathaus, it was to find a gathering of about a score awaiting them, mainly elderly men of prosperous appearance, of a quietly confident bearing and tending to be shrewd of eye, clad equally quietly but on the whole richly, all a deal less ostentatious than leaders of nations were apt to be. All stood to welcome Mary – Anna and Patrick remained behind for this meeting. Clearly princesses were unusual attenders here. Thomas was respectfully greeted also, but the King of Scots' sister was the magnet for all eyes, her good looks as obviously appreciated as was her status. Only German was spoken, and Nils sought to convey the exchange of compliments and courtesies as best he could. The spokesman for the senators was introduced as Wilhelm Schoenbach of this city, a portly individual of middle years, wearing a gold chain of office on which hung a handsome jewelled medallion.

When they were all sat round a great table, the Scots couple

216

placed on the chairman's right, he made a more formal speech of welcome. In translation it was evident that although he was announcing the Danish envoys as having come in response to the Hansa's request for assistance and co-operation, his primary interest this morning was in the princess and earl from Scotland, and in what they had come to say and propose.

Johansen gestured to Thomas, who rose.

Speaking slowly and in brief sentences, to give time for translation, he declared that he and his royal wife were glad to be here, appreciative of their kind reception and hopeful that they had something to offer the esteemed Hanseatic League, famous in all lands and providing notable service to all nations' trade, England's less than some, perhaps – but who knew if this might be amended? They had come, on a visit to the King of Denmark, to offer their services in any way possible, to the Hansa Senate, in especial in this matter of English infringements of the Icelandic trade monopoly.

That drew approving nods, but alert waiting as to more detailed proposals.

This, of course, was the difficulty. In his position, Thomas was only capable of uttering generalities at this stage, not knowing what he *could* offer, with any likelihood of fulfilment, an exile from his country and possibly by now a condemned man. All that he could say meantime was that he and his wife were prepared to act as ambassadors elsewhere in Europe, emphasising that the Scots were always concerned, as a matter of national policy, to limit English aggression whether in armed alliances or in trade. They had suffered the said aggression for centuries.

This, while well enough received, obviously did not greatly excite his hearers. Making an almost deliberately queenly gesture of the hand, Mary sought to come to his rescue.

Asking if she might be permitted to speak in this august company, she declared that although her husband, the Earl of Arran, was perhaps too modest to mention it, he was notably well placed to be an envoy to the princes of Europe. For he already knew many of them, and had established good relations. This was because, two years earlier, he had been empowered by the Scottish regency and parliament to visit the courts of most of the great nations – France, Brittany, Spain, the Low Countries, Burgundy, Saxony and the rest, as well as Denmark – to seek a suitable bride for her brother King James. In the end he had chosen the Princess

Margaret of Denmark; but on his questing tour he had made many friends amongst the highest in Christendom, including the Emperor himself, Frederick the Third, and so was admirably placed to help advance the Hansa cause.

This took Nils a deal of translating, but it was evident that she was making an impression. Thomas endeavoured to look suitably modest. Being so handsome a young man did no harm.

Mary went on carefully. There were, it seemed to her, two important aspects of Scottish trade which could possibly be used to assist: the great wool trade with the Low Countries, their nation's chiefest; and their major export of salt to England. Even when at active war with that realm, this export of salt went on, for the English needed salt and the Scots needed the English gold in return. If they were to halt that salt trade with England, this would gravely trouble that nation. And if they could persuade the Low Countries to halt their export of cloths and the like to England also, the English might well decide that their new efforts at Icelandic trade were scarcely worthwhile.

That had heads nodding approvingly. But would the Scots be prepared to do that? Schoenbach wondered.

Mary said that she would approach her royal brother, to urge it. Some inducement would be necessary, of course. For instance, if the League made some adjustments to its own export of salt, to allow the Scots to replace the English market? She understood that Lüneburg, near to here, a Hansa city, was the greatest exporter of mined salt in all Europe!

The senators eyed each other, and some smiled faintly. There were no head-shakings.

She went on, encouraged. The wool and cloth trade of the Low Countries could surely also be re-directed? Possibly only for a short time, until the English learned their lesson.

Her hearers looked more doubtful about that.

Thomas added his support. Surely this sort of damage to English pockets and purses would be better than enlisting armed forces from rulers for possible war?

Senator Schoenbach agreed that this last was so. But there were problems, especially with the Low Countries. Unfortunately, of recent years, a division had developed in the League. The western German states, the Low Countries and Burgundy had come to consider that the eastern cities based on Lübeck were gaining overmuch of the benefits of the League's activities. Bruges in especial was vaunting itself, with the support of Charles the Bold, Duke of Burgundy. So much so that these Hansa traders were now being called Westerlings and naming the Lübeck-based members Easterlings. This was of course a grave weakness for the League, and complicated the present situation anent England, for the English merchants were seeking to exploit this rivalry, making offers to the Westerlings and even seeking to establish trading centres at Calais and Antwerp. So some sort of show of strength on Lübeck's part was called for, not only against the English but to remind these Westerlings that the League must remain one, united.

Thomas leant forward at the mention of the Duke of Burgundy, eager now. Charles the Bold and he had become particularly friendly, he declared, on his bridal-tour. Indeed he had been able to aid the duke, by recommending his daughter, Mary, as bride for the Emperor's son Maximillian, she being a year or two old for King James.

This information commended itself to all present, and it was accepted that the Earl of Arran and his princess were most suitable ambassadors for the League – which would show its appreciation in due course.

With the senators moving on to the matter of King Christian making a formal declaration of war against England, and a demonstration expedition of his ships to Icelandic waters, as warning, the Scots recognised that their presence was no longer relevant, and excused themselves, departing amongst expressions of goodwill, and instructions to consider all Lübeck and its province at their disposal.

Thomas, once again, had occasion to compliment his wife on her wits. She certainly was a worthy daughter of a long line of kings, he declared.

They filled in the next few days, until the Danish deputation had completed their negotiations, by exploring the great city, the largest in all Germany next to Cologne, they were told; but also the surrounding countryside and territory, all of which they found interesting, Mary especially so, her first real opportunity to observe closely how the people lived in a foreign land, and to compare all with Scotland – not always to the latter's advantage. Hers was the sort of mind which was intrigued and concerned.

Most of both Schleswig and Holstein consisted of low, heathy moorland, with the population mainly concentrated on the coasts, although great use was made of canals to lead into the interior, something never done in Scotland, too hilly a country for the like. These canals linked inland towns with the sea and with each other, with much barge traffic. Most were maintained by the League. They had assumed that Lübeck was the capital of Schleswig-Holstein, but found that the much smaller town of Schleswig itself was, a quiet, old-fashioned place. From there they visited Kiel, inland from its bay, where was the university and the ancient fortress-castle of the Dukes of Holstein. The interior was all very evidently cattle-country, with the slow-living peasantry which went with stock-raising; whilst fishing was important around the extensive coastline on both east and west. The travellers had heard of the Jutes, Saxons, Angles and Wends, early invaders of the Celtic lands of Britain, followed by the later Normans, Norsemen at only one remove; now they were discovering where all these had come from.

They sailed back to Copenhagen in due course, the Scots at least satisfied with their visit.

18

Now more journeying was to be planned, major travel indeed. The League would provide the means, shipping and horses, with introductions to useful contacts in sundry lands, burgomasters, aldermen, rich merchants, senators, churchmen, well-disposed nobles. It all ought to be a notable experience, and Mary and Thomas looked forward to it.

Not so Anna, and therefore Patrick. For that young woman was in no condition to set out on prolonged and extended travel; and Patrick was torn between the desire to accompany Thomas and to remain with her, having duties towards them both. Thomas said that he must remain with Anna at Copenhagen, at least until the child was born, and rejoin him later perhaps. Nils Larsen, who agreed to accompany them again, at League expense, was no lord's esquire, however worthy a character. They certainly would miss Patrick, not only for himself but as attendant, to see to much that an earl and princess could not suitably do for themselves in visiting the courts of Europe. Anna said that she would be well enough here; and once the infant was born, if she could find a wet-nurse, she might even come to rejoin them herself.

There was endless discussion about this, while the preparations went on. That is, until one day, soon after King Christian's return from Norway, when all was abruptly changed. A ship, their old *Tay Pearl*, arrived from Scotland, bearing the Chancellor again, Lord Avondale, supported by the Lord Haliburton of Dirleton, a member of the Privy Council. If supported was the right word; supervised might be nearer it. For Avondale had grown to friendly terms with Thomas and Mary on their embassage; and his mission now was less than friendly. He came with King James's orders that his sister was to return to Scotland immediately, with or without her husband. There was to be no question about it, no delay – this was a royal command. And King Christian was directed to ensure it, under the terms of the treaty between the two realms.

Mary, appalled, scarcely believing her ears, drew a great

breath. "No!" she exclaimed. "'I refuse! I will not do it. *He* cannot do it. My brother cannot force me to leave my husband. I, his sister, do not recognise his royal command. This is not to be considered."

"Not only the King's command, Highness. But the Council's . . ."

"No, I say! A wife's first duty is to her husband. And Thomas most certainly is not going to return to Scotland in present circumstances. That is the end of it. I . . ."

It was not Avondale who gave her pause.

"Highness," Lord Haliburton said grimly, "His Grace's and those of the Council's instructions are that should you make refusal, we are to take the Earl of Arran along with you. King Christian to be charged to enforce this."

Mary stared. "But . . . this is beyond all! It is outrageous. You cannot do this . . ."

"It is a royal command, lady." Haliburton was a stern-faced, hard man of middle years, no doubt chosen as apt for this duty. "His Grace has been as kind as he might be towards my lord Earl here, since he is Your Highness's husband. He has made it possible for *you* to come back to Scotland, alone, leaving my lord at liberty here. Only if you *refuse*, are we to take you both. That is the kindest that His Grace could command, after the parliament's decision."

"Parliament . . . ?" That was Thomas, thick-voiced.

"Aye, parliament, my lord. You, along with your father and your uncles, have been condemned for high treason. By parliament. The Lord Boyd is fled to England. Sir Alexander Boyd is already taken and executed. The Abbot of Kilwinning is gone, none knows where. So – if you return with us to Scotland, my lord, it is to your death!"

Mary and Thomas looked at each other, wordless now.

"So, Highness, how say you?"

Mary found voice. "I say . . . I say that King Christian cannot force this on us. Will not. He is our friend. This is *his* realm, not my brother's . . ."

"He has no choice in the matter, lady. The terms of the treaty which both kings have signed declare that each will support the other in all things. This is the first demand under that treaty – and in King James's own written word and seal, which we carry. And you are His Grace's own sister. Refusal by King

Christian to accede would be to refute and negate the treaty, injure King James's marriage and endanger relations between the realms. King Christian cannot but agree, however he may feel towards you."

"I am sorry," Avondale said. "But that is the decision of King, parliament and Council."

"You must go, my dear. Alone," Thomas got out.

"No!"

All considered each other.

"I think that you should well consider the matter. Together," Avondale went on, unhappily. "*Before* we seek audience of King Christian. Tomorrow. With our royal letter."

Thomas nodded. He took Mary's arm to lead her out of the room, without another word, leaving the two emissaries standing.

There was no lack of words thereafter. Indeed, far into the night Mary and Thomas lay awake, going over and over the situation, agonised, undecided – or, at least, each decided, but differing, he that she must go, she that he must not and she *would* not.

It was the young woman who, at length, in desperation, came out with the suggestion. "Thomas, let us slip away. Both of us. Alone. From here. From Copenhagen. Try to get a ship back to Lübeck. Nils would aid us. There, the League would look after us. This of your troubles in Scotland would not hurt their cause, nor what you could do for them, as envoy. Let us flee Copenhagen. Secretly. They would never catch us, from here."

"We could not do that, my heart. Without harming Christian. He has been good to us. That would grievously injure his position. He would be held responsible. Forby, it would turn *you* into a hunted fugitive – and that I will not have. I have brought sufficient trouble upon you already. If you were so deliberately to disobey a royal command, even you would be held guilty of high treason. They might not hang you, but you could be imprisoned, if captured. So, a fugitive always. No, not that, my dear."

"I will go throw myself on Christian's mercy. He likes me – likes me overmuch indeed! He will not let them take me away, if I go and plead with him."

"He cannot help himself, in this. He is a king, a monarch, in treaty with another king. *You* know his position, lass, if any does,

223

you a king's daughter and sister. Where are your famed wits, my dear? Use them."

She knew in her head if not her heart that he was right.

"Oh, Thomas – to leave you! Leave you, an outlaw. Condemned. For how long? Before I can win back to you? I think that I *hate* James! To do this to us. He is weak. But he need not have done this. They could not *make* him do it . . ."

"Weak, yes. But, I think, lost without you. He relied on you, Mary. Lacking you, he has not the strength to withstand harsh men, our enemies. And he is young . . ."

"Not so very young, now. He will soon be of age. To rule as well as to reign. Then, perhaps, I can convince him, work on him. Yes, then I could sway him to grant you pardon. My father was but nineteen years when he took over rule. James will be nineteen in less than two years . . ."

"That is it, yes. Since it seems that you must go back, then prevail on James to remit the sentence of death passed on me. Pardon me, and allow me to return to Scotland. Two years is not so long to be parted – although I shall grudge every day of it. That is best, lass. And there are the children to think of . . ."

"The children, yes. Do not think that I ever forget them. Our little ones. Perhaps that is best. All that we can do . . ."

They left it at that, meantime. But still they found that sleep eluded them.

In the morning they had thought of no better solution, and had to convey their sad decision to Anna and Patrick. These two had not failed to hear of the situation, of course, and were equally unhappy, but had come to their own conclusions and decisions. If, as they had anticipated, Mary elected to go back to Scotland alone, then Anna would go with her. Nothing else was practicable. Patrick would go journeying with Thomas. *He* dare not go back to Scotland, either – he would be condemned along with his master, nothing more sure. It would be a sore parting, but needs must.

The other couple were in no position to refute that.

Christian sent for them after his interview with Avondale and Haliburton, less than his usual hearty self. He put the best face on it that he could, but it was obvious that he was embarrassed and unhappy. He took the attitude that all was settled, however unfortunate it was, that the princess was going back to her royal brother's care and that the earl was going on his travels for

224

the Hanseatic senators. Nothing was said of treason or death sentences. He was grieved to be losing them – and he gripped Mary to emphasise it – but they would assuredly meet again one day. Meantime they would have a farewell banquet, two evenings hence, for today he had to visit his wife at Helsingor, and the Scots lords wished to be away as soon as possible, with winter conditions coming to the Norse Sea.

So they had two days only.

Avondale and Haliburton, evidently taking it for granted that the pair had come to the only conclusion possible, now kept out of their way. Decisions taken, the two couples were not going to moon about in gloom, so that day they went to the Ostergade to get Nils Larsen to find Thomas a Hansa ship to convey him to Lübeck – for Thomas would not wish to linger here after Mary had gone. Then they wandered round the city and pretended that they were interested and enjoying all they saw, even buying keepsakes from the stalls.

That night they slept little more than on the previous one. As Mary said, hereafter they all would have plenty of time for sleeping. Every waking moment was precious.

Next day they hired a fishing boat, since Anna found much walking tiring, to take them through the intricate network of waterways which linked Copenhagen's docks area, and down the Inner Haven to the Killebo Strand, a great sheltered bay to the south-west, which they had been told of but had not yet visited, with the large island of Amager on the east, the most fruitful and densely populated rural area of Denmark reputedly, known as Copenhagen's kitchen-garden. This, then, they dutifully explored, even though their attention to all they saw was less than concentrated.

King Christian had, it proved later, gone to great lengths to make their last evening a memorable one, his way of expressing his regrets and inability to help. The feasting was beyond all previously offered, in richness and variety, the entertainment as lavish, singers, storytellers, dancers, acrobats, performing bears, even a troupe of dwarfs who posed, acted and mimicked naked, a highly suggestive presentation. Christian's own contribution, at least towards Mary, was in keeping, and grew the more so as the evening wore on, that young woman loth to repulse him in the circumstances and enduring as best she could. The unlimited schnapps, however, did come to her aid eventually, and before the evening was out the monarch had fallen asleep, admittedly a-lean against her, the arm which had been encircling her bosom dropped to her lap. Even when his guests, or some of them, made their escape, he did not awake.

Mary and Thomas were again distinctly less soporific, for who could tell when next they would lie in each other's arms – the *Tay Pearl* was to sail next day. They passed a bitter-sweet night.

In the morning, still abed, they said their private farewells, for the eventual leave-taking would inevitably be in front of others. Holding each other, halting words were the least of their exchange.

"Who would have thought that it would come to this, my dearest?" the man got out. "Parting, in a foreign land. Constrained by others . . ."

"Not truly parting, Thomas – only our bodies moving in different directions meantime. Ourselves, our love, our spirits, inseparable always, wherever our persons. Constrained, yes, but only our outer shells, these poor bodies. They can never separate *us*!"

"Lord, you name this dear, lovely body, this adored delight of mine, a poor shell! This, which I swore before God to cherish and protect, till the death. Aye, and beyond! Which I would indeed die for – may yet have to! But now I leave it . . . !"

"Hush, you. You are not leaving it. Others are taking it. But they cannot take *me*, the true me, the reality which is yours, for ever. This body – you love it, yes. And I rejoice that you do. But one day it will grow old and wither. Nothing more sure. But *I* will not. The part you love and hold. Wherever you are. The constraint is only for the body – and even so, only meantime. Who knows how soon we may come together again, in person as in love?"

"Aye. No doubt but you are right, lass. Would that I had your faith, your certainty. But . . . man's constraint is hard, hard to accept."

"And yet, was it not constraint, men's constraint, which brought us together, in the first place?"

"Dear God, yes, it was! My father's constraint of you and James. Aye, who am I to complain of constraints! We took you by force. I was wed to you by force – or, at least, against *your* will. Never mine. My father was a master of constraint, I cannot deny. For that I beg your forgiveness, Mary."

"No need. Not now. See how fair a flower has bloomed after so odd a planting, out of that constraint. It took time. Who knows what, in time, may come out of *this* constraint?"

"It did not take time, for me. My heart lurched at the first sight of you, that day near to Linlithgow. I loved you from the beginning. Not as I do now. My love grew, yes. But you smote my eyes and heart from that first meeting . . ."

She mustered a little laugh. "As you scarcely did to me! Oh, I saw you as a handsome, personable young man, a man to take the eye, a man to watch. Aye, to watch! You were *forward*, no? Assertive. Bold. And I was young, and a king's daughter . . ."

"Sakes, yes – I was over-eager. In too great a haste. But . . . I *had* to win you, see you. Myself win you. I knew that my father intended to wed you to me, from the first. Part of his plan. For power. Constraint again. And I did not want to wed a woman reluctant. In especial such a woman as I found *you*! So I had to press my cause, my own cause, not my father's. However much I seemed to be spurring ahead."

"And you succeeded. However much *I* fought you off. And I did seek to smother my dawning love for you. I confess it. I tried – and failed!"

"When did you realise it, lass? Realise that I meant something to you?"

"In my heart, if not my head, fairly soon. Or so it comes to me now, looking back."

"Before that wedding?"

"Oh, yes. I think that it may have been Anna who opened my eyes to it. That first day at Kilmarnock, at Dean Castle, when we went to collect her. Do you remember the matter? No – you will not, for she said it to me when you were not present. In her bedchamber, which I shared with her. When I told her that you were over-urgent towards me, she answered that I would be a match for you! Hastily she pointed out that she did not mean a match as marriage. Only that I could perhaps *out*match you, in my, my attitudes. That opened my eyes, I now think. Made me to realise that I did not *want* to outmatch you always, that I could accept you as leader. Not master, no. But to lead. And that a match between us, marriage, might be none so ill. Yes, I think that it was then . . ."

"So! That other night, that wedding night, you were not having to steel yourself? You were not abhorring it? It was not just a matter of needs must?"

"Did I act, sound, look as though I was?"

"No-o-o. But, myself, I was so beside myself that I knew little save my own hot need and desire for you. And my resolve, such as it was, not to hurt you if it was possible. A battle within me . . ."

"Perhaps your battle, then, was greater than mine, husband! Who knows? But, an inexperienced girl, I knew so little."

"You did not fail to act the woman then, Mary my heart!"

"Perhaps. But it was no great trial!"

"It, your beauty, overwhelmed me. Beauty of body, as beauty of feature. That I, Thomas Boyd, should have been so blest. My pride and joy, pride in your person and your looks and your spirit. Aye, and your wits. You, with the mind to outwit so many, in affairs of state as in lesser matters . . ."

"But not sufficient to counter my royal brother, it seems!"

"His is not wit, but weakness. James allowing himself to be forced by others. Using me, my life or my death, to constrain you. No wits in that. Only yielding to the wishes of hard men who seek power and advancement. None could take pride in that. My pride in you, lass, is otherwise . . ."

"All the pride is not yours, my love. I am proud, also. Proud of you. Proud of what you have done. You won Orkney and Shetland for Scotland. You were so good to James – and he repays you thus! You shone at the tournament. And you taught me much about my own body, kindly, patiently. I am proud to have borne your children, a great joy to me. Those bairns, Thomas. Young Jamie. And Grizel. They will link us always, part of each of us. We are blest in them."

"I scarce know them, to my sorrow. And they will grow without knowing *me*. That is hard . . ."

"Part of the price that we are having to pay for our love. A great price. But . . . perhaps the greater the love, the greater the price? If we loved less, how much less heavy the cost? We must hold on to that. But, who knows – it may not be for so long."

"Even two years could seem an eternity."

"It is only so many months. We have been parted before, for months, have we not? And even eternity is ours, for love is eternal. That is our sure anchor. Since God Himself is love, and His eternity ruled by love. Unlike this sorry world of men.

So, we cannot lose, Thomas – we cannot lose! Absence, here or hereafter, is no barrier to love, I do believe."

"You believe – then so must I, my heart. There is no more to be said, is there?"

So they held each other, silent now, until he rose to throw off the bedcovers.

King Christian himself came to escort them down to the dockside, a notable honour. He was excessively hearty, although not towards Avondale and Haliburton. He presented Mary with an ancient golden torque, a former Norseman's arm bracelet, as token of his affection and esteem; also entrusted her with a letter for his daughter. One day, he declared, he would come and see them in Scotland. He had chuckles and smiles for Anna too, patting her swelling frontage. He conducted them up the gangplank on to the ship.

There all was in readiness. Rob Carnegie greeted them with a sort of gruff but warm respect. The two lords took formal leave of the King, and Avondale had the grace to lead Haliburton below fairly promptly.

Their promptness seemed to communicate itself to Thomas Boyd also, for having got thus far, he appeared to be concerned to get the parting over as quickly as possible, Mary understanding all too well. Possibly Anna and Patrick felt the same.

Gripping his wife's hands in his, Thomas gazed into her lovely eyes, and for long moments his lips were tight as though sealed.

She helped him, as always. "Only a turn in our road, my love," she whispered. "That road has had many turns – but the end, the destination, is sure. A bend in it, only."

"God help us, yes! But – why?"

"He knows, if we do not. But . . . I will be waiting for you, husband. Whenever. Wherever. Waiting."

He nodded, then shook his head, wordless, features working. Fiercely he shook her, then all but flung her from him, there on the deck, and turned about to stride back to the gangway, and down, his bearing stiff as any ramrod.

She gulped and swallowed – and him safely gone, the tears welled out, hot.

Anna and Patrick were undergoing their own bitter ordeal. There it was the girl who broke away and ran, clumsily, for the companionway, sobbing.

229

Mary stood her ground.

For it was not over yet. A large ship cannot leave a quayside in moments, however ready and skilful the skipper and crew. Whether or not Thomas and Patrick would have departed forthwith, King Christian did not, and so they must wait there on the jetty also, endlessly it seemed, while the gangway was run in, the mooring cables loosed, the towing-barge manoeuvred into position to pull them down the canal, commands shouted.

So they stood, only some fifty yards apart still, although it might have been an endless yawning gulf already. And near as they were, Mary did not see him very clearly.

At last the *Tay Pearl* began to move, slowly, so very slowly, drawn by the barge's oarsmen away towards the Inner Haven. Thomas's arm rose, then, not to wave, not to salute, but to reach out towards her, hand open, cupped as though in mute appeal.

It was almost too much. Mary turned away for a moment, but forced herself to face him again. She spread her arms wide, and so remained. But her eyes were shut.

Fortunately Copenhagen itself came to their rescue, in this at least. Those narrow waterways amongst the docks and warehouses ensured that no lengthy views were possible. Quite quickly the quayside was hidden from the ship.

It was done.

Historical Note

Mary Stewart never saw Thomas Boyd again – not in this life, at least. Brought back to Scotland and reunited with her children, she was kept under strict guard and surveillance – as indeed, then, was King James – by a strong regency council determined that never again should one up-jumped family take over the rule of the realm and the control of a weak young monarch. She was not imprisoned nor maltreated, but was no free woman.

Thomas duly went journeying amongst the princes of Europe, and with some success, especially with Charles the Bold, Duke of Burgundy in the Low Countries, with whom he struck up a notable friendship, becoming that vigorous ruler's favoured representative, actually visiting England on his behalf, where he was recommended to the influential, by a letter which has survived, as "the most courteous, wisest, kindest and most bounteous knight, my lord Earl of Arran, clever, most perfect and truest to his lady of all knights". Whether he recognised himself in this description is not recorded. Nor is it recorded by what cause he died, five years later, in 1474, at Antwerp, whether by sickness, plague, poison or sharp steel. Duke Charles erected a handsome monument to his memory.

On the information of his death reaching Scotland, Mary was forcibly married, for the second time. This to James, first Lord Hamilton, he who had sought to halt the royal abduction at Linlithgow, if ineffectually. Sixth Lord of Cadzow, he had helped to pull down the House of Douglas, and in consequence gained great lands and possessions formerly belonging thereto. One of the new Council, he was also one of the greatest lechers in the land, and old enough to be Mary's father. He had innumerable bastards but only one legitimate daughter; but managed to produce a son and another daughter on his new wife – that son destined to create considerable upset in the Scottish crown succession, as giving the Hamilton family a claim to the throne by the Earls of Arran and Dukes of Chatelherault. Mary long survived this second husband, and as widow became a force to be reckoned with during the reign of one of the weakest of Scots monarchs, James the Third.

Of the Lady Annabella, wife of Sir John Gordon of Lochinvar, we hear no more.

Denmark never managed to redeem the Isles of Orkney and Shetland, which were incorporated in the realm of Scotland.

NIGEL TRANTER

UNICORN RAMPANT

The year 1617 was a fateful one for Scotland – and especially for young John Stewart of Methven, bastard son of the Duke of Lennox.

King James VI of Scotland and I of England made a rare and disastrous visit to the homeland of which he had been an absentee monarch for fourteen years. Knighted in a rash moment by the eccentric King Jamie, John became the reluctant servant of the Court. Much against his will he was commanded to return with the King to London, and was soon caught up in a net of murky political intrigue.

'I recommend it strongly'

Books in Scotland

HODDER AND STOUGHTON PAPERBACKS